History of Collins

In 1819, millworker William Collins from Glasgow,
Scotland, set up a company for printing and publishing
pamphlets, sermons, hymn books and prayer books. That
company was Collins and was to mark the birth of
HarperCollins Publishers as we know it today. The long
tradition of Collins dictionary publishing can be traced back
to the first dictionary William published in 1824, *Greek
and English Lexicon*. Indeed, from 1840 onwards, he began
to produce illustrated dictionaries and even obtained a
licence to print and publish the Bible.

Soon after, William published the first Collins novel,
Ready Reckoner, however it was the time of the Long
Depression, where harvests were poor, prices were high,
potato crops had failed and violence was erupting in
Europe. As a result, many factories across the country were
forced to close down and William chose to retire in 1846,
partly due to the hardships he was facing.

Aged 30, William's son, William II took over the
business. A keen humanitarian with a warm heart and a
generous spirit, William II was truly 'Victorian' in his
outlook. He introduced new, up-to-date steam presses and
published affordable editions of Shakespeare's works and
The Pilgrim's Progress, making them available to the
masses for the first time. A new demand for educational
books meant that success came with the publication of
travel books, scientific books, encyclopaedias and
dictionaries. This demand to be educated led to the later
publication of atlases and Collins also held the monopoly
on scripture writing at the time.

In the 1860s Collins began to expand and diversify

and the idea of 'books for the millions' was developed. Affordable editions of classical literature were published and in 1903 Collins introduced 10 titles in their Collins Handy Illustrated Pocket Novels. These proved so popular that a few years later this had increased to an output of 50 volumes, selling nearly half a million in their year of publication. In the same year, The Everyman's Library was also instituted, with the idea of publishing an affordable library of the most important classical works, biographies, religious and philosophical treatments, plays, poems, travel and adventure. This series eclipsed all competition at the time and the introduction of paperback books in the 1950s helped to open that market and marked a high point in the industry.

HarperCollins is and has always been a champion of the classics and the current Collins Classics series follows in this tradition – publishing classical literature that is affordable and available to all. Beautifully packaged, highly collectible and intended to be reread and enjoyed at every opportunity.

Life & Times

This is one of those works where it is essential to understand the historical context to gain insight into the author's motivation. *The Pilgrim's Progress*, by John Bunyan, was written in two parts – the first in 1678, the second in 1684. Bunyan was born in 1628, so he was already 50 years old when the first part was published. Those 50 years had seen a great deal of history played out in Britain, which goes a long way to explaining Bunyan's intent.

He was born a couple of years into the reign of King Charles I, which proved to be the beginning of a period of great turmoil. Due to the King's ill-judged actions, the English Civil War broke out in 1642 and would last until 1651, during which time hundreds of thousands died, either in the name of the monarchy or parliament. Charles was executed in 1649 and Oliver Cromwell took the role of Lord Protector from 1653 until his death in 1658. England then decided a monarchy was better than a republic and instated Charles II as the new king. The authorities even tried to erase the Protectorate from history by recording the start of Charles II's reign from 1649. To this day, England is the only nation to have rid itself of monarchy and then brought it back again.

By the time Bunyan was 30 years old he had witnessed the horrors of warfare, which had only served to exchange the selfishness of Charles I for the piousness of Cromwell. He was now witnessing the frivolity and excesses of Charles II. Understandably, he felt that English society had become so confused that it was slipping into moral and ethical bankruptcy. People wanted to put the past behind them at the expense of their religious fortitude. They had the Christian Bible for guidance, but they appeared no longer to heed its message. Bunyan set about putting things right by means of an allegorical tale that would make the reader think about the consequences of their behaviour. It would be a kind of practical guide or companion to the Bible, so that the layperson had a straightforward point of reference, instead of having to read and interpret the metaphorical words of the good book. In effect, *The Pilgrim's Progress* is a fable about what to expect in the afterlife if one chooses to act in one way or another during life.

Bunyan was a Protestant Christian. Following the restoration of the English monarchy, the nation became Anglican (Church of England) Christian under Charles II. Protestants had a puritanical approach to Christianity, while Anglicans were more progressive and open-minded. In 1664, the Conventicle Act was passed, which meant that it became illegal for anyone outside the Church of England to attend religious assemblies of more than five people. Bunyan found himself arrested for preaching and was subjected to two periods of imprisonment. It was his incarceration for his beliefs that inspired him to write *The Pilgrim's Progress*, because it was a way of preaching his message regardless of his own circumstances. Once published, his words would be a meme in society. The authorities could imprison the man, but not his thoughts.

During this period in history people were generally obsessed with death. It was, after all, never far away due to warfare and disease, and Christianity had indoctrinated populations with the concept that their conduct in life would determine whether they went to heaven or hell. This preoccupation with the afterlife pervaded all levels of society, so Bunyan's writings had a potentially wide readership. Bunyan had been exposed to the uncertainty of life in 1644 when both his mother and sister died. Shortly after this he had signed up with the parliamentary army, otherwise known as the Roundheads.

In his early twenties Bunyan began to reflect on his misspent youth and claimed that he had a calling to Christianity.

He struggled for a number of years to come to terms with reforming his own character, but eventually emerged with a clear understanding of his mission. It was the acknowledgement of his own lack of moral fibre in youth that prompted him to guide others in their own journey to redemption. He was a converted sinner surrounded by scores of other sinners, all wishing to be led to salvation.

Monotheism – the idea that a single god is responsible for everything – was a ubiquitous mindset in the Western world in Bunyan's time. No one questioned that accepted wisdom, largely because science was still in its infancy, so religions provided rounded explanations for the workings of the world. It would be some time before science demonstrated empirical explanations for phenomena previously attributed to the actions of an omnipotent entity.

The Pilgrim's Progress describes the quasi-literal spiritual journey of the central character, Christian, who meets various other characters and visits many places along the way. These characters and places represent good and bad qualities and concepts. Christian has to negotiate his way through a supernatural parallel world, from his hometown, The City of Destruction (Earth), to his intended destination, The Celestial City (Heaven). The second part of the book relates the same journey taken by his family.

The book thus falls into the genre of fantasy, albeit with a religious message. Bunyan used the word 'dream' to describe its manner of delivery. He clearly reasoned that it needed to be a good read first and foremost, to keep the reader engaged throughout. That way, the allegory would be effortlessly absorbed, making it far more accessible than the Bible. Of course, it also suited the tradition of public storytelling. As relatively few people were able to read, they would rely on an educated individual to entertain them with an interesting yarn. In that respect a journey is a useful device, as it allows the central characters to travel through different experiences and circumstances. In other words, there is a plot, which makes the reader or listener want to know what will happen next – the staple of all good stories.

It just so happened that the Popish Plot coincided with publication in England. It was alleged that the Catholic Church was infiltrating England and conspiring to assassinate Charles II. Bunyan's work fuelled the fire of anti-Catholic sentiment in England, a sentiment which lived on into the 20th century in some regions. When King James II took the throne in 1685 he introduced a policy of religious tolerance, because he had Catholic beliefs. He was widely detested by Protestants and this led to the Glorious Revolution in 1688, when James was overthrown by William III, who had come from Holland to restore the Protestant regime.

Catholicism fell from favour because it was seen as too extravagant to be godly. The term 'catholic' is used as a synonym for gaudy tastes, because Catholic churches were so adorned with colourful decoration that they were seen to detract from true faith. Protestantism, in contrast, was all about getting back to basics. Its churches were plain and simple, so that attention was centred on devotion and worship. Corruption was also rife in the Catholic Church, because priests were allowed to accept payments and gifts for their work as conduits to the Christian God. Protestant priests, on the other hand, were nourished by their devotion and made far more modest demands of their congregations.

Three years after the publication of the first part of *The Pilgrim's Progress* in England, it was published in America, where it enjoyed success among Protestant communities. Life in America was hard-going as it was still very much in its embryonic stages of development. Bunyan's work was viewed as a useful guide in an environment where hardships often led people to think selfishly and intolerantly.

Bunyan died as unpredictably as one could expect in his day. He developed a cold while riding to London. Within hours he was delirious with fever and died soon after of pneumonia. His death served to illustrate the importance of keeping up one's pursuit of godliness at all times, so as to be certain – even at very short notice – of favourable treatment in the afterlife.

THE PILGRIM'S PROGRESS

PREFACE

It may seem a very bold undertaking to change even a word of the book which, next to the Bible, has been read by more people, old and young, than any other book in the English language.

But, it must be remembered that, although *The Pilgrim's Progress* has come to be a children's book, and is read more often by young people than by those who are older, it was not the purpose of John Bunyan to write a book for children or even for the young.

The Pilgrim's Progress was a book for men and women; and it was aimed to teach the great truths of the gospel. Hence while most of it is written in a simple style,—as all books should be written,—it contains much that a child cannot understand; not often in the story, but in the conversations and discussions between the different persons. Some of these conversations are in reality short sermons on doctrines and teachings which Bunyan believed to be of great importance. But these are beyond the minds of children and give them great trouble when the book is read. They do not like to have them left out of the reading, thinking that they may lose something interesting. Many a young person has stumbled through the dull, doctrinal parts of the book, without understanding them; and even grown people find them in our time somewhat of a blemish upon the wonderful story, valuable as they were supposed to be in Bunyan's own time.

For many years it has been in my mind, not to re-write *The Pilgrim's Progress*, for that would destroy its greatest charm, but to change the words here and there to simpler ones, and to omit all the conversations and arguments concerning subjects belonging to the field of doctrine; in other words to place the story of *The Pilgrim's Progress* in such a form that every child ten years old can understand it. My purpose is to make it plain and interesting to children, leaving the older form of the book to be read by them when they become older.

Perhaps a short account of Bunyan's own life may add to the interest of his book. John Bunyan was born in 1628 at Elstow, a small village near Bedford, which is in the heart of England. His father was a poor man, traveling on foot from place to place mending pots and pans and the simple furniture of country kitchens, and the son followed the same trade, and was known as a "tinker." He tells us that he lived a wild life, and was especially known as one of the worst swearers in the region.

When the great Civil War broke out in England, in 1642, between King Charles the First and the Parliament, Bunyan became a soldier on the side of the Commonwealth, as the party against the king was called. He served in the army between 1644 and 1646.

In 1648, at the age of twenty years, he married a good young woman, who led him to prayer and to a new life. But it was hard for one who had led such a life as his had been to turn to God, and it cost the young man a great struggle. It seemed to him that his past sins were like a load upon his back, just as he afterward wrote of his "pilgrim," and it was long before he found peace.

He became a member of a little Baptist society, and soon

began to preach. Crowds came to hear him, drawn by his earnest spirit and his quaint striking manner. But when Charles the Second became king, no religious services were allowed except those of the Church of England, and all other meetings were forbidden. Bunyan however went on preaching, until he was sent to prison in Bedford. In Bedford jail he stayed twelve years. To find a means of living in jail, he made lace, and sold it as a support for himself and his blind daughter.

If the prison was hard for Bunyan his sufferings were made a blessing to untold millions, for while in Bedford jail he wrote *The Pilgrim's Progress*. This story was intended to be a parable, like many of our Saviour's teachings; that is, it put into the form of a story the life of one who turns from sin, finds salvation through Christ, and in the face of many difficulties makes his way through this world to heaven. Even a child who reads or listens to the book will see this meaning in part; and he will understand it better as he grows older.

In 1672 Bunyan was set free, and allowed to begin again his work as a Baptist minister, and he soon became one of the most popular preachers in all England. He died quite suddenly in 1688, when he was sixty years old, and is buried in an old graveyard now near the center of London, called Bunhill Fields Burial-ground. In the same ground is buried another great writer, Daniel Defoe, whose story of "Robinson Crusoe" ranks next to *The Pilgrim's Progress* in the number of its readers; also Isaac Watts, the author of many hymns sung in all the churches, and Mrs. Susanna Wesley, the mother of the great John Wesley. Four people who have left a deep mark upon the world, all lie near together in this small cemetery in London.

Every child should read *The Pilgrim's Progress* as a story if no more than a story; should read it until he knows it by heart. And the older he grows the deeper will be the meaning that he will see in it.

JESSE LYMAN HURLBUT.

PART I

PART I

CHAPTER 1

As I walked through the wilderness of this world, I lighted on a certain place where was a den, and laid me down in that place to sleep; and as I slept, I dreamed a dream. I dreamed, and behold, I saw a man clothed with rags, standing in a certain place, with his face from his own house, a book in his hand, and a great burden upon his back. I looked, and saw him open the book, and read therein; and as he read, he wept and trembled; and, not being able longer to contain, he brake out with a lamentable cry, saying, "What shall I do?"

In this plight, therefore, he went home, and restrained himself as long as he could, that his wife and children should not perceive his distress; but he could not be silent long, because that his trouble increased. Wherefore at length he brake his mind to his wife and children; and thus he began to talk to them: "Oh my dear wife," said he, "and you my sweet children, I, your dear friend, am in myself undone by reason of a burden that lieth hard upon me; moreover, I am told to a certainty that this our city will be burned with fire from heaven; in which fearful overthrow, both myself, with thee, my wife, and you, my sweet babes, shall miserably come to ruin, except some way of escape can be found whereby we may be delivered." At this all his family were sore amazed;

not for that they believed that what he had said to them was true, but because they thought that some frenzy or madness had got into his head; therefore, it drawing towards night, and they hoping that sleep might settle his brain, with all haste they got him to bed. But the night was as troublesome to him as the day; wherefore, instead of sleeping, he spent it in sighs and tears. So when the morning was come, they would know how he did. He told them, Worse and worse: he also set to talking to them again; but they began to be hardened. They also thought to drive away his madness by harsh and surly treatment of him: sometimes they would ridicule, sometimes they would chide, and sometimes they would quite neglect him. Wherefore he began to retire himself to his chamber, to pray for and pity them, and also to sorrow over his own misery; he would also walk solitary in the fields, sometimes reading, and sometimes praying; and thus for some days he spent his time.

CHRISTIAN'S DISTRESS OF MIND

Now, I saw, upon a time, when he was walking in the fields, that he was (as he was wont) reading in his book, and greatly distressed in his mind; and as he read, he burst out as he had done before, crying, "What shall I do to be saved?"

I saw also that he looked this way and that way, as if he would run; yet he stood still, because (as I perceived) he could not tell which way to go. I looked then, and saw a man named Evangelist coming to him, who asked, "Wherefore dost thou cry?"

He answered, "Sir, I read in the book in my hand, that I am condemned to die, and after that to come to judgment; and I find that I am not willing to do the first, nor able to do the second."

Then said Evangelist, "Why not willing to die, since this life is troubled with so many evils?" The man answered,

"Because I fear that this burden that is upon my back will sink me lower than the grave, and I shall fall into Tophet. And, sir, if I be not fit to go to prison, I am not fit to go to judgment, and from thence to death; and the thoughts of these things make me cry."

Then said Evangelist, "If this be thy condition, why standest thou still?"

He answered, "Because I know not whither to go." Then he gave him a parchment roll, and there was written within, "Flee from the wrath to come."

The man, therefore, read it, and looking upon Evangelist very carefully, said, "Whither must I fly?" Then said Evangelist (pointing with his finger over a very wide field), "Do you see yonder wicket-gate?" The man said, "No." Then said the other, "Do you see yonder shining light?" He said, "I think I do." Then said Evangelist, "Keep that light in your eye, and go up directly thereto; so shalt thou see the gate; at which, when thou knockest, it shall be told thee what thou shalt do." So I saw in my dream that the man began to run. Now, he had not run far from his own door, when his wife and children perceiving it, began to cry after him to return; but the man put his fingers in his ears, and ran on, crying, "Life! life! eternal life!" So he looked not behind him, but fled towards the middle of the plain.

CHRISTIAN FLEES FROM THE CITY

The neighbors also came out to see him run; and as he ran, some mocked, others threatened, and some cried after him to return; and among those that did so there were two that resolved to fetch him back by force. The name of the one was Obstinate, and the name of the other Pliable. Now, by this time the man was got a good distance from them; but, however, they were resolved to pursue him, which they did, and in a little time they overtook him. Then said the man,

"Neighbors, wherefore are ye come?" They said, "To persuade you to go back with us." But he said, "That can by no means be: you dwell," said he, "in the City of Destruction, the place also where I was born: I see it to be so; and, dying there, sooner or later, you will sink lower than the grave, into a place that burns with fire and brimstone. Be content, good neighbors, and go along with me."

OBST. "What!" said Obstinate, "and leave our friends and comforts behind us?"

CHRIS. "Yes," said Christian (for that was his name), "because that all which you forsake is not worthy to be compared with a little of that I am seeking to enjoy; and if you would go along with me, and hold it, you shall fare as I myself; for there, where I go, is enough and to spare. Come away, and prove my words."

OBST. What are the things you seek, since you leave all the world to find them?

CHRIS. I seek a place that can never be destroyed, one that is pure, and that fadeth not away, and it is laid up in heaven, and safe there, to be given, at the time appointed, to them that seek it with all their heart. Read it so, if you will, in my book.

OBST. "Tush!" said Obstinate, "away with your book; will you go back with us or no?"

CHRIS. "No, not I," said the other, "because I have put my hand to the plough."

OBST. Come, then, neighbor Pliable, let us turn again, and go home without him: there is a company of these crazy-headed fools, that, when they take a fancy by the end, are wiser in their own eyes than seven men that can render a reason.

PLI. Then said Pliable, "Don't revile; if what the good Christian says is true, the things he looks after are better than ours; my heart inclines to go with my neighbor."

OBST. What! more fools still? Be ruled by me, and go back; who knows whither such a brain-sick fellow will lead you? Go back, go back, and be wise.

CHRIS. Nay, but do thou come with thy neighbor Pliable; there are such things to be had which I spoke of, and many more glories besides. If you believe not me, read here in this book; and for the truth of what is told therein, behold, all is made by the blood of Him that made it.

PLI. "Well, neighbor Obstinate," said Pliable, "I begin to come to a point; I intend to go along with this good man, and to cast in my lot with him. But, my good companion, do you know the way to this desired place?"

CHRIS. I am directed by a man, whose name is Evangelist, to speed me to a little gate that is before us, where we shall receive directions about the way.

PLI. Come, then, good neighbor, let us be going. Then they went both together.

"And I will go back to my place," said Obstinate; "I will be no companion of such misled, fantastical fellows."

Now, I saw in my dream, that, when Obstinate was gone back, Christian and Pliable went talking over the plain; and thus they began:

DISCOURSES WITH PLIABLE

CHRIS. Come, neighbor Pliable, how do you do? I am glad you are persuaded to go along with me. Had even Obstinate himself but felt what I have felt of the powers and terrors of what is yet unseen, he would not thus lightly have given us the back.

PLI. Come, neighbor Christian, since there are none but us two here, tell me now further what the things are, and how to be enjoyed, whither we are going.

CHRIS. I can better understand them with my mind than speak

of them with my tongue; but yet, since you are desirous to know, I will read of them in my book.

PLI. And do you think that the words of your book are certainly true?

CHRIS. Yes, verily; for it was made by Him that cannot lie.

PLI. Well said; what things are they?

CHRIS. There is an endless kingdom to be enjoyed, and everlasting life to be given us, that we may live in that kingdom forever.

PLI. Well said; and what else?

CHRIS. There are crowns of glory to be given us, and garments that will make us shine like the sun in the sky.

PLI. This is very pleasant; and what else?

CHRIS. There shall be no more crying, nor sorrow; for he that is owner of the place will wipe all tears from our eyes.

PLI. And what company shall we have there?

CHRIS. There we shall be with seraphims and cherubims, creatures that shall dazzle your eyes to look on them. There also you shall meet with thousands and ten thousands that have gone before us to that place; none of them are hurtful, but all loving and holy; every one walking in the sight of God, and standing in His presence with acceptance for ever. In a word, there we shall see the elders with their golden crowns; there we shall see the holy women with their golden harps; there we shall see men that by the world were cut in pieces, burnt in flames, eaten of beasts, drowned in the seas, for the love they bear to the Lord of the place, all well, and clothed with everlasting life as with a garment.

PLI. The hearing of this is enough to delight one's heart. But are these things to be enjoyed? How shall we get to be sharers thereof?

CHRIS. The Lord, the Governor of the country, hath written that in this book; the substance of which is, If we be truly willing to have it, He will bestow it upon us freely.

PLI. Well, my good companion, glad am I to hear of these things; come on, let us mend our pace.

CHRIS. I cannot go so fast as I would, by reason of this burden that is on my back.

THE SLOUGH OF DESPOND

Now, I saw in my dream, that just as they had ended this talk, they drew nigh to a very miry slough or swamp, that was in the midst of the plain; and they, being heedless, did both fall suddenly into the bog. The name of the slough was Despond. Here, therefore, they wallowed for a time, being grievously bedaubed with the dirt; and Christian, because of the burden that was on his back, began to sink into the mire.

PLI. Then said Pliable, "Ah! neighbor Christian where are you now?"

CHRIS. "Truly," said Christian, "I do not know."

PLI. At this Pliable began to be offended, and angrily said to his fellow, "Is this the happiness you have told me all this while of? If we have such ill speed at our first setting out, what may we expect between this and our journey's end? May I get out again with my life, you shall possess the brave country alone for me." And with that, he gave a desperate struggle or two, and got out of the mire on that side of the swamp which was next to his own house: so away he went, and Christian saw him no more.

Wherefore Christian was left to tumble in the Slough of Despond alone; but still he tried to struggle to that side of the slough which was farthest from his own house, and next to the wicket-gate; the which, he did but could not get out because of the burden that was upon his back; but I beheld in my dream, that a man came to him whose name was Help, and asked him, What he did there?

CHRIS. "Sir," said Christian, "I was bid to go this way by a man called Evangelist, who directed me also to yonder gate, that I might escape the wrath to come; and as I was going there I fell in here."

HELP. But why did you not look for the steps?

CHRIS. Fear followed me so hard, that I fled the next way and fell in.

HELP. Then said he, "Give me thine hand." So he gave him his hand, and he drew him out, and set him upon solid ground, and bade him go on his way.

Then I stepped to him that plucked him out, and said, "Sir, wherefore, since over this place is the way from the City of Destruction to yonder gate, is it that this place is not mended, that poor travelers might go thither with more safety?" And he said unto me, "This miry slough is such a place as cannot be mended; it is the hollow whither the scum and filth that go with the feeling of sin, do continually run, and therefore it is called the Slough of Despond; for still, as the sinner is awakened by his lost condition, there arise in his soul many fears, and doubts, and discouraging alarms, which all of them get together and settle in this place; and this is the reason of the badness of the ground.

"It is not the pleasure of the King that this place should remain so bad. His laborers also have, by the direction of His Majesty's surveyors, been for about these sixteen hundred years employed about this patch of ground, if perhaps it might have been mended; yea, and to my knowledge," said he, "here have been swallowed up at least twenty thousand cart-loads, yea, millions, of wholesome teachings, that have at all seasons been brought from all places of the King's dominions (and they that can tell say they are the best materials to make good ground of the place), if so be it might have been mended; but it is the Slough of Despond still, and so will be when they have done what they can.

"True, there are, by the direction of the Lawgiver, certain good and substantial steps, placed even through the very midst of this slough; but at such time as this place doth much spew out its filth, as it doth against change of weather, these steps are hardly seen; or, if they be, men, through the dizziness of their heads, step aside, and then they are bemired to purpose, notwithstanding the steps be there; but the ground is good when they are got in at the gate."

Now, I saw in my dream, that by this time Pliable was got home to his house. So his neighbors came to visit him; and some of them called him wise man for coming back, and some called him a fool for risking himself with Christian; others again did mock at his cowardliness, saying "Surely since you began to venture, I would not have been so base to have given out for a few difficulties;" so Pliable sat sneaking among them. But at last he got more confidence; and then they all turned their tales, and began to abuse poor Christian behind his back. And thus much concerning Pliable.

WORLDLY WISEMAN'S COUNSEL

Now, as Christian was walking solitary by himself, he espied one afar off come crossing over the field to meet him; and their hap was to meet just as they were crossing the way of each other. The gentleman's name that met him was Mr. Worldly Wiseman: he dwelt in the town of Carnal Policy, a very great town, and also hard by from whence Christian came. This man, then, meeting with Christian, and having heard about him—(for Christian's setting forth from the City of Destruction was much noised abroad, not only in the town where he dwelt, but also it began to be the town-talk in some other places)—Mr. Worldly Wiseman therefore, having some guess of him, by beholding his laborious going, by noticing his sighs and groans, and the like, began thus to enter into some talk with Christian:

WORLD. How now, good fellow! whither away after this
burdened manner?

CHRIS. A burdened manner indeed, as ever I think poor creature had! And whereas you ask me, Whither away? I tell
you, sir, I am going to yonder wicket-gate before me; for
there, as I am informed, I shall be put into a way to be
rid of my heavy burden.

WORLD. Hast thou a wife and children?

CHRIS. Yes; but I am so laden with this burden, that I cannot
take that pleasure in them as formerly; methinks I am
as if I had none.

WORLD. Wilt thou hearken to me, if I give thee counsel?

CHRIS. If it be *good*, I will; for I stand in need of good counsel.

WORLD. I would advise thee, then, that thou with all speed
get thyself rid of thy burden; for thou wilt never be
settled in thy mind till then; nor canst thou enjoy the
blessings which God hath bestowed upon thee till then.

CHRIS. That is that which I seek for, even to be rid of this
heavy burden; but get it off myself I cannot; nor is there
any man in our country that can take it off my shoulders;
therefore am I going this way, as I told you, that I may
be rid of my burden.

WORLD. Who bid thee go this way to be rid of thy burden?

CHRIS. A man that appeared to me to be a very great and
honorable person; his name, as I remember, is Evangelist.

WORLD. I curse him for his counsel! there is not a more
dangerous and troublesome way in the world than is
that into which he hath directed thee; and that thou
shalt find, if thou wilt be ruled by his advice. Thou hast
met with something, as I perceive, already; for I see the
dirt of the Slough of Despond is upon thee; but that
slough is the beginning of the sorrows that do attend
those that go on in that way. Hear me: I am older than
thou: thou art like to meet with, in the way which thou
goest, wearisomeness, painfulness, hunger, perils,

nakedness, sword, lions, dragons, darkness, and, in a word, death, and what not. These things are certainly true, having been proved by the words of many people. And why should a man so carelessly cast away himself, by giving heed to a stranger?

CHRIS. Why, sir, this burden upon my back is more terrible to me than all these things which you have mentioned; nay, methinks I care not what I meet with in the way, if so be I can also meet with deliverance from my burden.

WORLD. How camest thou by the burden at first?

CHRIS. By reading this book in my hand.

WORLD. I thought so. And it has happened unto thee as unto other weak men, who, meddling with things too high for them, do suddenly fall into thy crazy thoughts, which thoughts do not only unman men, as thine I perceive have done thee, but they run them upon desperate efforts to obtain they know not what.

CHRIS. I know what I would obtain; it is ease for my heavy burden.

WORLD. But why wilt thou seek for ease this way, seeing so many dangers attend it? Especially since (hadst thou but patience to hear me,) I could direct thee to the getting of what thou desirest, without the dangers that thou in this way wilt run thyself into. Yea, and the remedy is at hand. Besides, I will add that, instead of those dangers, thou shalt meet with much safety, friendship, and content.

CHRIS. Sir, I pray, open this secret to me.

WORLD. Why, in yonder village (the village is named Morality), there dwells a gentleman whose name is Legality, a very wise man, and a man of very good name, that has skill to help men off with such burdens as thine is from their shoulders; yea, to my knowledge he hath done a great deal of good this way; aye, and besides, he hath skill to cure those that are somewhat crazed in their wits with their burdens. To him, as I said, thou mayest go, and be helped presently. His house is not quite a mile from this place; and if he should not be at home himself, he hath a pretty young man as his son, whose name is Civility, that can do it (to speak on) as well as the old gentleman himself. There, I say, thou mayest be eased of thy burden; and if thou art not minded to go back to thy former habitation (as indeed I would not wish thee), thou mayest send for thy wife and children to thee in this village, where there are houses now standing empty, one of which thou mayest have at a reasonable rate; provision is there also cheap and good; and that which will make thy life the more happy is, to be sure there thou shalt live by honest neighbors, in credit and good fashion.

Now was Christian somewhat at a stand; but presently he concluded, "If this be true which this gentleman hath said, my wisest course is to take his advice;" and with that, he thus further spake:

CHRIS. Sir, which is my way to this honest man's house?
WORLD. Do you see yonder high hill?
CHRIS. Yes, very well.
WORLD. By that hill you must go, and the first house you come at is his.

EVANGELIST AND CHRISTIAN

So Christian turned out of his way to go to Mr. Legality's house for help; but, behold, when he was got now hard by the hill, it seemed so high, and also that side of it that was next the wayside did hang so much over, that Christian was afraid to venture farther, lest the hill should fall on his head; wherefore there he stood still, and knew not what to do. Also his burden now seemed heavier to him than while he was in his way. There came also flashes of fire out of the hill, that made Christian afraid that he should be burnt: here, therefore, he sweat and did quake for fear. And now he began to be sorry that he had taken Mr. Worldly Wiseman's counsel; and with that, he saw Evangelist coming to meet him, at the sight also of whom he began to blush for shame. So Evangelist drew nearer and nearer; and, coming up to him, he looked upon him with a severe and dreadful countenance, and thus began to reason with Christian:

Evan. "What dost thou here, Christian?" said he; at which words Christian knew not what to answer; wherefore at present he stood speechless before him. Then said Evangelist further, "Art thou not the man that I found crying, without the walls of the City of Destruction?"

Chris. Yes, dear sir, I am the man.

Evan. Did not I direct thee the way to the little wicket-gate?

Chris. "Yes, dear sir," said Christian.

Evan. How is it, then, that thou art so quickly turned aside? For thou art now out of the way.

Chris. I met with a gentleman as soon as I had got over the Slough of Despond, who persuaded me that I might, in the village before me, find a man that could take off my burden.

Evan. What was he?

Chris. He looked like a gentleman, and talked much to me, and got me at last to yield: so I came hither, but when I beheld this hill, and how it hangs over the way, I suddenly made a stand, lest it should fall on my head.

Evan. What said that gentleman to you?

Chris. Why, he asked me whither I was going, and I told him.

Evan. And what said he then?

Chris. He asked me if I had a family, and I told him. But, said I, I am so laden with the burden that is on my back, that I cannot take pleasure in them as formerly.

EVAN. And what said he then?

CHRIS. He bid me with speed get rid of my burden; and I told him it was ease that I sought. And, said I, I am therefore going to yonder gate to receive further direction how I may get to the place of deliverance. So he said that he would show me a better way, and short, not so hard as the way, sir, that you sent me in; which way, said he, will direct you to a gentleman's house that hath skill to take off these burdens. So I believed him, and turned out of that way into this, if haply I might soon be eased of my burden. But, when I came to this place, and beheld things as they are, I stopped for fear (as I said) of danger; but I now know not what to do.

EVAN. Then said Evangelist, "Stand still a little, that I may show thee the words of God." So he stood trembling. Then said Evangelist, "God says in his book, 'See that ye refuse not him that speaketh; for if they escaped not who refused him that spake on earth, much more shall not we escape, if we turn away from Him that speaketh from heaven.' He said, moreover, 'Now, the righteous man shall live by faith in God, but if any man draw back, my soul shall have no pleasure in him.'" He also did thus apply them: "Thou art the man that art running into misery; thou hast begun to reject the counsel of the Most High, and to draw back thy foot from the way of peace, even almost to the danger of thy everlasting ruin."

Then Christian fell down at his feet as dead, crying, "Woe is me, for I am undone!" At the sight of which Evangelist caught him by the right hand, saying, "All manner of sin and evil words shall be forgiven unto men." "Be not faithless, but believing." Then did Christian again a little revive, and stood up trembling, as at first, before Evangelist.

Then Evangelist proceeded, saying, "Give more earnest heed to the things that I shall tell thee of. I will now show thee who it was that led thee astray, and who it was also to whom he sent thee. That man that met thee is one Worldly Wiseman; and rightly is he so called; partly because he seeks only for the things of this world (therefore he always goes to the town of Morality to church), and partly because he loveth that way best, for it saveth him from the Cross; and because he is of this evil temper, therefore he seeketh to turn you from my way though it is the right way.

"He to whom thou wast sent for ease, being by name Legality, is not able to set thee free from thy burden. No man was as yet ever rid of his burden by him; no, nor ever is like to be: ye cannot be set right by any such plan. Therefore, Mr. Worldly Wiseman is an enemy, and Mr. Legality is a cheat; and, for his son Civility, notwithstanding his simpering looks, he is but a fraud and cannot help thee. Believe me, there is nothing in all this noise that thou hast heard of these wicked men, but a design to rob thee of thy salvation, by turning thee from the way in which I had set thee." After this, Evangelist called aloud to the heavens for proof of what he had said; and with that there came words and fire out of the mountain under which poor Christian stood, which made the hair of his flesh stand up. The words were thus spoken: "As many as are of the works of the law are under the curse."

Now, Christian looked for nothing but death, and began to cry out lamentably; even cursing the time in which he met with Mr. Worldly Wiseman; still calling himself a thousand fools for listening to his counsel. He also was greatly ashamed to think that this gentleman's arguments should have the power with him so far as to cause him to forsake the right way. This done, he spoke again to Evangelist, in words and sense as follows:

CHRIS. Sir, what think you? Is there any hope? May I now go back, and go up to the wicket-gate? Shall I not be abandoned for this, and sent back from thence ashamed? I am sorry I have hearkened to this man's counsel; but may my sins be forgiven?

EVAN. Then said Evangelist to him, "Thy sin is very great, for by it thou hast committed two evils; thou hast forsaken the way that is good, to tread in forbidden paths. Yet will the man at the gate receive thee, for he has good will for men; only," said he, "take heed that thou turn not aside again, lest thou perish from the way, when his anger is kindled but a little."

CHAPTER 2

Then did Christian begin to go back to the right road; and Evangelist, after he had kissed him, gave him one smile, and bid him God speed; so he went on with haste, neither spake he to any man by the way; nor, if any asked him, would he give them an answer. He went like one that was all the while treading on forbidden ground, and could by no means think himself safe, till again he was got in the way which he had left to follow Mr. Worldly Wiseman's counsel: so after a time, Christian got up to the gate. Now, over the gate there was written, "Knock, and it shall be opened unto you."

He knocked, therefore, more than once or twice, saying:

> "May I now enter here? Will He within
> Open to sorry me, though I have been
> An undeserving rebel? Then shall I
> Not fail to sing His lasting praise on high."

GOODWILL OPENS THE GATE

At last there came a grave person to the gate named Goodwill, who asked who was there, and whence he came, and what he would have?

CHRIS. Here is a poor burdened sinner. I come from the City
of Destruction, but am going to Mount Zion, that I may
be set free from the wrath to come; I would therefore,
sir, since I am told that by this gate is the way thither,
know, if you are willing to let me in.

GOOD. "I am willing with all my heart," said he; and, with
that, he opened the gate.

So, when Christian was stepping in, the other gave him a pull.
Then said Christian, "What means that?" The other told him,
"A little distance from this gate there is erected a strong castle,
of which Beelzebub, the Evil One, is the captain; from whence
both he and they that are with him shoot arrows at those that
come up to this gate, if haply they may die before they can
enter in." Then said Christian, "I rejoice and tremble." So
when he was got in, the man of the gate asked him who
directed him thither.

CHRIS. Evangelist bid me come hither and knock, as I did;
and he said that you, sir, would tell me what I must do.

GOOD. An open door is set before thee, and no man can shut
it.

CHRIS. Now I begin to reap the benefit of the trouble which
I have taken.

GOOD. But how is it that you came alone?

CHRIS. Because none of my neighbors saw their danger, as I
saw mine.

GOOD. Did any of them know you were coming?

CHRIS. Yes, my wife and children saw me at the first, and
called after me to turn again; also some of my neighbors
stood crying and calling after me to return; but I put my
fingers in my ears, and so came on my way.

GOOD. But did none of them follow you, to persuade you to
go back?

CHRIS. Yes, both Obstinate and Pliable: but, when they saw

that they could not prevail, Obstinate went railing back, but Pliable came with me a little way.

GOOD. But why did he not come through?

CHRIS. We indeed came both together until we came to the Slough of Despond, into the which we also suddenly fell. And then was my neighbor Pliable discouraged, and would not venture farther. Wherefore, getting out again on the side next his own house, he told me I should win the brave country alone for him: so he went his way, and I came mine; he after Obstinate, and I to this gate.

GOOD. Then said Goodwill, "Alas, poor man! is the heavenly glory of so little worth with him, that he counteth it not worth running the risk of a few difficulties to obtain it?"

CHRIS. "Truly," said Christian, "I have said the truth of Pliable; and if I should also say the truth of myself, it will appear there is not betterment betwixt him and myself. 'Tis true, he went on back to his own house; but I also turned aside to go into the way of death, being persuaded thereto by the words of one Mr. Worldly Wiseman."

GOOD. Oh! did he light upon you? What! he would have had you seek for ease at the hands of Mr. Legality! They are both of them a very cheat. But did you take his counsel?

CHRIS. Yes, as far as I durst. I went to find out Mr. Legality, until I thought that the mountain that stands by his house would have fallen upon my head: wherefore there I was forced to stop.

GOOD. That mountain has been the death of many, and will be the death of many more; it is well you escaped being by it dashed in pieces.

CHRIS. Why, truly, I do not know what had become of me there, had not Evangelist happily met me again as I was musing in the midst of my dumps; but it was God's mercy that he came to me again, for else I had never come hither. But now I am come, such a one as I am, more fit indeed for death by that mountain, than thus to stand talking with my Lord. But, oh! what a favor this is to me, that yet I am to enter here!

Good. We make no objections against any, notwithstanding all that they have done before they come hither; they in no wise are cast out. And therefore, good Christian, come a little with me, and I will teach thee about the way thou must go. Look before thee: dost thou see this narrow way? That is the way thou must go. It was cast up by the men of old, prophets, Christ and His apostles, and it is as straight as a rule can make it: this is the way thou must go.

Chris. "But," said Christian, "are there no turnings nor windings by which a stranger may lose his way?"

Good. "Yes, there are many ways butt down upon this, and they are crooked and wide; but thus thou mayest distinguish the right from the wrong, the right only being straight and narrow."

Then I saw in my dream, that Christian asked him further if he could not help him off with his burden that was upon his back. For as yet he had not got rid thereof, nor could he by any means get it off without help.

He told him, "As to thy burden, be content to bear it until thou comest to the place of deliverance; for there it will fall from thy back of itself."

Then Christian began to gird up his loins, and to turn again to his journey.

So the other told him that as soon as he was gone some distance from the gate, he would come at the house of the Interpreter, at whose door he should knock, and he would show him excellent things. Then Christian took his leave of his friend, and he again bid him God speed.

HOUSE OF THE INTERPRETER

Then he went on till he came to the house of the Interpreter, where he knocked over and over. At last one came to the door, and asked who was there.

CHRIS. Sir, here is a traveler who was bid by a friend of the good man of this house to call here for his benefit; I would therefore speak with the master of the house.

So he called for the master of the house, who, after a little time, came to Christian, and asked him what he would have.

CHRIS. "Sir," said Christian, "I am a man that am come from the City of Destruction, and am going to Mount Zion; and I was told by the man that stands at the gate at the head of this way, that, if I called here, you would show me excellent things, such as would be helpful to me on my journey."

INTER. Then said the Interpreter, "Come in; I will show thee that which will be profitable to thee." So he commanded his man to light the candle, and bid Christian follow him; so he led him into a private room, and bid his man open a door; the which when he had done, Christian saw the picture of a very grave person hung up against the wall; and this was the fashion of it: it had eyes lifted up to heaven, the best of books in its hand, the law of truth was written upon its lips, the world was behind its back; it stood as if it pleaded with men, and a crown of gold did hang over its head.

CHRIS. Then said Christian, "What meaneth this?"

INTER. The man whose picture this is, is one of a thousand. He can say, in the words of the apostle Paul, "Though ye have ten thousand teachers in Christ, yet have you not many fathers; for in Christ Jesus I have been your father through the Gospel." And whereas thou seest him with his eyes lifted up to heaven, the best of books in his hand, and the law of truth writ on his lips, it is to show thee that his work is to know and unfold dark things to sinners; even as also thou seest him stand as if he pleaded with men. And whereas thou seest the world is cast behind him, and that a crown hangs over his head; that is to show thee that, slighting and despising the things that are in the world, for the love that he hath to his Master's service, he is sure in the world that comes next to have glory for his reward. Now, said the Interpreter, I have showed thee this picture first, because the man whose picture this is, is the only man whom the Lord of the place whither thou art going hath chosen to be thy guide, in all difficult places thou mayest meet with in thy way; wherefore take good heed to what I have showed thee, and bear well in thy mind what thou hast seen, lest in thy journey thou meet with some that pretend to lead thee right, but their way goes down to death.

Then he took him by the hand, and led him into a very large parlor, that was full of dust, because never swept; the which after he had looked at it a little while, the Interpreter called for a man to sweep. Now, when he began to sweep, the dust began so abundantly to fly about that Christian had almost therewith been choked. Then said the Interpreter to a girl that stood by, "Bring hither water, and sprinkle the room;" the which when she had done, it was swept and cleansed with ease.

CHRIS. Then said Christian, "What means this?"
INTER. The Interpreter answered, "This parlor is the heart of a man that was never made pure by the sweet grace of the Gospel. The dust is his sin, and inward evils that

have defiled the whole man. He that began to sweep at first is the law; but she that brought water, and did sprinkle it, is the Gospel. Now, whereas thou sawest that, as soon as the first began to sweep, the dust did fly so about that the room could not by him be cleansed, but that thou wast almost choked therewith; this is to show thee, that the law, instead of cleansing the heart (by its working) from sin, doth revive, put strength into, and increase it in the soul, even as it doth discover and forbid it, for it doth not give power to overcome. Again, as thou sawest the girl sprinkle the room with water, upon which it was cleansed with ease; this is to show thee, that when the Gospel comes, in the sweet and gracious power thereof, to the heart, then, I say, even as thou sawest the maiden lay the dust by sprinkling the floor with water, so is sin vanquished and subdued, and the soul made clean through the faith of it, and, consequently, fit for the King of Glory to dwell in."

I saw moreover in my dream, that the Interpreter took him by the hand, and led him into a little room where sat two little children, each one in his own chair. The name of the eldest was Passion, and the name of the other Patience. Passion seemed to be much discontented, but Patience was very quiet. The Christian asked, "What is the reason of the discontent of Passion?" The Interpreter answered, "The governor of them would have him stay for his best things till the beginning of next year; but he will have all now. Patience is willing to wait."

Then I saw that one came to Passion, and brought him a bag of treasure, and poured it down at his feet; the which he took up, and rejoiced therein, and withal laughed Patience to scorn. But I beheld but awhile, and he had wasted all away, and had nothing left him but rags.

CHRIS. Then said Christian to the Interpreter, "Explain this matter more fully to me."

INTER. So he said, "These two lads are pictures: Passion, of the men of this world; and Patience, of the men of that which is to come: for, as here thou seest, Passion will have all now, this year, that is to say in this world; so are the men of this world; they must have all their good things now; they cannot stay till the next year, that is, until the next world, for their portion of good. That proverb, 'A bird in the hand is worth two in the bush,' is of more weight with them than all the words in the Bible of the good of the world to come. But, as thou sawest that he had quickly wasted all away, and had presently left him nothing but rags, so will it be with all such men at the end of this world."

CHRIS. Then said Christian, "Now I see that Patience has the best wisdom, and that upon many accounts. 1. Because he stays for the best things. 2. And also because he will have the glory of his when the other has nothing but rags."

INTER. Nay, you may add another; this, the glory of the next world will never wear out; but these are suddenly gone. Therefore Passion had not so much reason to laugh at Patience because he had his good things at first, as Patience will have to laugh at Passion, because he had his best things last; for first must give place to last, because last must have his time to come; but last gives place to nothing, for there is not another to succeed: he, therefore, that hath his portion first, must needs have a time to spend it; but he that hath his portion last, must have it lastingly.

CHRIS. Then I see it is not best to covet things that are now, but to wait for things to come.

INTER. You say truth; "for the things that are seen soon pass away, but the things that are not seen endure forever."

Then I saw in my dream, that the Interpreter took Christian by the hand and led him into a place where was a fire burning against a wall, and one standing by it, always casting much water upon it, to quench it; yet did the fire burn higher and hotter.

CHRIS. Then said Christian, "What means this?"

INTER. The Interpreter answered, "This fire is the work of God that is wrought in the heart: he that casts water upon it to extinguish and put it out, is the devil; but, in that thou seest the fire notwithstanding burn higher and hotter, thou shalt also see the reason of that." So then he led him about to the other side of the wall, where he saw a man with a vessel of oil in his hand, of the which he did also continually cast, but secretly, into the fire.

CHRIS. Then said Christian, "What means this?"

INTER. The Interpreter answered, "This is Christ, who continually, with the oil of His grace, helps the work already begun in the heart; by the means of which notwithstanding what the devil can do, the souls of His people prove gracious still. And in that thou sawest that the man stood behind the wall to keep up the fire; this is to teach thee, that it is hard for the tempted to see how this work of grace is kept alive in the soul."

I saw also that the Interpreter took him again by the hand, and led him into a pleasant place, where was built a stately palace, beautiful to behold, at the sight of which Christian was greatly delighted. He saw also upon the top thereof certain persons walking, who were clothed all in gold.

Then said Christian, "May we go in thither?"

Then the Interpreter took him and led him up toward the door of the palace; and behold, at the door stood a great company of men, as desirous to go in, but durst not. There also sat a man at a little distance from the door, at a table-side, with a book and his ink-horn before him, to take the name of him that should enter therein; he saw also that in the doorway stood many men in armor to keep it, being resolved to do to the men that would enter what hurt and mischief they could. Now was Christian somewhat in amaze. At last, when every man started back for fear of the armed men, Christian saw a man of a very stout countenance come up to the man that sat there to write, saying, "Set down my name, sir:" the which when he had done, he saw the man draw his sword, and put a helmet upon his head, and rush toward the door upon the armed men, who laid upon him with deadly force; but the man, not at all discouraged, fell to cutting and hacking most fiercely. So that, after he had received and given many wounds to those that attempted to keep him out, he cut his way through them all and pressed forward into the palace; at which there was a pleasant voice heard from those that were within, even of those that walked upon the top of the palace, saying:

"Come in, come in; Eternal glory thou shalt win."

So he went in, and was clothed in such garments as they. Then Christian smiled, and said, "I think verily I know the meaning of this."

"Now," said Christian, "let me go hence." "Nay, stay," said the Interpreter, "until I have showed thee a little more; and after that thou shalt go on thy way." So he took him by the hand again, and led him into a very dark room, where there sat a man in an iron cage.

Now, the man, to look on, seemed very sad. He sat with his eyes looking down to the ground, his hands folded together; and he sighed as if he would break his heart. Then said Christian, "What means this?" At which the Interpreter bid him talk with the man.

Then said Christian to the man, "What art thou?" The man answered, "I am what I was not once."

CHRIS. What wast thou once?

MAN. The man said, "I was once a fair and flourishing Christian, both in mine own eyes, and also in the eyes of others; I was once, as I thought, fair for the Celestial City, and had even joy at the thoughts that I should get thither."

CHRIS. Well, but what art thou now?

MAN. I am now a man of despair, and am shut up in it, as in this iron cage. I cannot get out. Oh, *now* I cannot!

CHRIS. But how camest thou in this condition?

MAN. I left off to watch and be sober. I gave free reins to sin; I sinned against the light of the Word and the goodness of God; I have grieved the Spirit, and He is gone; I tempted the devil, and he has come to me; I have provoked God to anger, and He has left me; I have so hardened my heart that I *cannot* turn.

Then said Christian to the Interpreter, "But are there no hopes for such a man as this?" "Ask him," said the Interpreter.

CHRIS. Then said Christian, "Is there no hope, but you must be kept in the iron cage of despair?"

MAN. No, none at all.

CHRIS. Why? the Son of the Blessed is very pitiful.

MAN. I have crucified Him to myself afresh. I have despised His person. I have despised His holiness; I have counted His blood an unholy thing; I have shown contempt to the Spirit of mercy. Therefore I have shut myself out of all the promises of God, and there now remains to me nothing but threatenings, dreadful threatenings, fearful threatenings of certain judgment and fiery anger, which shall devour me as an enemy.

33

CHRIS. For what did you bring yourself into this condition?

MAN. For the desires, pleasures, and gains of this world; in the enjoyment of which I did then promise myself much delight; but now every one of those things also bite me, and gnaw me, like a burning worm.

CHRIS. But canst thou not now turn again to God?

MAN. God no longer invites me to come to Him. His Word gives me no encouragement to believe; yea, Himself hath shut me up in this iron cage; nor can all the men in the world let me out. O eternity! eternity! how shall I grapple with the misery that I must meet with in eternity?

INTER. Then said the Interpreter to Christian, "Let this man's misery be remembered by thee, and be an everlasting caution to thee."

THE DREAM OF THE JUDGMENT

CHRIS. "Well," said Christian, "this is fearful! God help me to watch and be sober, and to pray, that I may shun the cause of this man's misery. Sir, is it not time for me to go on my way now?"

INTER. Tarry till I show thee one thing more, and then thou shalt go on thy way.

So he took Christian by the hand again, and led him into a chamber, where there was one rising out of bed; and, as he put on his clothing, he shook and trembled. Then said Christian, "Why doth this man thus tremble?" The Interpreter then bid him tell to Christian the reason of his so doing. So he began, and said, "This night, as I was in my sleep, I dreamed, and behold, the heavens grew exceeding black; also it thundered and lightened in most fearful manner, that it put me into an agony. So I looked up in my dream, and saw the clouds rack at an unusual rate; upon which I heard a great sound of a trumpet, and saw also a Man sitting upon a cloud, attended with the thousands of heaven; they were all in flaming fire; also the heavens were in a burning flame. I heard then a great voice saying, 'Arise, ye dead, and come to judgment.' And with that the rocks rent, the graves opened, and the dead that were therein came forth: some of them were exceeding glad, and looked upward; and some thought to hide themselves under the mountains. Then I saw the Man that sat upon the cloud open the book and bid the world draw near. Yet there was, by reason of a fierce flame that issued out and came before Him, a certain distance betwixt Him and them, as betwixt the judge and the prisoners at the bar. I heard it also called out to them that stood around on the Man that sat on the cloud, 'Gather together the tares, the chaff, and stubble, and cast them into the burning lake. And, with that, the bottomless pit opened, just whereabout I stood; out of the mouth of which there came, in an abundant manner, smoke and coals of fire, with hideous noises. It was also said to the same persons, 'Gather my wheat into the garner.' And, with that, I saw many catched up and carried away into the clouds; but I was left behind. I also sought to hide myself, but I could not; for the Man that sat upon the cloud still kept His eye upon me; my sins also came into my mind, and my conscience did accuse me on every side. Upon this I awakened from my sleep."

Chris. But what was it that made you so afraid of this sight?

Man. Why I thought that the day of judgment was come, and that I was not ready for it. But this affrighted me most, that the angels gathered up several, and left me behind; also the pit of hell opened her mouth just where I stood. My conscience, too, troubled me; and, as I thought, the judge had always His eye upon me, showing anger in His countenance.

INTER. Then said the Interpreter to Christian, "Hast thou
    considered these things?"
CHRIS. Yes; and they put me in hope and fear.
INTER. Well, keep all things so in thy mind, that they may be
    as a goad in thy sides, to prick thee forward in the way
    thou must go.

Then Christian began to gird up his loins, and to address
himself to his journey. Then said the Interpreter, "The
Comforter be always with thee, good Christian, to guide thee
into the way that leads to the city."

So Christian went on his way, saying:

> "Here have I seen things rare and profitable;
> Things pleasant, dreadful; things to make me
>   stable
> In what I have begun to take in hand:
> Then let me think on them, and understand
> Wherefore they showed me where; and let
>   me be
> Thankful, O good Interpreter, to thee."

CHAPTER 3

Now, I saw in my dream that the highway up which Christian was to go was fenced on either side with a wall that was called Salvation. Up this way, therefore, did burdened Christian run, but not without great difficulty, because of the load on his back.

He ran thus till he came to a place somewhat ascending; and upon that place stood a Cross, and a little below, in the bottom, a tomb. So I saw in my dream, that just as Christian came up with the cross, his burden loosed from off his shoulders, and fell from off his back, and began to tumble, and so continued to do till it came to the mouth of the tomb, where it fell in, and I saw it no more.

Then was Christian glad and lightsome, and said with a merry heart, "He hath given me rest by His sorrow, and life by His death." Then he stood still awhile to look and wonder; for it was very surprising to him that the sight of the cross should thus ease him of his burden. He looked, therefore, and looked again, even till the springs that were in his head sent the water down his cheeks. Now, as he stood looking and weeping, behold, three Shining Ones came to him, and saluted him with "Peace be to thee." So the first said to him, "Thy sins be forgiven thee;" the second stripped him of his rags, and clothed him with a change of garments; the third also set a mark on his forehead, and gave him a roll with a seal upon it, which he bade him look on as he ran, and that he should give it in at the heavenly gate; so they went their way. Then Christian gave three leaps for joy, and went on, singing:

> "Thus far did I come laden with my sin;
> Nor could aught ease the grief that I was in,
> Till I came hither; what a place is this!
> Must here be the beginning of my bliss?
> Must here the burden fall from off my back?
> Must here the strings that bound it to me
>   crack?
> Blest cross! blest sepulchre! blest rather be
> The Man that was there put to shame for
>   me!"

SIMPLE, SLOTH, PRESUMPTION

I saw then in my dream that he went on thus, even until he came to the bottom, where he saw, a little out of the way, three men fast asleep, with fetters upon their heels. The name of one was Simple, of another Sloth, and of the third Presumption.

Christian, then, seeing them lie in this case, went to them, if perhaps he might awake them, and cried, "You are like them that sleep on the top of a mast; for the deep sea is under you, a gulf that hath no bottom: awake, therefore, and come away; be willing, also, and I will help you off with your irons." He also told them, "If he that goeth about like a roaring lion comes by, you will certainly become a prey to his teeth." With that they looked upon him, and began to reply in this sort: Simple said, "I see no danger." Sloth said, "Yet a little more sleep." And Presumption said, "Every tub must stand upon his own bottom." And so they lay down to sleep again, and Christian went on his way.

FORMALIST AND HYPOCRISY

Yet was he troubled to think that men in that danger should so little care for the kindness of him that so offered to help them, both by awakening of them, advising them, and offering to help them off with their irons. And, as he was troubled thereabout, he espied two men come tumbling over the wall on the left hand of the narrow way; and they made up apace to him. The name of one was Formalist, and the name of the other was Hypocrisy. So, as I said, they drew up unto him, who thus began talking with them:

Chris. Gentlemen, whence came you, and whither go you?

Form. and Hyp. We were born in the land of Vain-glory, and are going for praise to Mount Zion.

Chris. Why came you not in at the gate which standeth at the beginning of the way? Know ye not that it is written, "He that cometh not in by the door, but climbeth up some other way, the same is a thief and a robber?"

Form. and Hyp. They said that to go to the gate for entrance was, by all their countrymen, counted too far about; and that therefore their usual way was to make a short cut of it, and to climb over the wall as they had done.

Chris. But will it not be counted a trespass against the Lord of the city whither we are bound, thus to disobey His will?

Form. and Hyp. They told him, that as for that, he needed not trouble his head thereabout; for what they did they had custom for, and could show, if need were, testimony that could prove it for more than a thousand years.

Chris. "But," said Christian, "will it stand a trial at law?"

Form. and Hyp. They told him that custom, it being of so long standing as above a thousand years, would doubtless now be admitted as a thing according to law by a fair judge. "And besides," said they, "if we get into the way, what matter is it which way we may get in? If we are in, we are in: thou art but in the way, who, as we perceive, came in at the gate; and we are also in the way, that came tumbling over the wall: wherein, now, is thy condition better than ours?"

CHRIS. I walk by the rule of my Master; you walk by the rude working of your fancies. You are counted thieves already by the Lord of the way; therefore I doubt you will not be found true men at the end of the way. You come in by yourselves without His word, and shall go out by yourselves without His mercy.

To this they made him but little answer; only they bid him look to himself. Then I saw that they went on every man in his way, without much talking one with another; save that these two men told Christian, that, as to law and rules, they doubted not but that they should as carefully do them as he. "Therefore," said they, "we see not wherein thou differest from us, but by the coat which is on thy back, which was, as we believe given thee by some of thy neighbors to hide the shame of thy nakedness."

CHRIS. By laws and rules you will not be saved, since you came not in by the door. And as for this coat that is on my back, it was given to me by the Lord of the place whither I go; and that, as you say, to cover my nakedness with. And I take it as a token of His kindness to me; for I had nothing but rags before. And besides, thus I comfort myself as I go. Surely, think I, when I come to the gate of the city, the Lord thereof will know me for good, since I have His coat on my back; a coat that He gave me freely in the day that He stripped me of my rags. I have moreover, a mark in my forehead, of which perhaps you have taken no notice, which one of my Lord's most intimate friends fixed there the day that my burden fell off my shoulders. I will tell you, moreover, that I had then given me a roll sealed, to comfort me by reading as I go in the way; I was also bid to give it in at the heavenly gate, in token of my certain going in after it; all which things, I doubt, you want, and want them because you came not in at the gate.

To these things they gave him no answer; only they looked upon each other, and laughed. Then I saw that they went on all, save that Christian kept before, who had no more talk but with himself, and sometimes sighingly, and sometimes comfortably; also he would be often reading in the roll that one of the Shining Ones gave him, by which he was refreshed.

THE HILL OF DIFFICULTY

I beheld then that they all went on till they came to the foot of the Hill Difficulty, at the bottom of which was a spring. There were also in the same place two other ways, besides that which came straight from the gate; one turned to the left hand, and the other to the right, at the bottom of the hill; but the narrow way lay right up the hill, and the name of that going up the side of the hill is called Difficulty. Christian now went to the spring, and drank thereof to refresh himself, and then began to go up the hill, saying:

> "The hill, though high, I covet to ascend;
> The difficulty will not me offend,
> For I perceive the way to life lies here.
> Come, pluck up, heart, let's neither faint nor fear.
> Better, though *difficult*, the right way to go,
> Than wrong, though *easy*, where the end is woe."

The other two also came to the foot of the hill. But when they saw that the hill was steep and high, and that there were two other ways to go; and supposing also that these two ways might meet again with that up which Christian went, on the other side of the hill; therefore they were resolved to go in those ways. Now, the name of one of those ways was Danger, and the name of the other Destruction. So the one took the way which is called Danger, which led him into a great wood; and the other took directly up the way to destruction, which led him into a wide field, full of dark mountains, where he stumbled and fell, and rose no more.

I looked then after Christian, to see him go up the hill, where I perceived he fell from running to going, and from going to clambering upon his hands and his knees, because of the steepness of the place. Now, about the midway to the top of the hill was a pleasant arbor, made by the Lord of the hill for the refreshment of weary travelers. Thither, therefore, Christian got, where also he sat down to rest him; then he pulled his roll out of his bosom, and read therein to his comfort; he also now began afresh to take a review of the coat or garment that was given him as he stood by the cross. Thus pleasing himself a while, he at last fell into a slumber, and thence into a fast sleep, which detained him in that place until it was almost night; and in his sleep his roll fell out of his hand. Now, as he was sleeping, there came one to him, and awaked him, saying, "Go to the ant, thou sluggard; consider her ways, and be wise." And, with that, Christian suddenly started up, and sped on his way, and went apace till he came to the top of the hill.

TIMOROUS AND MISTRUST

Now, when he was got up to the top of the hill, there came two men running amain: the name of the one was Timorous, and of the other Mistrust; to whom Christian said, "Sirs, what's the matter? You run the wrong way." Timorous answered, that they were going to the city of Zion, and had got up that difficult place: "but," said he, "the farther we go, the more danger we meet with; wherefore we turned, and are going back again."

"Yes," said Mistrust, "for just before us lie a couple of lions in the way, whether sleeping or waking we know not; and we could not think, if we came within reach, but they would presently pull us in pieces."

CHRIS. Then said Christian, "You make me afraid; but whither shall I fly to be safe? If I go back to my own country, that is prepared for fire and brimstone, and I shall certainly perish there; if I can get to the Celestial City, I am sure to be in safety there: I must venture. To go back is nothing but death; to go forward is fear of death, and life everlasting beyond it. I will yet go forward." So Mistrust and Timorous ran down the hill, and Christian went on his way. But, thinking again of what he heard from the men, he felt in his bosom for his roll, and found it not. Then was Christian in great distress, and knew not what to do; for he wanted that which used to comfort him, and that which should have been his pass into the Celestial City. Here, therefore, he began to be greatly troubled, and knew not what to do. At last he bethought himself that he had slept in the arbor that is on the side of the hill; and, falling down upon his knees, he asked God's forgiveness for that his foolish act, and then went back to look for his roll. But all the way he went back, who can sufficiently set forth the sorrow of Christian's heart? Sometimes he sighed, sometimes he wept, and oftentimes he blamed himself for being so foolish to fall asleep in that place, which was erected only for a little refreshment from his weariness. Thus, therefore, he went back, carefully looking on this side and on that, all the way as he went, if happily he might find his roll that had been his comfort so many times in his journey. He went thus till he came again within sight of the arbor where he sat and slept; but that sight renewed his sorrow the more, by bringing again, even afresh, his evil of sleeping into his mind. Thus, therefore, he now went on, bewailing his sinful sleep, saying, "O wretched man that I am, that I should sleep in the day-time; that I should sleep in the midst of difficulty! that I should so indulge myself, as to use that rest for ease to my flesh which the Lord of the hill hath builded only for the relief of the spirits of pilgrims! How many steps have I taken in vain! Thus it happened to Israel; for their sin they were sent back again by the way of the Red Sea; and I am made to tread those steps with sorrow which I might have trod with delight, had it not been for this sinful sleep. How far might I have been on my way by this time! I am made to tread those steps thrice over which I needed not to have trod but once; yea, also, now I am like to be benighted, for the day is almost spent. Oh that I had not slept!"

CHRISTIAN RECOVERS HIS ROLL

Now, by this time he was come to the arbor again, where for awhile he sat down and wept; but at last (as Providence would have it), looking sorrowfully down under the settle, there he espied his roll, the which he, with trembling and haste, caught up, and put it into his bosom. But who can tell how joyful this man was when he had got his roll again? for this roll was the assurance of his life and acceptance at the desired haven. Therefore he laid it up in his bosom, giving thanks to God for directing his eye to the place where it lay, and with joy and tears betook himself again to his journey. But oh, how nimbly now did he go up the rest of the hill! Yet, before he got up, the sun went down upon Christian; and this made him again recall the folly of his sleeping to his remembrance; and thus he began again to condole with himself, "Oh, thou sinful sleep! how for thy sake am I like to be benighted in my journey. I must walk without the sun, darkness must cover the path of my feet, and I must hear the noise of the doleful creatures, because of my sinful sleep." Now also he remembered the story that Mistrust and Timorous told him, of how they were frighted with the sight of the lions. Then said Christian to himself again, "These beasts range in the night for their prey; and if they should meet with me in the dark, how should I avoid them? how should I escape being torn in pieces?" Thus he went on his way. But, while he was thus bewailing his unhappy mistake, he lifted up his eyes, and behold there was a very stately palace before him, the name of which was Beautiful, and it stood just by the highway side.

WATCHFUL THE PORTER

So I saw in my dream that he made haste, and went forward, that, if possible, he might get lodging there. Now, before he had gone far, he entered into a very narrow passage, which was about a furlong off the Porter's lodge; and looking very narrowly before him as he went, he espied two lions in the way. Now, thought he, I see the dangers by which Mistrust and Timorous were driven back. (The lions were chained, but he saw not the chains). Then he was afraid, and thought also himself to go back after them; for he thought nothing but death was before him. But the Porter at the lodge, whose name is Watchful, perceiving that Christian made a halt as if he would go back, cried out unto him, saying, "Is thy strength so small? fear not the lions, for they are chained, and are placed there for the trial of faith where it is, and for the finding out of those that have none: keep in the midst of the path, and no hurt shall come unto thee."

Then I saw that he went on trembling for fear of the lions; but, taking good heed to the words of the Porter, he heard them roar, but they did him no harm. Then he clapped his hands, and went on till he came and stood before the gate where the Porter was. Then said Christian to the Porter, "Sir, what house is this? and may I lodge here to-night?"

The Porter answered, "This house was built by the Lord of the hill, and He built it for the relief and security of pilgrims." The Porter also asked whence he was, and whither he was going.

CHRIS. I am come from the City of Destruction, and am going to Mount Zion; but, because the sun is now set, I desire, if I may, to lodge here to-night.

PORT. What is your name?

CHRIS. My name is now Christian, but my name at the first was Graceless.

PORT. But how doth it happen that you come so late? The sun is set.

CHRIS. I had been here sooner, but that, wretched man that I am, I slept in the arbor that stands on the hill-side. Nay, I had, notwithstanding that, been here much sooner, but that in my sleep I lost my roll, and came without it to the brow of the hill; and then, feeling for it and finding it not, I was forced with sorrow of heart to go back to the place where I slept my sleep, where I found it; and now I am come.

PORT. Well, I will call out one of the women of this place, who will, if she likes your talk, bring you in to the rest of the family, according to the rules of the house.

So Watchful the Porter rang a bell, at the sound of which came out of the door of the house a grave and beautiful young woman, named Discretion, and asked why she was called.

The Porter answered, "This man is on a journey from

the City of Destruction to Mount Zion; but, being weary and benighted, he asked me if he might lodge here to-night; so I told him I would call for thee, who, after speaking with him, mayest do as seemeth thee good, even according to the law of the house."

PIETY, PRUDENCE, CHARITY

Then she asked him whence he was, and whither he was going; and he told her. She asked him also how he got into the way; and he told her. Then she asked him what he had seen and met with on the way; and he told her. And at last she asked his name. So he said, "It is Christian; and I have so much the more a desire to lodge here to-night, because, by what I perceive, this place was built by the Lord of the hill for the relief and safety of pilgrims." So she smiled, but the water stood in her eyes; and after a little pause, she said, "I will call forth two or three of my family." So she ran to the door, and called out Prudence, Piety, and Charity, who, after a little more discourse with him brought him in to the family; and many of them, meeting him at the threshold of the house, said, "Come in, thou blessed of the Lord: this house was built by the Lord of the hill on purpose to entertain such pilgrims in." Then he bowed his head, and followed them into the house. So, when he was come in and sat down, they gave him something to drink, and agreed together, that, until supper was ready, some of them should talk with Christian, for the best use of the time; and they appointed Piety, Prudence, and Charity to talk with him; and thus they began:

PIETY. Come, good Christian, since we have been so loving to you to receive you into our house this night, let us, if perhaps we may better ourselves thereby, talk with you of all things that have happened to you in your pilgrimage.

CHRIS. With a very good will, and I am glad that you are so
well disposed.

PIETY. What moved you at first to betake yourself to a pilgrim's
life?

CHRISTIAN'S ADVENTURES

CHRIS. I was driven out of my native country by a dreadful
sound that was in mine ears; to wit, that certain destruction did await me, if I abode in that place where I was.

PIETY. But how did it happen that you came out of your country
this way?

CHRIS. It was as God would have it; for, when I was under
the fears of destruction, I did not know whither to go;
but by chance there came a man even to me, as I was
trembling and weeping, whose name is Evangelist, and
he directed me to the wicket-gate, which else I should
never have found, and so set me in the way that hath
led me directly to this house.

PIETY. But did you not come by the house of the Interpreter?

CHRIS. Yes, and did see such things there, the remembrance
of which will stick by me as long as I live, especially
three things; to wit, how Christ, in despite of Satan, the
Evil One maintains His work of grace in the heart; how
the man had sinned himself quite out of hopes of God's
mercy; and also the dream of him that thought in his
sleep the day of judgment was come.

PIETY. Why? did you hear him tell his dream?

CHRIS. Yes, and a dreadful one it was, I thought it made my
heart ache as he was telling of it; but yet I am glad I
heard of it.

PIETY. Was that all you saw at the house of the Interpreter?

CHRIS. No; he took me, and had me where he showed me a
stately palace; and how the people were clad in gold
that were in it; and how there came a venturous man,

and cut his way through the armed men that stood in the door to keep him out; and how he was bid to come in and win eternal glory. Methought those things did delight my heart. I would have stayed at that good man's house a twelvemonth, but that I knew I had farther to go.

PIETY. And what saw you else in the way?

CHRIS. Saw? Why, I went but a little farther, and I saw One, as I thought in my mind, hang bleeding upon a tree; and the very sight of Him made my burden fall off my back; for I groaned under a very heavy burden, and then it fell down from off me. It was a strange thing to me, for I never saw such a thing before; yea, and while I stood looking up (for then I could not forbear looking), three Shining Ones came to me. One of them told me that my sins were forgiven me; another stripped me of my rags, and gave me this broidered coat which you see; and the third set the mark which you see in my forehead, and gave me this sealed roll. (And, with that, he plucked it out of his bosom.)

PIETY. But you saw more than this, did you not?

CHRIS. The things that I have told you were the best; yet some other matters I saw; as namely I saw three men, Simple, Sloth, and Presumption, lie asleep, a little out of the way as I came, with irons upon their heels; but do you think I could wake them? I also saw Formalist and Hypocrisy come tumbling over the wall, to go, as they pretended, to Zion; but they were quickly lost, even as I myself did tell them, but they would not believe. But, above all, I found it hard work to get up this hill, and as hard to come by the lions' mouths; and truly, if it had not been for the good man the Porter, that stands at the gate, I do not know but that, after all, I might have gone back again; but now I thank God I am here, and I thank you for receiving of me.

Then Prudence thought good to ask him a few questions, and desired his answer to them.

Pru. Do you think sometimes of the country from whence you came?

Chris. Yes, but with much shame and detestation. Truly, if I had been mindful of that country from whence I came out, I might have had an opportunity to have returned; but now I desire a better country, that is, a heavenly one.

Pru. Do you not yet bear away with you in your thoughts some of the things that you did in the former time?

Chris. Yes, but greatly against my will; especially my inward and sinful thoughts, with which all my countrymen, as well as myself, were delighted. But now all those things are my grief; and, might I but choose mine own things, I would choose never to think of those things more; but when I would be doing that which is best, that which is worst is with me.

Pru. Do you not find sometimes as if those things were overcome, which at other times are your trouble?

Chris. Yes, but that is but seldom; but they are to me golden hours in which such things happen to me.

Pru. Can you remember by what means you find your annoyances, at times, as if they were overcome?

Chris. Yes; when I think what I saw at the cross, that will do it; and when I look upon my broidered coat, that will do it; also when I look into the roll that I carry in my bosom, that will do it; and when my thoughts wax warm about whither I am going, that will do it.

Pru. And what makes you so desirous to go to Mount Zion?

Chris. Why, there I hope to see Him alive that did hang dead on the cross; and there I hope to be rid of all these things that to this day are in me an annoyance to me. There, they say, there is no death; and there I shall dwell with such company as I like best. For, to tell you the truth, I love Him because I was by Him eased of my burden; and I am weary of my inward sickness. I would fain be where I shall die no more, and with the company that shall continually cry, "Holy, holy, holy!"

CHARITY TALKS WITH CHRISTIAN

CHAR. Then said Charity to Christian, "Have you a family? are you a married man?"

CHRIS. I have a wife and four small children.

CHAR. And why did you not bring them along with you?

CHRIS. Then Christian wept, and said, "Oh, how willingly would I have done it! but they were all of them utterly against my going on pilgrimage."

CHAR. But you should have talked to them, and endeavored to have shown them the danger of staying behind.

CHRIS. So I did, and told them also what God had shown to me of the destruction of our city; but I seemed to them as one that mocked, and they believed me not.

CHAR. And did you pray to God that He would bless your words to them?

CHRIS. Yes, and that with much affection; for you must think that my wife and poor children are very dear unto me.

CHAR. But did you tell them of your own sorrow and fear of destruction? for I suppose that you could see your destruction before you.

CHRIS. Yes, over, and over, and over. They might also see my fears in my countenance, in my tears, and also in my trembling under the fear of the judgment that did hang over our heads: but all was not enough to prevail with them to come with me.

CHAR. But what could they say for themselves why they came not?

CHRIS. Why, my wife was afraid of losing this world, and my

children were given to the foolish delights of youth; so, what by one thing, and what by another, they left me to wander in this manner alone.

CHAR. But did you not, with your vain life, hinder all that you by words used by way of persuasion to bring them away with you?

CHRIS. Indeed, I cannot commend my life, for I am conscious to myself of many failings therein. I know also, that a man, by his actions may soon overthrow what, by proofs or persuasion, he doth labor to fasten upon others for their good. Yet this I can say, I was very wary of giving them occasion, by any unseemly action, to make them averse to going on pilgrimage. Yea, for this very thing they would tell me I was too precise, and that I denied myself of things (for their sakes) in which they saw no evil. Nay, I think I may say that, if what they saw in me did hinder them, it was my great tenderness in sinning against God, or of doing any wrong to my neighbor.

CHAR. Indeed, Cain hated his brother because his own works were evil, and his brother's righteous; and, if thy wife and children have been offended with thee for this, they thereby show themselves to be resolutely opposed to good: thou hast freed thy soul from their blood.

Now I saw in my dream, that thus they sat talking together till supper was ready. So, when they had made ready, they sat down to meat. Now, the table was furnished with fat things, and wine that was well refined; and all their talk at the table was about the Lord of the hill; as, namely, about what He had done, and wherefore He did what He did, and why He had builded that house; and by what they said, I perceived that He had been a great warrior, and had fought with and slain him that had the power of death, but not without great danger to Himself, which made me love Him the more.

For, as they said, and as I believe (said Christian), He did it with the loss of much blood. But that which puts the glory of grace into all He did, was, that He did it out of pure love to this country. And, besides, there were some of them of the household that said they had seen and spoken with Him since He did die on the cross; and they have declared that they had it from His own lips, that He is such a lover of poor pilgrims, that the like is not to be found from the east to the west. They moreover gave an instance of what they affirmed; and that was, He had stripped Himself of His glory, that He might do this for the poor; and that they had heard Him say and affirm that He would not dwell in the mountains of Zion alone. They said, moreover, that He had made many pilgrims princes, though by nature they were beggars born, and their home had been the dunghill.

Thus they talked together till late at night; and after they had committed themselves to their Lord for protection, they betook themselves to rest. The Pilgrim they laid in a large upper chamber, whose window opened towards the sunrising. The name of the chamber was Peace, where he slept till break of day, and then he awoke and sang:

> "Where am I now? Is this the love and care
> Of Jesus, for the men that pilgrims are,
> Thus to provide that I should be forgiven,
> And dwell already the next door to heaven?"

THE VIRGINS READ TO CHRISTIAN

So in the morning they all got up; and after some more talking together, they told him that he should not depart till they had shown him the rarities of that place. And first they took him into the study, where they showed him records of the greatest age; in which, as I remember in my dream, they showed him first the history of the Lord of the hill, that He was the son of the Ancient of Days, and had lived from the beginning. Here also were more fully written the acts that He had done, and the names of many hundreds that He had taken into his service; and how he had placed them in such houses that could neither by length of days nor decays of nature be destroyed.

Then they read to him some of the worthy acts that some of His servants had done; as, how they had conquered kingdoms, wrought righteousness, obtained promises, stopped the mouths of lions, quenched the violence of fire, escaped the edge of the sword, out of weakness were made strong, waxed valiant in fight, and turned to flight the armies of the enemies.

They then read again in another part of the records of the house, where it was shown how willing their Lord was to receive into His favor any even any, though they in time past had done great wrongs to His person and rule. Here also were several other histories of many other famous things, of all which Christian had a view; as of things both ancient and modern, together with prophecies and foretellings of things that surely come to pass, both to the dread and wonder of enemies, and the comfort and happiness of pilgrims.

The next day they took him and led him into the armory, where they showed him all manner of weapons which their Lord had provided for pilgrims; as sword, shield, helmet, breast-plate, all-prayer, and shoes that would not wear out. And there was here enough of this to harness out as many men for the service of their Lord as there be stars in the heaven for multitude.

They also showed him some of the things with which some of His servants had done wonderful things. They showed him Moses' rod; the hammer and nail with which Jael slew Sisera; the pitchers, trumpets, and lamps too, with which Gideon put to flight the armies of Midian. Then they showed him the ox's goad wherewith Shamgar slew six hundred men. They showed him also the jaw-bone with which Samson did such mighty feats. They showed him, moreover, the sling and stone with which David slew Goliath of Gath, and the sword also with which their Lord will kill the Man of Sin, in the day that He shall rise up to the battle. They showed him, besides, many excellent things, with which Christian was much delighted. This done, they went to their rest again.

Then I saw in my dream that on the morrow he got up to go forward, but they desired him to stay till the next day also; "and then," said they, "we will, if the day be clear, show you the Delectable Mountains;" which they said would yet further add to his comfort, because they were nearer the desired haven than the place where at present he was. So he consented and stayed. When the morning was up, they led him to the top of the house, and bid him look south. So he did, and behold, at a great distance he saw a most pleasant mountainous country, beautified with woods, vineyards, fruits of all sorts, flowers also, with springs and fountains, very lovely to behold. Then he asked the name of the country. They said it was Immanuel's Land; "and it is as common," said they, "as this hill is, to and for all the pilgrims. And when thou comest there, from thence thou mayest see to the gate of the Celestial City, as the shepherds that live there will make appear."

Now he bethought himself of setting forward, and they were willing he should. "But first," said they, "let us go again into the armory." So they did; and when he came there, they dressed him from head to foot with armor of proof, lest perhaps he should meet with assaults in the way. He being, therefore, thus armed, walked out with his friends to the gate; and there he asked the Porter if he saw any pilgrim pass by. Then the Porter answered, "Yes."

CHRIS. "Pray, did you know him?" said he.
PORT. I asked his name, and he told me it was Faithful.
CHRIS. "Oh," said Christian, "I know him, he is my townsman,

my near neighbor; he comes from the place where I was
born. How far do you think he may be before?"

PORT. He has got by this time below the hill.

CHRIS. "Well," said Christian, "good Porter, the Lord be with
thee, and add to all thy blessings much increase for the
kindness thou has shown to me!"

Then he began to go forward; but Discretion, Piety, Charity,
and Prudence would accompany him down to the foot of the
hill. So they went on together repeating their former discourses,
till they came to go down the hill. Then said Christian, "As
it was difficult coming up, so far so as I can see, it is dangerous
going down." "Yes," said Prudence, "so it is; for it is a hard
matter for a man to go down the Valley of Humiliation, as
thou art now, and to catch no slip by the way; therefore,"
said they, "are we come out to accompany thee down the hill."
So he began to go down, but very warily; yet he caught a slip
or two.

Then I saw in my dream that these good companions,
when Christian was gone down to the bottom of the hill, gave
him a loaf of bread, a bottle of wine, and a cluster of raisins;
and then he went his way.

CHAPTER 4

But now, in this Valley of Humiliation, poor Christian was hard put to it; for he had gone but a little way before he espied a foul fiend coming over the field to meet him: his name is Apollyon. Then did Christian begin to be afraid, and to cast in his mind whether to go back or to stand his ground. But he considered again that he had no armor for his back, and therefore thought that to turn the back to him might give him greater advantage with ease to pierce him with darts; therefore he resolved to venture and stand his ground; for, thought he, had I no more in mine eye than the saving of my life, it would be the best way to stand. So he went on, and Apollyon met him. Now, the monster was hideous to behold: he was clothed with scales like a fish, and they are his pride; he had wings like a dragon, and feet like a bear, and out of his belly came fire and smoke; and his mouth was as the mouth of a lion. When he was come up to Christian, he beheld him with a disdainful countenance, and thus began to question with him:

APOLLYON STAYS CHRISTIAN

APOL. Whence come you, and whither are you bound?
CHRIS. I am come from the City of Destruction, which

is the place of all evil, and am going to the City of Zion.

APOL. By this I perceive that thou art one of my subjects; for all that country is mine, and I am the prince and God of it. How is it then that thou hast run away from thy king? Were it not that I hope that thou mayest do me more service, I would strike thee now at one blow to the ground.

CHRIS. I was indeed born in your kingdom; but your service was hard, and your wages such as a man could not live on; for the wages of sin is death; therefore, when I was come to years, I did as other thoughtful persons do, look out, if perhaps I might mend myself.

APOL. There is no prince that will thus lightly lose his subjects, neither will I as yet lose thee; but, since thou complainest of thy service and wages, be content to go back, and what our country will afford I do here promise to give thee.

CHRIS. But I have let myself to another, even to the King of princes; and how can I with fairness go back with thee?

APOL. Thou hast done in this according to the proverb, "changed a bad for a worse;" but it is common for those that have called themselves His servants, after awhile to give Him the slip, and return again to me. Do thou so too, and all shall be well.

CHRIS. I have given Him my faith, and sworn my service to Him; how, then, can I go back from this, and not be hanged as a traitor?

APOL. Thou didst the same to me, and yet I am willing to pass by all, if now thou wilt yet turn again and go back.

CHRIS. What I promised thee was in my youth, and besides, I count that the Prince under whose banner I now stand is able to set me free, yea, and to pardon also what I did as to my service with thee. And besides, O thou destroying Apollyon, to speak the truth, I like His service, His wages,

His servants, His government, His company, and country, better than thine; therefore leave off to persuade me further: I am His servant, and I will follow Him.

APOL. Consider again when thou art in cold blood, what thou art likely to meet with in the way that thou goest. Thou knowest that for the most part His servants come to an ill end, because they are disobedient against me and my ways. How many of them have been put to shameful deaths! And besides, thou countest His service better than mine; whereas He never came yet from the place where He is, to deliver any that served Him out of their hands; but as for me, how many times, as all the world very well knows, have I delivered, either by power or fraud, those that have faithfully served me, from Him and His, though taken by them! And so I will deliver thee.

CHRIS. His forbearing at present to deliver them is on purpose to try their love, whether they will cleave to Him to the end; and, as for the ill end thou sayest they come to, that is most glorious in their account. For, for present deliverance, they do not much expect it; for they stay for their glory, and then they shall have it when their prince comes in His and the glory of the angels.

APOL. Thou hast already been unfaithful in thy service to Him; and how dost thou think to receive wages of Him?

CHRIS. Wherein, O Apollyon, have I been unfaithful to Him?

APOL. Thou didst faint at first setting out, when thou wast almost choked in the Gulf of Despond. Thou didst attempt wrong ways to be rid of thy burden, whereas thou shouldst have stayed till thy Prince had taken it off. Thou didst sinfully sleep and lose thy choice things. Thou wast almost persuaded to go back at the sight of the lions. And when thou talkest of thy journey, and of what thou hast seen and heard, thou art inwardly desirous of glory to thyself in all that thou sayest or doest.

CHRIS. All this is true, and much more which thou hast left out; but the Prince whom I serve and honor is merciful and ready to forgive. But besides, these infirmities possessed me in thy own country; for there I sucked them in, and I have groaned under them, been sorry for them, and have obtained pardon of my Prince.

APOL. Then Apollyon broke out into a grievous rage, saying, "I am an enemy to this Prince; I hate His person, His laws, and people. I am come out on purpose to withstand thee."

CHRISTIAN THE CONQUEROR

CHRIS. Apollyon, beware what you do, for I am in the King's highway, the way of holiness: therefore take heed to yourself.

APOL. Then Apollyon straddled quite over the whole breadth of the way, and said, "I am void of fear in this matter. Prepare thyself to die; for I swear by my infernal den, that thou shalt go no farther: here will I spill thy soul." And, with that, he threw a flaming dart at his breast; but Christian held a shield in his hand, with which he caught, and so prevented the danger of that.

Then did Christian draw, for he saw it was time to bestir him; and Apollyon as fast made at him, throwing darts as thick as hail, by the which, notwithstanding all that Christian could do to avoid it, Apollyon wounded him in his head, his hand, and foot. This made Christian give a little back; Apollyon, therefore, followed his work amain, and Christian again took courage, and resisted as manfully as he could. This sore combat lasted for above half a day, even till Christian was almost quite spent. For you must know that Christian, by reason of his wounds, must needs grow weaker and weaker.

Then Apollyon, espying his opportunity, began to gather up close to Christian, and, wrestling with him, gave him a dreadful fall; and, with that, Christian's sword flew out of his hand. Then said Apollyon, "I am sure of thee now." And, with that, he had almost pressed him to death, so that Christian began to despair of life. But, as God would have it, while Apollyon was fetching his last blow, thereby to make a full end of this good man, Christian nimbly reached out his hand for his sword, and caught it, saying, "Rejoice not against me, O mine enemy: when I fall I shall arise;" and, with that, gave him a deadly thrust, which made him give back, as one that had received his mortal wound. Christian, perceiving that, made at him again, saying, "Nay, in all these things we are more than conquerors through Him that loved us." And, with that, Apollyon spread forth his dragon's wings, and sped him away, that Christian for a season saw him no more.

In this combat no man can imagine, unless he had seen and heard, as I did, what yelling and hideous roaring Apollyon made all the time of the fight: he spake like a dragon; and, on the other side, what sighs and groans burst from Christian's heart. I never saw him all the while give so much as one pleasant look, till he perceived he had wounded Apollyon with his two-edged sword; then, indeed, he did smile and look upward; but it was the dreadfullest sight that ever I saw.

CHRISTIAN GIVES THANKS

CHRIS. So, when the battle was over, Christian said, "I will here give thanks to Him that hath delivered me out of the mouth of the lion; to Him that did help me against Apollyon." And so he did, saying:

> "Great Satan, the captain of this fiend,
> Designed my ruin; therefore to this end
> He sent him harnessed out: and he with rage
> That hellish was, did fiercely me engage;

> But blessed angels helped me; and I,
> By dint of sword, did quickly make him fly:
> Therefore to God let me give lasting praise,
> And thank and bless His holy name always."

Then there came to him a hand with some of the leaves of the tree of life; the which Christian took, and laid upon the wounds that he had received in the battle, and was healed immediately. He also sat down in that place to eat bread, and to drink of the bottle that was given to him a little before: so, being refreshed, he went forth on his journey, with his sword drawn in his hand; "For," he said, "I know not but some other enemy may be at hand." But he met with no other harm from Apollyon quite through this valley.

Now, at the end of this valley was another, called the Valley of the Shadow of Death; and Christian must needs go through it, because the way to the Celestial City lay through the midst of it. Now this valley is a very solitary place; the prophet Jeremiah thus describes it: "A wilderness, a land of deserts and pits, a land of drought, and of the shadow of death, a land that no man" but a Christian "passeth through, and where no man dwelt."

Now here Christian was worse put to it than in his fight with Apollyon, as in the story you shall see.

I saw then in my dream, that when Christian was got to the borders of the Shadow of Death, there met him two men, children of them that brought up an evil report of the good land, making haste to go back; to whom Christian spake as follows:

CHRIS. Whither are you going?

MEN. They said, "Back, back! and we would have you to do so too, if either life or peace is prized by you."

CHRIS. "Why, what's the matter?" said Christian.

MEN. "Matter!" said they: "we were going that way as you

are going, and went as far as we durst: and indeed we were almost past coming back; for had we gone a little farther, we had not been here to bring the news to thee."

CHRIS. "But what have you met with?" said Christian.

MEN. Why, we were almost in the Valley of the Shadow of Death, but that by good hap we looked before us, and saw the danger before we came to it.

CHRIS. "But what have you seen?" said Christian.

MEN. Seen! why, the valley itself, which is as dark as pitch: we also saw there the hobgoblins, satyrs, and dragons of the pit; we heard also in that valley a continual howling and yelling, as of a people under unutterable misery, who there sat bound in affliction and irons; and over that hung the discouraging clouds of confusion; Death also does always spread his wings over it. In a word, it is every whit dreadful, being utterly without order.

CHRIS. Then said Christian, "I perceive not yet, by what you have said, but that this is my way to the desired haven."

MEN. Be it thy way, we will not choose it for ours.

So they parted, and Christian went on his way, but still with his sword drawn in his hand, for fear lest he should be attacked.

I saw then in my dream, as far as this valley reached, there was on the right hand a very deep ditch; that ditch is it into which the blind have led the blind in all ages, and have both there miserably perished. Again, behold, on the left hand there was a very dangerous quag, or marsh, into which, if even a good man falls, he finds no bottom for his foot to stand on: into that quag King David once did fall, and had no doubt there been smothered, had not He that is able plucked him out.

The pathway was here also exceedingly narrow, and therefore good Christian was the more put to it; for when he sought, in the dark, to shun the ditch, on the one hand he was ready to tip over into the mire on the other; also when he sought to escape the mire, without great carefulness he would be ready to fall into the ditch. Thus he went on, and I heard him here sigh bitterly, for besides the danger mentioned above, the pathway was here so dark, that ofttimes, when he lifted up his foot to go forward, he knew not where or upon what he should set it next.

A COMPANY OF FIENDS

About the midst of this valley I perceived the mouth of hell to be, and it stood also hard by the wayside. Now, thought Christian, what shall I do? And ever and anon the flame and smoke would come out in such abundance, with sparks and hideous noises (things that cared not for Christian's sword, as did Apollyon before), that he was forced to put up his sword, and betake himself to another weapon, called "All-Prayer." So he cried in my hearing, "O Lord, I beseech Thee, deliver my soul." Thus he went on a great while, yet still the flames would be reaching towards him; also he heard doleful voices, and rushings to and fro, so that sometimes he thought he should be torn in pieces, or trodden down like mire in the streets. This frightful sight was seen, and those dreadful noises were heard by him, for several miles together, and, coming to a place where he thought he heard a company of fiends coming forward to meet him, he stopped, and began to muse what he had best to do. Sometimes he had half a thought to go back; then again he thought he might be half-way through the valley. He remembered, also, how he had already vanquished many a danger, and that the danger of going back might be much more than going forward. So he resolved to go on; yet the fiends seemed to come nearer and nearer. But, when they were come even almost at him, he cried out with a most vehement voice, "I will walk in the strength of the Lord God." So they gave back, and came no farther.

VALLEY OF THE SHADOW OF DEATH

One thing I would not let slip: I took notice that now poor Christian was so confounded that he did not know his own voice; and thus I perceived it: just when he was come over against the mouth of the burning pit, one of the wicked ones got behind him, and stepped up softly to him, and whisperingly suggested many wicked words to him, which he verily thought had proceeded from his own mind. This put Christian more to it than anything he had met with before, even to think that he should now speak evil of Him that he had so much loved before. Yet, if he could have helped it, he would not have done it; but he had not the wisdom either to stop his ears, or to know from whence those wicked words came.

When Christian had traveled in this sorrowful condition some considerable time he thought he heard the voice of a man, as going before him, saying, "Though I walk through the Valley of the Shadow of Death I will fear no evil; for Thou art with me."

Then he was glad, and that for these reasons:

First,—Because he gathered from thence, that some who feared God were in this valley as well as himself.

Secondly,—For that he perceived God was with them, though in that dark and dismal state. And why not, thought he, with me, though by reason of the kindness that attends this place, I cannot perceive it?

Thirdly,—For that he hoped (could he overtake them) to have company by-and-by. So he went on, and called to him that was before; but he knew not what to answer, for that he also thought himself to be alone. And by-and-by the day broke. Then said

Christian, "He hath turned the shadow of death into the morning."

Now, morning being come, he looked back, not out of desire to return, but to see, by the light of the day, what dangers he had gone through in the dark. So he saw more perfectly the ditch that was on the one hand, and the quag that was on the other; also how narrow the way which led betwixt them both. Also now he saw the hobgoblins, and satyrs, and dragons of the pit, but all afar off; for after break of day they came not nigh; yet they were shown to him according to that which is written, "He showeth deep things out of darkness, and bringeth out to light the shadow of death."

Now was Christian much affected with his deliverance from all the dangers of his solitary way; which dangers, though he feared them much before, yet he saw them more clearly now, because the light of the day made them plain to him. And about this time the sun was rising, and this was another mercy to Christian; for you must note that, though the first part of the Valley of the Shadow of Death was dangerous, yet this second part, which he was yet to go, was if possible far more dangerous; for, from the place where he now stood, even to the end of the valley, the way was all along set so full of snares, traps, gins, and nets here, and so full of pits, pitfalls, deep holes, and shelvings down there, that, had it now been dark, as it was when he came the first part of the way, had he had a thousand souls, they had in reason been cast away. But, as I said just now the sun was rising. Then said he, "His candle shineth on my head, and by His light I go through darkness."

POPE AND PAGAN

In this light, therefore, he came to the end of the valley. Now, I saw in my dream that at the end of the valley lay blood, bones, ashes, and mangled bodies of men, even of pilgrims that had gone this way formerly; and, while I was musing what should be the reason, I espied a little before me a cave, where two giants, POPE and PAGAN, dwelt in old time; by whose power and tyranny, the men whose bones, blood, ashes, etc., lay there, were cruelly put to death. But by this place Christian went without danger, whereat I somewhat wondered; but I have learnt since, that Pagan has been dead many a day; and, as for the other, though he be yet alive, he is, by reason of age, also of the many shrewd brushes that he met with in his younger days, grown so crazy and stiff in his joints, that he can now do little more than sit in his cave's mouth, grinning at pilgrims as they go by, and biting his nails because he cannot come to them.

So I saw that Christian went on his way; yet, at the sight of the old man that sat at the mouth of the cave, he could not tell what to think, especially because he spoke to him, though he could not go after him, saying, "You will never mend till more of you be burned." But he held his peace, and set a good face on it, and so went by and caught no hurt. Then sang Christian:

"O, world of wonders (I can say no less),
That I should be preserved in that distress
That I have met with here! Oh, blessed be
That hand that from it hath delivered me!
Dangers in darkness, devils, hell, and sin,
Did compass me, while I this vale was in;
Yes, snares, and pits, and traps, and nets
    did lie
My path about, that worthless, silly I
Might have been catched, entangled, and
    cast down;
But, since I live, let Jesus wear the crown."

CHAPTER 5

Now as Christian went on his way, he came to a little ascent which was cast up on purpose that pilgrims might see before them: up there, therefore, Christian went; and looking forward, he saw Faithful before him upon his journey. Then said Christian aloud, "Ho, ho! so-ho! stay, and I will be your companion." At that Faithful looked behind him; to whom Christian cried, "Stay, stay, till I come up to you." But Faithful answered, "No, I am upon my life, and the avenger of blood is behind me."

CHRISTIAN JOINS FAITHFUL

At this Christian was somewhat moved; and putting to all his strength, he quickly got up with Faithful, and did also overrun him: so the last was first. Then did Christian boastfully smile, because he had gotten the start of his brother; but, not taking good heed to his feet, he suddenly stumbled and fell, and could not rise again until Faithful came up to help him.

Then I saw in my dream, they went very lovingly on together, and had sweet talk together of all things that had happened to them in their pilgrimage; and thus Christian began:

CHRIS. My honored and well-beloved brother Faithful, I am glad that I have overtaken you, and that God has so tempered our spirits that we can walk as companions in this so pleasant a path.

FAITH. I had thought, dear friend, to have had your company quite from our town; but you did get the start of me, wherefore I was forced to come thus much of the way alone.

CHRIS. How long did you stay in the City of Destruction before you set out after me on your pilgrimage?

WHAT WAS SAID IN THE CITY

FAITH. Till I could stay no longer; for there was great talk, presently after you were gone out, that our city would, in a short time, with fire from heaven, be burned down to the ground.

CHRIS. What! did your neighbors talk so?

FAITH. Yes, it was for a while in everybody's mouth.

CHRIS. What! and did no more of them but you come out to escape the danger?

FAITH. Though there was, as I said, a great talk thereabout, yet I do not think they did firmly believe it. For, in the heat of the talking I heard some of them deridingly speak of you, and of your desperate journey; for so they called this your pilgrimage. But I did believe, and do still, that the end of our city will be with fire and brimstone from above; and therefore I have made my escape.

CHRIS. Did you hear no talk of neighbor Pliable?

FAITH. Yes, Christian; I heard that he followed you till he came to the Slough of Despond, where, as some said, he fell in; but he would not be known to have so done; but I am sure he was soundly bedabbled with that kind of dirt.

CHRIS. And what said the neighbors to him?

FAITH. He hath, since his going back, been held greatly in derision, and that among all sorts of people: some do mock and despise him, and scarce any will set him on work. He is now seven times worse than if he had never gone out of the city.

CHRIS. But why should they be set so against him, since they also despise the way that he forsook?

FAITH. "Oh," they say, "hang him; he is a turncoat! he was not true to his profession!" I think God has stirred up even his enemies to hiss at him and laugh at him, because he hath forsaken the way.

CHRIS. Had you no talk with him before you came out?

FAITH. I met him once in the streets, but he leered away on the other side, as one ashamed of what he had done; so I spake not to him.

CHRIS. Well, at my first setting out, I had hopes of that man, but now I fear he will perish in the overthrow of the city. For it has happened to him according to the true proverb, "The dog is turned to his vomit again, and the sow that was washed to her wallowing in the mire."

FAITH. These are my fears of him too; but who can hinder that which will be?

CHRIS. "Well, neighbor Faithful," said Christian, "let us leave him, and talk of things that more immediately concern ourselves. Tell me now what you have met with in the way as you came; for I know you have met with some things, or else it may be writ for a wonder."

FAITH. I escaped the slough that I perceive you fell into, and got up to the gate without that danger; only I met with one whose name was Wanton, that had like to have done me a mischief.

CHRIS. It was well you escaped her net: Joseph was hard put to it by her, and he escaped her as you did; but it had like to have cost him his life. But what did she do to you?

FAITH. You cannot think (but that you know something) what a flattering tongue she had; she lay at me hard to turn aside with her, promising me all manner of enjoyment.

CHRIS. Nay, she did not promise you the enjoyment of a good conscience.

FAITH. You know what I mean—not the enjoyment of the soul, but of the body.

CHRIS. Thank God you have escaped her: the abhorred of the Lord shall fall into her ditch.

FAITH. Nay, I know not whether I did wholly escape her or no.

CHRIS. Why, I suppose you did not consent to her desires?

FAITH. No, not to defile myself; for I remembered an old writing that I had seen which saith, "Her steps take hold of hell." So I shut mine eyes, because I would not be bewitched with her looks. Then she railed on me, and I went my way.

CHRIS. Did you meet with no other assault as you came?

FAITHFUL AND ADAM THE FIRST

FAITH. When I came to the foot of the hill called Difficulty, I met with a very aged man, who asked me what I was and whither bound. I told him that I was a pilgrim, going to the Celestial City. Then said the old man, "Thou lookest like an honest fellow: wilt thou be content to dwell with me, for the wages that I shall give thee?" Then I asked him his name, and where he dwelt. He said his name was Adam the First, and that he dwelt in the town of Deceit. I asked him then what was his work, and what the wages that he would give. He told me that his work was many delights; and his wages, that I should be his heir at last. I further asked him what house he kept, and what other servants he had. So he told me that his house was filled with all the dainties of the world, and that his servants were his own children. Then I asked him how many children he had. He said that he had but three daughters, the Lust of the Flesh, the Lust of the Eyes, and the Pride of Life, and that I should marry them if I would. Then I asked, how long time he would have me live with him? And he told me, As long as he lived himself.

CHRIS. Well, and what conclusion came the old man and you to at last?

FAITH. Why, at first I found myself somewhat inclinable to go with the man, for I thought he spake very fair; but looking in his forehead, as I talked with him, I saw there written, "Put off the old man with his deeds."

CHRIS. And how then?

FAITH. Then it came burning hot into my mind, whatever he said, and however he flattered, when he got home to his house he would sell me for a slave. So I bid him forbear, for I would not come near the door of his house. Then he reviled me, and told me that he would send such a one after me that should make my way bitter to my soul. So I turned to go away from him; but, just as I turned myself to go thence, I felt him take hold of my flesh, and give me such a deadly twitch back, that I thought he had pulled part of me after himself: this made me cry, "O wretched man!" So I went on my way up the hill. Now, when I had got about half-way up, I looked behind me, and saw one coming after me, swift as the wind; so he overtook me just about the place where the settle stands.

CHRIS. "Just there," said Christian, "did I sit down to rest me; but being overcome with sleep, I there lost this roll out of my bosom."

FAITH. But, good brother, hear me out. So soon as the man overtook me, he was but a word and a blow; for down he knocked me, and laid me for dead. But, when I was a little come to myself again, I asked him wherefore he served me so. He said, because of my secret inclining to Adam the First. And, with that, he struck me another deadly blow on the breast, and beat me down backwards; so I lay at his feet as dead as before. So, when I came to myself again, I cried him mercy; but he said, "I know not how to show mercy;" and, with that, he knocked me down again. He had doubtless made an end of me, but that One came by, and bid him forbear.

CHRIS. Who was that that bid him forbear?

FAITH. I did not know him at first; but, as He went by, I perceived the holes in His hands and His side; then I concluded that He was our Lord. So I went up the hill.

CHRIS. That man that overtook you was Moses. He spareth none, neither knoweth he how to show mercy to those that disobey his law.

FAITH. I know it very well: it was not the first time that he has met with me. It was he that came to me when I dwelt securely at home, and that told me he would burn my house over my head if I stayed there.

CHRIS. But did not you see the house that stood there, on the top of that hill on the side of which Moses met you?

FAITH. Yes, and the lions too, before I came at it. But, for the lions, I think they were asleep, for it was about noon; and because I had so much of the day before me I passed by the Porter, and came down the hill.

CHRIS. He told me, indeed, that he saw you go by; but I wished you had called at the house, for they would have showed you so many rarities, that you would scarce have forgot them to the day of your death. But pray tell me, did you meet nobody in the Valley of Humility?

FAITH. Yes, I met with one Discontent, who would willingly have persuaded me to go back again with him: his reason was, for that the valley was altogether without honor. He told me, moreover, that there to go was the way to disoblige all my friends, as Pride, Arrogancy, Self-Conceit, Worldly-Glory, with others, who he knew, as he said, would be very much offended if I made such a fool of myself as to wade through this valley.

CHRIS. Well, and how did you answer him?

FAITH. I told him that, although all these that he named might claim kindred of me, and that rightly (for, indeed, they were my relations according to the flesh), yet, since I became a pilgrim, they have disowned me, as I also have rejected them; and therefore they were to me now no more than if they had never been of my lineage. I told him, moreover, that as to this valley, he had quite misrepresented the thing; for before honor is humility, and a haughty spirit before a fall. "Therefore," said I, "I had rather go through this valley to the honor that was so accounted by the wisest, than choose that which he esteemed most worthy of our affections."

CHRIS. Met you with nothing else in that valley?

SHAME A BOLD VILLAIN

FAITH. Yes, I met with Shame; but, of all the men that I met with in my pilgrimage, he I think, bears the wrong name. The others would take "No" for an answer, at least after some words of denial; but this bold-faced Shame would never have done.

CHRIS. Why, what did he say to you?

FAITH. What? why, he objected against religion itself. He said it was a pitiful, low, sneaking business for a man to mind religion. He said that a tender conscience was an unmanly thing; and that for a man to watch over his words and ways, so as to tie up himself from that liberty that the brave spirits of the times accustom themselves unto, would make him the ridicule of all the people in our time. He objected also, that but a few of the mighty, rich, or wise were ever of my opinion; nor any of them neither, before they were persuaded to be fools, to venture the loss of all for nobody else knows what. He, moreover, objected the base and low estate and condition of those that were chiefly the pilgrims of the times in which they lived; also their ignorance, and want of understanding in all worldly knowledge. Yea, he did hold me to it at that rate also, about a great many more things than here I relate; as, that it was a shame to sit whining and mourning under a sermon, and a shame to come sighing and groaning home; that it was a shame to ask my neighbor forgiveness for petty faults, or to give back what I had taken from any. He said also that religion made a man grow strange to the great, because of a few vices (which he called by finer names), and because religion made him own and respect the base, who were of the same religious company; "and is not this," said he, "a shame?"

CHRIS. And what did you say to him?

FAITH. Say? I could not tell what to say at first. Yea, he put me so to it that my blood came up in my face; even this Shame fetched it up, and had almost beat me quite off. But at last I began to consider that that which is highly esteemed among men is had in abomination with God. And I thought again, This Shame tells me what men are, but it tells me nothing what God, or the Word of God is. And I thought, moreover, that at the day of doom we shall not be doomed to death or life according to the spirits of the world, but according to the wisdom and law of the Highest. Therefore, thought I, what God says is best—is best, though all the men in the world are against it. Seeing, then, that God prefers His religion; seeing God prefers a tender conscience; seeing they that make themselves fools for the kingdom of heaven are wisest, and that the poor man that loveth Christ is richer than the greatest man in the world that hates Him; Shame, depart! thou art an enemy to my salvation. Shall I listen to thee against my sovereign Lord? how, then, shall I look Him in the face at His coming? Should I now be ashamed of His way and servants how can I expect the blessing? But, indeed, this Shame was a bold villain: I could scarce shake him out of my company; yea, he would be haunting of me, and continually whispering me in the ear with some one or other of the weak things that attend religion. But at last I told him it was in vain to attempt further in this business; for those things that he despised, in those did I see most glory; and so, at last, I got past this persistent one. And when I had shaken him off, then I began to sing,

> "The trials that those men do meet withal,
> That are obedient to the heavenly call,
> Are manifold, and suited to the flesh,
> And come, and come, and come again afresh;
> That now, or some time else, we by them
>   may
> Be taken, overcome, and cast away.
> Oh, let the pilgrims, let the pilgrims then,
> Be vigilant and quit themselves like men!"

CHRIS. I am glad, my brother, that thou didst withstand this villain so bravely: for of all, as thou sayest, I think he has the wrong name; for he is so bold as to follow us in the streets, and to attempt to put us to shame before all men; that is, to make us ashamed of that which is good. But, if he was not himself bold, he would never attempt to do as he does. But let us still resist him; for, notwithstanding all his bold words, he promoteth the fool, and none else. "The wise shall inherit glory," said Solomon; "but shame shall be the promotion of fools."

FAITH. I think we must cry to Him for help against Shame who would have us to be valiant for truth upon the earth.

CHRIS. You say true. But did you meet nobody else in that valley?

FAITH. No, not I; for I had sunshine all the rest of the way through that, and also through the Valley of the Shadow of Death.

CHRIS. It was well for you! I am sure it fared far otherwise with me. I had for a long season, as soon almost as I entered into that valley, a dreadful combat with that foul fiend Apollyon; yea, I thought verily he would have killed me, especially when he got me down, and crushed me under him, as if he would have crushed me to pieces. For, as he threw me, my sword flew out of my hand; nay, he told me he was sure of me; and I cried to God, and He heard me, and delivered me out of all my troubles. Then I entered into the Valley of the Shadow of Death, and had no light for almost half the way through it. I thought I should have been killed there over and over: but at last day broke, and the sun rose, and I went through that which was behind with far more ease and quiet.

TALKATIVE OVERTAKEN

Moreover, I saw in my dream that, as they went on, Faithful, as he chanced to look on one side, saw a man whose name is Talkative walking at a distance beside them; for in this place there was room enough for them all to walk. He was a tall man, and something better looking at a distance than near at hand. To this man Faithful spoke himself in this manner:

FAITH. Friend, whither away? Are you going to the heavenly country?

TALK. I am going to that same place.

FAITH. That is well; then I hope we may have your good company.

TALK. With a very good will, will I be your companion.

FAITH. Come on, then, and let us go together, and let us spend our time in talking of things that are profitable.

TALK. To talk of things that are good, to me is very acceptable, with you or with any other; and I am glad that I have met with those that incline to so good a work; for, to speak the truth, there are but few who care thus to spend their time as they are in their travels, but choose much rather to be speaking of things to no profit; and this has been a trouble to me.

FAITH. That is, indeed, a thing to be lamented; for what things so worthy of the use of the tongue and mouth of men on earth, as are the things of the God of heaven?

TALK. I like you wonderfully well, for your saying is full of the truth; and I will add, What thing is so pleasant, and what so profitable, as to talk of the things of God? What things so pleasant? that is, if a man hath any delight in things that are wonderful. For instance, if a man doth delight to talk of the history or the mystery of things, or if a man doth love to talk of miracles, wonders, or signs, where shall he find things written so delightful, or so sweetly penned, as in the Holy Scripture?

FAITH. That's true; but to be profited by such things in our talk should be that which we design.

TALKATIVE SELF-DECEIVED

TALK. That is it that I said; for to talk of such things is most profitable; for, by so doing, a man may get knowledge of many things; as of the folly of earthly things, and the benefit of things above. Besides, by this a man may learn what it is to turn from sin, to believe, to pray, to suffer, or the like; by this, also, a man may learn what are the great promises and comforts of the Gospel, to his own enjoyment. Further, by this a man may learn to answer false opinions, to prove the truth, and also to teach the ignorant.

FAITH. All this is true; and glad am I to hear these things from you.

TALK. Alas! the want of this is the cause that so few understand the need of faith, and the necessity of a work of grace in their soul, in order to eternal life.

FAITH. But, by your leave, heavenly knowledge of these is the gift of God; no man attaineth to them by human working, or only by the talk of them.

TALK. All that I know very well, for a man can receive nothing except it be given him from heaven; I could give you a hundred scriptures for the confirmation of this.

FAITH. "Well, then," said Faithful, "what is that one thing that we shall at this time found our talk upon?"

TALK. What you will. I will talk of things heavenly or things earthly; things in life or things in the gospel; things sacred or things worldly; things past or things to come; things foreign or things at home; things necessary or things accidental, provided that all be done to our profit.

FAITH. Now did Faithful begin to wonder; and, stepping to Christian (for he walked all this while by himself), he said to him, but softly, "What a brave companion have we got! Surely this man will make a very excellent pilgrim."

FAITHFUL DISPUTES TALKATIVE

CHRIS. At this Christian modestly smiled, and said, "This man with whom you are so taken will deceive with this tongue of his twenty of them that know him not."

FAITH. Do you know him, then?

CHRIS. Know him? Yes, better than he knows himself.

FAITH. Pray what is he?

CHRIS. His name is Talkative; he dwelleth in our town. I wonder that you should be a stranger to him: only I consider that our town is large.

FAITH. Whose son is he? and whereabout doth he dwell?

CHRIS. He is the son of one Say-well. He dwelt in Prating Row, and is known to all that are acquainted with him by the name of Talkative of Prating Row; and notwithstanding his fine tongue, he is but a sorry fellow.

FAITH. Well, he seems to be a very pretty man.

CHRIS. That is, to them that have not a thorough acquaintance with him, for he is best abroad; near home he is ugly enough. Your saying that he is a pretty man brings to my mind what I have observed in the work of the painter, whose pictures show best at a distance, but very near more unpleasing.

FAITH. But I am ready to think you do but jest, because you smiled.

CHRIS. God forbid that I should jest (though I smiled) in this matter, or that I should accuse any falsely. I will give you a further discovery of him. This man is for any company, and for any talk. As he talketh now with you, so will he talk when he is on the ale-bench; and the more drink he hath in his crown, the more of these things he hath in his mouth. Religion hath no place in his heart, or house, or conversation: all he hath lieth in his tongue, and his religion is to make a noise therewith.

FAITH. Say you so? Then am I in this man greatly deceived.

CHRIS. Deceived! you may be sure of it. Remember the proverb, "They say, and do not;" but the kingdom of God is not in word, but in power. He talketh of prayer, of turning to God, of faith, and of the new birth; but he knows but only to talk of them. I have been in his family, and have seen him both at home and abroad, and I know what I say of him is the truth. His house is as empty of religion as the white of an egg is of savor. There is there neither prayer nor sign of turning from sin; yea, the brute, in his kind, serves God far better than he. He is the very stain, reproach, and shame of religion to all that know him. It can hardly have a good word in all that end of the town where he dwells, through him. Thus say the common people that know him: "A saint abroad, and a devil at home." His poor family finds it so: he is such a fault-finder, such a railer at, and so unreasonable with his servants, that they neither know how to do for or speak to him. Men that have any dealings with him say, it is better to deal with a Turk than with him, for fairer dealing they shall have at their hands. This Talkative, if it be possible, will go beyond them, cheat, beguile, and overreach them. Besides, he brings up his sons to follow his steps; and, if he findeth in any of them a foolish timorousness (for so he calls the first appearance of a tender conscience), he calls them fools and blockheads, and by no means will employ them in much, or speak to their commendation before others. For my part, I am of opinion that he has, by his wicked life, caused many to stumble and fall, and will be, if God prevent not, the ruin of many more.

FAITH. Well, my brother, I am bound to believe you, not only because you say you know him, but also because like a Christian you make your reports of men. For I cannot think you speak these things of ill-will, but because it is even so as you say.

CHRIS. Had I known him no more than you, I might, perhaps, have thought of him as at first you did; yea, had he received this report only from those that are enemies to religion, I should have thought it had been a slander, a lot that often falls from bad men's mouths upon good men's names and professions. But all these things, yea, and a great many more as bad, of my own knowledge I can prove him guilty of. Besides, good men are ashamed of him: they can neither call him brother nor friend; the very naming of him among them makes them blush, if they know him.

FAITH. Well, I see that saying and doing are two things, and hereafter I shall better observe the difference between them.

CHRIS. They are two things, indeed, and are as diverse as are the soul and the body; for, as the body without the soul is but a dead carcase, so *saying*, if it be alone, is but a dead carcase also. The soul of religion is the practical part. "Pure religion and undefiled before God and the Father is this, to visit the fatherless and the widows in their affliction, and to keep himself unspotted from the world." This, Talkative is not aware of: he thinks that hearing and saying will make a good Christian, and thus he deceiveth his own soul. Hearing is but as the sowing of the seed; talking is not sufficient to prove that fruit is indeed in the heart and life. And let us assure ourselves that, at the day of doom, men shall be judged according to their fruits.

FAITH. Well, I was not so fond of his company at first, but I am as sick of it now. What shall we do to be rid of him?

CHRIS. Take my advice, and do as I bid you, and you shall find that he will soon be sick of your company too, except God shall touch his heart and turn it.

FAITH. What would you have me to do?

CHRIS. Why, go to him, and enter into some serious conversation about the power of religion and ask him plainly (when he has approved of it, for that he will) whether this thing be set up in his heart, house or conduct.

FAITH. Then Faithful stepped forward again, and said to Talkative, "Come, what cheer? How is it now?"

TALK. Thank you, well: I thought we should have had a great deal of talk by this time.

FAITH. Well, if you will, we will fall to it now; and, since you left it with me to state the question, let it be this: How doth the saving grace of God show itself when it is in the heart of man?

TALK. I perceive, then, that our talk must be about the power of things. Well, it is a very good question, and I shall be willing to answer you. And take my answer in brief, thus. First, where the grace of God is in the heart, it causeth there a great outcry against sin. Secondly,—

FAITH. Nay, hold; let us consider of one at once. I think you should rather say, it shows itself by inclining the soul to hate its sin.

TALK. Why, what difference is there between crying out against and hating sin?

FAITH. Oh! a great deal. A man may cry out against sin in order to appear good; but he cannot hate it except by a real dislike for it. I have heard many cry out against sin in the pulpit, who yet can abide it well enough in the heart, house, and life. Some cry out against sin, even as the mother cries out against her child in her lap, when she calleth it a naughty girl, and then falls to hugging and kissing it.

TALK. You are trying to catch me, I perceive.

FAITH. No, not I; I am only for setting things right. But what is the second thing whereby you would prove a discovery of a work of God in the heart?

TALK. Great knowledge of hard things in the Bible.

TALKATIVE PARTS COMPANY

FAITH. This sign should have been first; but, first or last, it is also false; for knowledge, great knowledge, may be obtained in the mysteries of the Gospel, and yet no work of grace in the soul. Yea, if a man have all knowledge, he may yet be nothing, and so, consequently, be no child of God. When Christ said, "Do ye know all these things?" and the disciples had answered, "Yes," He added, "Blessed are ye if ye do them." He doth not lay the blessing in the knowledge of them, but in the doing of them. For there is a knowledge that is not attended with doing: "He that knoweth his master's will, and doeth it not." A man may know like an angel, and yet be no Christian; therefore your sign of it is not true. Indeed, to know is a thing that pleaseth talkers and boasters; but to do is that which pleaseth God.

TALK. You are trying to catch me again: this is not profitable.

FAITH. Well, if you please, name another sign how this work of grace showeth itself where it is.

TALK. Not I; for I see we shall not agree.

FAITH. Well, if you will not, will you give me leave to do it?

TALK. You may say what you please.

FAITH. God's work in the soul showeth itself either to him that hath it or to standers by. To him that has it, it is shown by making him see and feel his own sins. To others who are standing by it is shown by his life, a life of doing right in the sight of God. And now, sir, as to this brief account of the work of grace, and also the showing of it, if you have aught to object, object; if not, then give me leave to ask you a second question.

TALK. Nay, my part is not now to object, but to hear; let me, therefore, have your second question.

FAITH. It is this: Have you felt your own sins, and have you turned from them? And do your life and conduct show it the same? Or is your religion in word or in tongue, and not in deed and truth? Pray, if you incline to answer me in this, say no more than you know the God above will say Amen to, and also nothing but what your conscience can approve you in; for not he that commendeth himself is approved, but whom the Lord commendeth. Besides, to say I am thus and thus, when my conduct and all my neighbors tell me I lie, is great wickedness.

TALK. Then Talkative at first began to blush; but, recovering himself, thus he replied: "This kind of discourse I did not expect; nor am I disposed to give an answer to such questions, because I count not myself bound thereto, unless you take upon you to be a questioner; and though you should do so, yet I may refuse to make you my judge. But, I pray, will you tell me why you ask me such questions?"

FAITH. Because I saw you forward to talk, and because I knew not that you had aught else but notion. Besides, to tell you all the truth, I have heard of you that you are a man whose religion lies in talk, and that your life gives this your mouth-profession the lie. They say you are a spot among Christians, and that religion fareth the worse for your ungodly conduct; that some already have stumbled at your wicked ways, and that more are in danger of being destroyed thereby: your religion, and an alehouse, and greed for gain, and uncleanness, and swearing, and lying, and vain company-keeping, etc., will stand together. You are a shame to all who are members of the church.

TALK. Since you are ready to take up reports, and to judge so rashly as you do, I cannot but conclude you are some peevish or cross man, not fit to be talked with; and so adieu.

CHRIS. Then came up Christian, and said to his brother, "I told you how it would happen; your words and his heart could not agree. He had rather leave your company than reform his life. But he is gone, as I said: let him go; the loss is no man's but his own: he has saved us the trouble of going from him; for he continuing (as I suppose he will do) as he is, he would have been but a blot in our company. Besides, the Apostle says, 'From such withdraw thyself.'"

FAITH. But I am glad we had this little talk with him; it may happen that he will think of it again: however, I have dealt plainly with him, and so am clear of his blood, if he perisheth.

CHRIS. You did well to talk so plainly to him as you did. There is but little of this faithful dealing with men now-a-days; and that makes religion to be despised by so many; for they are these talkative fools, whose religion is only in word, and are vile and vain in their life, that, being so much admitted into the fellowship of the godly, do puzzle the world, blemish Christianity, and grieve the sincere. I wish that all men would deal with such as you have done; then should they either be made more suitable to religion, or the company of saints would be too hot for them.

FAITH. Then did Faithful say,

> "How Talkative at first lifts up his plumes!
> How bravely doth he speak! How he
>   presumes
> To drive down all before him! But so soon
> As Faithful talks of heart-work, like the
>   moon
> That's past the full, into the wane he goes;
> And so will all but he who heart-work
>   knows."

Thus they went on, talking of what they had seen by the way, and so made that way easy, which would otherwise, no doubt, have been tedious to them; for now they went through a wilderness.

CHAPTER 6

Now, when they were got almost quite out of this wilderness, Faithful chanced to cast his eye back, and espied one coming after him, and he knew him. "Oh!" said Faithful to his brother, "who comes yonder?" Then Christian looked, and said, "It is my good friend Evangelist." "Ay, and my good friend, too," said Faithful; "for it was he that set me the way to the gate." Now was Evangelist come up unto them, and thus saluted them:

EVAN. Peace be with you, dearly beloved, and peace be to your helpers.

CHRIS. Welcome, welcome, my good Evangelist: the sight of thy face brings to my thought thy former kindness and unwearied laboring for my eternal good.

FAITH. "And a thousand times welcome," said good Faithful: "thy company, O sweet Evangelist, how desirable is it to us poor pilgrims!"

EVAN. Then said Evangelist, "How hath it fared with you, my friends, since the time of our last parting? What have you met with, and how have you behaved yourselves?"

Then Christian and Faithful told him of all things that had happened to them in the way; and how, and with what difficulty, they had arrived to that place.

Evan. "Right glad am I," said Evangelist, "not that you met with trials, but that you have been victors, and for that you have, notwithstanding many weaknesses, continued in the way to this very day. I say, right glad am I of this thing, and that for my own sake and yours. I have sowed, and you have reaped; and the day is coming when 'both he that sowed and they that reaped shall rejoice together;' that is, if you faint not. The crown is before you, and it is an uncorruptible one: so run that you may obtain it. Some there be that set out for this crown, and after they have gone far for it, another comes in and takes it from them: 'Hold fast, therefore, that you have; let no man take your crown.'"

Then Christian thanked him for his words, but told him withal that they would have him speak further to them, for their help the rest of the way; and the rather, for that they well knew that he was a prophet, and could tell them of things that might happen unto them, and also how they might resist and overcome them. To which request Faithful also consented. So Evangelist began as followeth:

EVANGELIST EXHORTS CHRISTIAN

Evan. My sons, you have heard, in the words of the truth of the Gospel, that you must "through many trials enter into the kingdom of heaven;" and again, that "in every city bonds and afflictions await you;" and therefore you cannot expect that you should go long on your pilgrimage without them in some sort or other. You have found something of the truth of these words upon you already, and more will immediately follow; for now, as you see, you are almost out of this wilderness, and therefore you will soon come into a town that you will by-and-by see before you; and in that town you will be hardly beset with enemies who will strain hard but they will kill you; and be you sure that one or both of you must seal the truth which you hold with blood: but be you faithful unto death, and the King will give you a crown of life. He that shall die there, although his death will be unnatural, and his pain, perhaps, great, he will yet have the better of his fellow; not only because he will be arrived at the Celestial City soonest, but because he will escape many miseries that the other will meet with in the rest of his journey. But when you are come to the town, and shall find fulfilled what I have here related, then remember your friend, and quit yourselves like men, and commit the keeping of your souls to God in well-doing, as unto a faithful Creator.

THE PILGRIMS AT VANITY FAIR

Then I saw in my dream, that, when they were got out of the wilderness, they presently saw a town before them, and the name of that town is Vanity; and at the town there is a fair kept, called Vanity Fair. It is kept all the year long. It beareth the name of Vanity Fair, because the town where it is kept is lighter than vanity, and also because all that is there sold, or that cometh thither, is vanity; as is the saying of the Wise, "All that cometh is vanity."

This is no newly begun business, but a thing of ancient standing. I will show you the original of it.

Almost five thousand years ago, there were pilgrims walking to the Celestial City, as these two honest persons are; and Beelzebub, Apollyon, and Legion, with their companions, perceiving by the path that the pilgrims made that their way to the city lay through this town of Vanity, they contrived here to set up a fair; a fair wherein should be sold all sorts of vanity, and that it should last all the year long. Therefore at this fair are all such things sold as houses, lands, trades, places, honors, preferments, titles, countries, kingdoms, lusts, pleasures, and delights of all sorts, as wives, husbands, children, masters, servants, lives, blood, bodies, souls, silver, gold, pearls, precious stones, and what not.

And, moreover, at this fair there are at all times to be seen jugglings, cheats, games, plays, fools, apes, knaves, and rogues, and that of every kind.

Here are to be seen, too, and that for nothing, thefts, murders, false swearers, and that of a blood-red color.

And, as in other fairs of less moment there are several rows and streets under their proper names, where such and such wares are vended; so here likewise you have the proper places, rows, streets (namely, countries and kingdoms), where the wares of this fair are soonest to be found. Here are the Britain Row, the French Row, the Italian Row, the Spanish Row, the German Row, where several sorts of vanities are to be sold. But, as in other fairs some one commodity is as the chief of all the fair, so the ware of Rome and her goods are greatly promoted in this fair; only our English nation, with some others, have taken dislike thereat.

Now, as I said, the way to the Celestial City lies just through this town where this lusty fair is kept; and he that would go to the city, and yet not go through this town, "must needs go out of the world." The Prince of princes Himself, when here, went through this town to His own country, and that upon a fair day too; yea, and as I think, it was Beelzebub, the chief lord of this fair, that invited Him to buy of his vanities; yea, would have made Him lord of the fair, would He but have done him reverence as He went through the town. Yea, because He was such a person of honor, Beelzebub had Him from street to street, and showed Him all the kingdoms of the world in a little time, that he might, if possible, allure that Blessed One to ask for and buy some of his vanities; but He had no mind to the merchandise, and therefore left the town without laying out so much as one farthing upon these vanities. This fair, therefore, is an ancient thing of long-standing, and a very great fair.

Now, these pilgrims, as I said, must needs go through this fair. Well, so they did; but, behold, even as they entered into the fair, all the people in the fair were moved and the town itself, as it were, in a hubbub about them, and that for several reasons; for,

First,—The pilgrims were clothed with such kind of garments as were different from the raiment of any that traded in that fair. The people, therefore, of the fair, made a great gazing upon them: some said they were fools; some, they were bedlams; and some, they were outlandish men.

Secondly,—And, as they wondered at their apparel, so they did likewise at their speech; for few could understand what they said. They naturally spoke the language of Canaan; but they that kept the fair were the men of this world. So that from one end of the fair to the other, they seemed barbarians each to the other.

Thirdly,—But that which did not a little amuse the store-keepers was, that these pilgrims set very light by all their wares. They cared not so much as to look upon them; and if they called upon them to buy, they would put their fingers in their ears, and cry, "Turn away mine eyes from beholding

vanity," and look upwards, signifying that their
trade and traffic were in heaven.

One chanced, mockingly, beholding the actions of the men,
to say unto them, "What will you buy?" But they, looking
gravely upon him, said, "We buy the truth." At that there
was an occasion taken to despise the men the more: some
mocking, some taunting, some speaking reproachfully, and
some calling on others to smite them. At last things came to
a hubbub and great stir in the fair, insomuch that all order
was confounded. Now was word presently brought to the
great one of the fair, who quickly came down, and deputed
some of his most trusty friends to take these men for trial
about whom the fair was almost overturned. So the men were
brought to trial, and they that sat upon them asked them
whence they came, whither they went, and what they did
there in such an unusual garb. The men told them that they
were pilgrims and strangers in the world, and that they were
going to their own country, which was the heavenly Jerusalem,
and that they had given no occasion to the men of the town,
nor yet to the merchants, thus to abuse them, and to hinder
them in their journey, except it was for that, when one asked
them what they would buy, they said they would buy the
truth. But they that were appointed to examine them did not
believe them to be any other than crazy people and mad, or
else such as came to put all things into a confusion in the fair.
Therefore they took them and beat them, and besmeared them
with dirt, and then put them into the cage, that they might
be made a spectacle to all the men of the fair. There, therefore,
they lay for some time, and were made the objects of any
man's sport, or malice, or revenge; the great one of the fair
laughing still at all that befell them. But, the men being
patient, and "not rendering railing for railing, but contrariwise
blessing," and giving good words for bad, and kindness for
injuries done, some men in the fair that were more observing

and less opposed than the rest, began to check and blame the baser sort for their continual abuses done by them to the men. They, therefore, in an angry manner, let fly at them again, counting them as bad as the men in the cage, and telling them that they seemed to be in league with them, and should be made partakers of their misfortunes. The others replied, that, for aught they could see, the men were quiet and sober, and intended nobody any harm; and that there were many that traded in their fair that were more worthy to be put into the cage, yea, and pillory too, than were the men that they had abused. Thus, after divers words had passed on both sides (the men behaving themselves all the while very wisely and soberly before them,) they fell to some blows, and did harm to one another. Then were these two poor men brought before the court again, and there charged as being guilty of the late hubbub that had been in the fair. So they beat them pitifully, and hanged irons upon them, and led them in chains up and down the fair, for an example and terror to others, lest any should speak in their behalf, or join themselves unto them. But Christian and Faithful behaved themselves yet more wisely, and received the wrongs and shame that were cast upon them with so much meekness and patience, that it won to their side (though but few in comparison of the rest) several of the men in the fair. This put the other party in yet a greater rage, insomuch that they resolved upon the death of these two men. Wherefore they threatened that neither cage nor irons should serve their turn, but that they should die for the abuse they had done, and for deceiving the men of the fair.

THE PILGRIMS IN STOCKS

Then were they remanded to the cage again, until further order should be taken with them. So they put them in, and made their feet fast in the stocks.

Here, therefore, they called again to mind what they had

heard from their faithful friend Evangelist, and were more confirmed in their way and sufferings, by what he told them would happen to them. They also now comforted each other, that whose lot it was to suffer, even he should have the best of it; therefore each man secretly wished he might have that privilege. But, committing themselves to the all-wise disposal of Him that ruleth all things, with much content they abode in the condition in which they were, until they should be otherwise disposed of.

LORD HATE-GOOD

Then a convenient time being appointed, they brought them forth to their trial, in order to their being condemned. When the time was come, they were brought before their enemies, and placed on trial. The judge's name was Lord Hate-good: the charges against both were one and the same in substance, though somewhat varying in form; the contents whereof were this: "That they were enemies to and disturbers of their trade; that they had made riots and divisions in the town, and had won a party to their own most dangerous opinions, in contempt of the law of their prince."

Then Faithful began to answer, that he had only set himself against that which had set itself against Him that is higher than the highest. "And," said he, "as for disturbances, I make none, being myself a man of peace; the parties that were won to us, were won by beholding our truth and inno-cence, and they are only turned from the worse to the better. And, as to the king you talk of, since he is Beelzebub, the enemy of our Lord, I defy him and all his angels."

THE PILGRIMS ON TRIAL

Then it was made known that they that had aught to say for their lord the king against the prisoner at the bar should forthwith appear and give in their evidence. So there came in three witnesses; to wit, Envy, Superstition, and Pickthank. They were then asked if they knew the prisoner at the bar, and what they had to say for their lord the king against him.

Then stood forth Envy, and said to this effect: "My lord, I have known this man a long time, and will attest upon my oath before this honorable bench that he is—"

JUDGE. Hold! Give him his oath.

ENVY. So they sware him. Then said he, "My lord, this man, notwithstanding his name, Faithful is one of the vilest men in our country. He cares for neither prince nor people, law nor custom, but doth all that he can to possess all men with certain of his disloyal notions, which he in the general calls principles of faith and holiness. And in particular, I heard him once myself affirm that Christianity and the customs of our town of Vanity were opposite, and could not be reconciled. By which saying, my lord, he doth at once not only condemn all our laudable doings, but us in the doing of them."

JUDGE. Then did the judge say to him, "Hast thou any more to say?"

ENVY. My lord, I could say much more, only I would not be tiresome to the court. Yet, if need be, when the other gentlemen have given in their evidence, rather than anything shall be wanting that will dispatch him, I will have more to speak against him. So he was bid stand by.

Then they called Superstition, and bade him look upon the prisoner. They also asked what he could say for their lord the king against him. Then they sware him: so he began:

SUPER. My lord, I have no great acquaintance with this man, nor do I desire to have further knowledge of him. However, this I know, that he is a very pestilent fellow, from some discourse the other day that I had with him in this town; for then, talking with him, I heard him say that our religion was naught, and such by which a man could by no means please God. Which saying of his, my lord, your lordship very well knows what necessarily thence will follow; to wit, that we still do worship in vain, are yet in our sins, and finally shall be destroyed: and this is that which I have to say.

Then was Pickthank sworn, and bid say what he knew, in behalf of their lord the king, against the prisoner at the bar.

PICK. My lord, and you gentlemen all, this fellow I have known a long time, and have heard him speak things that ought not to be spoken, for he hath railed on our noble prince Beelzebub, and hath spoken contemptuously of his honorable friends, whose names are, the Lord Old-man, the Lord Carnal-Delight, the Lord Luxurious, the Lord Desire-of-Vain-Glory, my old Lord Lust, Sir Having Greedy, with all the rest of our nobility and he hath said, moreover, that, if all men were of his mind, if possible there is not one of these noblemen should have any longer a being in this town. Besides, he has not been afraid to rail on you, my lord, who are now appointed to be his judge, calling you an ungodly villain, with many other such-like abusive terms, with which he hath bespattered most of the gentry of our town.

JUDGE. When this Pickthank had told his tale, the judge directed his speech to the prisoner at the bar, saying, "Thou runagate, heretic, and traitor! hast thou heard what these honest gentlemen have witnessed against thee?"

FAITH. May I speak a few words in my own defense?

JUDGE. Sirrah, sirrah, thou deservest to live no longer, but to be slain immediately upon the place; yet, that all men may see our gentleness towards thee, let us hear what thou, vile runagate, hast to say.

FAITH. 1. I say, then, in answer to what Mr. Envy hath spoken, I have never said aught but this, that what rule, or laws, or custom, or people were flat against the Word of God, are opposite to Christianity. If I have said amiss in this, convince me of my error, and I am ready here before you to take back my words.

2. As to the second, to wit, Mr. Superstition and his charge against me, I said only this, that in the worship of God there is required true faith. But there can be no true faith without a knowledge of the will of God. Therefore, whatever is thrust into the worship of God that is not agreeable to the word of God will not profit to eternal life.

3. As to what Mr. Pickthank hath said, I say (avoiding terms, as that I am said to rail, and the like), that the prince of this town, with all the rabblement his attendants, by this gentleman named, are more fit for a being in hell than in this town and country. And so the Lord have mercy upon me!

Then the judge called to the jury (who all this while stood by to hear and observe), "Gentlemen of the jury, you see this man about whom so great an uproar hath been made in this town; you have also heard what these worthy gentlemen have witnessed against him; also you have heard his reply and confession. It lieth now in your breast to hang him or to save his life; but yet I think meet to instruct you into our law.

"There was an act made in the days of Pharaoh, the great servant to our prince, that, lest those of a contrary religion should multiply and grow too strong for him, their males should be thrown into the river. There was also an act made in the days of Nebuchadnezzar the Great, another of his servants, that whoever would not fall down and worship his golden image should be thrown into a fiery furnace. There was also an act made in the days of Darius, that whoso for some time called upon any god but him should be cast into the lions' den. Now, the substance of these laws this rebel has broken, not only in thought (which is not to be borne,) but also in word and deed, which must, therefore, needs be intolerable. You see he disputeth against our religion; and for the reason that he hath confessed he deserveth to die the death."

FAITHFUL DIES AT THE STAKE

Then went the jury out, whose names were Mr. Blind-man, Mr. No-good, Mr. Malice, Mr. Love-lust, Mr. Live-loose, Mr. Heady, Mr. High-mind, Mr. Enmity, Mr. Liar, Mr. Cruelty, Mr. Hate-light, and Mr. Implacable, who every one gave in his private voice against him among themselves, and afterwards unanimously concluded to bring him in guilty before the Judge. And first among themselves, Mr. Blind-man, the foreman, said, "I see clearly that this man is a heretic." Then said Mr. No-good, "Away with such a fellow from the earth!" "Ay," said Mr. Malice, "for I hate the very look of him." Then said Mr. Love-lust, "I could never endure him." "Nor I," said Mr. Live-loose; "for he would always be condemning my way." "Hang him, hang him!" said Mr. Heady. "A sorry scrub," said Mr. High-mind. "My heart riseth against him," said Mr. Enmity. "He is a rogue," said Mr. Liar. "Hanging is too good for him," said Mr. Cruelty. "Let us dispatch him out of the way," said Mr. Hate-light. Then said Mr. Implacable, "Might I have all the world given to me, I could not be reconciled to him; therefore let us forthwith bring him in guilty of death."

And so they did: therefore he was presently condemned to be had from the place where he was, to the place from whence he came, and there to be put to the most cruel death that could be invented.

They therefore brought him out, to do with him according

to their law; and first they scourged him, then they buffeted him, then they lanced his flesh with knives; after that they stoned him with stones, then pricked him with their swords, and, last of all, they burned him to ashes at the stake. Thus came Faithful to his end.

Now, I saw that there stood behind the multitude a chariot and a couple of horses waiting for Faithful, who (so soon as his enemies had slain him) was taken up into it, and straightway was carried up through the clouds with sound of trumpet the nearest way to the Celestial Gate. But as for Christian, he had some delay, and was sent back to prison; so he there remained for a space. But He who overrules all things, having the power of their rage in his own hand, so wrought it about that Christian for that time escaped them, and went his way. And as he went, he sang, saying,

> "Well, Faithful, thou hast faithfully professed
> Unto thy Lord, with whom thou shalt be
>   blest,
> When faithless ones, with all their vain
>   delights,
> Are crying out under their hellish plights.
> Sing, Faithful, sing, and let thy name
>   survive;
> For though they killed thee, thou art yet
>   alive."

CHAPTER 7

Now, I saw in my dream, that Christian went forth not alone; for there was one whose name was Hopeful (being so made by looking upon Christian and Faithful in their words and behavior in their sufferings at the fair,) who joined himself unto him, and, entering into a brotherly pledge told him that he would be his companion. Thus one died to show faithfulness to the truth, and another rises out of his ashes to be a companion with Christian in his pilgrimage. This Hopeful also told Christian that there were many more of the men in the fair that would take their time and follow after.

BY-ENDS OF FAIR-SPEECH

So I saw that, quickly after they were got out of the fair, they overtook one that was going before them, whose name was By-ends; so they said to him, "What countryman, sir? and how far go you this way?" He told them that he came from the town of Fair-speech, and he was going to the Celestial City; but told them not his name.

CHRIS. "From Fair-speech! are there any that be good live there?"

By. "Yes," said By-ends, "I hope."

Chris. Pray, sir, what may I call you?

By. I am a stranger to you, and you to me: if you be going this way, I shall be glad of your company; if not, I must be content.

Chris. This town of Fair-speech, I have heard of it; and, as I remember, they say it's a wealthy place.

By. Yes, I will assure you that it is; and I have very many rich kindred there.

Chris. Pray, who are your kindred there? if a man may be so bold.

By. Almost the whole town; but in particular my Lord Turnabout, my Lord Timeserver, my Lord Fair-speech, from whose ancestors that town first took its name; also Mr. Smooth-man, Mr. Facing-both-ways, Mr. Anything; and the parson of our parish, Mr. Two-tongues, was my mother's own brother by father's side; and to tell you the truth, I am become a gentleman of good quality; yet my great-grandfather was but a waterman, looking one way and rowing another, and I got most of my estate by the same occupation.

Chris. Are you a married man?

By. Yes, and my wife is a very virtuous woman, the daughter of a virtuous woman; she was my Lady Feigning's daughter: therefore she came of a very honorable family, and is arrived to such a pitch of breeding, that she knows how to carry it to all, even to prince and peasant. 'Tis true we somewhat differ in religion from those of the stricter sort, yet but in two small points: First, we never strive against wind and tide; secondly, we are always most zealous when Religion is well dressed and goes in his silver slippers: we love much to walk with him in the street if the sun shines and the people praise him.

Then Christian stepped a little aside to his fellow Hopeful, saying, "It runs in my mind that this is one By-ends, of

Fair-speech; and if it be he, we have as very a knave in our company as dwelleth in all these parts." Then said Hopeful, "Ask him; methinks he should not be ashamed of his name." So Christian came up with him again, and said, "Sir, you talk as if you knew something more than all the world doth; and if I take not my mark amiss, I deem I have half a guess of you. Is not your name Mr. By-ends, of Fair-speech?"

BY. This is not my name; but, indeed, it is a nickname that is given me by some that cannot abide me, and I must be content to bear it as a reproach, as other good men have borne theirs before me.

CHRIS. But did you never give an occasion to men to call you by this name?

BY. Never, never! The worst that ever I did to give them an occasion to give me this name was, that I had always the luck to jump in my judgment with the present way of the times, whatever it was, and my chance was to gain thereby. But if things are thus cast upon me, let me count them a blessing; but let not the malicious load me therefore with reproach.

CHRIS. I thought, indeed, that you were the man that I heard of; and, to tell you what I think, I fear this name belongs to you more properly than you are willing we should think it doth.

BY. Well, if you will thus imagine, I cannot help it: you shall find me a fair company-keeper if you still admit me your companion.

CHRIS. If you will go with us, you must go against wind and tide; the which, I perceive, is against your opinion; you must also own Religion in his rags, as well as when in his silver slippers; and stand by him, too, when bound in irons, as well as when he walketh the streets with applause.

BY. You must not impose or lord it over my faith; leave it to my liberty, and let me go with you.

CHRIS. Not a step farther, unless you will do in what I declare as we do.

BY. Then said By-ends, "I never desert my old principles, since they are harmless and profitable. If I may not go with you, I must do as I did before you overtook me, even go by myself, until some overtake me that will be glad of my company."

MONEY-LOVE'S PRINCIPLES

Now, I saw in my dream that Christian and Hopeful forsook him, and kept their distance before him; but one of them, looking back, saw three men following Mr. By-ends; and, behold, as they came up with him, he made them a very low bow, and they also gave him a compliment. The men's names were Mr. Hold-the-world, Mr. Money-love, and Mr. Save-all; men that Mr. By-ends had been formerly acquainted with; for in their boyhood they were schoolfellows, and taught by one Mr. Gripe-man a schoolmaster in Love-gain, which is a market town in the county of Coveting, in the North. This schoolmaster taught them the art of getting, either by violence, cheating, flattery, lying, or by putting on a pretence of religion; and these four gentlemen had learned much of the art of their master, so that they could each of them have kept such a school themselves.

Well, when they had, as I said, thus saluted each other, Mr. Money-love said to Mr. By-ends, "Who are they upon the road before us?" for Christian and Hopeful were yet within view.

BY. They are a couple of far countrymen, that, after their mode, are going on pilgrimage.

MONEY. Alas! why did they not stay, that we might have had their good company? for they, and we, and you, sir, I hope, are all going on pilgrimage.

BY. We are so, indeed; but the men before us are so rigid, and love so much their own notions, and do also so lightly esteem the opinions of others, that, let a man be ever so godly, yet, if he agrees not with them in all things, they thrust him quite out of their company.

SAVE. That is bad; but we read of some that are righteous overmuch, and such men's rigidness makes them to judge and condemn all but themselves. But I pray, what and how many were the things wherein you differed?

BY. Why, they, after their headstrong manner conclude that it is their duty to rush on their journey all weathers; and I am for waiting for wind and tide. They are for taking the risk of all for God at a clap; and I am for taking all advantages to secure my life and property. They are for holding their notions, though all other men be against them; but I am for religion in what and so far as, the times and my safety will bear it. They are for Religion when in rags and contempt; but I am for him when he walks in his golden slippers, in the sunshine, and with applause.

HOLD. Ay, and hold you there still, good Mr. By-ends; for, for my part, I can count him but a fool, that, having the liberty to keep what he has, shall be so unwise as to lose it. Let us be wise as serpents. It is best to make hay while the sun shines. You see how the bee lieth still all winter, and bestirs her only when she can have profit and pleasure. God sends sometimes rain and sometimes sunshine; if they be such fools to go through the rain, yet let us be content to take fair weather along with us. For my part, I like that religion best that will stand with the safety of God's good blessings unto us; for who can imagine, that is ruled by his reason, since God has bestowed upon us the good things of this life, but that He would have us keep them for His sake? Abraham and Solomon grew rich in religion; and Job says that "a good man should lay up gold as dust;" but he must not be such as the men before us, if they be as you have described them.

SAVE. I think that we are all agreed in this matter, and therefore there needs no more words about it.

MONEY. No, there needs no more words about this matter, indeed; for he that believes neither Scripture nor reason (and you see we have both on our side), neither knows his own liberty nor seeks his own safety.

And so these four men, Mr. By-ends, Mr. Money-love, Mr. Save-all, and old Mr. Hold-the-world, walked on together, while Christian and Hopeful were far in advance.

CHRISTIAN AND HOPEFUL

Then Christian and Hopeful went on till they came to a delicate plain, called Ease, where they went with much content; but that plain was but narrow, so they were quickly got over it. Now at the farther side of that plain was a little hill, called Lucre, and in that hill a silver mine, which some of them that had formerly gone that way, because of the rarity of it, had turned aside to see; but going too near the brink of the pit, the ground, being deceitful under them, broke, and they were slain; some also had been maimed there, and could not to their dying day be their own men again.

Then I saw in my dream that a little off the road, over against the silver mine, stood Demas (gentleman-like) to call to passengers to come and see; who said to Christian and his fellow, "Ho! turn aside hither, and I will show you a thing."

CHRIS. What thing so deserving as to turn us out of the way?

DEMAS. Here is a silver mine, and some digging in it for treasure; if you will come, with a little pains you may richly provide for yourselves.

HOPE. Then said Hopeful, "Let us go see."

CHRIS. "Not I," said Christian. "I have heard of this place before now, and how many have there been slain; and besides, that treasure is a snare to those that seek it, for it hindereth them in their pilgrimage."

CHRIS. Then Christian called to Demas, saying, "Is not the place dangerous? Hath it not hindered many in their pilgrimage?"

DEMAS. Not very dangerous, except to those that are careless. But withal, he blushed as he spake.

CHRIS. Then said Christian to Hopeful, "Let us not stir a step, but still keep on our way."

HOPE. I will warrant you, when By-ends comes up, if he hath the same invitation as we, he will turn in thither to see.

CHRIS. No doubt thereof, for his principles lead him that way; and a hundred to one but he dies there.

DEMAS. Then Demas called out again, saying, "But will you not come over and see?"

CHRIS. Then Christian roundly answered, saying, "Demas, thou art an enemy to the right ways of the Lord of this way, and hast been already condemned for thine own turning aside, by one of His Majesty's judges; and why seekest thou to have us condemned also? Besides, if we at all turn aside, our Lord the King will certainly hear thereof, and will there put us to shame where we should stand with boldness before Him."

Demas cried again that he also was one of their company, a pilgrim like themselves, and that, if they would tarry a little, he also himself would walk with them.

CHRIS. Then said Christian, "What is thy name? Is it not the same by the which I have called thee?"

DEMAS. Yes, my name is Demas; I am the son of Abraham.

CHRIS. I know you: Gehazi was your great-grandfather, and

Judas your father, and you have trod in their steps. It is but a devilish prank that thou usest: thy father was hanged for a traitor, and thou deservest no better reward. Assure thyself that when we come to the King, we will tell him of this thy behavior. Thus they went their way.

By this time By-ends and his companions were come again within sight, and they at the first beck went over to Demas. Now, whether they fell into the pit by looking over the brink thereof, or whether they went down to dig, or whether they were smothered in the bottom by the damps that commonly arise, of these things I am not certain; but this I observed, that they never were seen again in the way. Then sang Christian:

> "By-ends and silver Demas both agree;
> One calls; the other runs, that he may be
> A sharer in his lucre; so these two
> Take up in this world, and no farther go."

Now, I saw that just on the other side of the plain the pilgrims came to a place where stood an old monument hard by the highway-side; at the sight of which they were both concerned, because of the strangeness of the form thereof; for it seemed to them as if it had been a woman changed into the shape of a pillar. Here, therefore, they stood looking and looking upon it, but could not for a time tell what they should make thereof. At last Hopeful espied written above, upon the head thereof, a writing in an unusual hand; but he, being no scholar, called to Christian (for he was learned,) to see if he could pick out the meaning; so he came, and after a little laying of letters together, he found the same to be this, "Remember Lot's wife." So he read it to his fellow; after which, they both concluded that that was the pillar of salt into which Lot's wife was turned, for her looking back with a covetous heart when she was going from Sodom. Which sudden and amazing sight gave them occasion for speaking thus:

CHRIS. Ah, my brother! this is a seasonable sight. It came just in time to us after the invitation which Demas gave us to come over to view the hill Lucre; and, had we gone over, as he desired us, and as thou wast inclining to do, my brother, we had, for aught I know, been made ourselves, like this woman, a spectacle for those that shall come after to behold.

HOPE. I am sorry that I was so foolish, and am made to wonder that I am not now as Lot's wife; for wherein was the difference betwixt her sin and mine? She only looked back, and I had a desire to go see. Let God's goodness be praised; and let me be ashamed that ever such a thing should be in mine heart.

CHRIS. Let us take notice of what we see here, for our help for time to come. This woman escaped one judgment, for she fell not by the destruction of Sodom; yet she was destroyed by another, as we see: she is turned into a pillar of salt.

HOPE. What a mercy is it that neither thou, but especially I, am not made myself this example! This gives reason to us to thank God, to fear before Him and always to remember Lot's wife.

RIVER OF THE WATER OF LIFE

I saw, then, that they went on their way to a pleasant river, which David the King called "the river of God," but John, "the river of the water of life." Now their way lay just upon the bank of this river; here, therefore, Christian and his companion walked with great delight; they drank also of the water of the river, which was pleasant and enlivening to their weary spirits. Besides, on the banks of this river on either side were green trees that bore all manner of fruit; and the leaves of the trees were good for medicine; with the fruit of these trees they were also much delighted; and the leaves they ate to prevent illness, especially such diseases that come to those that heat their blood by travels. On either side of the river was also a meadow, curiously beautified with lilies, and it was green all the year long. In this meadow they lay down and slept, for here they might lie down safely. When they awoke, they gathered again of the fruit of the trees and drank again of the water of the river, and they lay down again to sleep. This they did several days and nights. Then they sang:

> "Behold ye, how these crystal streams do
>   glide,
> To comfort pilgrims by the highway-side;
> The meadows green, besides their fragrant
>   smell,
> Yield dainties for them; and he who can tell
> What pleasant fruit, yea, leaves, these trees
>   do yield,
> Will soon sell all, that he may buy this
>   field."

So when they were disposed to go on (for they were not as yet at their journey's end,) they ate and drank, and departed.

Now, I beheld in my dream that they had not journeyed far, but the river and the way for a time parted, at which they were not a little sorry; yet they durst not go out of the way. Now the way from the river was rough, and their feet tender by reason of their travels; so the souls of the pilgrims were much discouraged because of the way. Wherefore, still as they went on they wished for a better way. Now, a little before them there was, on the left hand of the road, a meadow, and a stile to go over into it, and that meadow is called By-path Meadow. Then said Christian to his fellow, "If this meadow lieth along by our wayside, let's go over it." Then he went to the stile to see; and behold, a path lay along by the way on the other side of the fence. "It is according to my wish," said Christian; "here is the easiest going. Come, good Hopeful, and let us go over."

HOPE. But how if this path should lead us out of the way?

VAIN-CONFIDENCE

CHRIS. "That is not likely," said the other. "Look, doth it not go along by the wayside?" So Hopeful, being persuaded by his fellow, went after him over the stile. When they were gone over, and were got into the path, they found it very easy to their feet; and withal, they, looking before them, espied a man walking as they did, and his name was Vain-Confidence: so they called after him, and asked him whither that way led. He said, "To the Celestial Gate." "Look," said Christian, "did not I tell you so? By this you may see we are right." So they followed, and he went before them. But, behold, the night came on, and it grew very dark; so that they that were behind lost sight of him that went before. He, therefore, that went before (Vain-Confidence by name) not seeing the way before him, fell into a deep pit, which was on purpose there made by the prince of those grounds to catch careless fools, withal and was dashed in pieces with his fall.

Now Christian and his fellow heard him fall. So they called to know the matter; but there was none to answer, only they heard a groaning. Then said Hopeful, "Where are we now?" Then was his fellow silent, as mistrusting that he had led him out of the way; and now it began to rain, and thunder, and lighten in a most dreadful manner, and the water rose amain.

Then Hopeful groaned in himself, saying, "Oh that I had kept on my way!"

CHRIS. Who could have thought that this path should have led us out of the way?

HOPE. I was afraid on't at the very first, and therefore gave you that gentle caution. I would have spoken plainer, but that you are older than I.

CHRIS. Good brother, be not offended. I am very sorry I have brought thee out of the way, and that I have put thee into such great danger. Pray, my brother, forgive me: I did not do it of any evil intent.

HOPE. Be comforted, my brother, for I forgive thee, and believe, too, that this shall be for our good.

CHRIS. I am glad I have with me a merciful brother; but we must not stand still: let us try to go back again.

HOPE. But, good brother, let me go before.

CHRIS. No, if you please; let me go first, that, if there be any danger, I may be first therein, because by my means we are both gone out of the way.

HOPE. "No, you shall not go first; for your mind being troubled may lead you out of the way again." Then for their encouragement they heard the voice of one saying, "Let thine heart be towards the highway, even the way that thou wentest; turn again." But by this time the waters were greatly risen, by reason of which the way of going back was very dangerous. (Then I thought that it is easier going out of the way when we are in, than going in when we are out.) Yet they undertook to go back; but it was so dark, and the flood so high, that, in their going back, they had like to have been drowned nine or ten times.

GIANT DESPAIR

Neither could they, with all the skill they had, get again to the stile that night. Wherefore, at last lighting under a little shelter, they sat down there until daybreak; but, being weary, they fell asleep. Now, there was, not far from the place where they lay, a castle, called Doubting Castle the owner whereof was Giant Despair, and it was in his grounds they now were sleeping; wherefore he, getting up in the morning early, and walking up and down in his fields, caught Christian and Hopeful asleep in his grounds. Then, with a grim and surly voice, he bid them awake, and asked them whence they were, and what they did in his grounds. They told him they were pilgrims, and that they had lost their way. Then said the giant, "You have this night trespassed on me by trampling in and lying on my grounds, and therefore you must go along with me." So they were forced to go, because he was stronger than they. They had also but little to say, for they knew themselves in fault. The giant, therefore, drove them before him, and put them into his castle, into a very dark dungeon, nasty and smelling vilely to the spirits of these two men. Here, then, they lay from Wednesday morning till Saturday night, without one bit of bread or drop of drink, or light, or any to ask how they did; they were, therefore, here in evil case, and were far from friends and people whom they knew. Now, in this place Christian had double sorrow, because it was through his thoughtless haste that they were brought into this distress.

THE PILGRIMS IN A DUNGEON

Now, Giant Despair had a wife, and her name was Diffidence. So, when he was gone to bed, he told his wife what he had done; to wit, that he had taken a couple of prisoners and cast them into his dungeon for trespassing on his grounds. Then he asked her also what he had best to do further to them. So she asked him what they were, whence they came, and whither they were bound; and he told her. Then she advised him, that when he arose in the morning, he should beat them without any mercy. So, when he arose, he getteth him a grievous crab-tree cudgel, and goes down into the dungeon to them, and there first fell to abusing them as if they were dogs, although they never gave him a word of distaste. Then he falls upon them, and beats them fearfully, in such sort that they were not able to help themselves, or to turn them upon the floor. This done, he withdraws and leaves them there to sorrow over their misery and to mourn under their distress. So all that day they spent their time in nothing but sighs and bitter grief. The next night she, talking with her husband about them further, and understanding that they were yet alive, did advise him to tell them to make away with themselves. So, when morning was come, he goes to them in a surly manner, as before and, perceiving them to be very sore with the stripes that he had given them the day before, he told them that, since they were never like to come out of that place, their only way would be forthwith to make an end of themselves, either with knife, halter, or poison: "For why," said he, "should you choose life, seeing it is attended with so much bitterness?" But they desired him to let them go. With that, he looked ugly upon them, and rushing to them, had doubtless made an end of them himself, but that he fell into one of his fits (for he sometimes, in sunshiny weather, fell into fits), and lost for a time the use of his hands, wherefore he withdrew, and left them as before to consider what to do. Then did the prisoners consult between themselves, whether it was best to take his advice or no; and thus they began to discourse:

CHRIS. "Brother," said Christian, "what shall we do? The life we now live is miserable. For my part, I know not whether is best, to live thus, or to die out of hand. My soul chooseth strangling rather than life, and the grave is more easy for me than this dungeon. Shall we be ruled by the giant?"

HOPEFUL CHEERS CHRISTIAN

HOPE. Indeed, our present condition is dreadful; and death would be far more welcome to me than thus for ever to abide. But yet, let us think: the Lord of the country to which we are going hath said, "Thou shalt do no murder," no, not to another man's person; much more, then, are we forbidden to take his advice to kill ourselves. Besides, he that kills another can but commit murder upon his body; but for one to kill himself is to kill body and soul at once. And, moreover, my brother, thou talkest of ease in the grave; but hast thou forgotten the hell, whither, for certain, the murderers go? for "no murderer hath eternal life." And let us consider again, that all the law is not in the hand of Giant Despair: others, so far as I can understand, have been taken by him as well as we, and yet have escaped out of his hand. Who knows but that God, who made the world, may cause that Giant Despair may die? or that, at some time or other, he may forget to lock us in? or that he may, in a short time, have another of his fits before us, and he may lose the use of his limbs? and if ever that should come to pass again, for my part, I am resolved to pluck up the heart of a man, and try to my utmost to get from under his hand. I was a fool that I did not try to do it before. But however, my brother, let us be patient, and endure awhile: the time may come that may give us a happy release; but let us not be our own murderers.

With these words, Hopeful at present did calm the mind of his brother; so they continued together in the dark that day, in their sad and doleful condition.

Well, towards evening, the giant goes down into the dungeon again, to see if his prisoners had taken his counsel. But, when he came there, he found them alive; and truly, alive was all; for now, what for want of bread and water, and by reason of the wounds they received when he beat them, they could do little but breathe. But, I say, he found them alive; at which he fell into a grievous rage, and told them that, seeing they had disobeyed his counsel, it should be worse with them than if they had never been born.

At this they trembled greatly, and I think that Christian fell into a swoon; but, coming a little to himself again, they renewed their discourse about the giant's advice and whether yet they had best to take it or no. Now, Christian again seemed for doing it; but Hopeful made his second reply as followeth:

HOPE. "My brother," said he, "rememberest thou not how valiant thou hast been heretofore? Apollyon could not crush thee, nor could all that thou didst hear, or see, or feel in the Valley of the Shadow of Death. What hardship, terror, and amazement hast thou already gone through! and art thou now nothing but fear? Thou seest that I am in the dungeon with thee, a far weaker man by nature than thou art; also this giant has wounded me as well as thee, and hath also cut off the bread and water from my mouth; and, with thee, I mourn without the light. But let us have a little more patience. Remember how thou showedst thyself the man at Vanity Fair, and wast neither afraid of the chain, nor cage, nor yet of bloody death. Wherefore, let us (at least to avoid the shame that it becomes not a Christian to be found in) bear up with patience as well as we can."

Now, night being come again, and the giant and his wife being in bed, she asked him concerning the prisoners, and if they had taken his advice: to which he replied, "They are sturdy rogues; they choose rather to bear all hardship than to make away with themselves." Then said she, "Take them unto the castle-yard to-morrow, and show them the bones and skulls of those that thou hast already killed; and make them believe, ere a week comes to an end, thou wilt tear them also in pieces, as thou hast done their fellows before them."

So when the morning was come, the giant goes to them again, and takes them into the castle-yard and shows them as his wife had bidden him. "These," said he, "were pilgrims, as you are, once, and they trespassed in my grounds as you have done; and when I thought fit, I tore them in pieces; and so within ten days I will do you. Go, get you down to your den again." And, with that, he beat them all the way thither. They lay, therefore, all day on Saturday in a lamentable case, as before. Now, when night was come, and when Mrs. Diffidence and her husband, the giant were got to bed, they began to renew their talking of their prisoners; and withal, the old giant wondered that he could neither by his blows nor counsel bring them to an end. And, with that, his wife replied, "I fear," said she, "that they live in hope that some will come to relieve them; or that they have picklocks about them, by the means of which they hope to escape." "And sayest thou so, my dear?" said the giant: "I will therefore search them in the morning."

THE PILGRIMS ESCAPE

Well, on Saturday about midnight, they began to pray, and continued in prayer till almost break of day.

Now, a little before it was day, good Christian, as one half amazed, brake out into this earnest speech: "What a fool," quoth he, "am I to lie in a foul-smelling dungeon, when I may as well walk at liberty! I have a key in my bosom called Promise, that will, I am sure, open any lock in Doubting

Castle." Then said Hopeful, "That is good news, good brother: pluck it out of thy bosom, and try."

Then Christian pulled it out of his bosom, and began to try at the dungeon door, whose bolt, as he turned the key, gave back, and the door flew open with ease, and Christian and Hopeful both came out. Then he went to the outward door that leads into the castle-yard, and with his key opened that door also. After, he went to the iron gate, for that must be opened too; but that lock went exceedingly hard, yet the key did open it. Then they thrust open the gate to make their escape with speed; but that gate, as it opened, made such a creaking, that it waked Giant Despair who, hastily rising to pursue his prisoners, felt his limbs to fail; for his fits took him again, so that he could by no means go after them. Then they went on, and came to the King's highway again, and so were safe because they were out of Giant Despair's rule.

Now, when they were gone over the stile, they began to contrive with themselves what they should do at that stile to prevent those that should come after from falling into the hands of Giant Despair. So they agreed to build there a pillar, and to engrave upon the side thereof this sentence: "Over this stile is the way to Doubting Castle, which is kept by Giant Despair, who despiseth the King of the Celestial Country, and seeks to destroy His holy pilgrims." Many, therefore, that followed after, read what was written, and escaped the danger. This done, they sang as follows:

> "Out of the way we went, and then we found
> What 'twas to tread upon forbidden ground:
> And let them that come after have a care,
> Lest heedlessness make them as we to fare;
> Lest they for trespassing his prisoners are
> Whose Castle's Doubting, and whose name's
>   Despair."

CHAPTER 8

THE DELECTABLE MOUNTAINS

They went then till they came to the Delectable Mountains, which mountains belong to the Lord of that hill of which we have spoken before. So they went up to the mountains to behold the gardens and orchards, the vineyards and fountains of water, where also they drank and washed themselves, and did freely eat of the vineyards. Now there were on the tops of these mountains shepherds feeding their flocks, and they stood by the highway-side. The pilgrims, therefore, went to them, and leaning upon their staves (as is common with weary pilgrims when they stand to talk with any by the way), they asked, "Whose delightful mountains are these, and whose be the sheep that feed upon them?"

SHEP. These mountains are Immanuel's Land, and they are within sight of His city; and the sheep also are His, and He laid down His life for them.

CHRIS. Is this the way to the Celestial City?

SHEP. You are just in your way.

CHRIS. How far is it thither?

SHEP. Too far for any but those who shall get thither indeed.

CHRIS. Is the way safe or dangerous?

SHEP. Safe for those for whom it is to be safe; but sinners shall fall therein.

CHRIS. Is there in this place any relief for pilgrims that are weary and faint in the way?

SHEP. The Lord of these mountains hath given us a charge not to be forgetful to care for strangers; therefore the good of the place is before you.

I saw also in my dream that when the shepherds perceived that they were wayfaring men, they also put questions to them (to which they made answer as in other places), as, "Whence came you?" and "How got you into the way?" and, "By what means have you so persevered therein? for but few of them that begin to come hither do show their faces on these mountains." But when the shepherds heard their answers, being pleased therewith they looked very lovingly upon them, and said, "Welcome to the Delectable Mountains!"

The shepherds, I say, whose names were Knowledge, Experience, Watchful, and Sincere, took them by the hand and took them to their tents, and made them partake of what was ready at present. They said moreover, "We would that you should stay here awhile, to be acquainted with us, and yet more to cheer yourselves with the good of these Delectable Mountains." They then told them that they were content to stay. So they went to rest that night, because it was very late.

THE SHEPHERDS CONDUCT THEM

Then I saw in my dream that in the morning the shepherds called up Christian and Hopeful to walk with them upon the mountains. So they went forth with them and walked a while, having a pleasant prospect on every side. Then said the shepherds one to another, "Shall we show these pilgrims some wonders?" So, when they had concluded to do it, they had them first to the top of the hill called Error, which was very steep on the farthest side, and bid them look down to the bottom. So Christian and Hopeful looked down, and saw at the bottom several men dashed all to pieces by a fall they had had from the top. Then said Christian, "What meaneth this?" Then the shepherds answered, "Have you not heard of them that were made to err, by hearkening to Hymeneus and Philetus, as concerning the faith of the rising from the dead?" They answered, "Yes." Then said the shepherds, "Those you see lie dashed to pieces at the bottom of this mountain are they; and they have continued to this day unburied, as you see, for an example to others to take heed how they clamber too high, or how they come too near the brink of this mountain."

Then I saw that they had them to the top of another mountain, and the name of that is Caution and bid them look afar off; and when they did, they perceived, as they thought, several men walking up and down among the tombs that were there; and they perceived that the men were blind, because they stumbled sometimes upon the tombs, and because they could not get out from among them. Then said Christian, "What means this?"

The shepherds then answered, "Did you not see a little below these mountains a stile that led into a meadow on the left hand side of this way?" They answered, "Yes." Then said the shepherds, "From that stile there goes a path that leads directly to Doubting Castle, which is kept by Giant Despair; and these men" (pointing to them among the tombs) "came once on pilgrimage, as you do now, even until they came to that same stile. And because the right way was rough in that place, they chose to go out of it into that meadow, and there were taken by Giant Despair, and cast into Doubting Castle, where, after they had been kept a while in the dungeon, he at last did put out their eyes, and led them among those tombs, where he has left them to wander to this very day, that the saying of the Wise Man might be fulfilled, 'He that wandereth out of the way of knowledge, shall remain in the congregation of the dead.'" Then Christian and Hopeful looked upon one another with tears gushing out, but yet said nothing to the shepherds.

Then I saw in my dream, that the shepherds had them to another place in a bottom, where was a door on the side of a hill; and they opened the door, and bid them look in. They looked in, therefore, and saw that within it was very dark and smoky; they also thought that they heard there a rumbling noise, as of fire, and a cry of some tormented, and that they smelt the scent of brimstone. Then said Christian, "What means this?" The shepherds told them, "This is a by-way to hell, a way that hypocrites go in at: namely, such as sell their birthright, with Esau; such as sell their master, with Judas; such as blaspheme the Gospel, with Alexander; and that lie and deceive with Ananias and Sapphira his wife."

HOPE. Then said Hopeful to the shepherds, "I perceive that these had on them, even every one, a show of pilgrimage, as we have now; had they not?"

SHEP. Yes, and held it a long time too.

HOPE. How far might they go on in pilgrimage in their day, since they notwithstanding were thus miserably cast away?

SHEP. Some farther, and some not so far as these mountains.

Then said the pilgrims one to another, "We have need to cry to the Strong for strength."

SHEP. Ay, and you will have need to use it when you have it, too.

GATE OF THE CELESTIAL CITY

By this time the pilgrims had a desire to go forward, and the shepherds a desire they should; so they walked together towards the end of the mountains. Then said the shepherds one to another, "Let us here show to the pilgrims the gate of the Celestial City, if they have skill to look through our perspective glass." The pilgrims then lovingly accepted the motion; so they had them to the top of a high hill called Clear, and gave them their glass to look.

Then they tried to look; but the remembrance of that last thing, that the shepherds had showed them, made their hands shake, by means of which hindrance they could not look steadily through the glass; yet they thought they saw something like the gate, and also some of the glory of the place. Thus they went away, and sang this song:

> "Thus by the shepherds secrets are revealed,
> Which from all other men are kept
>   concealed.
> Come to the shepherds, then, if you would
>   see
> Things deep, things hid, and that mysterious
>   be."

When they were about to depart, one of the shepherds gave them a note of the way. Another of them bid them beware of the Flatterer. The third bid them take heed that they slept not upon the Enchanted Ground. And the fourth bid them God speed.

So I awoke from my dream.

CHAPTER 9

THEY OVERTAKE IGNORANCE

And I slept, and dreamed again, and saw the same two pilgrims going down the mountains along the highway towards the city. Now, a little below these mountains, on the left hand, lieth the country of Conceit; from which country there comes into the way in which the pilgrims walked a little crooked lane. Here, therefore, they met with a very brisk lad, that came out of that country, and his name was Ignorance. So Christian asked him from what parts he came, and whither he was going.

IGNOR. Sir, I was born in the country that lieth off there a little on the left hand, and I am going to the Celestial City.

CHRIS. But how do you think to get in at the gate? for you may find some difficulty there.

IGNOR. As other people do.

CHRIS. But what have you to show at the gate, that may cause that the gate should be opened to you?

IGNOR. I know my Lord's will, and have been a good liver; I pay every man his own; I pray, fast, pay money to the church and give to the poor, and have left my country for whither I am going.

CHRIS. But thou camest not in at the wicket-gate that is at the head of this way: thou camest in hither through that same crooked lane; and therefore I fear, however thou mayest think of thyself, when the reckoning day shall come, thou wilt have laid to thy charge that thou art a thief and a robber, instead of getting admittance into the city.

IGNOR. Gentlemen, ye be utter strangers to me: I know you not: be content to follow the custom of your country, and I will follow the custom of mine. I hope all will be well. And, as for the gate that you talk of, all the world knows that that is a great way off of our country. I cannot think that any man in all our parts doth so much as know the way to it; nor need they matter whether they do or no, since we have, as you see, a fine, pleasant green lane, that comes down from our country, the next way into the way.

When Christian saw that the man was wise in his own opinion, he said to Hopeful, whisperingly, "There is more hope of a fool than of him." And said, moreover "When he that is a fool walketh by the way, his wisdom faileth him, and he saith to every one that he is a fool. What! shall we talk further with him, or outgo him at present, and so leave him to think of what he hath heard already, and then stop again for him afterwards, and see if by degrees we can do any good to him?"

Then said Hopeful:

> "Let Ignorance a little while now muse
> On what is said, and let him not refuse
> Good counsel to embrace, lest he remain
> Still ignorant of what's the chiefest gain.

> God saith, those that no understanding have
> (Although He made them), them He will not
> save."

Hope. He further added, "It is not good, I think, to say all to him at once: let us pass him by, if you will, and talk to him by and by, even as he is able to bear it."

So they both went on, and Ignorance he came after. Now, when they had passed him a little way, they entered into a very dark lane, where they met a man whom seven devils had bound with seven strong cords, and were carrying of him back to the door that they saw on the side of the hill. Now good Christian began to tremble, and so did Hopeful his companion; yet, as the devils led away the man, Christian looked to see if he knew him; and he thought it might be one Turn-away, that dwelt in the town of Apostasy. But he did not perfectly see his face, for he did hang his head like a thief that is found; but being gone past, Hopeful looked after him, and espied on his back a paper with this inscription, "One who was wicked while claiming to be good, and turned away from God."

THREE STURDY ROGUES

Then said Christian to his fellow, "Now I call to remembrance that which was told of a thing that happened to a good man hereabout. The name of that man was Little-Faith, but a good man, and dwelt in the town of Sincere. The thing was this: At the entering in at this passage, there comes down from Broad-way Gate a lane called Dead Man's Lane; so-called because of the murders that are commonly done there; and this Little-Faith, going on pilgrimage as we do now, chanced to sit down there, and slept. Now, there happened at that time to come down that lane, from

Broad-way Gate, three sturdy rogues, and their names were Faint-heart, Mistrust, and Guilt, three brothers; and they espying Little-Faith, where he was, came galloping up with speed. Now, the good man was just awaked from his sleep, and was getting up to go on his journey. So they came up all to him, and with threatening language bid him stand. At this, Little-Faith looked as white as a sheet and had neither power to fight nor fly. Then said Faint-heart, 'Deliver thy purse;' but, he making no haste to do it (for he was loth to lose his money) Mistrust ran up to him, and, thrusting his hand into his pocket, pulled out thence a bag of silver. Then he cried out, 'Thieves! thieves!' With that, Guilt, with a great club that was in his hand, struck Little-Faith on the head, and with that blow felled him flat to the ground, where he lay bleeding as one that would bleed to death. All this while the thieves stood by. But, at last, they hearing that some were upon the road, and fearing lest it should be one Great-Grace, that dwells in the city of Good-Confidence, they betook themselves to their heels, and left this good man to shift for himself. Now, after a while, Little-Faith came to himself, and, getting up, made shift to scramble on his way. This was the story."

HOPE. But did they take from him all that ever he had?

CHRIS. No; the place where his jewels were they never ransacked; so those he kept still. But as I was told, the good man was much afflicted for his loss, for the thieves got most of his spending money. That which they got not, as I said, were jewels; also he had a little odd money left, but scarce enough to bring him to his journey's end. Nay, if I was not misinformed, he was forced to beg as he went, to keep himself alive, for his jewels he might not sell; but, beg and do what he could, he went, as we say, often with a hungry stomach the most part of the rest of the way.

HOPE. But is it not a wonder they got not from him his certificate, by which he was to receive admission at the Celestial Gate?

CHRIS. It is a wonder; but they got not that, though they missed it not through any cunning of his; for he, being dismayed by their coming upon him, had neither power nor skill to hide anything; so it was more by good providence than by his endeavor, that they missed of that good thing.

HOPE. But it must needs be a comfort to him that they got not his jewels from him.

CHRIS. It might have been great comfort to him, had he used it as he should; but they that told me the story said, that he made but little use of it all the rest of the way, and that because of the alarm that he had in their taking away his money. Indeed, he forgot it a great part of the rest of his journey; and besides, when at any time it came into his mind, and he began to be comforted therewith, then would fresh thoughts of his loss come again upon him, and those thoughts would swallow up all.

HOPEFUL REBUKED

HOPE. Alas, poor man! this could not but be a great grief unto him.

CHRIS. Grief! ay, a grief indeed. Would it not have been so to any of us, had we been used as he, to be robbed and wounded too, and that in a strange place, as he was? It is a wonder he did not die with grief, poor heart! I was told that he scattered almost all the rest of the way with nothing but doleful and bitter complaints; telling also to all that overtook him, or that he overtook in the way as he went, where he was robbed, and how; who they were that did it, and what he had lost; how he was wounded, and that he hardly escaped with life.

HOPE. But it is a wonder that his necessities did not put him upon selling or pawning some of his jewels, that he might have wherewith to relieve himself in his journey.

CHRIS. Thou talkest like one whose head is thick to this very day. For what should he pawn them, or to whom should he sell them? In all that country where he was robbed, his jewels were not accounted of; nor did he want that relief which could from thence be administered to him. Besides, had his jewels been missing at the gate of the Celestial City, he had (and that he knew well enough) been shut out from an inheritance there; and that would have been worse to him than the coming and villainy of ten thousand thieves.

HOPE. But, Christian, these three fellows, I am persuaded in my heart, are but a company of cowards: would they have run else, think you, as they did at the noise of one that was coming on the road? Why did not Little-Faith pluck up a greater heart? He might, methinks, have stood one brush with them, and have yielded when there had been no remedy.

CHRIS. That they are cowards many have said, but few have found it so in the time of trial. As for a great heart, Little-Faith had none; and I perceive by thee, my brother, hadst thou been the man concerned, thou art but for a brush, and then to yield. And, verily, since this is the height of thy courage now they are at a distance from us, should they appear to thee as they did to him, they might put thee to second thoughts. But consider again, they are but journeymen-thieves; they serve under the king of the bottomless pit, who, if need be, will come in to their aid himself, and his voice is as the roaring of a lion. I myself have been engaged as this Little-Faith was, and I found it a terrible thing. These three villains set upon me: and I beginning like a Christian to resist, they gave but a call, and in came their master. I would, as the saying is, have given my life for a penny, but that, as God would have it, I was clothed with armor of proof. Ay, and yet, though I was so protected, I found it hard work to quit myself like a man. No man can tell what in that combat attends us, but he that hath been in the battle himself.

LITTLE-FAITH AND GREAT-GRACE

HOPE. Well, but they ran, you see, when they did but suppose that one Great-Grace was in the way.

CHRIS. True, they have often fled, both they and their master, when Great-Grace hath but appeared; and no marvel, for he is the King's champion. But I trow you will put some difference between Little-Faith and the King's champion? All the King's subjects are not His champions, nor can they when tried do such feats of war as he. Is it meet to think that a little child should handle Goliath as David did? or that there should be the strength of an ox in a wren? Some are strong, some are weak; some have great faith, some have little: this man was one of the weak, and therefore he went to the wall.

HOPE. I would it had been Great-Grace for their sakes.

CHRIS. If it had been he, he might have had his hands full; for I must tell you that though Great-Grace is excellent good at his weapons, and has, and can, so long as he keeps them at sword's point, do well enough with them; yet, if they get within him, even Faint-heart, Mistrust, or the other, it shall go hard but they will throw up his heels. And when a man is down, you know, what can he do?

Whoso looks well upon Great-Grace's face will see those scars and cuts there, that shall easily give proof of what I say. Yea, once I heard that he should say (and that when he was in the combat), "We despaired even of life." How did these sturdy rogues and their fellows make David groan, mourn, and roar! Yea, Heman, and Hezekiah too, though champions in their days, were forced to bestir when by these attacked; and yet, notwithstanding, they had their coats soundly brushed by them. Peter, upon a time, would go try what he could do; but though some do say of him that he is the prince of the apostles, they handled him so that they made him at last afraid of a sorry girl.

LITTLE-FAITH AMONG THIEVES

Besides, their king is at their whistle—he is never out of hearing; and if at any time they be put to the worst, he, if possible, comes in to help them; and of him it is said, "The sword of him that layeth at him cannot hold; the spear, the dart, nor the habergeon. He esteemeth iron as straw, and brass as rotten wood. The arrow cannot make him flee; sling-stones are turned with him into stubble. Darts are counted as stubble: he laugheth at the shaking of a spear." What can a man do in this case? It is true, if a man could at every turn have Job's horse, and had skill and courage to ride him, he might do notable things. For his neck is clothed with thunder. He will not be afraid as the grasshopper: "the glory of his nostrils is terrible. He paweth in the valley, and rejoiceth in his strength: he goeth on to meet the armed men. He mocketh at fear, and is not affrighted, neither turneth he his back from the sword. The quiver rattleth against him, the glittering spear and the shield. He swalloweth the ground with fierceness and rage; neither believeth he that it is the sound of the trumpet. He saith among the trumpets, Ha! ha! and he smelleth the battle afar off, the thunder of the captains, and the shouting."

But for such footmen as thee and I are, let us never desire to meet with an enemy, nor vaunt as if we could do better, when we hear of others that have been foiled, nor be tickled at the thoughts of our manhood; for such commonly come by the worst when tried. Witness Peter, of whom I made mention before: he would swagger, ay, he would; he would, as his vain mind prompted him to say, do better and stand more for his Master than all men; but who so foiled and run down by those villains as he?

Then Christian sang:

> "Poor Little-Faith! hast been among the
>   thieves?
> Wast robbed? Remember this: whoso
>   believes
> And gets more faith, shall then a victor be
> Over ten thousand; else, scarce over three."

So they went on, and Ignorance followed. They went then till they came to a place where they saw a way put itself into their way, and seemed withal to lie as straight as the way which they should go; and here they knew not which of the two to take, for both seemed straight before them; therefore here they stood still to consider. And, as they were thinking about the way, behold, a man, black of flesh, but covered with a very light robe, came to them, and asked them why they stood there. They answered they were going to the Celestial City, but knew not which of these ways to take. "Follow me," said the man; "it is thither that I am going." So they followed him to the way that but now came into the road, which by degrees turned and turned them so from the city that they desired to go to, that, in a little time, their faces were turned away from it; yet they followed him. But by-and-by, before they were aware, he led them both within the folds of a net, in which they were both so entangled that they knew not what to do; and with that, the white robe fell off the black man's back. Then they saw where they were. Wherefore, there they lay crying some time, for they could not get themselves out.

CHRIS. Then said Christian to his fellow, "Now do I see myself in an error. Did not the shepherds bid us beware of flatterers? As is the saying of the Wise Man, so we have found it this day: 'A man that flattereth his neighbor, spreadeth a net at his feet.'"

A SHINING ONE APPEARS

HOPE. They also gave us a note of directions about the way, for our more sure finding thereof; but therein we have also forgotten to read, and have not kept ourselves from the paths of the destroyer. Thus they lay bewailing themselves in the net. At last they espied a Shining One coming towards them with a whip of small cord in his hand. When he was come to the place where they were, he asked them whence they came, and what they did there. They told him that they were poor pilgrims going to Zion, but were led out of their way by a black man clothed in white, "Who bid us," said they, "follow him, for he was going thither too." Then said he with the whip, "It is Flatterer, a false prophet, that hath changed himself into an angel of light." So he rent the net, and let the men out. Then said he to them, "Follow me, that I may set you in your way again." So he led them back to the way which they had left to follow the Flatterer. Then he asked them, saying, "Where did you lie the last night?" They said, "With the shepherds upon the Delectable Mountains." He asked them then if they had not of those shepherds

a note of direction for the way. They answered, "Yes."
"But did you not," said he, "when you were at a stand,
pluck out and read your note?" They answered, "No."
He asked them, "Why?" They said they forgot. He
asked them, moreover, if the shepherds did not bid
them beware of the Flatterer. They answered, "Yes;
but we did not imagine," said they, "that this fine-
spoken man had been he."

Then I saw in my dream, that he commanded them to lie
down; which when they did, he whipped them sore, to teach
them the good way wherein they should walk; and, as he
whipped them, he said, "As many as I love, I rebuke and
chasten; be zealous, therefore, and repent." This done, he
bid them go on their way, and take good heed to the other
directions of the shepherds. So they thanked him for all his
kindness, and went softly along the right way, singing:

> "Come hither, you that walk along the way,
> See how the pilgrims fare that go astray;
> They catchèd are in an entangling net,
> 'Cause they good counsel lightly did forget;
> 'Tis true, they rescued were; but yet, you
>   see,
> They're scourged to boot: let this your
>   caution be."

Now, after awhile they perceived afar off, one coming softly
and alone, all along the highway, to meet them. Then said
Christian to his fellow, "Yonder is a man with his back towards
Zion, and he is coming to meet us."

HOPE. I see him: let us take heed to ourselves lest he should
prove a flatterer also.

THEY MEET ATHEIST

So he drew nearer and nearer, and at last came up to them. His name was Atheist, and he asked them whither they were going.

CHRIS. We are going to Mount Zion.

Then Atheist fell into a very great laughter.

CHRIS. What is the meaning of your laughter?

ATHEIST. I laugh to see what ignorant persons you are, to take upon yourselves so tedious a journey, and yet are like to have nothing but your travel for your pains.

CHRIS. Why, man, do you think we shall not be received?

ATHEIST. Received! There is no such a place as you dream of in all this world.

CHRIS. But there is in the world to come.

ATHEIST. When I was at home in mine own country, I heard as you now affirm, and, from that hearing, went out to see, and have been seeking this city these twenty years, but find no more of it than I did the first day I set out.

CHRIS. We have both heard and believe that there is such a place to be found.

ATHEIST. Had not I, when at home, believed I had not come thus far to seek; but, finding none (and yet I should had there been such a place to be found, for I have gone to seek it farther than you), I am going back again, and will seek to refresh myself with the things that I then cast away for hopes of that which I now see is not.

CHRIS. Then said Christian to Hopeful his fellow, "Is it true which this man hath said?"

HOPE. Take heed; he is one of the flatterers. Remember what it hath cost us once already for hearkening to such kind of fellows. What! no Mount Zion? Did we not see from the Delectable Mountains the gate of the city? Also, are we not now to walk by faith? Let us go on, lest the man with the whip overtake us again. I say, my brother, cease to hear him, and let us believe to the saving of the soul.

CHRIS. My brother, I did not put the question to thee for that I doubted of the truth of our belief myself, but to prove thee, and to fetch from thee a fruit of the honesty of thy heart. As for this man, I know that he is blinded. Let thee and me go on, knowing that we have belief of the truth, and no lie is of the truth.

HOPE. Now do I rejoice in hope of the glory of God.

So they turned away from the man, and he, laughing at them, went his way.

I then saw in my dream that they went till they came into a certain country, whose air naturally tended to make one drowsy if he came a stranger into it. And here Hopeful began to be very dull and heavy of sleep; wherefore he said unto Christian, "I do now begin to grow so drowsy, that I can scarcely hold up mine eyes; let us lie down here, and take one nap."

CHRIS. "By no means," said the other, "lest sleeping, we never awake more."

HOPE. Why, my brother? sleep is sweet to the laboring man: we may be refreshed if we take a nap.

CHRIS. Do not you remember that one of the shepherds bid us beware of the Enchanted Ground? He meant by that that we should beware of sleeping; wherefore let us not sleep as others, but let us watch and be sober.

HOPE. I acknowledge myself in fault; and had I been here alone, I had, by sleeping, run the danger of death. I see it is true that the Wise Man saith, "Two are better than one." Hitherto hath thy company been my help; and thou shalt have a good reward for thy labor.

CHRIS. "Now, then," said Christian, "to prevent drowsiness in this place, let us talk about something profitable."

HOPE. With all my heart.

HOPEFUL NARRATES CONVERSION

CHRIS. Where shall we begin?

HOPE. Where God began with us. But do you begin, if you please.

CHRIS. I will sing you first this song:

> "When saints do sleepy grow, let them come
>   hither,
> And hear how these two pilgrims talk
>   together;
> Yea, let them learn of them, in any wise,
> Thus to keep ope their drowsy, slumbering
>   eyes.
> Saints' fellowship, if it be managed well,
> Keeps them awake, and that in spite of hell."

CHRIS. Then Christian began, and said, "I will ask you a question. How came you to think at first of doing as you do now?"

HOPE. Do you mean, how came I at first to look after the good of my soul?

CHRIS. Yes, that is my meaning.

HOPE. I continued a great while in the delight of those things which were seen and sold at our fair; things which I believe now would have, had I continued in them still, drowned me in ruin and destruction.

CHRIS. What things were they?

HOPE. All the treasures and riches of the world. Also I delighted much in rioting, revelling, drinking, swearing, lying, uncleanness, Sabbath-breaking, and what not, that tended to destroy the soul. But I found at last, by hearing and considering of things that are holy, which indeed I heard of you, as also of beloved Faithful, that was put to death for his faith, and good living in Vanity Fair, that the end of these things is death; and that, for these things' sake, the wrath of God cometh upon those who disobey him.

CHRIS. And did you presently fall under the power of this feeling?

HOPE. No; I was not willing presently to know the evil of sin, nor the destruction that follows upon the doing of it; but tried, when my mind at first began to be shaken with the Word, to shut mine eyes against the light thereof.

CHRIS. But what was the cause of your waiting so long?

HOPE. The causes were,—Firstly, I was ignorant that this was the work of God upon me. Secondly, Sin was yet very sweet to my flesh, and I was loth to leave it. Thirdly, I could not tell how to part with mine old companions, their presence and actions were so desirable unto me. Fourthly, The hours in which these feelings were upon me, were such troublesome and such heart-affrighting hours, that I could not bear, no, not so much as the remembrance of them upon my heart.

CHRIS. Then, as it seems, sometimes you got rid of your trouble?

HOPE. Yes, verily, but it would come into my mind again, and then I should be as bad, nay, worse than I was before.

CHRIS. Why, what was it that brought your sins to mind again?

HOPE. Many things; as,

1. If I did but meet a good man in the streets; or,
2. If I have heard any read in the Bible; or,
3. If mine head did begin to ache; or,
4. If I were told that some of my neighbors were sick; or,
5. If I heard the bell toll for some that were dead; or,

6. If I thought of dying myself; or,
7. If I heard that sudden death happened to others;
8. But especially when I thought of myself that I must quickly come to judgment.

CHRIS. And could you at any time with ease get off the guilt of sin, when by any of these ways it came upon you?

HOPE. No, not I; for then they got faster hold of my conscience; and then, if I did but think of going back to sin (though my mind was turned against it,) it would be double torment to me.

CHRIS. And how did you do then?

HOPE. I thought I must endeavor to mend my life; for else, thought I, I am sure to be lost forever.

CHRIS. And did you endeavor to mend?

HOPE. Yes, and fled from not only my sins, but sinful company too, and betook me to religious duties, as praying, reading, weeping for sin, speaking truth to my neighbors, etc. These things did I, with many others, too much here to tell.

CHRIS. And did you think yourself well then?

HOPE. Yes, for a while; but, at the last, my trouble came tumbling upon me again, and that over the neck of all my trying to do right.

CHRIS. How came that about, since you were now doing right, as far as you knew?

HOPE. There were several things brought it upon me; especially such sayings as these: "All our righteousness are as filthy rags;" "By the works of the law shall no flesh be made righteous;" "When ye shall have done all those things which are commanded you, say, We are unprofitable;" with many more such like. From whence I began to reason with myself thus: If all my righteousness are filthy rags, if by the deeds of the law no man can be made righteous, and if, when we have done *all*, we are yet unprofitable, then it is but a folly to think of heaven by the law. I further thought thus; If a man runs a hundred pounds into the shopkeeper's debt, and after that shall pay for all that he shall buy; yet his old debt stands still in the book uncrossed; for the which the shopkeeper may sue him, and cast him into prison till he shall pay the debt.

CHRIS. Well, and how did you apply this to yourself?

HOPE. Why, I thought thus with myself: I have by my sins run a great way into God's book, and my now reforming will not pay off that score. Therefore I should think still, under all my present trying. But how shall I be freed from that punishment that I have brought myself in danger of by my former sins.

CHRIS. A very good application; but pray go on.

HOPE. Another thing that hath troubled me ever since my late turning from sin is, that if I look narrowly into the best of what I do now, I still see sin, new sin, mixing itself with the best of that I do; so that now I am forced to conclude that, notwithstanding my former fond opinion of myself and duties, I have committed sin enough in one duty to send me to hell, though my former life had been faultless.

CHRIS. And what did you do then?

HOPE. Do! I could not tell what to do, till I brake my mind to Faithful; for he and I were well acquainted. And he told me, that unless I could obtain the righteousness of a Man that never had sinned, neither mine own nor all the righteousness of the world could save me.

CHRIS. And did you think he spake true?

HOPE. Had he told me so when I was pleased and satisfied with mine own trying, I had called him fool for his pains; but now, since I see mine own weakness and the sin which cleaves to my best performance, I have been forced to be of his opinion.

CHRIS. But did you think, when at first he suggested it to you, that there was such a Man to be found, of whom it might justly be said that He never committed sin?

HOPE. I must confess the words at first sounded strangely; but after a little more talk and company with him I had full certainty about it.

CHRIS. And did you ask him what Man this was, and how you must be made righteous by Him?

HOPE. Yes, and he told me it was the Lord Jesus, that dwelleth on the right hand of the Most High. And thus, said he, you must be made right by Him, even by trusting what He hath done by Himself in the days of His flesh, and suffered when He did hang on the tree. I asked him further, How that Man's righteousness could be of that power to help another before God? And he told me He was the mighty God, and did what He did, and died the death also, not for Himself, but for me; to whom His doings, and the worthiness of them, should be given if I believed on Him.

CHRIS. And what did you do then?

HOPE. I made my objections against my believing, for that I thought He was not willing to save me.

CHRIS. And what said Faithful to you then?

HOPE. He bid me go to Him and see. Then I said it was too much for me to ask for. But he said No, for I was invited to come. Then he gave me a book of Jesus' own writing to encourage me the more freely to come; and he said concerning that book, that every word and letter thereof stood firmer than heaven and earth. Then I asked him what I must do when I came; and he told me I must entreat on my knees, with all my heart and soul, the Father to reveal Him to me. Then I asked him further how I must make my prayer to Him; and he said, Go, and thou shalt find Him upon a mercy-seat, where He sits all the year long to give pardon and forgiveness to them that come. I told him that I knew not what to say when I came; and he bid me say to this effect: God be merciful to me a sinner, and make me to know and believe in Jesus Christ; for I see that if His righteousness had not been, or I have not faith in that righteousness, I am utterly cast away. Lord, I have heard that Thou art a merciful God, and hast given that Thy Son Jesus Christ should be the Saviour of the world; and, moreover, that Thou art willing to bestow Him upon such a poor sinner as I am. And I am a sinner indeed. Lord, take therefore this opportunity, and show Thy grace in the salvation of my soul, through Thy Son Jesus Christ. Amen.

CHRIS. And did you do as you were bidden?

HOPE. Yes, over, and over, and over.

CHRIS. And did the Father show His son to you?

HOPE. Not at the first, nor second, nor third, nor fourth, nor fifth; no, nor at the sixth time neither.

CHRIS. What did you do then?

HOPE. What! why, I could not tell what to do.

CHRIS. Had you no thoughts of leaving off praying?

HOPE. Yes; a hundred times twice told.

CHRIS. And what was the reason you did not?

HOPE. I believed that that was true which had been told me; to wit, that without the righteousness of this Christ, all the world could not save me; and therefore, thought I with myself, if I leave off I die, and I can but die at the throne of grace. And withal, this came into my mind: "Though it tarry, wait for it; because it will surely come, it will not tarry." So I continued praying until the Father showed me His Son.

CHRIS. And how was He shown unto you?

HOPE. I did not see Him with my bodily eyes, but with the eyes of my heart, and thus it was: One day I was very sad, I think sadder than at any one time in my life; and this sadness was through a fresh sight of the greatness and vileness of my sins. And, as I was then looking for nothing but hell and the everlasting loss of my soul, suddenly, as I thought, I saw the Lord Jesus look down from heaven upon me, and saying, "Believe on the Lord Jesus Christ, and thou shalt be saved."

But I replied, "Lord, I am a great, a very great sinner." And He answered, "My grace is sufficient for thee." Then I said, "But, Lord, what is believing?" And then I saw from that saying, "He that cometh to me shall never hunger, and he that believeth on me shall never thirst," that believing and coming was all one; and that he that came, that is, ran out in his heart and desire after salvation by Christ, he indeed believed in Christ. Then the water stood in mine eyes, and I asked further, "But, Lord, may such a great sinner as I am be indeed accepted of Thee, and be saved by thee?" and I heard Him say, "And him that cometh to me I will in no wise cast out." Then said I, "But how Lord, must I consider of Thee in my coming to Thee, that my faith may be placed aright upon Thee?" Then he said, "Christ Jesus came into the world to save sinners. He is the end of the law for righteousness to every one that believes. He died for our sins, and rose again for our righteousness. He loved us, and washed us from our sins in His own blood. He is Mediator between God and us. He ever liveth to plead for us." From all which I gathered that I must look for righteousness in His person, and for satisfaction for my sins by His blood; that what He did in obedience to His Father's law, and in submitting to the penalty thereof, was not for Himself, but for him that will accept it for his salvation, and be thankful. And now was my heart full of joy, mine eyes full of tears, and mine affections running over with love to the name, people, and ways of Jesus Christ.

CHRIS. This was a revelation of Christ to your soul indeed. But tell me particularly what effect this had upon your spirit.

HOPE. It made me see that all the world, notwithstanding all the righteousness thereof, is in a state of condemnation. It made me see that God the Father, though He be just, can justly forgive the coming sinner. It made me greatly ashamed of the vileness of my former life, and confounded me with the sense of my own ignorance; for there never came thought into my heart before now, that showed me so the beauty of Jesus Christ. It made me love a holy life, and long to do something for the honor and glory of the name of the Lord Jesus. Yea, I thought that had I now a thousand gallons of blood in my body, I could spill it all for the sake of the Lord Jesus.

CHAPTER 10

I saw then in my dream that Hopeful looked back, and saw Ignorance, whom they had left behind, coming after. "Look," said he to Christian, "how far yonder youngster loitereth behind."

CHRIS. Ay, ay, I see him: he careth not for our company.

HOPE. But I think it would not have hurt him, had he kept pace with us hitherto.

CHRIS. That is true; but I warrant you he thinks otherwise.

HOPE. That I think he doth; but, however, let us tarry for him. So they did.

CHRIS. Then Christian said to him, "Come away, man; why do you stay so behind?"

IGNOR. I take my pleasure in walking alone, even more a great deal than in company, unless I like it the better.

Then said Christian to Hopeful (but softly), "Did I not tell you he cared not for our company? But, however," said he, "come up, and let us talk away the time in this solitary place." Then, directing his speech to Ignorance, he said, "Come how do you? How stands it between God and your soul now?"

IGNOR. I hope well; for I am always full of good thoughts, that come into my mind to comfort me as I walk.

CHRIS. What good motions? pray tell us.

IGNOR. Why, I think of God and heaven.

CHRIS. So do the devils and lost souls.

IGNOR. But I think of them and desire them.

CHRIS. So do many that are never like to come there. "The soul of the sluggard desireth and hath nothing."

IGNOR. But I think of them, and leave all for them.

CHRIS. That I doubt, for leaving of all is a very hard matter; yea, a harder matter than many are aware of. But why, or by what, art thou persuaded that thou hast left all for God and heaven?

IGNOR. My heart tells me so.

CHRIS. The Wise Man says, "He that trusteth in his own heart is a fool."

IGNOR. This is spoken of an evil heart; but mine is a good one.

CHRIS. But how dost thou prove that?

IGNOR. It comforts me in the hopes of heaven.

CHRIS. That may be through its deceitfulness; for a man's heart may minister comfort to him in the hopes of that thing for which he has yet no ground to hope.

IGNOR. But my heart and life agree together; and therefore my hope is well grounded.

CHRIS. Who told thee that thy heart and life agree together?

IGNOR. My heart tells me so.

CHRIS. Ask my fellow if I be a thief! Thy heart tells thee so! Except the Word of God telleth thee in this matter, other testimony is of no value.

IGNOR. But is it not a good heart that hath good thoughts? and is not that a good life that is according to God's commandments?

CHRIS. Yes, that is a good heart that hath good thoughts, and that is a good life that is according to God's commandments; but it is one thing, indeed, to have these, and another thing only to think so.

IGNOR. Pray, what count you good thoughts, and a life according to God's commandments?

CHRIS. There are good thoughts of many kinds: some respecting ourselves, some God, some Christ, and some other things.

IGNOR. You go so fast, I cannot keep pace with you. Do you go on before: I must stay awhile behind.

Then they said:

> "Well, Ignorance, wilt thou yet foolish be,
> To slight good counsel, ten times given thee?
> And if thou yet refuse it, thou shalt know,
> Ere long, the evil of thy doing so.
> Remember, man, in time; stoop, do not fear;
> Good counsel, taken well, saves; therefore
>   hear:
> But, if thou yet shalt slight it, thou wilt be
> The loser, Ignorance, I'll warrant thee."

Then Christian addressed himself thus to his fellow:

CHRIS. Well, come, my good Hopeful; I perceive that thou and I must walk by ourselves again.

THE TWO PILGRIMS PROCEED

So I saw in my dream that they went on apace before, and Ignorance he came hobbling after. Then said Christian to his companion, "It pities me much for this poor man: it will certainly go ill with him at last."

HOPE. Alas! there are abundance in our town in his condition, whole families, yea, whole streets, and that of pilgrims, too; and if there be so many in our parts, how many, think you, must there be in the place where he was born?

CHRIS. Indeed, the Word saith, "He hath blinded their eyes, lest they should see."

HOPE. Well said; I believe you have said the truth. Are we now almost got past the Enchanted Ground?

CHRIS. Why, art thou weary of our talking?

HOPE. No, verily; but that I would know where we are.

CHRIS. We have not now above two miles farther to go thereon. Well, we will leave at this time our neighbor Ignorance by himself, and fall upon another subject.

HOPE. With all my heart; but you shall still begin.

CHRIS. Well, then, did you not know, about ten years ago, one Temporary in your parts, who was a forward man in religion then?

HOPE. Know him! yes; he dwelt in Graceless, a town about two miles off of Honesty, and he dwelt next door to one Turnback.

CHRIS. Right, he dwelt under the same roof with him. Well, that man was much awakened once: I believe that then he had some sight of his sins, and of the punishment that was due thereto.

HOPE. I am of your mind; for (my house not being above three miles from him) he would ofttimes come to me, and that with many tears. Truly, I pitied the man, and was not altogether without hope of him; but one may see, it is not every one that cries "Lord! Lord!"

CHRIS. He told me once that he was resolved to go on pilgrimage as we do now; but all of a sudden he grew acquainted with one Save-self, and then he became a stranger to me, for at that time he gave up going on pilgrimage.

CHAPTER 11

BEULAH LAND

Now I saw in my dream, that by this time the pilgrims were got over the Enchanted Ground, and entering into the country of Beulah, whose air was very sweet and pleasant: the way lying directly through it, they enjoyed themselves there for a season. Yea, here they heard continually the singing of birds and saw every day the flowers appear on the earth, and heard the voice of the turtle in the land. In this country the sun shineth night and day; wherefore this was beyond the Valley of the Shadow of Death, and also out of the reach of Giant Despair; neither could they from this place so much as see Doubting Castle. Here they were within sight of the City they were going to; also here met them some of the inhabitants thereof; for in this land the Shining Ones commonly walked, because it was upon the borders of heaven. Here they had no want of corn and wine; for in this place they met with abundance of what they had sought for in all their pilgrimage. Here they heard voices from out of the City, loud voices, saying, "Say ye to the daughter of Zion, Behold, thy salvation cometh! Behold, His reward is with Him!" Here all the inhabitants of the country called them "The holy people, and redeemed of the Lord, sought out," etc.

Now, as they walked in this land, they had more rejoicing than in parts more remote from the kingdom to which they were bound; and drawing near to the City, they had yet a more perfect view thereof. It was builded of pearls and precious stones, also the streets thereof were paved with gold; so that by reason of the natural glory of the City, and the reflection of the sunbeams upon it, Christian with desire fell sick; Hopeful also had a fit or two of the same disease, wherefore here they lay by it awhile, crying out because of their pangs, "If you see my Beloved tell Him that I am sick of love."

But being a little strengthened, and better able to bear their sickness, they walked on their way, and came yet nearer and nearer, where were orchards, vineyards, and gardens, and their gates opened into the highway. Now, as they came up to these places, behold, the gardener, stood in the way; to whom the pilgrims said, "Whose goodly vineyards and gardens are these?" He answered, "They are the King's, and are planted here for His own delight, and also for the solace of pilgrims." So the gardener had them into the vineyards, and bid them refresh themselves with the dainties. He also showed them there the King's walks, and the arbors where He delighted to be; and here they tarried and slept.

Now I beheld in my dream, that they talked more in their sleep at this time than ever they did in all their journey; and being in thought thereabout, the gardener said even to me, "Wherefore dost thou meditate at the matter? It is the nature of the fruit of the grapes of these vineyards to go down so sweetly as to cause the lips of them that are asleep to speak."

So I saw, when they awoke they undertook to go up to the City. But, as I said, the reflection of the sun upon the City (for the City was pure gold) was so extremely glorious, that they could not, as yet, with open face behold it, but through a glass made for that purpose. So I saw that, as they went on, there met them two men in raiment that shone like gold, also their faces shone as the light.

These men asked the pilgrims whence they came; and they told them. They also asked them where they had lodged, what difficulties and dangers, what comforts and pleasures, they had met in the way; and they told them. Then said the men that met them, "You have but two difficulties more to meet with, and then you are in the City."

Christian, then, and his companion, asked the men to go along with them; so they told them that they would. "But," said they, "you must obtain it by your own faith." So I saw in my dream that they went on together till they came in sight of the gate.

A RIVER INTERVENES

Now I further saw, that betwixt them and the gate was a river; but there was no bridge to go over, and the river was very deep. At the sight, therefore, of this river, the pilgrims were much stunned; but the men that went with them said, "You must go through, or you cannot come at the gate."

The pilgrims then began to inquire if there was no other way to the gate; to which they answered, "Yes; but there hath not any save two, to wit, Enoch and Elijah, been permitted to tread that path since the foundation of the world, nor shall until the last trumpet shall sound." The pilgrims then, especially Christian, began to be anxious in his mind, and looked this way and that; but no way could be found by them by which they might escape the river. Then they asked the men if the waters were all of a depth. They said, "No," yet they could not help them in that case; "for," said they, "you shall find it deeper or shallower as you believe in the King of the place."

They then addressed themselves to the water; and, entering, Christian began to sink, and crying out to his good

150

friend Hopeful, he said, "I sink in deep waters; the billows go over my head; all His waves go over me."

Then said the other, "Be of good cheer, my brother; I feel the bottom, and it is good." Then said Christian, "Ah! my friend, the sorrows of death have compassed me about; I shall not see the land that flows with milk and honey." And with that, a great darkness and horror fell upon Christian, so that he could not see before him. Also here he in a great measure lost his senses, so that he could neither remember nor orderly talk of any of those sweet refreshments that he had met with in the way of his pilgrimage. But all the words that he spake still tended to show that he had horror of mind, and heart-fears that he should die in that river, and never obtain entrance in at the gate. Here also, as they that stood by perceived, he was much in the troublesome thoughts of the sins that he had committed, both since and before he began to be a pilgrim. It was also observed that he was troubled with the sight of demons and evil spirits; for ever and anon he would intimate so much by words.

Hopeful, therefore, here had much ado to keep his brother's head above water; yea, sometimes he would be quite gone down, and then, ere a while he would rise up again half dead. Hopeful would also endeavor to comfort him, saying, "Brother, I see the gate, and men standing by to receive us;" but Christian would answer, "It is you, it is you they wait for: you have been hopeful ever since I knew you." "And so have you," said he to Christian. "Ah, brother," said he, "surely, if I were right, He would now arise to help me; but for my sins He hath brought me into this snare, and hath left me." Then said Hopeful, "My brother, these troubles and distresses that you go through in these waters are no sign that God hath forsaken you; but are sent to try you, whether you will call to mind that which hitherto you have received of His goodness, and live upon Him in your distresses."

Then I saw in my dream that Christian was in thought awhile. To whom also Hopeful added these words, "Be of good cheer, Jesus Christ maketh thee whole." And, with that, Christian brake out with a loud voice, "Oh, I see Him again; and He tells me, 'When thou passest through the waters, I will be with thee; and through the rivers, they shall not overflow thee.'" Then they both took courage; and the enemy was, after that, as still as a stone, until they were gone over. Christian, therefore, presently found ground to stand upon; and so it followed that the rest of the river was but shallow. Thus they got over.

TWO SHINING MEN

Now, upon the bank of the river, on the other side, they saw the two Shining Men again, who there waited for them. Wherefore, being come out of the river, they saluted them, saying, "We are heavenly spirits, sent forth to help those that shall be heirs of salvation." Thus they went along towards the gate. Now, you must note that the City stood upon a mighty hill; but the pilgrims went up that hill with ease, because they had these two men to lead them up by the arms; also they had left their mortal garments behind them in the river; for though they went in with them, they came out without them. They therefore went up here with much activity and speed, though the foundation upon which the City was framed was higher than the clouds. They therefore went up through the regions of the air, sweetly talking as they went, being comforted because they had safely got over the river, and had such glorious companions to attend them.

MOUNT ZION

The talk they had with the Shining Ones, was about the glory of the place; who told them that the beauty and glory of it were such as could not be put into words. "There," said they, "is the Mount Zion, the heavenly Jerusalem, the innumerable company of angels, and the spirits of good men made perfect. You are going now," said they, "to the Paradise of God, wherein you shall see the tree of life, and eat of the never-fading fruits thereof; and when you come there, you shall have white robes given you, and your walk and talk shall be every day with the King, even all the days of an eternal life. There you shall not see again such things as you saw when you were in the lower region upon the earth; to wit, sorrow, sickness, affliction, and death; 'for the former things are passed away.' You are going now to Abraham, to Isaac, and to Jacob, and to the prophets, men that God hath taken away from the evil to come, and that are now resting upon their beds, each one walking in his righteousness." The men then asked, "What must we do in the holy place?" To whom it was answered, "You must there receive the comfort of all your toil, and have joy for all your sorrow; you must reap what you have sown, even the fruit of all your prayers, and tears, and sufferings for the King by the way. In that place you must wear crowns of gold, and enjoy the perpetual sight and visions of the Holy One; for there you shall see Him as He is. There also you shall serve Him continually with praise, with shouting and thanksgiving, whom you desired to serve in the world, though with much difficulty, because of the weakness of your bodies. There your eyes shall be delighted with seeing and your ears with hearing the pleasant voice of the Mighty One. There you shall enjoy your friends again that are gone thither before you; and there you shall with joy receive even every one that follows into the holy place after you. There also you shall be clothed with glory and majesty, and put into a state fit to ride out with the King of Glory. When He shall come with sound of trumpet in the clouds, as upon the wings of the wind, you shall come with Him; and when He shall sit upon the throne of judgment, you shall sit by Him; yea, and when He shall pass sentence upon all the workers of evil, let them be angels or men, you also shall have a voice in that judgment because they were His and your enemies. Also, when He shall again return to the City, you shall go too, with sound of trumpet, and be ever with Him."

Now, while they were thus drawing towards the gate, behold, a company of the heavenly host came out to meet them; to whom it was said by the other two Shining Ones, "These are the men that have loved our Lord when in the world, and that have left all for His holy name; and He hath sent us to fetch them, and we have brought them thus far on their desired journey, that they may go in and look their Redeemer in the face with joy." Then the heavenly host gave a great shout, saying, "Blessed are they which are called to the marriage supper of the Lamb." There came out also at this time to meet them several of the King's trumpeters, clothed in white and shining raiment who, with melodious noises and loud, made even the heavens to echo with their sound. These trumpeters saluted Christian and his fellow with ten thousand welcomes from the world; and this they did with shouting and sound of trumpet.

THE CELESTIAL CITY

This done, they compassed them round on every side; some went before, some behind, and some on the right hand, some on the left (as it were to guard them through the upper regions), continually sounding as they went, with melodious noise, in notes on high: so that the very sight was to them that could behold it as if heaven itself was come down to meet them. Thus, therefore, they walked on together; and, as they walked, ever and anon these trumpeters, even with joyful sound, would, by mixing their music, with looks and gestures, still signify to Christian and his brother how welcome they were into their company, and with what gladness they came to meet them. And now were these two men as it were in heaven before they came at it, being swallowed up with the sight of angels, and with hearing of their melodious notes. Here also they had the City itself in view, and thought they heard all the bells therein to ring, and welcome them thereto. But, above all, the warm and joyful thoughts that they had about their own dwelling there with such company, and that for ever and ever, oh! by what tongue or pen can their glorious joy be expressed?

And thus they came up to the gate. Now, when they were come up to the gate, there was written over it in letters of gold, "BLESSED ARE THEY THAT DO HIS COMMANDMENTS, THAT THEY MAY HAVE RIGHT TO THE TREE OF LIFE, AND MAY ENTER IN THROUGH THE GATES INTO THE CITY."

Then I saw in my dream, that the Shining Men bid them call at the gate: the which when they did, some from above looked over the gate: such as Enoch, Moses, and Elijah, and others, to whom it was said, "These pilgrims are come from the City of Destruction, for the love that they bear to the King of this place." And then the pilgrims gave in unto them each man his certificate, which they had received in the beginning; those therefore were carried in to the King, who, when He had read them, said, "Where are the men?" To whom it was answered, "They are standing without the gate." The King then commanded to open the gate, "that the righteous nation," said He, "which keepeth the truth, may enter in."

Now, I saw in my dream, that these two men went in at the gate; and lo! as they entered, their looks were changed so that their faces became bright; and they had garments put on that shone like gold. There were also that met them with harps and crowns, and gave them to them—the harps to praise withal, and the crowns in token of honor. Then I heard in my dream that all the bells in the City rang again for joy, and that it was said unto them, "Enter ye into the joy of your Lord." I also heard the men themselves, that they sang with a loud voice, saying, "Blessing, and honor, and glory, and power, be unto Him that sitteth upon the throne, and unto the Lamb, for ever and ever!"

Now, just as the gates were opened to let in the men, I looked in after them, and behold, the City shone like the sun; the streets also were paved with gold; and in them walked many men with crowns on their heads, palms in their hands, and golden harps to sing praises withal.

There were also of them that had wings, and they answered one another without ceasing, saying, "Holy, holy, holy is the Lord!" And, after that, they shut up the gates; which when I had seen, I wished myself among them.

IGNORANCE FAILS TO ENTER

Now while I was gazing upon all these things, I turned my head to look back, and saw Ignorance come up to the river-side; but he soon got over, and that without half the difficulty which the other two men met with. For it happened that there was then in the place one Vain-Hope, a ferryman, that with his boat helped him over; so he, as the others I saw, did ascend the hill, to come up to the gate; only he came alone, neither did any man meet him with the least encouragement. When he was come up to the gate, he looked up to the writing that was above, and then began to knock, supposing that entrance should have been quickly given to him; but he was asked by the men that looked over the top of the gate, "Whence came you? and what would you have?" He answered, "I have eaten and drunk in the presence of the King, and He has taught in our streets." Then they asked him for his certificate, that they might go in and show it to the King: so he fumbled in his bosom for one, and found none. Then said they, "Have you none?" But the man answered never a word. So they told the King; but He would not come down to see him, but commanded the two Shining Ones that conducted Christian and Hopeful to the City, to go out and take Ignorance, and bind him hand and foot, and have him away. Then they took him up, and carried him through the air to the door that I saw in the side of the hill, and put him in there. Then I saw that there was a way to hell, even from the gates of heaven, as well as from the City of Destruction!

So I awoke, and behold, it was a dream.

CONCLUSION

Now, reader, I have told my dream to thee,
See if thou canst interpret it to me,
Or to thyself or neighbor; but take heed
Of misinterpreting; for that, instead
Of doing good, will but thyself abuse:
By misinterpreting, evil ensues.
Take heed also that thou be not extreme
In playing with the outside of my dream;
Nor let my figure or similitude
Put thee into a laughter or a feud.
Leave this for boys and fools; but as for thee,
Do thou the substance of my matter see.
Put by the curtains, look within my veil;
Turn up my metaphors, and do not fail,
There, if thou seekest them, such things to find
As will be helpful to an honest mind.
What of my dross thou findest there, be bold
To throw away; but yet preserve the gold.
What if my gold be wrapped up in ore?—
None throws away the apple for the core.
But if thou shalt cast all away as vain,
I know not but t'will make me dream again.

PART II

PART II

CHAPTER 1

Courteous Companions,–

Some time since, to tell you my dream that I had of Christian the Pilgrim, and of his dangerous journey towards the Celestial Country, was pleasant to me and profitable to you. I told you then, also, what I saw concerning his wife and children, and how unwilling they were to go with him on pilgrimage, insomuch that he was forced to go on his progress without them; for he durst not run the danger of that destruction which he feared would come by staying with them in the City of Destruction; wherefore, as I then showed you, he left them and departed.

Now, it hath so happened, through the abundance of business, that I have been much hindered and kept back from my wonted travels into those parts whence he went, and so could not, till now, obtain an opportunity to make further inquiry after those whom he left behind, that I might give you an account of them. But, having had some concerns that way of late, I went down again thitherward. Now, having taken up my lodgings in a wood about a mile off the place, as I slept I dreamed again.

THE AUTHOR AND MR. SAGACITY

And as I was in my dream, behold, an aged gentleman came by where I lay; and, because he was to go some part of the way that I was travelling, methought I got up and went with him. So, as we walked, and as travelers usually do, it was as if we fell into discourse; and our talk happened to be about Christian and his travels; for thus I began with the old man:

"Sir," said I, "what town is that there below, that lieth on the left hand of our way?"

Then said Mr. Sagacity (for that was his name), "It is the City of Destruction; a populous place, but possessed with a very ill-conditioned and idle sort of people."

"I thought that was that city," quoth I: "I went once myself through that town, and therefore know that this report you give of it is true."

SAG. Too true! I wish I could speak truth in speaking better of them that dwell therein.

"Well, sir," quoth I, "then I perceive you to be a well-meaning man, and so one that takes pleasure to hear and tell of that which is good. Pray, did you never hear what happened to a man some time ago of this town (whose name was Christian), that went on pilgrimage up towards the higher regions?"

SAG. Hear of him! Ay, and I also heard of the difficulties, troubles, wars, captivities, cries, groans, frights and fears that he met with and had in his journey. Besides, I must tell you all our country rings of him: there are but few houses that have heard of him and his doings but have sought after and got the record of his pilgrimage. Yea, I think I may say that his hazardous journey has got many wellwishers to his ways; for though, when he was here, he was a fool in every man's mouth, yet now he is gone he is highly commended of all. For 'tis said he lives bravely where he is: yea, many of them that are resolved never to run his risks yet have their mouths water at his gains.

"They may," quoth I, "well think, if they think anything that is true, that he liveth well where he is; for he now lives at and in the Fountain of Life, and has what he has without labor and sorrow; for there is no grief mixed therewith. But, pray, what talk have the people about him?"

SAG. Talk! the people talk strangely about him: some say that he now walks in white; that he has a chain of gold about his neck; that he has a crown of gold beset with pearls upon his head. Others say that the Shining Ones, that sometimes showed themselves unto him in his journey, are become his companions, and that he is as familiar with them in the place where he is, as here one neighbor is with another. Besides, it is confidently spoken concerning him, that the King of the place where he is has bestowed upon him already a very rich and pleasant dwelling at court, and that he every day eateth and drinketh and walketh with Him, and receiveth of the smiles and favors of Him that is judge of all there. Moreover, it is expected of some, that his Prince, the Lord of that country, will shortly come into these parts, and will know the reason, if they can give any, why his neighbors set so little by him, and had him so much in derision, when they perceived that he would be a Pilgrim. For they say, now he is so in the affections of his Prince, and that his Sovereign is so much concerned with the wrongs that were cast upon Christian when he became a Pilgrim, that He will look upon all as if done unto Himself; and no marvel, for it was for the love that he had to his Prince that he ventured as he did.

SAGACITY TELLS OF CHRISTIANA

"I daresay," quoth I; "I am glad on't; I am glad for the poor man's sake, for that he now has rest from his labor, and for that he reapeth the benefit of his tears with joy, and for that he has got beyond gunshot of his enemies, and is out of the reach of them that hate him. I also am glad for that a rumor of these things is noised abroad in this country: who can tell but that it may work some good effect on some that are left behind? But pray, sir, while it is fresh in my mind, do you hear anything of his wife and children? Poor hearts! I wonder in my mind what they do."

SAG. Who? Christiana and her sons? They are like to do as well as did Christian himself; for, though they all played the fool at first, and would by no means be persuaded by either the tears or entreaties of Christian, yet, second thoughts have wrought wonderfully with them, so they have packed up, and are also gone after him.

"Better and better," quoth I: "but, what! wife and children and all?"

SAG. It is true: I can give you an account of the matter, for I was upon the spot at the instant, and was thoroughly acquainted with the whole affair.

"Then," said I, "a man, it seems, may report it for a truth?"

SAG. You need not fear to declare it. I mean, that they are all gone on pilgrimage, both the good woman and her four boys. And, since (we are, as I perceive) going some considerable way together, I will give you an account of the whole matter.

This Christiana (for that was her name from the day that she, with her children betook themselves to a pilgrim's life) after her husband had gone over the river, and she could hear of him no more, her thoughts began to work in her mind. First, for that she had lost her husband, and of that the loving bond of that relation was utterly broken betwixt them. For you know (said he to me) it is only natural that the living should have many sad thoughts, in the remembrance of the loss of loving relations. This, therefore, of her husband, did cost her many a tear. But this was not all; for Christiana did also begin to consider with herself, whether unbecoming behavior towards her husband was not one cause that she saw him no more, and that in such sort he was taken away from her. And, upon this, came into her mind, by swarms, all her unkind, unnatural, and ungodly treatment of her dear friend; which also troubled her conscience, and did load her with guilt. She was, moreover, much broken with recalling to remembrance the restless groans, brinish tears, and self-bemoanings of her husband, and how she did harden her heart against all his entreaties and loving persuasions of her and her sons to go with him; yea, there was not anything that Christian either said to her or did before her, all the while that his burden did hang on his back, but it returned upon her like a flash of lightning, and rent her heart in sunder. Specially that bitter outcry of his, "What shall I do to be saved?" did ring in her ears most dolefully.

Then said she to her children, "Sons, we are all undone. I have sinned away your father, and he is gone; he would have had us with him, but I would not go myself; I also have hindered you of life."

With that, the boys fell all into tears, and cried out to go after their father.

"Oh," said Christiana, "that it had been but our lot to go with him! then had it fared well with us, beyond what it is like to do now. For though I formerly foolishly imagined, concerning the troubles of your father, that they came from a foolish fancy that he had, or for that he was overrun with melancholy humors; yet now it will not out of my mind but that they sprang from another cause; and it was this, that the light of life was given him, by the help of which, as I perceive, he has escaped the snares of death."

OF CHRISTIANA'S DREAM

Then they all wept again, and cried out, "Oh, woe worth the day!"

The next night Christiana had a dream; and, behold, she saw as if a broad parchment were opened before her, in which were recorded the sum of her ways; and the times, as she thought, looked very black upon her. Then she cried out aloud in her sleep, "Lord, have mercy upon me a sinner!" and the little children heard her.

After this, she thought she saw two very ill-favored ones standing by her bed-side, and saying, "What shall we do with this woman? for she cries out for mercy waking and sleeping: if she be suffered to go on as she begins, we shall lose her as we have lost her husband. Wherefore we must, by one way or other, seek to take her off from the thoughts of what shall be hereafter; else, all the world cannot help but she will become a pilgrim."

Now she awoke in a great sweat; also a trembling was upon her; but after a while, she fell to sleeping again. And then she thought she saw Christian her husband in a place of bliss, among many immortals, with a harp in his hand, standing and playing upon it before One that sat upon a throne, with a rainbow about His head.

She saw, also, as if he bowed his head with his face to the paved work that was under the Prince's feet, saying, "I heartily thank my Lord and King for bringing of me into this place." Then shouted a company of them that stood round about, and harped with their harps; but no man living could tell what they said, but Christian and his companions.

Next morning, when she was up, and had prayed to God and talked with her children a while, one knocked hard at the door; to whom she spake out, saying, "If thou comest in God's name, come in." So he said, "Amen," and opened the door, and saluted her with "Peace be to this house!" The which, when he had done, he said, "Christiana, knowest thou wherefore I am come?" Then she blushed and trembled, also her heart began to wax warm with desires to know from whence he came, and what was his errand to her. So he said unto her, "My name is Secret: I dwell with those that are on high. It is talked of where I dwell, as if thou hadst a desire to go thither; also there is a report that thou art aware of the evil thou hast formerly done to thy husband, in hardening thy heart against his way, and in keeping of these thy babes in their ignorance. Christiana, the Merciful One hath sent me to tell thee, that He is a God ready to forgive, and that He taketh delight to pardon offences. He also would have thee know that He inviteth thee to come into His presence, to His table, and that He will feed thee with the fat of His house, and with the heritage of Jacob thy father.

"There is Christian, thy husband that was, with legions more, his companions, ever behold that face that doth minister life to beholders; and they will be glad when they shall hear the sound of thy feet step over thy Father's threshold."

CHRISTIANA IS SENT FOR

Christiana at this was greatly abashed in herself, and bowed her head to the ground.

This visitor proceeded, and said, "Christiana, here is also a letter for thee, which I have brought from thy husband's King." So she took it, and opened it; but it smelt after the manner of the best perfume; also it was written in letters of gold. The contents of the letter were these: "That the King would have her to do as Christian her husband; for that was the way to come to His City, and to dwell in His presence with joy for ever."

At this the good woman was quite overcome; so she cried out to her visitor, "Sir, will you carry me and my children with you, that we also may worship this King?"

Then said the visitor, "Christiana, the bitter is before the sweet. Thou must through troubles, as did he that went before thee, enter the Celestial City. Wherefore I advise thee to do as did Christian thy husband: go to the wicket-gate yonder over the plain, for that stands in the head of the way up which you must go; and I wish thee all good speed. Also I advise that thou put this letter in thy bosom, that thou read therein to thyself, and to thy children, until you have got it by rote of heart: for it is one of the songs that thou must sing while thou art in this house of thy pilgrimage. Also this thou must deliver in at the farther gate."

Now, I saw in my dream, that this old gentleman, as he told me the story, did himself seem to be greatly affected therewith. He moreover went on, and said:

So Christiana called her sons together, and began thus to address herself unto them: "My sons, I have, as you may perceive, been of late under much trouble in my soul about the death of your father: not for that I doubt at all of his happiness, for I am satisfied now that he is well. I have also been much affected with the thoughts of mine own state and yours, which I verily believe is by nature miserable. My treatment also of your father in his distress is a great load to my conscience, for I hardened both mine own heart and yours against him, and refused to go with him on pilgrimage.

"The thoughts of these things would now kill me outright, but for a dream which I had last night, and but for the encouragement that this stranger has given me this morning. Come, my children, let us pack up, and be gone to the gate that leads to the Celestial Country, that we may see your father, and be with him and his companions in peace, according to the laws of that land."

Then did her children burst out into tears, for joy that the heart of their mother was so inclined. So their visitor bade them farewell; and they began to prepare to set out for their journey.

MRS. TIMOROUS AND CHRISTIANA

But while they were thus about to be gone, two of the women that were Christiana's neighbors came up to the house, and knocked at the door. To whom she said as before, "if you come in God's name, come in." At this the women were stunned; for this kind of language they used not to hear, or to perceive to drop from the lips of Christiana. Yet they came in; but, behold they found the good woman preparing to be gone from her house.

So they began, and said, "Neighbor, pray what is your meaning by this?"

Christiana answered and said to the eldest of them, whose name was Mrs. Timorous, "I am preparing for a journey."

This Timorous was daughter to him that met Christian upon the Hill Difficulty, and would have had him go back for fear of the lions.

TIM. For what journey, I pray you?

CHR. Even to go after my good husband. And with that she fell a weeping.

TIM. I hope not so, good neighbor. Pray, for your poor children's sake, do not so unwomanly cast away yourself.

CHR. Nay, my children shall go with me; not one of them is willing to stay behind.

169

TIM. I wonder in my very heart what or who has brought you into this mind!

CHR. Oh, neighbor, knew you but as much as I do, I doubt not but that you would go with me.

TIM. Prithee, what new knowledge hast thou got that so worketh off thy mind from thy friends, and that tempteth thee to go nobody knows where?

CHR. Then Christiana replied, "I have been sorely afflicted since my husband's departure from me, but especially since he went over the river. But that which troubleth me most is my unkind treatment of him when he was under his distress. Besides, I am now as he was then: nothing will serve me but going on pilgrimage. I was a-dreaming last night that I saw him. Oh that my soul was with him! He dwelleth in the presence of the King of the country; he sits and eats with Him at His table; he has become a companion of immortals, and has a house now given him to dwell in, to which the best palaces on earth, if compared, seem to me but as a dung-hill. The Prince of the place has also sent for me, with promises of entertainment if I shall come to Him; His messenger was here even now, and has brought me a letter which invites me to come." And with that she plucked out the letter, and read it, and said to them, "What now will you say to this?"

MERCY ALSO DESIRES TO GO

TIM. Oh, the madness that hath possessed thee and thy husband, to run yourselves upon such difficulties! You have heard, I am sure, what your husband did meet with, even in a manner at the first step that he took on his way, as our neighbor Obstinate can yet testify, for he went along with them, yea, and Pliable too; until they, like wise men, were afraid to go any farther. We also heard, over and above, how he met with the lions, Apollyon, the Shadow of Death, and many other things. Nor is the danger he met with at Vanity Fair to be forgotten by thee. For if he, though a man, was so hard put to it, what canst thou, being but a poor woman, do? Consider also that these four sweet babes are thy children, thy flesh and thy bones. Wherefore, though thou shouldest be so rash as to cast away thyself, yet, for the sake of thy children, keep thou at home.

But Christiana said unto her, "Tempt me not, my neighbor. I have now a price put into my hands to get gain, and I should be a fool of the greatest size if I should have no heart to strike in with the opportunity. And for that you tell me of all these troubles which I am like to meet with in the way, they are so far off from being to me a discouragement, that they show I am in the right. The bitter must come before the sweet, and that also will make the sweet the sweeter. Wherefore, since you came not to my house in God's name, as I said, I pray you to be gone, and not to disquiet me further."

Then Timorous reviled her, and said to her fellow, "Come, neighbor Mercy, let us leave her in her own hands, since she scorns our counsel and company." But Mercy was at a stand, and could not so readily comply with her neighbor, and that for a twofold reason:

1. Her heart yearned over Christiana; so she said within herself, "If my neighbor will needs be gone, I will go a little way with her, and help her."

2. Her heart yearned over her own soul; for what Christiana had said had taken hold upon her mind. Wherefore she said within herself again, "I will yet have more talk with this Christiana, and if I find truth and life in what she shall say, myself, with my heart, shall also go with her." Wherefore Mercy began thus to reply to her neighbor Timorous:

MER. Neighbor, I did indeed come with you to see Christiana this morning; and since she is, as you see, taking her last farewell of her country, I think to walk this sunshiny morning a little with her, to help her on her way.

But she told her not of the second reason, but kept that to herself.

TIM. Well, I see you have a mind to go a-fooling too; but take heed in time, and be wise. While we are out of danger, we are out; but when we are in, we are in.

So Mrs. Timorous returned to her house, and Christiana betook herself to her journey. But when Timorous was got home to her house, she sends for some of her neighbors; to wit, Mrs. Bat's-eyes, Mrs. Inconsiderate, Mrs. Light-mind, and Mrs. Know-nothing. So, when they were come to her house, she falls to telling of the story of Christiana and of her intended journey. And thus she began her tale:

MRS. TIMOROUS' NEIGHBORS

TIM. Neighbors, having had little to do this morning, I went to give Christiana a visit; and when I came at the door, I knocked, as you know it is our custom; and she answered, "If you come in God's name come in." So in I went, thinking all was well; but when I came in I found her preparing herself to depart the town, she and also her children. So I asked her what was her meaning by that. And she told me, in short, that she was now of a mind to go on pilgrimage, as did her husband. She told me also a dream that she had, and how the King of the country where her husband was had sent her an inviting letter to come thither.

Then said Mrs. Know-nothing, "And, what! do you think she will go?"

TIM. Ay, go she will, whatever comes on't; and methinks I know it by this: for that which was my great reason in persuading her to stay at home (that is, the troubles she was like to meet with in the way) is one great reason with her to put her forward on her journey. For she told me, in so many words, "The bitter goes before the sweet; yea, and forasmuch as it so doth, it makes the sweet the sweeter."

MRS. BAT'S-EYES. "Oh, this blind and foolish woman!" said she; "will she not take warning by her husband's trials? For my part, I see, if he were here again, he would rest him content in a whole skin, and never run so many dangers for nothing."

Mrs. Inconsiderate also replied, saying, "Away with such fantastical fools from the town! a good riddance, for my part, I say, of her! Should she stay where she dwells, and retain this in her mind, who could live quietly by her? for she will either be dumpish, or unneighborly, or talk of such matters as no wise body can abide. Wherefore, for my part, I shall never be sorry for her departure: let her go, and let better come in her room. It was never a good world since these whimsical fools dwelt in it."

Then Mrs. Light-mind added as followeth: "Come, put this kind of talk away. I was yesterday at Madam Wanton's, where we were as merry as the maids. For who do you think should be there, but I and Mrs. Love-the-Flesh, and three or four more, with Mr. Lechery, Mrs. Filth, and some others. So there we had music and dancing, and what else was meet to fill up the pleasure. And, I dare say, my lady herself is an admirable well-bred gentlewoman, and Mr. Lechery is as pretty a fellow."

CHAPTER 2

The Wicket-Gate

By this time Christiana was got on her way, and Mercy went along with her. So as they went, her children being there also, Christiana began to discourse. "And, Mercy," said Christiana, "I take this as an unexpected favor, that thou shouldest set forth out of doors with me, to accompany me a little in my way."

MER. Then said young Mercy (for she was but young), "If I thought it would be a good purpose to go with you, I would never go near the town any more."

CHR. "Well, Mercy," said Christiana, "cast in thy lot with me: I well know what will be the end of our pilgrimage: my husband is where he would not but be for all the gold in the Spanish mines. Nor shalt thou be turned away, though thou goest but upon my invitation. The King who hath sent for me and my children is One that delighteth in mercy. Besides, if thou wilt, I will hire thee, and thou shalt go along with me as my servant; yet we will have all things in common betwixt thee and me, only go along with me."

MER. But how shall I be sure that I also shall be welcomed? Had I this hope but from one that can tell, I would have

no hesitation at all, but would go, being helped by Him
that can help, though the way be never so tedious.

CHR. Well, loving Mercy, I will tell thee what thou shalt do:
go with me to the wicket-gate, and there I will further
inquire for thee; and if there thou dost not meet with
encouragement, I will be content that thou shalt return
to thy place: I also will pay thee for thy kindness which
thou showest to me and my children, in the accompanying
of us in our way as thou dost.

MERCY GOES WITH CHRISTIANA

MER. Then will I go thither, and will take what shall follow;
and the Lord grant that my lot may there fall, even as
the King of heaven shall have His heart upon me!

Christiana was then glad at her heart, not only that she had
a companion, but also for that she had prevailed with this
poor maid to fall in love with her own salvation. So they went
on together and Mercy began to weep.

Then said Christiana, "Wherefore weepeth my sister so?"

MER. "Alas!" said she, "who can but lament, that shall but
rightly consider what a state and condition my poor
relations are in, that yet remain in our sinful town? And
that which makes my grief the more heavy is, because
they have no one to teach them nor to tell them what is
to come."

CHR. Tenderness becometh pilgrims; and thou dost for thy
friends as my good Christian did for me when he left
me: he mourned for that I would not heed nor regard
him; but his Lord and ours did gather up his tears, and
put them into His bottle; and now both I and thou,
and these my sweet babes, are reaping the fruit and
benefit of them I hope, Mercy, that these tears of thine

will not be lost; for the Truth hath said that "they that sow in tears shall reap in joy," in singing; and "he that goeth forth and weepeth, bearing precious seed, shall doubtless come again with rejoicing, bringing his sheaves with him."

Then said Mercy:

"Let the Most Blessèd be my guide,
If 't be His blessèd will,
Unto His gate, into His fold,
Up to His holy hill.
And never let Him suffer me
To swerve or turn aside
From His free grace and holy ways,
Whate'er shall me betide.
And let Him gather them of mine
That I have left behind:
Lord, make them pray they may be Thine,
With all their heart and mind."

Now my old friend proceeded, and said, "But when Christiana came to the Slough of Despond, she began to be at a stand; 'For,' said she, 'this is the place in which my dear husband had like to have been smothered with mud.' She perceived also that, notwithstanding the command of the King to make this place for pilgrims good, yet it was rather worse than formerly." So I asked if that was true.

"Yes," said the old gentleman, "too true, for many there be that pretend to be the King's laborers, and say they are for mending the King's highway, that bring dirt and dung instead of stones, and so mar instead of mending. Here Christiana, therefore, with her boys, did make a stand. But said Mercy, 'Come, let us venture, only let us be wary.' Then they looked well to their steps, and made shift to get staggeringly over. Yet Christiana had to have been in, and that not once nor twice.

"Now, they had no sooner got over, but they thought they heard words that said unto them, 'Blessed is she that believeth, for there shall be a performance of those things which were told her from the Lord.'

"Then they went on again; and said Mercy to Christiana, 'Had I as good ground to hope for a loving reception at the wicket-gate as you, I think no Slough of Despond would discourage me.'

" 'Well,' said the other, 'You know your trouble, and I know mine; and, good friend, we shall have enough evil before we come at our journey's end. For can it be imagined that the people that design to attain such excellent glories as we do, and that are so envied that happiness as we are, but that we shall meet with what fears, with what troubles and afflictions they can possibly assault us with, that hate us?' "

AT THE WICKET-GATE

And now Mr. Sagacity left me to dream out my dream by myself. Wherefore, methought I saw Christiana, and Mercy, and the boys, go all of them up to the gate; to which when they were come they betook themselves to a short debate about how they must manage their calling at the gate, and what should be said unto him that did open unto them: so it was concluded, since Christiana was the eldest, that she should knock for entrance, and that she should speak to him that did open, for the rest. So Christiana began to knock, and, as her poor husband did, she knocked and knocked again. But instead of any that answered, they all thought that they heard as if a dog came barking upon them; a dog, and a great one too: and this made the women and children afraid, nor durst they for a while to knock any more, for fear the mastiff should fly upon them. Now, therefore, they were greatly tumbled up and down in their minds, and knew not what to do. Knock they durst not, for fear of the dog; go back they durst not, for fear the keeper of the gate should espy them as they so went, and should be offended with them. At last they thought of knocking again, and knocked more loudly than they did at first. Then said the Keeper of the gate, "Who is there?" So the dog left off to bark, and He opened unto them.

Then Christiana made low obeisance, and said, "Let not our Lord be offended with His handmaidens, for that we have knocked at His princely gate."

Then said the Keeper, "Whence come ye? and what is it that you would have?"

Christiana answered, "We are come from whence Christian did come, and upon the same errand as he; to wit, to be, if it shall please you, graciously admitted by this gate into the way that leads to the Celestial City. And I answer, my Lord, in the next place, that I am Christiana, once the wife of Christian, that now is gotten above."

With that the Keeper of the gate did marvel, saying, "What! is she now become a pilgrim, that, but a while ago hated that life?"

Then she bowed her head, and said, "Yes; and so are these my sweet babes also."

Then He took her by the hand, and let her in, and said also, "Suffer the little children to come unto me;" and with that He shut up the gate. This done, He called to a trumpeter that was above, over the gate, to entertain Christiana with shouting and sound of trumpet for joy. So he obeyed, and sounded, and filled the air with his melodious notes.

Now, all this while poor Mercy did stand without trembling and crying, for fear that she was rejected. But when Christiana had got admittance for herself and her boys, then she began to make intercession for Mercy.

MERCY FALLS IN A SWOON

CHR. And she said, "My Lord, I have a companion of mine that stands yet without, that is come hither upon the same account as myself, one that is much troubled in her mind, for that she comes, as she thinks, without sending for; whereas I was sent to by my husband's King to come."

Now Mercy began to be very impatient, for each minute was as long to her as an hour; wherefore she prevented Christiana from asking for her more fully by knocking at the gate herself. And she knocked then so loud that she made Christiana to start. Then said the Keeper of the gate, "Who is there?" And said Christiana, "It is my friend."

So He opened the gate and looked out; but Mercy was fallen down without in a swoon, for she fainted, and was afraid that no gate would be opened to her.

Then he took her by the hand, and said, "Maiden, I bid thee arise."

"Oh, sir," said she, "I am faint: there is scarce life left in me."

But He answered that "One once said, 'When my soul fainted within me, I remembered the Lord; and my prayer came in unto Thee, into Thy holy temple.' Fear not, but stand upon thy feet, and tell me wherefore thou art come."

MER. I am come for that unto which I was never invited, as my friend Christiana was. Hers was from the King, and mine was but from her. Wherefore I fear I presume.
KEEP. Did she desire thee to come with her to this place?
MER. Yes; and, as my Lord sees, I am come. And if there is any grace and forgiveness of sins to spare, I beseech that I, Thy poor handmaiden, may be partaker thereof.

MERCY PERMITTED TO ENTER

Then He took her again by the hand, and led her gently in, and said, "I pray for all them that believe on me, by what means soever they come unto me." Then said He to those that stood by, "Fetch something, and give it to Mercy to smell on, thereby to stay her fainting." So they fetched her a bundle of myrrh, and a while after she was revived.

And now was Christiana and her boys and Mercy received of the Lord at the head of the way, and spoke kindly unto by Him. Then said they yet further unto Him, "We are sorry for our sins, and beg of our Lord His pardon and further information what we must do."

"I grant pardon," said He, "by word and deed: by word, in the promise of forgiveness; by deed, in the way I obtained it. Take the first from my lips with a kiss, and the other as it shall be revealed."

Now, I saw in my dream, that He spake many good words unto them, whereby they were greatly gladded. He also had them up to the top of the gate, and showed them by what deed they were saved; and told them withal that that sight they would have again as they went along the way, to their comfort.

So He left them a while in a summer parlor below, where they entered into a talk by themselves; and thus Christiana began:

"O Lord, how glad am I that we are got in hither!"

Mer. So you well may; but I of all have cause to leap for joy.
Chr. I thought one time as I stood at the gate, because I knocked, and none did answer, that all our labor had been lost, specially when that ugly cur made such a heavy barking against us.
Mer. But my worst fear was after I saw that you were taken into His favor, and that I was left behind. Now, thought I, it is fulfilled which is written, "Two women shall be

grinding at the mill; the one shall be taken, and the other left." I had much ado to forbear crying out, "Undone! undone!" And afraid I was to knock any more: but when I looked up to what was written over the gate, I took courage. I also thought that I must either knock again or die; so I knocked, but I cannot tell how, for my spirit now struggled betwixt life and death.

CHR. Can you not tell how you knocked? I am sure your knocks were so earnest, that the very sound of them made me start. I thought I never heard such knocking in all my life; I thought you would come in by violent hands, or take the kingdom by storm.

MER. Alas! to be in my case, who that so was could but have done so? You saw that the door was shut upon me, and that there was a most cruel dog thereabout. Who, I say, that was so faint-hearted as I, would not have knocked with all their might? But, pray, what said my Lord to my rudeness? Was He not angry with me?

CHR. When He heard your lumbering noise, He gave a wonderful innocent smile; I believe what you did pleased Him well enough, for He showed no sign to the contrary. But I marvel in my heart why he keeps such a dog; had I known that afore, I should not have had heart enough to have ventured myself in this manner. But now we are in, we are in, and I am glad with all my heart.

MER. I will ask, if you please, next time He comes down, why He keeps such a filthy cur in His yard. I hope He will not take it amiss.

"Ay, do," said the children, "and persuade Him to hang him, for we are afraid he will bite us when we go hence."

So at last He came down to them again, and Mercy fell to the ground on her face before Him, and worshiped, and said, "Let my Lord accept the offering of praise which I now offer unto Him with my lips."

MERCY EXPRESSES HER FEARS

So He said unto her, "Peace be to thee; stand up." But she continued upon her face, and said, "Righteous art Thou, O Lord, when I plead with Thee; yet let me talk with Thee of Thy judgments. Wherefore dost Thou keep so cruel a dog in Thy yard, at the sight of which such women and children as we are ready to fly from the gate with fear?" He answered and said, "That dog has another owner; he also is kept close in another man's ground, only my pilgrims hear his barking: he belongs to the castle which you see there at a distance, but can come up to the walls of this place. He has frighted many an honest pilgrim from worse to better, by the great voice of his roaring. Indeed, he that owneth him doth not keep him out of any good-will to me or mine, but with intent to keep the pilgrims from coming to me, and that they may be afraid to come and knock at this gate for entrance. Sometimes also he has broken out, and has worried some that I love; but I take all at present patiently. I also give my pilgrims timely help, so that they are not delivered up to his power, to do with them what his doggish nature would prompt him to. But, what! my beloved one, I should suppose, hadst thou known even so much beforehand, thou wouldst not have been afraid of a dog. The beggars that go from door to door will, rather than lose a supposed alms, run the danger of the bawling, barking, and biting too, of a dog; and shall a dog in another man's yard, a dog whose barking I turn to the profit of pilgrims, keep any one from coming to me? I deliver them from the lions, their darling from the power of the dog."

MER. Then said Mercy, "I confess my ignorance, I spake what I understood not: I acknowledge that Thou doest all things well."

CHR. Then Christiana began to talk of their journey, and to inquire after the way.

So He fed them, and washed their feet, and set them in the way of His steps, according as He had dealt with her husband before.

So I saw in my dream that they walked on in their way, and had the weather very comfortable to them.

Then Christiana began to sing:

"Blessed be the day that I began
A pilgrim for to be;
And blessèd also be the man
That thereto movèd me.
'Tis true 'twas long ere I began
To seek to live for ever;
But now I run fast as I can:
'Tis better late than never.
Our tears to joy, our fears to faith,
Are turnèd, as we see;
Thus our beginning (as one saith)
Shows what our end will be."

Now, there was, on the other side of the wall that fenced in the way up which Christiana and her companions were to go, a garden, and that garden belonged to him whose was that barking dog, of whom mention was made before. And some of the fruit-trees that grew in that garden shot their branches over the wall; and, being mellow, they that found them did gather them up and oft eat of them to their hurt. So Christiana's boys, as boys are apt to do, being pleased with the trees, and the fruit that did hang thereon, did bend the branches down, and pluck the fruit, and begin to eat. Their mother did also chide them for so doing; but still the boys went on.

"Well," said she, "my sons, you do wrong, for that fruit is none of ours;" but she did not know that it did belong to the enemy: I'll warrant you, if she had, she would have been ready to die for fear. But that passed, and they went on their way.

THE ILL-FAVORED ONES

Now, by that they were gone about two bow-shots from the place that led them unto the way, they espied two very ill-favored ones coming down apace to meet them. With that, Christiana, and Mercy her friend, covered themselves with their veils, and so kept on their journey; the children also went on before; so that, at last, they met together. Then they that came down to meet them came just up to the women, as if they would embrace them; but Christiana said, "Stand back, or go peaceably by, as you should."

Yet these two, as men that are deaf, regarded not Christiana's words, but began to lay hands upon them. At that, Christiana, waxing very wroth, spurned at them with her feet. Mercy also, as well as she could, did what she could to shift them. Christiana again said to them, "Stand back, and be gone; for we have no money to lose, being pilgrims, as you see, and such, too, as live upon the charity of our friends."

ILL-FAV. Then said one of the two men, "We make no assault upon you for money, but are come out to tell you that, if you will grant one small request which we shall ask, we will make women of you for ever."

CHR. Now Christiana, imagining what they should mean, made answer again, "We will neither hear nor regard, nor yield to what you shall ask. We are in haste, and cannot stay; our business is a business of life or death."

So again she and her companions made a fresh attempt to go past them; but they letted them in their way.

ILL-FAV. And they said, "We intend no hurt to your lives; it is another thing we would have."

CHR. "Ay," quoth Christiana, "you would have us body and soul, for I know it is for that you are come; but we will die rather upon the spot, than to suffer ourselves to be brought into such snares as shall risk the loss of our well-being hereafter." And, with that, they both shrieked out, and cried, "Murder! murder!" and so put themselves under those laws that are provided for the protection of women. But the men still made their approach upon them, with design to prevail against them. They therefore cried out again.

A RELIEVER APPEARS

Now, they being, as I said, far from the gate in at which they came, their voices were heard from where they were, thither; wherefore some of the house came out, and, knowing it was Christiana's tongue, they made haste to her relief. But by the time that they were got within sight of them, the women were in a very great terror; the children also stood crying by. Then did he that came in for their relief call out to the ruffians, saying, "What is that thing you do? Would you make my Lord's people to do wrong?" He also attempted to take them, but they did make their escape over the wall into the garden of the man to whom the great dog belonged; so the dog became their protector. This Reliever then came up to the women and asked them how they did.

So they answered, "We thank thy Prince, pretty well, only we have been somewhat affrighted: we thank thee also for that thou camest in to our help, otherwise we had been overcome."

Rel. So, after a few more words, this Reliever said as followeth: "I marvelled much when you were entertained at the gate above, being ye knew that ye were but weak women, that you asked not the Lord for a conductor. Then might you have avoided these troubles and dangers; for He would have granted you one."

CHR. "Alas!" said Christiana, "we were taken so with our present blessing, that dangers to come were forgotten by us. Besides, who could have thought that, so near the King's palace, there could have lurked such naughty ones? Indeed, it had been well for us had we asked our Lord for one; but, since our Lord knew it would be for our profit, I wonder He sent not one along with us."

REL. It is not always necessary to grant things not asked for, lest, by so doing, they become of little value; but when the want of a thing is felt, then he who needs it feels its preciousness; and so when it is given it will be used. Had my Lord granted you a conductor, you would not either have so bewailed that oversight of yours, in not asking for one, as now you have occasion to do. So all things work for good, and tend to make you more wary.

CHR. Shall we go back again to my Lord, and confess our folly, and ask one?

REL. Your confession of your folly I will present Him with. To go back again you need not; for, in all places where you shall come, you will find no want at all; for, in every one of my Lord's lodgings, which He has prepared for the care of His pilgrims, there is sufficient to furnish them against all attempts whatsoever. But, as I said, He will be asked of by them, to do it for them. And 'tis a poor thing that is not worth asking for.

THE PILGRIMS PROCEED

When he had thus said, he went back to his place, and the pilgrims went on their way.

MER. Then said Mercy, "What a sudden blank is here! I made account we had been past all danger, and that we should never see sorrow more."

CHR. "Thy innocence, my sister," said Christiana to Mercy, "may excuse thee much; but as for me, fault is so much the greater, for that I saw the danger before I came out of the doors, and yet did not provide for it when provision might have been had. I am, therefore, much to be blamed."

MER. Then said Mercy, "How knew you this before you came from home? Pray, open to me this riddle."

CHR. Why, I will tell you. Before I set foot out of doors, one night, as I lay in my bed, I had a dream about this; for methought I saw two men, as like these as ever any in the world could look, stand at my bed's feet, plotting how they might prevent my salvation. I will tell you their very words. They said (it was when I was in my troubles), "What shall we do with this woman? for she cries out waking and sleeping for forgiveness: if she be suffered to go on as she begins, we shall lose her as we have lost her husband." This, you know, might have made me take heed, and have provided when provision might have been had.

MER. "Well," said Mercy, "as by this neglect we have been made to behold our own imperfections, so our Lord has taken occasion thereby to make manifest the riches of His grace; for He, as we see, has followed us with unasked kindness, and has delivered us from their hands that were stronger than we, of His mere good pleasure."

CHAPTER 3

The Interpreter's House

THE INTERPRETER'S HOUSE

Thus, now, when they had talked away a little more time, they drew near to a house which stood in the way, which house was built for the relief of pilgrims, as you will find more fully related in the first part of these records of the Pilgrim's Progress. So they drew on towards the house (the house of the Interpreter); and, when they came to the door, they heard a great talk in the house. Then they gave ear, and heard, as they thought, Christiana mentioned by name; for you must know that there went along, even before her, a talk of her and her children's going on pilgrimage. And this was the more pleasing to them, because they had heard she was Christian's wife, that woman who was some time ago so unwilling to hear of going on pilgrimage. Thus, therefore, they stood still, and heard the good people within commending her, who, they little thought, stood at the door. At last Christiana knocked, as she had done at the gate before. Now, when she had knocked, there came to the door a young maiden, and opened the door and looked; and, behold, two women were there.

MAID. Then said the maid to them, "With whom would you speak in this place?"

CHR. Christiana answered, "We understand that this is a place prepared for those that are become pilgrims, and we now at this door are such; wherefore we pray that we may be partakers of that for which we at this time are come; for the day, as thou seest, is very far spent, and we are loth to-night to go any farther."

MAID. Pray, what may I call your name, that I may tell it to my lord within?

CHR. My name is Christiana: I was the wife of that pilgrim that some years ago did travel this way; and these be his four children. This young woman is my companion, and is going on pilgrimage too.

INNOCENT. Then Innocent ran in (for that was her name,) and said to those within, "Can you think who is at the door? There are Christiana and her children, and her companion, all waiting for entertainment here."

Then they leaped for joy, and went and told their master. So he came to the door, and looking upon her, he said, "Art thou that Christiana whom Christian the good man left behind him, when he betook himself to a pilgrim's life?"

CHR. I am that woman that was so hard-hearted as to slight my husband's troubles, and then left him to go on his journey alone; and these are his four children. But now also I am come, for I am convinced that no way is right but this.

INTER. Then is fulfilled that which also is written of the man that said to his son, "Go, work to-day in my vineyard;" and he said to his father, "I will not;" but afterwards he repented, and went.

CHR. Then said Christiana, "So be it: Amen. God make it a true saying upon me, and grant that I may be found

at the last of Him in peace, without spot and blame-
less!"

INTER. But why standest thou thus at the door? Come in,
thou blessed one. We were talking of thee but now;
for tidings have come to us before how thou art become
a pilgrim. Come, children, come in; come, maiden,
come in.

So he had them all into the house.

PILGRIMS ENTERTAINED

So when they were within, they were bidden to sit down and
rest them; the which when they had done, those that attended
upon the pilgrims in the house came into the room to see
them. And one smiled, and another smiled, and they all smiled
for joy that Christiana was become a pilgrim. They also looked
upon the boys; they stroked them over the faces with the
hand, in token of their kind reception of them; they also
carried it lovingly to Mercy, and bid them all welcome into
their master's house.

After a while, because supper was not ready, the
Interpreter took them into his significant rooms, and showed
them what Christian, Christiana's husband, had seen some
time before. Here, therefore, they saw the man in the cage,
the man and his dream, the man that cut his way through
his enemies, and the picture of the biggest of them all, together
with the rest of those things that were then so profitable to
Christian.

This done, and after those things had been seen and
thought of by Christiana and her company, the Interpreter
takes them apart again, and has them first into a room where
was a man that could look no way but downwards, with a
muck-rake in his hand. There stood also one over his head,
with a celestial crown in his hand, and proffered to give him

that crown for his muck-rake; but the man did neither look up nor regard, but raked to himself the straws, the small sticks, and the dust of the floor.

Then said Christiana, "I persuade myself that I know somewhat the meaning of this; for this is a figure of a man of this world. Is it not, good sir?"

INTER. "Thou hast said the right," said he; "and his muck-rake doth show his worldly mind. And whereas thou seest him rather give heed to rake up straws and sticks, and the dust of the floor, than to do what he says that calls to him from above with the celestial crown in his hand; it is to show that heaven is but a fable to some, and that things here are counted the only things substantial. Now, whereas it was also showed thee that the man could look no way but downwards; it is to let thee know that earthly things, when they are with power upon men's minds, quite carry their hearts away from God."

CHR. Then said Christiana, "Oh, deliver me from this muck-rake!"

INTER. "That prayer," said the Interpreter, "has lain by till it is almost rusty. 'Give me not riches' is scarce the prayer of one of ten thousand. Straws, and sticks, and dust, with most, are the great things now looked after."

With that, Mercy and Christiana wept, and said, "It is, alas! too true."

INTERPRETER'S ALLEGORIES

When the Interpreter had showed them this, he had them into the very best room in the house; a very brave room it was. So he bid them look round about, and see if they could find anything there. Then they looked round and round; for there was nothing to be seen but a very great spider on the wall, and that they overlooked.

MER. Then said Mercy, "Sir, I see nothing."

But Christiana held her peace.

INTER. "But," said the Interpreter, "look again."

She therefore looked again, and said, "Here is not anything but an ugly spider, who hangs by her hands upon the wall."

Then said he, "Is there but one spider in all this spacious room?"

Then the water stood in Christiana's eyes, for she was a woman quick of mind; and she said, "Yes, my lord; there is here more than one; yea, and spiders whose venom is far more destructive than that which is in her."

The Interpreter then looked pleasantly upon her, and said, "Thou hast said the truth."

This made Mercy blush and the boys to cover their faces; for they all began now to understand the riddle.

Then said the Interpreter again, "The spider taketh hold with her hands (as you see), and is in kings' palaces. And wherefore is this recorded, but to show you that, how full of the venom of sin soever you be, yet you may, by the hand of faith, lay hold of and dwell in the best room that belongs to the king's house above."

CHR. "I thought," said Christiana, "of something of this; but I could not imagine it all. I thought that we were like spiders, and that we looked like ugly creatures, in what fine rooms soever we were: but that by this spider, this venomous and ill-favored creature, we were to learn how to act faith, that came not into my mind; and yet she has taken hold with her hands, and, as I see, dwelleth in the best room in the house. God has made nothing in vain."

Then they seemed all to be glad, but the water stood in their eyes; yet they looked one upon another, and also bowed before the Interpreter.

He had them then into another room, where were a hen and chickens, and bid them observe a while. So one of the chickens went to the trough to drink; and every time she drank, she lifted up her head and her eyes toward heaven. "See," said he, "what this little chick doth; and learn of her to acknowledge whence your mercies come, by receiving them with looking up. Yet again," said he, "observe and look."

So they gave heed, and perceived that the hen did walk in a fourfold method towards her chickens. First, she had a common call, and that she hath all day long. Secondly, she had a special call, and that she had but sometimes. Thirdly, she had a brooding note. And, fourthly she had an outcry.

INTER. "Now," said he, "compare this hen to your King, and these chickens to His obedient ones: for, answerable to her, He Himself hath His methods which He walketh in toward His people. By His common call, He gives nothing; by His special call, He always has something to give; He also has a brooding voice for them that are under His wing; and He hath an outcry, to give the alarm when He seeth the enemy come. I chose, my darlings, to lead you into the room where such things are, because you are women, and they are easy for you."

CHR. "And, sir," said Christiana, "pray let us see some more."

So he had them into the slaughter-house, where the butcher was killing a sheep; and, behold, the sheep was quiet, and took her death patiently. Then said the Interpreter, "You must learn of this sheep to suffer, and to put up with wrongs without murmurings and complaints. Behold how quietly she takes her death; and, without objecting, she suffereth her skin to be pulled over her ears. Your King doth call you His sheep."

After this, he led them into his garden, where was great variety of flowers; and he said, "Do you see all these?" So Christiana said, "Yes." Then said he again, "Behold, the flowers are diverse in stature, in quality, and color, and smell, and virtue, and some are better than others; also, where the gardener has set them, there they stand, and quarrel not one with another."

Again, he had them into his field, which he had sowed with wheat and corn; but when they beheld, the tops of all were cut off, and only the straw remained. He said again, "This ground was made rich, and was ploughed, and sowed; but what shall we do with the crop?" Then said Christiana, "Burn some, and make muck of the rest." Then said the Interpreter again, "Fruit, you see, is that thing you look for; and, for want of that, you send it to the fire, and to be trodden under foot of men. Beware that in this you condemn not yourselves."

Then, as they were coming in from abroad, they espied a little robin with a great spider in his mouth. So the Interpreter said, "Look here." So they looked, and Mercy wondered; but Christiana said, "What a disparagement is it to such a pretty little bird as the robin-redbreast is; he being also a bird above many, that loveth to maintain a kind of sociableness with man! I had thought they had lived upon crumbs of bread, or upon other such harmless matter. I like him worse than I did."

The Interpreter then replied, "This robin is an emblem very apt, to set forth some people by; for to sight they are as this robin, pretty of note, color, and conduct. They seem also to have a very great love for those that are sincere followers of Christ; and above all other to desire to associate with them, and to be in their company, as if they could live upon the good man's crumbs. They pretend, also, that therefore it is that they frequent the house of the godly and the appointments of the Lord; but, when they are by themselves, as the robin, they can catch and gobble up spiders, they can change their diet, drink wickedness, and swallow down sin like water."

So, when they were come again into the house, because supper as yet was not ready, Christiana again desired that the Interpreter would either show, or tell of, some other things that were profitable.

Then the Interpreter began, and said, "The fatter the sow is the more she desires the mire; the fatter the ox is, the more thoughtlessly he goes to the slaughter; and the more healthy the lusty man is, the more prone he is unto evil. There is a desire in women to go neat and fine; and it is a comely thing to be adorned with that which in God's sight is of great price. 'Tis easier watching a night or two than to sit up a whole year together; so 'tis easier for one to begin to profess well than to hold out as he should to the end. Every ship-master, when in a storm, will willingly cast that over-board which is of the smallest value in the vessel; but who will throw the best out first? None but he that feareth not God. One leak will sink a ship, and one sin will destroy a sinner. He that forgets his friends is ungrateful unto him but he that forgets his Saviour is unmerciful to himself. He that lives in sin, and looks for happiness hereafter, is like him that soweth weeds, and thinks to fill his barn with wheat or barley. If a man would live well, let him bring before him his last day, and make it always his company-keeper. Whispering, and change of thoughts, prove that sin is in the world. If the world, which God sets light by, is counted a thing of that worth with men, what is heaven, that God commendeth! If the life that is attended with so many troubles is so loth to be let go by us, what is the life above! Everybody will cry up the goodness of men; but who is there that is, as he should be, affected with the goodness of God?"

When the Interpreter had done, he takes them out into his garden again, and had them to a tree, whose inside was all rotten and gone, and yet it grew and had leaves.

Then said Mercy, "What means this?"

"This tree," said he, "whose outside is fair, and whose inside is rotten, is that to which many may be compared that are in the garden of God, who with their mouths speak high in behalf of God, but indeed will do nothing for Him; whose leaves are fair, but their heart good for nothing but to be tinder for the devil's tinder-box."

Now supper was ready, the table spread, and all things set on the board; so they sat down, and did eat when one had given thanks. And the Interpreter did usually entertain those that lodged with him with music at meals; so the minstrels played. There was also one that did sing, and a very fine voice he had. His song was this:

> "The Lord is only my support,
> And He that doth me feed;
> How can I then want anything
> Whereof I stand in need?"

DISCOURSE AT SUPPER

When the song and music were ended, the Interpreter asked Christiana what it was that first did move her to betake herself to a pilgrim's life. Christiana answered, "First, the loss of my husband came into my mind, at which I was heartily grieved; but all that was but natural affection. Then, after that, came the troubles and pilgrimages of my husband into my mind, and also how unkindly I had behaved to him as to that. So guilt took hold of my mind, and would have drawn me into the pond, to drown myself, but that, just at the right time, I had a dream of the well-being of my husband, and a letter sent by the King of that country where my husband dwells, to come to him. The dream and the letter together so wrought upon my mind, that they forced me to this way."

INTER. But met you with no opposition afore you set out of doors?

CHR. Yes, a neighbor of mine, one Mrs. Timorous: she was akin to him that would have persuaded my husband to go back for fear of the lions. She all-to-be-fooled me for, as she called it, my intended desperate adventure; she also urged what she could to dishearten me from it—the hardship and troubles that my husband met with in the way; but all this I got over pretty well. But a dream that I had of two ill-looked ones, that I thought did plot how to make me fail in my journey, that hath troubled me much: yea, it still runs in my mind, and makes me afraid of every one that I meet, lest they should meet me to do me a mischief, and to turn me out of my way. Yea, I may tell my Lord, though I would not have everybody know it, that, between this and the gate by which we got into the way, we were both so sorely attacked that we were made to cry out "murder;" and the two that made this attack upon us were like the two that I saw in my dream.

Then said the Interpreter, "Thy beginning is good; thy latter end shall greatly increase." So he addressed himself to Mercy, and said unto her, "And what moved thee to come hither, sweetheart?"

Then Mercy blushed and trembled, and for a while continued silent.

INTER. Then said he, "Be not afraid; only believe, and speak thy mind."

MER. So she began, and said, "Truly, sir, my lack of knowledge is that which makes me wish to be in silence, and that also that fills me with fears of coming short at last. I cannot tell of visions and dreams, as my friend Christiana can nor know I what it is to mourn for my refusing the advice of those that were good relations."

INTER. What was it, then, dear heart, that hath prevailed with thee to do as thou hast done?

MER. Why, when our friend here was packing up to be gone from our town, I and another went accidentally to see her. So we knocked at the door and went in. When we were within, and seeing what she was doing, we asked her what was her meaning. She said she was sent for to go to her husband; and then she up and told us how she had seen him in a dream, dwelling in a wonderful place, among immortals, wearing a crown, playing upon a harp, eating and drinking at his Prince's table, and singing praises to Him for bringing him thither, and so on. Now, methought while she was telling these things unto us, my heart burned within me. And I said in my heart, If this be true, I will leave my father and my mother, and the land of my birth, and will, if I may, go along with Christiana. So I asked her further of the truth of these things, and if she would let me go with her; for I saw now that there was no dwelling but with the danger of ruin any longer in our town. But yet I came away with a heavy heart; not for that I was unwilling to come away, but for that so many of my relations were left behind. And I am come with all the desire of my heart, and will go, if I may, with Christiana, unto her husband and his King.

INTER. Thy setting out is good, for thou hast given credit to the truth: thou art a Ruth, who did, for the love she bare to Naomi and to the Lord her God, leave father and mother, and the land of her birth, to come out and go with a people that she knew not heretofore. The Lord bless thy work, and a full reward be given thee of the

Lord God of Israel, under whose wings thou art come to trust.

Now supper was ended, and preparation was made for bed: the women were laid singly alone, and the boys by themselves. Now, when Mercy was in bed, she could not sleep for joy, for that now her doubts of missing at last were removed farther from her than ever they were before. So she lay blessing and praising God, who had had such favor for her.

In the morning they arose with the sun, and prepared themselves for their departure; but the Interpreter would have them tarry a while: "For," said he, "you must orderly go from hence." Then said he to the maid that first opened to them, "Take them and have them into the garden, to the bath, and there wash them, and make them clean from the soil which they have gathered by traveling."

Then Innocent the maid took them and had them into the garden, and brought them to the bath; so she told them they must wash and be clean, for so her master would have the women to do that called at his house as they were going on pilgrimage. Then they went in and washed, yea, they and the boys and all; and they came out of that bath, not only sweet and clean, but also much enlivened, and strengthened in their joints. So, when they came in, they looked fairer a deal than when they went out to the washing.

When they were returned out of the garden from the bath, the Interpreter took them, and looked upon them, and said unto them, "Fair as the moon." Then he called for the seal wherewith they used to be sealed that were washed in this bath. So the seal was brought, and he set his mark upon them, that they might be known in the places whither they were yet to go; and the mark was set between their eyes. This seal added greatly to their beauty, for it was an ornament to their faces. It also added to their glory, and made their countenances more like those of angels.

CLOTHED IN WHITE RAIMENT

Then said the Interpreter again to the maid that waited upon these women, "Go into the vestry, and fetch out garments for these people." So she went and fetched out white raiment and laid it down before him; so he commanded them to put it on; it was fine linen, white and clean. When the women were thus adorned, they seemed to be afraid one of the other, for that they could not see that glory each one had in herself, which they could see in each other. Now, therefore, they began to esteem each other better than themselves. For "You are fairer than I am," said one; and "You are more beautiful than I am," said another. The children also stood amazed, to see into what fashion they were brought.

The Interpreter then called for a man-servant of his, one Great-heart, and bid him take sword, and helmet, and shield, and "Take these my daughters," said he, "and conduct them to the house called Beautiful, at which place they will rest next." So he took his weapons, and went before them; and the Interpreter said, "God speed!" Those also that belonged to the family sent them away with many a good wish. So they went on their way and sang:

> "This place hath been our second stage:
> Here we have heard and seen
> Those good things that from age to age
> To others hid have been.
> The Dunghill-raker, Spider, Hen,
> The Chicken, too, to me
> Have taught a lesson: let me then
> Conformèd to it be.
> The Butcher, Garden, and the Field,
> The Robin and his bait,
> Also the Rotten Tree, doth yield
> Me argument of weight:

To move me for to watch and pray,
To strive to be sincere,
To take my cross up day by day,
And serve the Lord with fear."

CHAPTER 4

The Cross and the Consequences

Now, I saw in my dream that they went on, and Great-heart before them. So they went, and came to the place where Christian's burden fell off his back and tumbled into a sepulchre. Here, then, they made a pause, and here also they blessed God. "Now," said Christiana, "comes to my mind what was said to us at the gate, to wit, that we should have pardon by word and deed: by word, that is, by the promise; by deed, that is, in the way it was obtained. What the promise is, of that I know something; but what it is to have pardon by deed, or in the way that it was obtained, Mr. Great-heart, I suppose you know; wherefore, if you please, let us hear you speak thereof."

GREAT-HEART DISCOURSES

GREAT. Pardon by the deed done, is pardon obtained by some one for another that hath need thereof; not by the person pardoned, but in the way, saith another, in which I have obtained it. So then, to speak to the question at large, the pardon that you, and Mercy, and these boys have obtained, was obtained by another; to wit, by Him that let you in at the gate. And He hath obtained it in this double way: He has shown righteousness to cover you, and spilt His blood to wash you in.

CHR. This is brave! Now I see that there was something to be learnt by our being pardoned by word and deed. Good Mercy, let us labor to keep this in mind; and, my children, do you remember it also. But, sir, was not this it that made my good Christian's burden fall from off his shoulders, and that made him give three leaps for joy?

GREAT. Yes, it was the belief of this that cut off those strings that could not be cut by other means; and it was to give him proof of the virtue of this that he was suffered to carry his burden to the Cross.

CHR. I thought so; for though my heart was lightsome and joyous before, yet it is ten times more lightsome and joyous now. And I am persuaded by what I have felt, though I have felt but little as yet, that, if the most burdened man in the World was here, and did see and believe as I now do, it would make his heart merry and blithe.

GREAT. There is not only comfort and the ease of a burden brought to us by the sight and consideration of these, but an endeared love born in us by it; for who can, if he doth but once think that pardon comes, not only by promise, but thus, but be affected with the way and means of his redemption, and so love the Man that hath wrought it for him?

CHR. True: methinks it makes my heart bleed, to think that He should bleed for me. Oh, Thou loving One! Oh, Thou blessed One! Thou deservest to have me: Thou hast bought me. Thou deservest to have me all: Thou hast paid for me ten thousand times more than I am worth. No marvel that this made the water stand in my husband's eyes, and that it made him trudge so nimbly on. I am persuaded he wished me with him; but, vile wretch that I was! I let him come all alone.

Oh, Mercy, that thy father and mother were here! yea, and Mrs. Timorous also! Nay, I wish now with all my heart that here was Madam Wanton too. Surely, surely, their hearts would be affected; nor could the fear of the one, nor the powerful passions of the other, prevail with them to go home again, and refuse to become good pilgrims.

GREAT. You speak now in the warmth of your affections: will it, think you, be always thus with you? Besides, this is not given to every one, nor to every one that did see your Jesus bleed. There were that stood by, and that saw the blood run from His heart to the ground, and yet were so far off this, that instead of lamenting, they laughed at Him, and instead of becoming His disciples, did harden their hearts against him. So that all that you have, my daughters, you have by a peculiar feeling made by a thinking upon what I have spoken to you. This you have, therefore, by a special grace.

SIMPLE, SLOTH, PRESUMPTION

Now, I saw still in my dream, that they went on till they were come to the place that Simple, and Sloth, and Presumption lay and slept in, when Christian went by on pilgrimage; and, behold, they were hanged up in irons a little way off on the other side.

MER. Then said Mercy to him that was their guide and conductor, "What are those three men? and for what are they hanged there?"

GREAT. These three men were men of very bad qualities: they had no mind to be pilgrims themselves, and whomsoever they could they hindered. They were for sloth and folly themselves, and whomsoever they could persuade with, they made so too, and withal taught them to presume that they should do well at last. They were asleep when Christian went by; and, now you go by, they are hanged.

MER. But could they persuade any to be of their opinion?

GREAT. Yes, they turned several out of the way. There was Slow-pace that they persuaded to do as they. They also prevailed with one Short-wind, with one No-heart, with one Linger-after-lust, and with one Sleepy-head, and with a young woman—her name was Dull—to turn out of the way and become as they. Besides, they brought up an ill report of your Lord, persuading others that He was a hard task-master. They also brought up an evil report of the good land, saying it was not half so good as some pretended it was. They also began to speak falsely about His servants, and to count the very best of them meddlesome, troublesome busy-bodies. Further, they would call the bread of God, husks; the comforts of His children, fancies; the travel labor of pilgrims, things to no purpose.

CHR. "Nay," said Christiana, "if they were such, they never shall be bewailed by me: they have but what they deserve; and I think it is well that they hang so near the highway, that others may see and take warning. But had it not been well if their crimes had been engraven on some plate of iron or brass, and left here where they did their mischiefs, for a caution to other bad men?"

GREAT. So it is, as you well may perceive, if you will go a little to the wall.

MER. No, no: let them hang, and their names rot, and their crimes live for ever against them. I think it a high favor that they were hanged afore we came hither who knows, else, what they might have done to such poor women as we are?

Then she turned it into a song, saying:

> "Now, then, you three, hang there, and be a
>   sign
> To all that shall against the truth combine;
> And let him that comes after fear this end,
> If unto pilgrims he is not a friend.
> And thou, my soul, of all such men beware
> That unto holiness opposers are."

Thus they went on till they came at the foot of the Hill Difficulty, where again their good friend Mr. Great-heart took an occasion to tell them of what happened there when Christian himself went by. So he had them first to the spring. "Lo," saith he, "this is the spring that Christian drank of before he went up this hill: and then it was clear and good; but now it is dirty with the feet of some that are not desirous that pilgrims here should quench their thirst." Thereat Mercy said, "And why are they so envious, I wonder?" But said their guide, "It will do if taken up and put into a vessel that is sweet and good; for then the dirt will sink to the bottom, and the water come out by itself more clear." Thus, therefore, Christiana and her companions were compelled to do. They took it up, and put it into an earthen pot, and so let it stand till the dirt was gone to the bottom, and then they drank thereof.

TWO DANGEROUS PATHS

Next he showed them the two by-ways that were at the foot of the hill, where Formality and Hypocrisy lost themselves. And said he, "These are dangerous paths. Two were here cast away when Christian came by; and although, as you see, these ways are since stopped up with chains, posts, and a ditch, yet there are that will choose to adventure here, rather than take the pains to go up this hill."

CHR. The way of transgressors is hard. It is a wonder that they can get into those ways without danger of breaking their necks.

GREAT. They will venture: yea, if at any time any of the King's servants doth happen to see them, and doth call unto them, and tell them that they are in the wrong ways, and do bid them beware the danger, then they will rail-ingly return them answer, and say, "As for the word that thou hast spoken unto us in the name of the King, we will not hearken unto thee; but we will certainly do whatsoever thing goeth forth out of our own mouth." Nay, if you look a little farther, you shall see that these ways are warned against enough, not only by these posts, and ditch, and chain, but also by being hedged up; yet they will choose to go there.

CHR. They are idle: they love not to take pains: up-hill way is unpleasant to them. So it is fulfilled unto them as it is written, "The way of the slothful man is a hedge of thorns." Yea, they will rather choose to walk upon a snare than go up this hill, and the rest of this way to the City.

Then they set forward, and began to go up the hill; and up the hill they went. But, before they got to the top, Christiana began to pant, and said, "I dare say this is a breathing hill: no marvel if they that love their ease more than their souls choose to themselves a smoother way." Then said Mercy, "I must sit down;" also the least of the children began to cry. "Come, come," said Great-heart, "sit not down here, for a little above is the Prince's arbor." Then took he the little boy by the hand, and led him up thereto.

THE ARBOR ON THE HILL

When they were come to the arbor, they were very willing to sit down, for they were all in a pelting heat. Then said

Mercy, "How sweet is rest to them that labor, and how good is the Prince of pilgrims to provide such resting-places for them! Of this arbor I have heard much, but I never saw it before. But here let us beware of sleeping; for, as I have heared, for that it cost poor Christian dear."

Then said Mr. Great-heart to the little ones, "Come, my pretty boys, how do you do? what think you now of going on pilgrimage?"

"Sir," said the least, "I was almost beat out of heart; but I thank you for lending me a hand at my need. And I remember now what my mother has told me, namely, 'That the way to heaven is as up a ladder, and the way to hell is as down a hill.' But I rather go up the ladder to life, than the hill to death."

Then said Mercy, "But the proverb, is, 'To go down the hill is easy.'"

But James said (for that was his name), "The day is coming when, in my opinion, going down-hill will be the hardest of all."

"That's a good boy," said his master; "thou hast given her a right answer."

Then Mercy smiled, but the little boy did blush.

CHR. "Come," said Christiana, "will you eat a bit, a little to sweeten your mouths, while you sit here to rest your legs? for I have here a piece of pomegranate, which Mr. Interpreter put in my hand just when I came out of his doors: he gave me also a piece of a honeycomb, and a little bottle of spirits."

"I thought he gave you something," said Mercy, "because he called you aside."

"Yes, so he did," said the other; "but, Mercy, it shall still be as I said it should, when at first we came from home; thou shalt be a sharer in all the good that I have, because thou so willingly didst become my companion."

Then she gave to them, and they did eat, both Mercy and the boys. And said Christiana to Mr. Great-heart, "Sir, will you do as we and take some refreshment?"

But he answered, "You are going on pilgrimage, and presently I shall return; much good may have do to you: at home I eat the same every day."

Now, when they had eaten and drunk, and had chatted a little longer, their guide said to them, "The day wears away; if you think good, let us prepare to be going." So they got up to go, and the little boys went before; but Christiana forgot to take her bottle of spirits with her, so she sent her little boy back to fetch it.

Then said Mercy, "I think this is a losing place: here Christian lost his roll, and here Christiana left her bottle behind her. Sir, what is the cause of this?"

So their guide made answer, and said, "The cause is sleep or forgetfulness: some sleep when they should keep awake, and some forget when they should remember. And this is the very cause why often at the resting-places some pilgrims, in some things, come off losers. Pilgrims should watch, and remember what they have already received, under their greatest enjoyments; but, for want of doing so, ofttimes their rejoicing ends in tears, and their sunshine in a cloud: witness the story of Christian at this place."

MISTRUST AND TIMOROUS

When they were come to the place where Mistrust and Timorous met Christian, to persuade him to go back for fear of the lions, they perceived as it were a stage, and before it, towards the road, a broad plate, with a copy of verses written thereon, and underneath the reason of the raising up of that stage in that place rendered. The verses were these:

> "Let him that sees this stage take heed
> Unto his heart and tongue;
> Lest, if he do not, here he speed
> As some have, long agone."

The words underneath the verses were, "This stage was built to punish such upon, who, through timorousness or mistrust, shall be afraid to go farther on pilgrimage. Also on this stage both Mistrust and Timorous were burned through the tongue with a hot iron, for endeavoring to hinder Christian in his journey."

Then said Mercy, "This is much like to the saying of the Beloved, 'What shall be given unto thee, or what shall be done unto thee, thou false tongue? Sharp arrows of the mighty, with coals of juniper.'"

So they went on till they came within sight of the lions. Now, Mr. Great-heart was a strong man, so he was not afraid of a lion. But yet, when they were come up to the place where the lions were, the boys, that went before, were glad to cringe behind, for they were afraid of the lions so they stepped back, and went behind.

At this their guide smiled, and said, "How now, my boys! do you love to go before when no danger doth approach, and love to come behind so soon as the lions appear?"

Now, as they went up, Mr. Great-heart drew his sword, with intent to make a way for the pilgrims in spite of the lions. Then there appeared one that, it seems, had taken upon him to back the lions; and he said to the pilgrims' guide, "What is the cause of your coming hither?" Now, the name of that man was Grim, or Bloody-man, because of his slaying of pilgrims; and he was of the race of the giants.

GREAT. Then said the pilgrims' guide, "These women and children are going on pilgrimage, and this is the way they must go; and go it they shall, in spite of thee and the lions."

GRIM. This is not their way, neither shall they go therein. I am come forth to withstand them, and to that end will back the lions.

GREAT-HEART OVERCOMES GRIM

Now, to say truth, by reason of the fierceness of the lions, and of the grim carriage of him that did back them, this way had of late lain much unoccupied, and was almost all grown over with grass.

CHR. Then said Christiana, "Though the highways have been unoccupied heretofore, and though the travellers have been made in times past to walk through by-paths, it must not be so now I am risen. 'Now I am risen a mother in Israel.'"

GRIM. Then he swore by the lions, "But it should," and therefore bid them turn aside, for they should not passage there.

But Great-heart their guide made first his approach unto Grim, and laid so heavily at him with his sword, that he forced him to a retreat.

GRIM. Then said he that attempted to back the lions, "Will you slay me upon mine own ground?"

GREAT. It is the King's highway that we are in, and in His way it is that thou hast placed thy lions; but these women, and these children, though weak, shall hold on their way in spite of thy lions.

And, with that, he gave him again a downright blow, and brought him upon his knees. With this blow he also broke his helmet, and with the next he cut off an arm. Then did the giant roar so hideously, that his voice frighted the women, and yet they were glad to see him lie sprawling upon the ground. Now, the lions were chained, and so of themselves could do nothing.

Wherefore, when old Grim, that intended to back them, was dead, Mr. Great-heart said to the pilgrims, "Come now, and follow me, and no hurt shall happen to you from the lions." They therefore went on; but the women trembled as they passed by them: the boys also looked as if they would die; but they all got by without further hurt.

CHAPTER 5

The Palace Beautiful

Now, then, they were within sight of the Porter's lodge, and they soon came up unto it; but they made the more haste after this to go thither, because it is dangerous travelling there in the night. So, when they were come to the gate, the guide knocked, and the Porter cried, "Who is there?" But as soon as the guide had said "It is I," he knew his voice, and came down, for the guide had oft before that come thither as a conductor of pilgrims. When he was come down he opened the gate; and, seeing the guide stand just before it (for he saw not the women, for they were behind him), he said unto him, "How now, Mr. Great-heart! what is your business here so late to-night?"

"I have brought," said he, "some pilgrims hither, where, by my Lord's commandment, they must lodge. I had been here some time ago, had I not been opposed by the giant that did use to back the lions; but I, after a long and tedious combat with him, have cut him off, and have brought the pilgrims hither in safety."

PORT. Will you not go in, and stay till morning?
GREAT. No, I will return to my Lord to-night.
CHR. Oh, sir, I know not how to be willing you should leave

213

us in our pilgrimage: you have been so faithful and so loving to us, you have fought so stoutly for us, you have been so hearty in counselling of us, that I shall never forget your favor towards us.

MER. Then said Mercy, "Oh that we might have thy company to our journey's end! How can such poor women as we hold out in a way so full of troubles as this way is, without a friend and defender?"

JAMES. Then said James, the youngest of the boys, "Pray, sir, be persuaded to go with us, and help us, because we are so weak, and the way so dangerous as it is."

GREAT. I am at my Lord's commandment. If he shall allot me to be your guide quite through, I will willingly wait upon you. But here you failed at first; for when he bid me come thus far with you, then you should have begged me of him to have gone quite through with you, and he would have granted your request. However, at present I must withdraw; and so, good Christiana, Mercy, and my brave children, adieu.

Then the Porter, Mr. Watchful, asked Christiana of her country and of her kindred. And she said, "I come from the City of Destruction. I am a widow woman, and my husband is dead: his name was Christian, the pilgrim."

"How!" said the Porter, "was he your husband?"

A JOYFUL RECEPTION

"Yes," said she, "and these are his children, and this" (pointing to Mercy) "is one of my townswomen."

Then the Porter rang his bell, as at such times he is wont, and there came to the door one of the maids, whose name was Humble-mind; and to her the Porter said, "Go, tell it within that Christiana, the wife of Christian, and her children, are come hither on pilgrimage."

She went in, therefore, and told it. But oh, what a noise for gladness was there within when the maid did but drop that word out of her mouth!

So they came with haste to the Porter, for Christiana stood still at the door. Then some of those within said unto her, "Come in, Christiana, come in, thou wife of that good man; come in, thou blessed woman; come in, with all that are with thee."

So she went in, and they followed her that were her children and her companions. Now, when they were gone in, they were had into a very large room, where they were bidden to sit down. So they sat down, and the chief of the house were called to see and welcome the guests. Then they came in and understanding who they were did salute each other with a kiss, and said, "Welcome, ye that bear the grace of God; welcome to us, your friends!"

Now, because it was somewhat late, and because the pilgrims were weary with their journey, and also made faint with the sight of the fight, and of the terrible lions, therefore they desired, as soon as might be, to prepare to go to rest. "Nay," said those of the family, "refresh yourselves first with a morsel of meat;" for they had prepared for them a lamb, with the accustomed sauce belonging thereto, for the Porter had heard before of their coming, and had told it to them within. So, when they had supped, and ended their prayer with a psalm, they desired they might go to rest.

"But let us," said Christiana, "if we may be so bold as to choose, be in that chamber that was my husband's when he was here."

So they had them up thither, and they lay all in a room. When they were at rest, Christiana and Mercy entered into discourse about things that were convenient.

CHR. Little did I think once, when my husband went on pilgrimage, that I should ever have followed.

MER. And you as little thought of lying in his bed, and in his chamber to rest, as you do now.

CHR. And much less did I ever think of seeing his face with comfort, and of worshipping the Lord the King with him; and yet now I believe I shall.

MER. Hark! don't you hear a noise?

CHR. Yes, it is, as I believe, a noise of music, for joy that we are here.

MER. Wonderful! Music in the house, music in the heart, and music also in heaven, for joy that we are here!

MERCY'S DREAM

Thus they talked a while, and then betook themselves to sleep. So in the morning, when they were awake, Christiana said to Mercy, "What was the matter, that you did laugh in your sleep to-night? I suppose you were in a dream."

MER. So I was, and a sweet dream it was; but are you sure I laughed?

CHR. Yes, you laughed heartily; but, prithee, Mercy, tell me thy dream.

MER. I was dreaming that I sat all alone in a solitary place, and was bemoaning of the hardness of my heart. Now, I had not sat there long, but methought many were gathered about me to see me, and to hear what it was that I said. So they hearkened, and I went on bemoaning the hardness of my heart. At this, some of them laughed at me, some called me fool, and some thrust me about. With that, methought I looked up, and saw one coming with wings towards me. So he came directly to me, and said, "Mercy, what aileth thee?" Now, when he had heard me make my complaint, he said, "Peace be to thee;" he also wiped mine eyes with his handkerchief, and clad me in silver and gold. He put a chain about my neck, and ear-rings in mine ears, and a beautiful crown upon my head. Then he took me by the hand, and said, "Mercy, come after me." So he went up, and I followed, till we came to a golden gate. Then he knocked; and when they within opened, the man went in, and I followed him up to a throne upon which One sat; and He said to me, "Welcome, daughter!" The place looked bright and twinkling, like the stars, or rather like the sun; and I thought that I saw your husband there. So I awoke from my dream. But did I laugh?

CHR. Laugh! ay, and well you might, to see yourself so well. For you must give me leave to tell you, that I believe it was a good dream; and that, as you have begun to find the first part true, so you shall find the second at last. "God speaks once, yea, twice, yet man perceiveth it not; in a dream, in a vision of the night, when deep sleep falleth upon men, in slumberings upon the bed." We need not, when abed, to lie awake to talk with God: He can visit us while we sleep, and cause us then to hear His voice. Our heart oftentimes wakes when we sleep; and God can speak to that, either by words, by proverbs, or by signs and similitudes, as well as if one was awake.

MER. Well, I am glad of my dream; for I hope ere long to see it fulfilled, to the making of me laugh again.

CHR. I think it is now high time to rise, and to know what we must do.

MER. Pray, if they invite us to stay, a while, let us willingly accept of the proffer. I am the willinger to stay a while here, to grow better acquainted with these maids. Methinks Prudence, Piety, and Charity have very lovely and sober countenances.

CHR. We shall see what they will do.

So, when they were up and ready, they came down; and they asked one another of their rest, and if it was comfortable or not.

MER. "Very good," said Mercy; "it was one of the best nights' lodging that ever I had in my life."

Then said Prudence and Piety, "If you will be persuaded to stay here a while, you shall have what the house will afford."

CHAR. "Ay, and that with a very good will," said Charity.

So they consented, and stayed there about a month, or above, and became very profitable one to another.

MR. BRISK VISITS MERCY

Now, by that these pilgrims had been at this place a week, Mercy had a visitor that pretended some good-will unto her; and his name was Mr. Brisk; a man of some breeding, and that pretended to religion, but a man that stuck very close to the world. So he came once or twice, or more, to Mercy, and offered love unto her. Now, Mercy was a fair countenance, and therefore the more alluring.

Her mind also was, to be always busying of herself in doing; for, when she had nothing to do for herself, she would be making of hose and garments for others, and would bestow them upon them that had need. And Mr. Brisk, not knowing where or how she disposed of what she made, seemed to be greatly taken, for that he found her never idle. "I will warrant her a good housewife," quoth he to himself.

Mercy then told the matter to the maidens that were of the house, and inquired of them concerning him; for they did know him better than she. So they told her that he was a very busy young man, and one who pretended to serve the Lord, but was, as they feared, a stranger to the power of that which is good.

"Nay, then," said Mercy, "I will look no more on him; for I purpose never to have a clog to my soul."

Prudence then replied that "There needed no great matter of discouragement to be given to him; her continuing so as she had begun to do for the poor would quickly cool his courage."

So, the next time he comes, he finds her at her old work, a-making of things for the poor. Then said he, "What! always at it?"

"Yes," said she, "either for myself or for others."

"And what canst thou earn a day?" quoth he.

"I do these things," said she, "that I may be rich in good works, laying up in store for myself a good foundation against the time to come, that I may lay hold on eternal life."

"Why, prithee, what doest thou with them?" said he.

"Clothe the naked," said she.

With that, his countenance fell. So he forbore to come at her again. And when he was asked the reason why, he said that "Mercy was a pretty lass, but troubled with too much working for others."

MERCY REJECTS THE SUITOR

When he had left her, Prudence said, "Did I not tell thee that Mr. Brisk would soon forsake thee? yea, he will raise up an ill report of thee; for, notwithstanding his pretence to serve bad and his seeming love to Mercy, yet Mercy and he are of tempers so different, that I believe they will never come together."

MER. I might have had husbands afore now, though I spake not of it to any; but they were such as did not like my ways, though never did any of them find fault with my person. So they and I could not agree.

PRUD. Mercy in our days is little set by, any further than as to its name: the practice, which is set forth by thy works, there are but few that can abide.

MER. "Well," said Mercy, "if nobody will have me, I will die a maid, or my works shall be to me as a husband; for I cannot change my nature; and to have one that lies cross to me in this, that I purpose never to admit of as long as I live. I had a sister, named Bountiful, that was married to one of these selfish people; but he and she could never agree; but, because my sister was resolved to do as she had begun, that is, to show kindness to the poor, therefore her husband first cried her down in public, and then turned her out of his doors."

PRUD. And yet he was a church-member, I warrant you?

MER. Yes, such a one as he was; and of such as he the world is now full; but I am for none of them at all.

MATTHEW FALLS SICK

Now Matthew, the eldest son of Christiana, fell sick, and his sickness was sore upon him for he was much pained in his bowels; so that he was with it, at times, pulled as it were both ends together.

There dwelt also not far from thence one Mr. Skill, an ancient and well-approved physician. So Christiana desired it and they sent for him, and he came. When he was entered the room, and had a little observed the boy, he concluded that he was sick of the gripes. Then he said to his mother, "What diet has Matthew of late fed upon?"

"Diet!" said Christiana, "nothing but that which is wholesome."

The physician answered, "This boy has been tampering with something that lies in his stomach undigested, and that will not away without means. And I tell you he must be purged, or else he will die."

SAM. Then said Samuel, "Mother, what was that which my brother did gather up and eat, so soon as we were come from the gate that is at the head of this way? You know that there was an orchard on the left hand, on the other side of the wall, and some of the trees hung over the wall, and my brother did pull down the branches and did eat."

CHR. "True, my child," said Christiana, "he did take thereof and did eat; naughty boy as he was, I did chide him, and yet he would eat thereof."

SKILL. I knew he had eaten something that was not wholesome food; and that food, to wit, that fruit, is even the most hurtful of all. It is the fruit of Beelzebub's orchard. I do marvel that none did warn you of it: many have died thereof.

CHR. Then Christiana began to cry, and she said, "Oh, naughty boy! and oh, careless mother! What shall I do for my son?"

SKILL. Come, do not be too much dejected; the boy may do well again, but he must purge and vomit.

CHR. Pray, sir, try the utmost of your skill with him, whatever it costs.

SKILL. Nay, I hope I shall be reasonable.

DOCTOR SKILL PRESCRIBES

So he made him a purge, but it was too weak; it was said, it was made of the blood of a goat, the ashes of an heifer, and with some of the juice of hyssop, etc. When Mr. Skill had seen that that purge was too weak, he made him one to the purpose. It was made [the name was written in Latin] *ex carne et sanguine Christi*; (you know physicians give strange medicines to their patients)—and it was made up into pills, with a promise or two, and a proportionable quantity of salt. Now, he was to take them three at a time, fasting, in half a quarter of a pint of the tears of sorrow.

When this potion was prepared and brought to the boy, he was loth to take it, though torn with the gripes as if he should be pulled in pieces.

"Come, come," said the physician, "you must take it."

"It goes against my stomach," said the boy.

"I must have you take it," said his mother.

"I shall vomit it up again," said the boy.

"Pray, sir," said Christiana to Mr. Skill, "how does it taste?"

"It has no ill taste," said the doctor; and with that she touched one of the pills with the tip of her tongue.

"O Matthew," said she, "this potion is sweeter than honey. If thou lovest thy mother, if thou lovest thy brothers, if thou lovest Mercy, if thou lovest thy life, take it."

So, with much ado, after a short prayer for the blessing of God upon it, he took it, and it wrought kindly with him. It caused him to purge, it caused him to sleep and rest quietly; it put him into a fine heat and breathing sweat, and did quite rid him of his gripes. So, in a little time he got up, and walked about with a staff, and would go from room to room, and talk with Prudence, Piety, and Charity, of his sickness, and how he was healed.

So, when the boy was healed, Christiana asked Mr. Skill, saying, "Sir, what will content you for your pains and care to and of my child?"

And he said, "You must pay the Master of the College of Physicians, according to the rules made in that case and provided."

CHR. "But, sir," said she, "what is this pill good for else?"

SKILL. It is an universal pill: it is good against all the diseases that pilgrims are troubled with; and when it is well prepared, it will keep good time out of mind.

CHR. Pray, sir, make me up twelve boxes of them; for if I can get these, I will never take other physic.

SKILL. These pills are good to prevent diseases, as well as to cure when one is sick. Yea, I dare say it, and stand to it, that if a man will but use this physic as he should, it will make him live for ever. But, good Christiana, thou must give these pills no other way than as I have prescribed; for if you do, they will do no good. So he gave unto Christiana physic for herself and her boys, and for Mercy; and bid Matthew take heed how he ate any more green plums; and kissed them and went his way.

It was told you before, that Prudence bid the boys, if at any time they would, they should ask her some questions that might be profitable, and she would say something to them.

MATT. Then Matthew, who had been sick, asked her, "Why, for the most part, physic should be bitter to our palates?"

PRUD. To show how unwelcome the Word of God, and the effects thereof, are to a sinful heart.

MATT. Why does physic, if it does good, purge and cause that we vomit?

PRUD. To show that the Word, when it works effectually, cleanseth the heart and mind. For look, what the one doth to the body, the other doth to the soul.

MATT. What should we learn by seeing the flame of our fire go upwards, and by seeing the beams and sweet influences of the sun strike downwards?

PRUD. By the going up of the fire, we are taught to ascend to heaven by fervent and hot desires. And by the sun's sending his heat, beams, and sweet influences downwards, we are taught that the Saviour of the world, though high reaches down with His grace and love to us below.

MATT. Where have the clouds their water?

PRUD. Out of the sea.

MATT. What may we learn from that?

PRUD. That ministers should fetch their teaching from God.

MATT. Why do they empty themselves upon the earth?

PRUD. To show that ministers should give out what they know of God to the world.

MATT. Why is the rainbow caused by the sun?

PRUD. To show that the promise of God's grace is made sure to us in Christ.

MATT. Why do the springs come from the sea to us through the earth?

PRUD. To show that the grace of God comes to us through the body of Christ.

MATT. Why do some of the springs rise out of the tops of high hills?

PRUD. To show that the spirit of grace shall spring up in some that are great and mighty, as well as in many that are poor and low.

MATT. Why doth the fire fasten upon the candle-wick?

PRUD. To show that, unless grace doth kindle upon the heart, there will be no true light of life in us.

MATT. Why is the wick, and tallow, and all, spent to maintain the light of the candle?

PRUD. To show that body, and soul, and all, should be at the service of, and spend themselves to maintain in good condition, that grace of God that is in us.

MATT. Why doth the pelican pierce her own breast with her bill?

PRUD. To nourish her young ones with her blood, and thereby to show that Christ the Blessed so loveth His young (His people), as to save them from death by His blood.

MATT. What may one learn by hearing the cock to crow?

PRUD. Learn to remember Peter's sin and Peter's sorrow. The cock's crowing shows also that day is coming on: let, then, the crowing of the cock put thee in mind of that last and terrible day of judgment.

Now, about this time, their month was out; wherefore they signified to those of the house that it was convenient for them to be up and going. Then said Joseph to his mother, "It is convenient that you forget not to send to the house of Mr. Interpreter, to pray him to grant that Mr. Great-heart should be sent unto us, that he may be our conductor the rest of our way."

"Good boy," said she, "I had almost forgot." So she drew up a petition, and prayed Mr. Watchful the Porter to send it by some fit man to her good friend Mr. Interpreter, who, when it was come, and he had seen the contents of the petition, said to the messenger, "Go, tell them that I will send him."

When the family where Christiana was saw that they had a purpose to go forward, they called the whole house together, to give thanks to their King for sending of them such profitable guests as these. Which done, they said unto Christiana, "And shall we not show thee something, according, as our custom is to do to pilgrims, on which thou mayest meditate when thou art upon the way?"

THE PILGRIMS VIEW CURIOSITIES

So they took Christiana, her children, and Mercy, into the closet, and showed them one of the apples that Eve did eat of, and that which she also did give to her husband, and that for the eating of which they were both turned out of Paradise, and asked her what she thought that was.

Then Christiana said, "It is food or poison, I know not which."

So they opened the matter to her, and she held up her hands and wondered.

Then they had her to a place, and showed her Jacob's ladder. Now, at that time there were some angels ascending upon it. So Christiana looked and looked, to see the angels go up, and so did the rest of the company. Then they were going into another place, to show them something else; but James said to his mother, "Pray bid them stay here a little longer, for this is a curious sight." So they turned again, and stood feeding their eyes with this so pleasing a prospect.

After this they had them into a place where did hang up a golden anchor. So they bid Christiana take it down; "For," said they, "you shall have it with you, for it is of absolute necessity that you should, that you may lay hold of that within the veil, and stand steadfast, in case you should meet with turbulent weather." So they were glad thereof.

Then they took them, and had them to the mount upon which Abraham our father had offered up Isaac his son, and showed them the altar, the wood, the fire, and the knife; for they remain to be seen to this very day. When they had seen it, they held up their hands, and blessed themselves, and said, "Oh! what a man for love to his Master, and for denial to himself, was Abraham!"

After they had showed them all these things, Prudence took them into the dining-room, where stood a pair of excellent virginals; so she played upon them, and turned what she had showed them into this excellent song, saying:

> "Eve's apple we have showèd you—
> Of that be you aware;
> You have seen Jacob's ladder too,
> Upon which angels are.
> An anchor you receivèd have:
> But let not these suffice,
> Until with Abra'm, you have gave
> Your best a sacrifice."

GREAT-HEART CONDUCTS THEM

Now, about this time, one knocked at the door. So the Porter opened, and behold, Mr. Great-heart was there; but when he was come in, what joy was there! For it came now fresh again into their minds, how, but a while ago, he had slain old Grim Bloody-man, the giant, and had delivered them from the lions.

Then said Mr. Great-heart to Christiana and to Mercy, "My lord has sent each of you a bottle of wine, and also some parched corn, together with a couple of pomegranates; he has also sent the boys some figs and raisins, to refresh you in your way."

Then they addressed themselves to their journey; and Prudence and Piety went along with them. When they came at the gate, Christiana asked the Porter if any one of late went by.

He said, "No; only one some time since, who also told me that, of late, there had been a great robbery committed on the King's highway as you go. But he saith the thieves are taken, and will shortly be tried for their lives."

Then Christiana and Mercy were afraid; but Matthew said, "Mother, fear nothing as long as Mr. Great-heart is to go with us, and to be our conductor."

Then said Christiana to the Porter, "Sir, I am much obliged to you for all the kindnesses that you have shown me since I came hither, and also for that you have been so loving and kind to my children. I know not how to gratify your kindness; wherefore, pray, as a token of my respects to you, accept of this small mite."

So she put a gold angel in his hand; and he made her a low obeisance, and said, "Let thy garments be always white, and let thy head want no ointment. Let Mercy live and not die, and let not her works be few." And to the boys he said, "Do you flee youthful passions, and follow after godliness with them that are grave and wise, so shall you put gladness into your mother's heart, and obtain praise of all that are sober-minded."

So they thanked the Porter, and departed.

Now I saw in my dream that they went forward until they were come to the brow of the hill; where Piety, bethinking herself, cried out, "Alas! I have forgot what I intended to bestow upon Christiana and her companions: I will go back and fetch it." So she ran and fetched it. While she was gone,

Christiana thought she heard, in a grove a little way off on the right hand, a most curious melodious note, with words much like these:

> "Through all my life Thy favor is
> So frankly showed to me,
> That in Thy house for evermore
> My dwelling-place shall be."

And listening still, she thought she heard another answer it, saying:

> "For why? the Lord our God is good;
> His mercy is for ever sure;
> His truth at all times firmly stood,
> And shall from age to age endure."

So Christiana asked Prudence what it was that made those curious notes. "They are," said she, "our country birds: they sing these notes but seldom, except it be at the spring, when the flowers appear and the sun shines warm, and then you may hear them all day long. I often," said she, "go out to hear them; we also ofttimes keep them tame in our house. They are very fine company for us when we are melancholy; also they make the woods, and groves, and solitary places, places desirable to be in."

By this time Piety was come again. So she said to Christiana, "Look here: I have brought thee a plan of all those things that thou hast seen at our house, upon which thou mayest look when thou findest thyself forgetful, and call those things again to remembrance for thy teaching and comfort."

CHAPTER 6

The Valley of Humiliation

Now they began to go down the hill into the Valley of Humiliation. It was a steep hill, and the way was slippery; but they were very careful, so they got down pretty well. When they were down in the valley, Piety said to Christiana, "This is the place where Christian, your husband, met with the foul fiend Apollyon, and where they had that dreadful fight that they had: I know you cannot but have heard thereof. But be of good courage: as long as you have here Mr. Greatheart to be your guide and conductor, we hope you will fare the better."

So when these two had given the pilgrims unto the care of their guide, he went forward, and they went after.

GREAT. Then said Mr. Great-heart, "We need not to be so afraid of this valley, for here is nothing to hurt us, unless we procure it to ourselves. It is true that Christian did here meet with Apollyon, with whom he had also a sore combat; but that fray was the fruit of those slips that he got in his going down the hill; for they that get slips there, must look for combats here. And hence it is that this valley has got so hard a name. For the common people, when they hear that some frightful thing has befallen such a one in such a place, are of an opinion that that place is haunted with some foul fiend or evil spirit; when, alas! it is for the fruit of their doing that such things do befall them there. This Valley of Humiliation is of itself as fruitful a place as any the crow flies over; and I am persuaded, if we could hit upon it, we might find, somewhere hereabouts, something that might give us an account why Christian was so hardly beset in this place."

Then James said to his mother, "Lo, yonder stands a pillar, and it looks as if something was written thereon: let us go and see what it is." So they went, and found there written, "Let Christian's slips before he came hither, and the battles that he met with in this place, be a warning to those that come after."

"Lo!" said their guide, "did not I tell you that there was something hereabouts that would give intimation of the reason why Christian was so hard beset in this place?" Then turning himself to Christiana, he said, "No disgrace to Christian, more than to many others whose hap and loss his was; for it is easier going up than down this hill; and that can be said but of few hills in all these parts of the world. But we will leave the good man: he is at rest; he also had a brave victory over his enemy. Let Him that dwelleth above grant that we fare no worse, when we come to be tried, than he.

"But we will come again to this Valley of Humiliation. It is the best and most fruitful piece of ground in all these parts. It is fat ground, and, as you see, consisteth much in meadows; and if a man was to come here in the summer-time, as we do now, if he knew not anything before thereof, and if he also delighted himself in the sight of his eyes, he might see that that would be delightful to him. Behold how green this valley is, also how beautified with lilies! I have also known many laboring men that have got good estates in this valley of Humiliation; for 'God resisteth the proud, but giveth grace to the humble.' Indeed, it is a very fruitful soil, and doth bring forth by handfuls. Some also have wished that the next way to their Father's house were here, that they might be troubled no more with either hills or mountains to go over; but the way is the way, and there's an end."

Now, as they were going along and talking, they espied a boy feeding his father's sheep. The boy was in very mean clothes, but of a very fresh and well-favored countenance; and as he sat by himself he sang. "Hark," said Mr. Great-heart, "to what the shepherd's boy saith." So they hearkened, and he said:

> "He that is down needs fear no fall
> He that is low, no pride;
> He that is humble ever shall
> Have God to be his guide.
> "I am content with what I have
> Little be it or much:
> And, Lord, contentment still I crave
> Because Thou savest much.
> "Fulness to such a burden is,
> That go on pilgrimage;
> Here little, and hereafter bliss,
> Is best from age to age."

Then said their guide, "Do you hear him? I will dare to say that this boy lives a merrier life, and wears more of that herb called heart's-ease in his bosom, than he that is clad in silk and velvet. But we will proceed in our account of this valley.

"In this valley our Lord formerly had His country house: He loved much to be here. He loved also to walk these meadows, for He found the air was pleasant. Besides, here a man shall be free from the noise and from the hurryings of

231

this life. All states are full of noise and confusion, only the Valley of Humiliation is that empty and solitary place. Here a man shall not be so let and hindered in his thoughts as in other places he is apt to be. This is a valley that nobody walks in but those that love a pilgrim's life. And though Christian had the hard hap to meet here with Apollyon, and to enter with him into a brisk encounter, yet I must tell you that in former times men have met with angels here, have found pearls here, and have in this place found the words of life.

"Did I say, our Lord had here in former days His country house, and that He loved here to walk? I will add, in this place, and to the people that love to tread these grounds, He has left a yearly sum of money, to be faithfully paid them at certain seasons, for their support by the way, and for their further encouragement to go on their pilgrimage."

SAM. Now, as they went on, Samuel said to Mr. Great-heart, "Sir, I perceive that in this valley my father and Apollyon had their battle; but whereabout was the fight? for I perceive this valley is large."

FORGETFUL GREEN

GREAT. Your father had that battle with Apollyon at a place yonder before us, in a narrow passage just beyond Forgetful Green. And, indeed, that place is the most dangerous place in all these parts. For, if at any time the pilgrims meet with any brunt, it is when they forget what favors they have received, and how unworthy they are of them. This is the place also where others have been hard put to it. But more of the place when we are come to it; for I persuade myself, that to this day there remains either some sign of the battle, or some monument to testify that such a battle there was fought.

MER. Then said Mercy, "I think that I am as well in this valley as I have been anywhere else in all our journey: the place, methinks, suits with my spirit. I love to be in such places, where there is no rattling with coaches nor rumbling with wheels. Methinks here one may, without much trouble, be thinking what he is, whence he came, what he has done, and to what the King has called him. Here one may think and break at heart, and melt in one's spirit, until one's eyes become like the fish-pools in Heshbon. They that go rightly through this Valley of Baca, make it a well; the rain that God sends down from heaven upon them that are here also filleth the pools. This valley is that from whence also the King will give to His their vineyards; and they that go through it shall sing, as Christian did, for all he met with Apollyon."

GREAT. "'Tis true," said their guide; "I have gone through this valley many a time, and never was better than when here. I have also been a conductor to several pilgrims, and they have confessed the same. 'To this man will I look,' saith the King, 'even to him that is poor and of a contrite spirit, and that trembleth at my word.'"

Now they were come to the place where the afore-mentioned battle was fought. Then said the guide to Christiana, her children, and Mercy, "This is the place; on this ground Christian stood, and up there came Apollyon against him. And look—did not I tell you?—here is some of your husband's blood upon these stones to this day. Behold, also, how here and there are yet to be seen upon the place some of the shivers of Apollyon's broken darts. See also how they did beat the ground with their feet as they fought, to make good their places against each other; how also, with their by-blows, they did split the very stones in pieces. Verily, Christian did here play the man, and showed himself as stout as could, had he been there, even Hercules himself. When Apollyon was beat, he made his retreat to the next valley, that is called the Valley of the Shadow of Death, unto which we shall come soon. Lo, yonder also stands a monument, on which is engraven this battle, and Christian's victory, to his fame throughout all ages."

VALLEY OF SHADOW OF DEATH

So, because it stood just on the way-side before them, they stepped to it, and read the writing, which word for word was this:

> "Hard by here was a battle fought,
> Most strange, and yet most true;
> Christian and Apollyon sought
> Each other to subdue.
> "The man so bravely played the man,
> He made the fiend to fly;
> Of which a monument I stand,
> The same to testify."

When they had passed by this place, they came upon the borders of the Shadow of Death. This valley was longer than the other; a place also most strangely haunted with evil things, as many are able to testify; but these women and children went the better through it, because they had daylight, and because Mr. Great-heart was their conductor.

When they were entered upon this valley, they thought that they heard a groaning, as of dead men—a very great groaning. They thought also that they did hear words of moaning spoken, as of some in extreme torment. These things made the boys to quake; the women also looked pale and wan; but their guide bid them be of good comfort.

So they went on a little farther, and they thought that they felt the ground begin to shake under them, as if some hollow place was there; they heard also a kind of hissing, as of serpents; but nothing as yet appeared. Then said the boys, "Are we not yet at the end of this doleful place?" But the guide also bid them be of good courage, and look well to their feet; "lest haply," said he, "you be taken in some snare."

Now James began to be sick; but I think the cause thereof was fear; so his mother gave him some of that glass of spirits that had been given her at the Interpreter's house, and three of the pills that Mr. Skill had prepared; and the boy began to revive. Thus they went on till they came to about the middle of the valley; and then Christiana said, "Methinks I see something yonder upon the road before us, a thing of such a shape as I have not seen." Then said Joseph, "Mother, what is it?" "An ugly thing, child, an ugly thing," said she. "But, mother, what is it like?" said he. "'Tis like I cannot tell what," said she, "and now it is but a little way off." Then said she, "It is nigh!"

RESIST THE DEVIL

"Well, well," said Mr. Great-heart, "let them that are most afraid keep close to me." So the fiend came on, and the conductor met it; but, when it was just come to him, it vanished to all their sights. Then remembered they what had been said some time ago, "Resist the devil, and he will flee from you."

They went therefore on, as being a little refreshed. But they had not gone far before Mercy, looking behind her, saw, as she thought, something most like a lion, and it came a great padding pace after; and it had a hollow voice of roaring, and at every roar that it gave it made all the valley echo, and all their hearts to ache, save the heart of him that was their guide. So it came up, and Mr. Great-heart went behind, and put the pilgrims all before him. The lion also came on apace, and Mr. Great-heart addressed himself to give him battle.

But, when he saw that it was determined that resistance should be made, he also drew back, and came no farther.

They then went on again, and their conductor did go before them, till they came to a place where was cast up a pit the whole breadth of the way; and before they could be prepared to go over that, a great mist and darkness fell upon them, so that they could not see. Then said the pilgrims, "Alas! what now shall we do?" But their guide made answer, "Fear not, stand still, and see what an end will be put to this also." So they stayed there, because their path was marred. They then also thought that they did hear more apparently the noise and rushing of the enemies; the fire also, and the smoke of the pit, were much easier to be discerned. Then said Christiana to Mercy, "Now I see what my poor husband went through. I have heard much of this place, but I never was here before now. Poor man! he went here all alone in the night; he had night almost quite through the way; also these fiends were busy about him, as if they would have torn him in pieces. Many have spoken of it, but none can tell what the Valley of the Shadow of Death should mean, until they come in it themselves. 'The heart knoweth its own bitterness, and a stranger intermeddleth not with its joy.' To be here is a fearful thing."

GREAT. This is like doing business in great waters, or like going down into the deep. This is like being in the heart of the sea, and like going down to the bottoms of the mountains. Now it seems as if the earth, with its bars, were about us for ever. But let them that walk in darkness and have no light, trust in the name of the Lord, and stay upon their God. For my part, as I have told you already, I have gone often through this valley, and have been much harder put to it than now I am; and yet, you see, I am alive. I would not boast, for that I am not mine own saviour; but I trust we shall have a good deliverance.

Come, let us pray for light to Him that can lighten our darkness, and that can rebuke not only these, but all the Satans in hell.

So they cried and prayed, and God sent light and deliverance; for there was now no hindrance in their way, no, not there where but now they were stopped with a pit. Yet they were not got through the valley; so they went on still; and behold, great stinks and loathsome smells, to the great annoyance of them. Then said Mercy to Christiana, "It is not so pleasant being here as at the gate, or at the Interpreter's, or at the house where we lay last."

"Oh, but," said one of the boys, "it is not so bad to go through here as it is to abide here always; and, for aught I know, one reason why we must go this way to the house prepared for us is, that our home might be made the sweeter to us."

"Well said, Samuel," quoth the guide; "thou hast now spoke like a man."

"Why, if ever I get out here again," said the boy, "I think I shall prize light and good way better than ever I did in all my life."

Then said the guide, "We shall be out by-and-by."

So on they went, and Joseph said, "Cannot we see to the end of this valley as yet?"

AMONG THE SNARES

Then said the guide, "Look to your feet, for we shall presently be among the snares."

So they looked to their feet, and went on; but they were troubled much with the snares. Now, when they were come among the snares, they espied a man cast into the ditch on the left hand, with his flesh all rent and torn.

Then said the guide, "That is one Heedless, that was

going this way; he has lain there a great while. There was one Take-heed with him when he was taken and slain, but he escaped their hands. You cannot imagine how many are killed hereabouts; and yet men are so foolishly venturous as to set out lightly on pilgrimage, and to come without a guide. Poor Christian! it is a wonder that he here escaped; but he was beloved of his God, also he had a good heart of his own, or else he could never have done it."

GREAT-HEART ENCOUNTERS MAUL

Now they drew towards the end of the way; and just where Christian had seen the cave when he went by, out thence came forth Maul, a giant. This Maul did use to spoil young pilgrims by deceiving them; and he called Great-heart by his name, and said unto him, "How many times have you been forbidden to do these things?"

Then said Mr. Great-heart, "What things?"

"What things!" quoth the giant; "you know what things; but I will put an end to your trade."

"But pray," said Mr. Great-heart, "before we fall to it, let us understand wherefore we must fight."

Now the women and children stood trembling, and knew not what to do.

Quoth the giant, "You rob the country, and rob it with the worst of thefts."

"These are but random words," said Mr. Great-heart; "tell what robberies I have done, man."

Then said the giant, "Thou practicest the craft of a kidnapper: thou gatherest up women and children, and carriest them into a strange country, to the weakening of my master's kingdom."

But now Great-heart replied, "I am a servant of the God of heaven; my business is to persuade sinners to turn to God. I am commanded to do my best to turn men, women, and children from darkness to light, and from the power of Satan unto God; and if this be indeed the ground of thy quarrel, let us fall to it as soon as thou wilt."

THE GIANT IS SLAIN

Then the giant came up, and Mr. Great-heart went to meet him; and as he went, he drew his sword, but the giant had a club. So without more ado they fell to it; and, at the first blow, the giant struck Mr. Great-heart down upon one of his knees. With that, the women and children cried out. So Mr. Great-heart, recovering himself, laid about him in full lusty manner, and gave the giant a wound in his arm. Thus he fought for the space of an hour, to that height of heat, that the breath came out of the giant's nostrils as the heat doth out of a boiling cauldron.

Then they sat down to rest them; but Mr. Great-heart betook himself to prayer. Also the women and children did nothing but sigh and cry all the time that the battle did last.

When they had rested them, and taken breath, they both fell to it again; and Mr. Great-heart with a blow fetched the giant down to the ground. "Nay, hold, and let me recover," quoth he. So Mr. Great-heart fairly let him get up: so to it they went again; and the giant missed but little of breaking Mr. Great-heart's skull with his club.

Mr. Great-heart seeing that, runs to him in the full heat of his spirit, and pierceth him under the fifth rib. With that the giant began to faint, and could hold up his club no longer. Then Mr. Great-heart seconded his blow, and smote the head of the giant from his shoulders. Then the women and the children rejoiced, and Mr. Great-heart also praised God for the deliverance He had wrought.

When this was done, they amongst them erected a pillar, and fastened the giant's head thereon, and wrote under it in letters that passengers might read:

"He that did wear this head, was one
That pilgrims did misuse;
He stopped their way, he spared none,
But did them all abuse;
Until that I, Great-heart, arose,
The pilgrims' guide to be;
Until that I did him oppose
That was their enemy."

Now, I saw that they went to the high ground that was a little way off, cast up to be a prospect for pilgrims. That was the place from whence Christiana had the first sight of Faithful his brother. Wherefore here they sat down and rested. They also here did eat and drink and make merry, for that they had gotten deliverance from this so dangerous an enemy. As they sat thus and did eat, Christiana asked the guide if he had caught no hurt in the battle. Then said Mr. Great-heart, "No, save a little on my flesh; yet that also shall be so far from being to my harm that it is at present a proof of my love to my Master and you, and shall be a means, by grace, to increase my reward at last."

CHR. But were you not afraid, good sir, when you saw him come out with his club?

GREAT. "It is my duty," said he, "to mistrust my own ability, that I may have trust in Him who is stronger than all."

CHR. But what did you think when he fetched you down to the ground at the first blow?

GREAT. "Why, I thought," replied he, "that so my Master Himself was served; and yet He it was that conquered at the last."

MATT. When you all have thought what you please, I think God has been wonderful good unto us, both in bringing us out of this valley, and in delivering us out of the hand of this enemy. For my part, I see no reason why we should distrust our God any more, since He has now, and in such a place as this, given us such proof of His love as this.

OLD HONEST

Then they got up and went forward. Now, a little before them stood an oak; and under it, when they came to it, they found an old pilgrim fast asleep. They knew that he was a pilgrim by his clothes, and his staff, and his girdle.

So the guide, Mr. Great-heart, awaked him; and the old gentleman, as he lifted up his eyes, cried out, "What's the matter? what are you, and what is your business here?"

GREAT. Come, man, be not so hot; here are none but friends.

Yet the old man gets up, and stands upon his guard, and will know of them what they are. Then said the guide, "My name is Great-heart; I am the guide of these pilgrims, that are going to the Celestial Country."

HONEST. Then said Mr. Honest, "I cry you mercy: I feared that you had been of the company of those that some time ago did rob Little-Faith of his money; but now I look better about me I perceive you are honester people."

GREAT. Why, what would or could you have done to have helped yourself, if we indeed had been of that company?

HON. Done! why, I would have fought as long as breath had been in me; and, had I so done, I am sure you could never have given me the worst on't, for a Christian can never be overcome unless he shall yield of himself.

GREAT. "Well said, Father Honest," quoth the guide; "for by this I know thou art a cock of the right kind, for thou hast said the truth."

HON. And by this also I know that thou knowest what true

pilgrimage is; for all others do think that we are the
soonest overcome of any.

CONVERSES WITH HONEST

GREAT. Well, now we are so happily met, pray let me crave
your name, and the name of the place you came from.

HON. My name I cannot; but I came from the town of
Stupidity; it lieth about four degrees beyond the City of
Destruction.

GREAT. Oh! are you that countryman? then I deem I have half
a guess of you: your name is old Honesty, is it not?

HON. So the old gentleman blushed, and said, "Not Honesty,
but Honest is my name; and I wish that my nature may
agree to what I am called. But, sir," said the old
gentleman, "how could you guess that I am such a man,
since I came from such a place?"

GREAT. I had heard of you before by my Master; for He knows
all things that are done on the earth. But I have often
wondered that any should come from your place, for
your town is worse than is the City of Destruction itself.

HON. Yes, we lie more off from the sun, and so are more cold
and senseless. But were a man in a mountain of ice, yet if
the Sun of Righteousness should rise upon him, his frozen
heart shall feel a thaw; and thus it hath been with me.

GREAT. I believe it, Father Honest, I believe it; for I know the
thing is true.

Then the old gentleman saluted all the pilgrims with a holy
kiss of love, and asked them their names, and how they had
fared since they had set out on their pilgrimage.

CHR. Then said Christiana, "My name I suppose you have
heard of: good Christian was my husband, and these are
his children."

But can you think how the old gentleman was taken when she told him who she was? He skipped, he smiled, he blessed them with a thousand good wishes, saying:

Hon. I have heard much of your husband, and of his travels and wars which he underwent in his days. Be it spoken to your comfort, the name of your husband rings all over these parts of the world: his faith, his courage, his enduring, and his sincerity under all, have made his name famous. Then he turned him to the boys, and asked of them their names, which they told him. Then he said unto them, "Matthew, be thou like Matthew the publican, not in vice, but in virtue. Samuel," said he, "be thou like Samuel the prophet, a man of faith and prayer. Joseph," said he, "be thou like Joseph in Potiphar's house, pure, and one that flees from temptation. And James, be thou like James the Just, and like James the brother of our Lord." Then they told him of Mercy, and how she had left her town and her kindred to come along with Christiana and with her sons. At that, the old honest man said, "Mercy is thy name? by Mercy shalt thou be sustained and carried through all those difficulties that shall attack thee in thy way, till thou shalt come thither where thou shalt look the Fountain of Mercy in the face with comfort."

All this while the guide, Mr. Great-heart, was very well pleased and smiled upon his companion.

THEY DISCUSS MR. FEARING

Now, as they walked along together, the guide asked the old gentleman if he did not know one Mr. Fearing, that came on pilgrimage out of his parts.

Hon. "Yes, very well," said he. "He was a man that had the root of the matter in him; but he was one of the most troublesome pilgrims that ever I met with in all my days."

Great. I perceive you knew him, for you have given a very right character of him.

Hon. Knew him! I was a great companion of his; I was with him most an end: when he first began to think upon what would come upon us hereafter, I was with him.

Great. I was his guide from my master's house to the gates of the Celestial City.

Hon. Then you knew him to be a troublesome one?

Great. I did so; but I could very well bear it, for men of my calling are oftentimes entrusted with the conduct of such as he was.

Hon. Well, then, pray let us hear a little of him, and how he managed himself under your conduct.

Great. Why, he was always afraid that he should come short of whither he had a desire to go. Everything frightened him that he heard anybody speak of, if it had but the least appearance of opposition in it. I hear that he lay roaring at the Slough of Despond for above a month together; nor durst he, for all he saw several go over before him, venture, though they, many of them, offered to lend him their hand. He would not go back again neither. The Celestial City, he said, he should die if he came not to it; and yet was discouraged at every difficulty, and stumbled at every straw that anybody cast in his way. Well, after he had lain at the Slough of Despond a great while, as I have told you, one sunshine morning, I don't know how, he ventured, and so got over; but, when he was over, he would scarce believe it. He had, I think, a Slough of Despond in his mind, a slough that he carried everywhere with him, or else he could never have been as he was. So he came up to the gate (you know what I mean) that stands at the head of this way, and here also he stood a good while before he would venture to knock. When the gate was opened, he would give back, and give place to others, and say that he was not worthy. For, for all he got before some to the gate, yet many of them went in before him. There the poor man would stand shaking and shrinking: I dare say it would have pitied one's heart to have seen him. Nor would he go back again. At last, he took the hammer that hanged on the gate in his hand, and gave a small rap or two; then One opened to him, but he shrank back as before. He that opened stepped out after him, and said, "Thou trembling one, what wantest thou?" With that, he fell down to the ground. He that spoke to him wondered to see him so faint; so He said to him, "Peace be to thee: up, for I have set open the door to thee; come in, for thou are blessed." With that, he got up, and went in trembling; and when he was in, he was ashamed to show his face. Well, after he had been entertained there a while, as you know how the manner is, he was bid go on his way, and also told the way he should take. So he came till he came to our house; but as he behaved himself at the gate, so he did at my master the Interpreter's door. He lay thereabout in the cold a good while before he would venture to call: yet he would not go back; and the nights were long and cold then. Nay, he had a note of need in his bosom to my master, to receive him and grant him the comfort of his house, and also to allow him a stout and valiant conductor, because he was himself so chicken-hearted a man; and yet, for all that, he was afraid to call at the door. So he lay up and down thereabouts, till, poor man, he was almost starved; yea, so great was his fear, though he had seen several others for knocking get in, yet he was afraid to venture. At last, I think I looked out of the window, and perceiving a man to be up and down about the door,

I went out to him, and asked what he was; but, poor man, the water stood in his eyes; so I perceived what he wanted. I went therefore in, and told it in the house, and we showed the things to our Lord: so he sent me out again, to entreat him to come in; but I dare say I had hard work to do it. At last he came in; and I will say that for my Lord, he carried it wonderful lovingly to him. There were but few good bits at the table, but some of it was laid upon his trencher. Then he presented the note; and my Lord looked thereon, and said his desire should be granted. So, when he had been there a good while, he seemed to get some heart, and to be a little more comfortable. For my master, you must know, is one of very tender heart, specially to them that are afraid; wherefore he carried it so towards him as might tend most to his encouragement. Well, when he had a sight of the things of the place, and was ready to take his journey to go to the City, my Lord, as he did to Christian before, gave him a bottle of spirits, and some comfortable things to eat. Thus we set forward, and I went before him; but the man was but of few words, only he would sigh aloud.

GREAT-HEART'S REMINISCENCES

When we were come to the place where the three fellows were hanged, he said that he doubted that that would be his end also. Only he seemed glad when he saw the Cross and the sepulchre. There, I confess, he desired to stay a little to look; and he seemed, for a little while after, to be a little cheery. When we came at the Hill Difficulty, he made no stick at that, nor did he much fear the lions, for you must know that his trouble was not about such things as those; his fear was about his acceptance at last.

I got him in at the House Beautiful, I think, before

he was willing. Also, when he was in, I brought him acquainted with the damsels that were of the place; but he was ashamed to make himself much for company. He desired much to be alone; yet he always loved good talk, and often would get behind the screen to hear it. He also loved much to see ancient things, and to be pondering them in his mind. He told me, afterwards, that he loved to be in those two houses from which he came last; to wit, at the gate, and that of the Interpreter; but that he durst not be so bold as to ask.

When we went also from the House Beautiful, down the hill into the Valley of Humiliation, he went down as well as ever I saw a man in my life: for he cared not how mean he was, so he might be happy at last. Yea, I think there was a kind of sympathy betwixt that valley and him; for I never saw him better in all his pilgrimage than when he was in that valley.

Here he would lie down, embrace the ground, and kiss the very flowers that grew in this valley. He would now be up every morning by break of day, tracing and walking to and fro in this valley.

But when he was come to the entrance of the Valley of the Shadow of Death, I thought I should have lost my man: not for that he had any inclination to go back—that he always abhorred; but he was ready to die for fear. "Oh, the hobgoblins will have me! the hobgoblins will have me!" cried he, and I could not beat him out of it. He made such a noise and such an outcry here, that, had they but heard him, it was enough to encourage them to come and fall upon us.

But this I took very great notice of, that this valley was as quiet while we went through it as ever I knew it before or since. I suppose those enemies here had now a special check from our Lord, and a command not to meddle until Mr. Fearing had passed over it.

FEARING AT VANITY FAIR

It would be too tedious to tell you of all, I will therefore only mention a passage or two more. When he was come at Vanity Fair, I thought he would have fought with all the men in the fair. I feared there we should both have been knocked on the head, so hot was he against their fooleries. Upon the Enchanted Ground he was also very wakeful. But, when he was come at the river where was no bridge, there again he was in a heavy case. Now, now, he said, he should be drowned for ever, and so never see that face with comfort that he had come so many miles to behold.

And here also I took notice of what was very remarkable: the water of that river was lower at this time than ever I saw it in all my life: so he went over at last, not much above wetshod. When he was going up to the gate, I began to take leave of him, and to wish him a good reception above. So he said, "I shall, I shall." Then parted we asunder, and I saw him no more.

Hon. Then it seems he was well at last?

Great. Yes, yes; I never had a doubt about him. He was a man of choice spirit; only he was always kept very low, and that made his life so burthensome to himself and so troublesome to others. He was, above many, tender of sin: he was so afraid of doing injuries to others, that he often would deny himself of that which was lawful because he would not offend.

Hon. But what should be the reason that such a good man should be all his days so much in the dark?

Great. There are two sorts of reasons for it. One is, the wise God will have it so; some must pipe, and some must weep. Now Mr. Fearing was one that played upon this bass. He and his fellows sound the sackbut, whose notes are more doleful than the notes of other music are;

though, indeed, some say the bass is the ground of music. And, for my part, I care not at all for that profession which begins, not in heaviness of mind. The first string that the musician usually touches is the bass, when he intends to put all in tune. God also plays upon this string first, when He sets the soul in tune for Himself. Only here was the imperfection of Mr. Fearing: he could play upon no other music but this till toward his latter end.

I make bold to talk thus in figures, for the ripening of the wits of young readers, and because, in the book of the Revelation, the saved are compared to a company of musicians, that play upon their trumpets and harps, and sing their songs before the throne.

HON. He was a very zealous man, as one may see by the relation which you have given of him. Difficulties, lions, or Vanity Fair he feared not at all; it was only sin, death, and hell that were to him a terror, because he had some doubts about his interest in that Celestial Country.

GREAT. You say right: those were the things that were his troublers, and they, as you have well observed, arose from the weakness of his mind thereabout, not from weakness of spirit as to the practical part of a pilgrim's life. I dare believe that, as the proverb is, he would have bit a firebrand, had it stood in his way; but the things with which he was oppressed no man ever yet could shake off with ease.

CHR. Then said Christiana, "This relation of Mr. Fearing has done me good. I thought nobody had been like me; but I see there was some semblance betwixt this good man and I: only we differed in two things. His troubles were so great that they broke out; but mine I kept within. His also lay so hard upon him, they made him that he could not knock at the houses provided for entertainment; but my trouble was always such as made me knock the louder."

MER. If I might also speak my heart, I must say that something of him has also dwelt in me; for I have ever been more afraid of the lake, and the loss of a place in Paradise, than I have been of the loss of other things. Oh, thought I, may I have the happiness to have a habitation there, it is enough, though I part with all the world to win it!

MATT. Then said Matthew, "Fear was one thing that made me think that I was far from having that within me which makes me sure of being saved. But if it were so with such a good man as he, why may it not also go well with me?"

JAMES. "No fears, no grace," said James, "Though there is not always grace where there is the fear of hell, yet, to be sure, there is no grace where there is no fear of God."

GREAT. Well said, James; thou hast hit the mark. For the fear of God is the beginning of wisdom; and, to be sure, they that want the beginning have neither middle nor end. But we will here conclude our discourse of Mr. Fearing, after we have sent after him this farewell:

"Well, Master Fearing, thou didst fear
Thy God, and wast afraid
Of doing anything while here
That would have thee betrayed.
"And didst thou fear the lake and pit?
Would others did so too!
For, as for them that want thy wit,
They do themselves undo."

HONEST TELLS OF MR. SELF-WILL

Now I saw that they still went on in their talk; for, after Mr. Great-heart had made an end with Mr. Fearing, Mr. Honest began to tell them of another, but his name was Mr. Self-will.

"He pretended himself to be a pilgrim," said Mr. Honest, "but I persuade myself he never came in at the gate that stands at the head of the way."

GREAT. Had you ever any talk with him about it?

HON. Yes, more than once or twice; but he would always be like himself, self-willed. He neither cared for man, nor argument, nor yet example; what his mind prompted him to, that he would do, and nothing else could he be got to do.

GREAT. Pray, what principles did he hold? for I suppose you can tell.

HON. He held that a man might follow the sins as well as the virtues of pilgrims; and that, if he did both, he should be certainly saved.

GREAT. How! If he had said it is possible for the best to be guilty of the vices, as well as to partake of the virtues, of pilgrims, he could not much have been blamed; for, indeed, we are free from no sin absolutely, but on condition that we watch and strive. But this, I perceive, is not the thing; but, if I understood you right, your meaning is that he was of opinion that it was allowable so to be.

HON. Ay, ay, so I mean, and so he believed and acted.

GREAT. But what grounds had he for his so saying?

HON. Why, he said he had the Scripture for his warrant.

HONEST QUOTES SELF-WILL

GREAT. Prithee, Mr. Honest, present us with a few particulars.

HON. So I will. He said, To have to do with other men's wives had been practiced by David, God's beloved; and therefore he could do it. He said, To have more women than one was a thing that Solomon practiced; and therefore he could do it. He said that Sarah lied, and so did Rahab; and therefore he could do it. He said that the disciples went at the bidding of their Master, and took away the owner's ass; and therefore he could do so too. He said that Jacob got the inheritance of his father in a way of guile and cheating; and therefore he could do so too.

GREAT. Highly base, indeed! And you are sure he was of this opinion?

HON. I have heard him plead for it, bring Scripture for it, bring argument for it, and so on.

GREAT. An opinion that is not fit to be with any allowance in the world!

HON. You must understand me rightly: he did not say that *any* man might do this; but that they who had the virtues of those that did such things, might also do the same.

GREAT. But what more false than such a conclusion? For this is as much as to say that, because good men heretofore have sinned through weakness or forgetfulness, therefore he had an allowance to do it of a purpose; or if, because a child, by the blast of the wind, or for that it stumbled at a stone, fell down and defiled itself in the mire, therefore he might wilfully lie down and wallow like a boar therein. Who could have thought that any one could so far have been blinded by the power of sin. But what is written must be true: they "stumble at the Word, being disobedient; whereunto also they were appointed." His supposing that such may have the godly man's virtues, who accustom themselves to their vices, is also a delusion as strong as the other. To eat up the sin of God's people as a dog licks up filth, is no sign of one that is possessed with their virtues. Nor can I believe that one who is of this opinion can have faith or love in him. But I know you have made strong objections against him: prithee, what can he say for himself?

HON. Why, he says, "To do this openly and by way of opinion, seems abundantly more honest than to do it and yet hold contrary to it in opinion."

GREAT. A very wicked answer. For, though to let loose the bridle to lusts while our opinions are against such things is bad; yet to sin, and plead a toleration so to do, is worse. The one stumbles beholders accidentally, the other *pleads* them into the snare.

HON. There are many of this man's mind, that have not this man's mouth; and that makes going on pilgrimage of so little esteem as it is.

GREAT. You have said the truth, and it is to be lamented; but he that feareth the King of Paradise shall come out of them all.

CHR. There are strange opinions in the world. I know one that said it was time enough to turn from sin when they come to die.

GREAT. Such are not overwise. That man would have been loth, might he have had a week to run twenty miles in for his life, to have deferred that journey to the last hour of that week.

HON. You say right; and yet the most of them who count themselves pilgrims do indeed do thus. I am, as you see, an old man, and have been a traveller in this road many a day, and I have taken notice of many things. I have seen some that have set out as if they would drive all the world afore them, who yet have, in a few days, died as they in the wilderness, and so never got sight of the promised land. I have seen some that have promised nothing at first, setting out to be pilgrims, and that one would have thought could not have lived a day, that have yet proved very good pilgrims. I have seen some that have run hastily forward, that again have, after a little time, run just as fast back again. I have seen some who have spoken very well of a pilgrim's life at first, that, after a while, have spoken as much against it. I have heard some, when they first set out for Paradise, say positively there is such a place, who, when they have been almost there, have come back again, and said there is none. I have heard some boast what they would do in case they should be opposed, that have, even at a false alarm, fled faith, the pilgrim's way, and all.

Now, as they were thus in their way, there came one running to meet them, and said, "Gentlemen, and you of the weaker sort, if you love life, shift for yourselves, for the robbers are before you."

GREAT. "They be the three that set upon Little-Faith heretofore. Well," said he, "we are ready for them."

THE PILGRIMS PROCEED

So they went on their way. Now they looked at every turning when they should have met with the villains; but whether they heard of Mr. Great-heart, or whether they had some other game, they came not up to the pilgrims.

CHAPTER 7

Entertained by Gaius

Christiana then wished for an inn for herself and her children, because they were weary.

Then said Mr. Honest, "There is one a little before us, where a very honorable disciple, one Gaius, dwells." So they all concluded to turn in thither, and the rather because the old gentleman gave him so good a report. When they came to the door, they went in, not knocking, for folks use not to knock at the door of an inn. Then they called for the master of the house, and he came to them; so they asked if they might lie there that night.

GAIUS. Yes, gentlemen, if you be true men, for my house is for none but pilgrims.

Then were Christiana, Mercy, and the boys the more glad, for that the Innkeeper was a lover of pilgrims. So they called for rooms, and he showed them one for Christiana, and her children, and Mercy, and another for Mr. Great-heart and the old gentleman.

GREAT. "Good Gaius, what hast thou for supper? for these pilgrims have come far to-day, and are weary."

GAIUS. "It is late, so we cannot conveniently go out to seek food; but such as we have you shall be welcome to, if that will content."

GREAT. We will be content with what thou hast in the house; forasmuch as I have proved thee, thou art never without that which is suitable.

Then he went down and spake to the cook, whose name was Taste-that-which-is-good, to get ready supper for so many pilgrims. This done, he came up again, saying, "Come, my good friends, you are welcome to me, and I am glad that I have a house to entertain you in; and, while supper is making ready, if you please, let us entertain one another with some good talking together."

So they all said, "Content."

GAIUS. "Whose wife is this aged matron? and whose daughter is this young damsel?"

GREAT. The woman is the wife of one Christian, a pilgrim of former times; and these are his four children. The maid is one of her acquaintance, one that she hath persuaded to come with her on pilgrimage. The boys take all after their father, and wish to tread in his steps; yea, if they do but see any place where the old pilgrim hath lain, or any print of his foot, it bringeth joy to their hearts, and they are eager to lie or tread in the same.

FAMILY OF THE CHRISTIANS

GAIUS. "Is this Christian's wife, and are these Christian's children? I knew your husband's father; yea, also his father's father. Many have been good of this stock; their ancestors dwelt first at Antioch. Christian's ancestors, the early fathers from whom he came (I suppose you have heard your husband talk of them) were very worthy men. They have, above any that I know, showed themselves men of great virtue and courage, for the Lord of pilgrims, His ways, and them that loved Him. I have heard of many of your husband's relations that have stood all trials for the sake of the truth. Stephen, who was one of the first of the family from whence your husband sprang, was knocked on the head with stones. James, another of this generation, was slain with the edge of the sword. To say nothing of Paul and Peter, men anciently of the family from whence your husband came; there was Ignatius, who was cast to the lions; Romanus, whose flesh was cut by pieces from his bones; and Polycarp, that played the man in the fire; there was he that was hanged up in a basket in the sun for the wasps to eat; and he whom they put into a sack, and cast him into the sea to be drowned. It would be utterly impossible to count up all of that family who have suffered injuries and death for the love of a pilgrim's life. Nor can I but be glad to see that thy husband has left behind him four such boys as these. I hope they will bear out their father's name, and tread in their father's steps, and come to their father's end."

GREAT. Indeed, sir, they are likely lads; they seem to choose heartily their father's ways.

GAIUS. That is it that I said; wherefore Christian's family is like still to spread abroad upon the face of the ground, and yet to be numerous upon the face of the earth. Wherefore let Christiana look out some damsels for her sons, to whom they may be married, etc., that the name of their father and the house of his family may never be forgotten in the world.

HON. 'Tis pity this family should fall and die out of the world.

GAIUS. Fall it cannot, but be diminished it may; but let Christiana take my advice, and that is the way to uphold it. "And Christiana," said this Innkeeper, "I am glad to see thee and thy friend Mercy together here, a lovely couple. And may I advise, take Mercy into a nearer relation to thee; if she will, let her be given to Matthew, thy eldest son. It is the way to give you a family in the earth."

So this match was arranged, and in process of time they were married; but more of that hereafter.

Gaius also proceeded, and said, "I will now speak on the behalf of women, to take away their reproach. For as death and the curse came into the world by a woman, so also did life and health: 'God sent forth His Son, born of a woman.' I will say again, that when the Saviour was come, women rejoiced in Him before either man or angel. I read not that man ever gave unto Christ so much as one penny; but the women followed Him, and ministered to Him of their substance. 'Twas a woman that washed His feet with tears, and a woman that anointed His body to the burial. They were women that wept when He was going to the cross, and women that followed Him from the cross; and that sat over against the sepulchre when He was buried. They were women that were first with Him at His resurrection-morn, and women that brought tidings first to His disciples that He was risen from the dead. Women, therefore, are highly favored, and show by these things that they are sharers with us in the grace of life."

THE SUPPER AT GAIUS'S HOUSE

Now the cook sent up to signify that supper was almost ready, and sent one to lay the cloth, the dishes, and to set the salt and bread in order.

Then said Matthew, "The sight of this cloth, and of this forerunner of the supper, awaketh in me a greater appetite to my food than I had before."

GAIUS. So let all teaching truth to thee in this life awaken in thee a greater desire to sit at the supper of the great King in His kingdom; for all preaching, books, and services here, are but as the laying of the dishes, and as setting of salt upon the board, when compared with the feast which our Lord will make for us when we come to His house.

So supper came up. And first a heave-shoulder and a wave-breast were set on the table before them, to show that they must begin their meal with prayer and praise to God. The heave-shoulder David lifted up his heart to God with; and with the wave-breast, where his heart lay, he used to lean upon his harp when he played. These two dishes were very fresh and good, and they all ate heartily well thereof.

The next they brought up was a bottle of wine, red as blood. So Gaius said to them, "Drink freely: this is the true juice of the vine, that makes glad the heart of God and man." So they drank and were merry. The next was a dish of milk, well crumbed; but Gaius said, "Let the boys have that, that they may grow thereby."

Then they brought up in course of dish of butter and honey. Then said Gaius, "Eat freely of this, for this is good to cheer up and strengthen your judgments and understandings. This was our Lord's dish when He was a child: 'Butter and honey shall He eat, that He may know to refuse the evil and choose the good.'"

Then they brought them up a dish of apples, and they were very good tasted fruit. Then said Matthew, "May we eat apples, since they were such by and with which the serpent deceived our first mother Eve?"

Then said Gaius:

> "Apples were they with which we were
> beguiled;

> Yet sin, not apples, hath our souls defiled.
> Apples forbid, if ate, corrupt the blood;
> To eat such, when commanded, does us
>   good.
> Drink of His flagons, then, thou Church, His
>   dove,
> And eat His apples who are sick of love."

Then said Matthew, "I made the objection, because I, a while since, was sick with eating of fruit."

GAIUS. Forbidden fruit will make you sick; but not what our Lord has allowed.

While they were thus talking, they were presented with another dish, and it was a dish of nuts. Then said some at the table, "Nuts spoil tender teeth, specially the teeth of children;" which, when Gaius heared, he said;

> "Hard texts are nuts (I will not call them
>   cheaters),
> Whose shells do keep their kernels from the
>   eaters;
> Ope then the shells, and you shall have the meat:
> They here are brought for you to crack and eat."

Then were they very merry, and sat at the table a long time, talking of many things. Then said the old gentleman, "My good landlord, while we are cracking your nuts, if you please, do you open this riddle;

> "A man there was, though some did count
>   him mad,
> The more he cast away, the more he had."

Then they all gave good heed, wondering what good Gaius would say: so he sat still awhile, and then thus replied:

> "He that bestows his goods upon the poor
> Shall have as much again, and ten times
>   more."

Then said Joseph, "I dare say, sir, I did not think you could have found it out."

"Oh!" said Gaius, "I have been trained up in this way a great while: nothing teaches like experience, I have learned of my Lord to be kind, and have found by experience that I have gained thereby. 'There is that scattereth, and yet increaseth; and there is that withholdeth more than is meet, but it tendeth to poverty.' 'There is that maketh himself rich, yet hath nothing; there is that maketh himself poor, yet hath great riches.'"

MERCY AND MATTHEW

Then Samuel whispered to Christiana, his mother, and said, "Mother, this is a very good man's house; let us stay here a good while, and let my brother Matthew be married here to Mercy before we go any farther." The which Gaius, the host, overhearing, said, "With a very good will, my child."

So they stayed there more than a month, and Mercy was given to Matthew to wife. While they stayed here, Mercy, as her custom was, would be making coats and garments to give to the poor, by which she brought up a very good report upon the pilgrims.

But to return again to our story. After supper, the lads desired a bed, for that they were weary with travelling. Then Gaius called to show them their chamber; but said Mercy, "I will have them to bed." So she had them to bed, and they slept well; but the rest sat up all night, for Gaius and they were such suitable company, that they could not tell how to part.

Then, after much talk of their Lord, themselves, and their journey, old Mr. Honest, he that put forth the riddle to Gaius, began to nod.

Then said Great-heart, "What, sir! you begin to be drowsy? Come, rub up. Now, here's a riddle for you."

Then said Mr. Honest, "Let us hear it."

Then said Mr. Great-heart:

> "He that will kill, must first be overcome;
> Who live abroad would, first must die at
>   home."

"Ha!" said Mr. Honest, "it is a hard one; hard to explain, and harder to do. But come, landlord," said he, "I will, if you please, leave my part to you: do you expound it, and I will hear what you say."

"No," said Gaius, "it was put to you, and it is expected you should answer it." Then said the old gentleman:

> "He first by grace must conquered be,
> That sin would mortify;
> And who that lives would convince me,
> Unto himself must die."

Thus they sat talking till break of day. Now, when the family were up, Christiana bade her son James read a chapter; so he read the fifty-third of Isaiah.

"Well," said Gaius, "now you are here, and since, as I know Mr. Great-heart is good at his weapons, if you please, after we have refreshed ourselves we will walk into the fields, to see if we can do any good. About a mile from hence there is one Slay-good, a giant, that doth much annoy the King's highway in these parts; and I know whereabout his haunt is.

He is master of a number of thieves: 'twould be well if we could clear these parts of him."

So they consented and went; Mr. Great-heart with his sword, helmet, and shield, and the rest with spears and staves.

SLAY-GOOD DESTROYED

When they were come to the place where he was, they found him with one Feeble-minded in his hands, whom his servants had brought unto him, having taken him in the way. Now the giant was picking his pockets, with a purpose after that to pick his bones; for he was of the nature of flesh-eaters.

Well, so soon as he saw Mr. Great-heart and his friends at the mouth of his cave with their weapons, he demanded what they wanted.

GREAT. We want thee, for we are come to revenge the quarrel of the many that thou hast slain of the pilgrims, when thou has dragged them out of the King's highway; wherefore come out of thy cave.

So he armed himself and came out; and to battle they went, and fought for above an hour, and then stood still to take wind.

SLAY. Then said the giant, "Why are you here on my ground?"
GREAT. To revenge the blood of pilgrims, as I told thee before.

FEEBLE-MIND RESCUED

So they went to it again, and the giant made Mr. Great-heart give back; but he came up again, and in the greatness of his mind he let fly with such stoutness at the giant's head and sides, that he made him let his weapon fall out of his hand. So he smote him, and slew him, and cut off his head, and brought it away to the inn. He also took Feeble-mind, the pilgrim, and brought him with him to his lodgings. When they were come home, they showed his head to the family, and then set it up as they had done others before, for a terror to those that should attempt to do as he hereafter.

Then they asked Mr. Feeble-mind how he fell into his hands.

FEEBLE. Then said the poor man, "I am a sickly man, as you see; and because death did usually once a day knock at my door, I thought I should never be well at home: so I betook myself to a pilgrim's life, and have travelled hither from the town of Uncertain, where I and my father were born. I am a man of no strength at all of body, nor yet of mind, but would, if I could, though I can but crawl, spend my life in the pilgrims' way. When I came at the gate that is at the head of the way, the Lord of that place did entertain me freely; neither objected He against my weakly looks, nor against my feeble mind, but gave me such things as were necessary for my journey, and bid me hope to the end. When I came to the house of the Interpreter, I received much kindness there; and because the Hill Difficulty was judged too hard for me, I was carried up that by one of his servants. Indeed, I have found much relief from pilgrims: though none were willing to go so softly as I am forced to do, yet still as they came on they bid me be of good cheer, and said that it was the will of their Lord that comfort should be given to the feeble-minded, and so went on their own pace. When I was come to Assault Lane, then this giant met with me, and bid me prepare for an encounter. But, alas! feeble one that I was, I had more need of a cordial; so he came up and took me. I believed not that he should kill me. Also when he got me into his den, since I went not with him willingly, I believed I should come out alive again; for I have heard that not any pilgrim that is taken captive by violent hands, if he keeps heart-whole towards his Master, is, by the laws of Providence, to die by the hands of the enemy. Robbed I looked to be, and robbed to be sure I am; but I have, as you see, escaped with life, for the which I thank my King as author, and you as the means. Other brunts I also look for; but this I have resolved on—to wit, to run when I can, to go when I cannot run, and to creep when I cannot go. As to the principal thing, I thank Him that loves me, I am fixed: my way is before me, my mind is beyond the river that has no bridge, though I am, as you see, but of a feeble mind."

HON. Then said old Mr. Honest, "Have not you some time ago been acquainted with one Mr. Fearing, a pilgrim?"

FEEBLE. Acquainted with him! yes; he came from the town of Stupidity, which lies four degrees northward of the City of Destruction, and as many off of where I was born; yet we were well acquainted, for indeed he was my uncle, my father's brother. He and I have been much of a temper: he was a little shorter than I, but yet we were much of a complexion.

HON. I perceive you know him, and I am apt to believe also that you are related one to another; for you have his whitely look, a cast like his with your eye, and your speech is much alike.

FEEBLE. Most have said so that have known us both; and besides, what I have read in him I have for the most part found in myself.

GAIUS. "Come, sir," said good Gaius, "be of good cheer: you are welcome to me and to my house. What thou hast a mind to, call for freely; and what thou wouldst have my servants do for thee, they will do it with a ready mind."

Then said Mr. Feeble-mind, "This is an unexpected favor, and as the sun shining out of a very dark cloud. Did Giant Slay-good intend me this favor when he stopped me, and resolved to let me go no farther? Did he intend that, after he had rifled my pockets, I should go to Gaius, mine host? Yet so it is."

Now, just as Feeble-mind and Gaius were thus in talk, there came one running, and called at the door, and said, that "About a mile and a half off there was one Mr. Not-right, a pilgrim, struck dead upon the place where he was, with a thunderbolt."

FEEBLE. "Alas!" said Mr. Feeble-mind, "is he slain? He overtook me some days before I came so far as hither, and would be my company-keeper. He also was with me when Slay-good, the giant, took me; but he was nimble of his heels, and escaped; but it seems he escaped to die, and I was taken to live.

"What, one would think, doth seek to slay
    outright,
Ofttimes delivers from the saddest plight,
That very Providence, whose face is death,
Doth ofttimes to the lowly life bequeath.
I was taken, he did escape and flee;
Hands crossed gives death to him, and life to
    me."

PHŒBE AND JAMES

Now, about this time, Matthew and Mercy were married; also Gaius gave his daughter Phœbe to James, Matthew's brother, to wife; after which time, they yet stayed about ten days at Gaius's house, spending their time and the seasons like as pilgrims use to do.

When they were to depart, Gaius made them a feast, and they did eat and drink and were merry. Now, the hour was come that they must be gone, wherefore Mr. Great-heart called for the bill of charges. But Gaius told him that at his house it was not the custom of pilgrims to pay for their entertainment. He boarded them by the year, but looked for his pay from the Good Samaritan, who had promised him, at His return, whatsoever charge he was at with them, faithfully to repay him.

Then said Mr. Great-heart to him,

GREAT. Beloved, thou doest faithfully, whatsoever thou doest to the brethren and to strangers, which have borne witness of thy liberal giving before the Church; whom if thou yet bring forward on their journey after a godly sort, thou shalt do well.

Then Gaius took his leave of them all, and his children, and particularly of Mr. Feeble-mind. He also gave him something to drink by the way.

Now, Mr. Feeble-mind, when they were going out of the door, made as if he intended to linger. The which when Mr. Great-heart espied, he said, "Come, Mr. Feeble-mind, pray do you go along with us: I will be your conductor, and you shall fare as the rest."

FEEBLE. Alas! I want a suitable companion. You are all lusty and strong, but I, as you see, am weak; I choose, therefore, rather to come behind, lest, by reason of my many weaknesses, I should be both a burden to myself and to you. I am, as I said, a man of a weak and feeble mind, and shall be injured and made weak at that which others can bear. I shall like no laughing; I shall like no gay attire; I shall like no unprofitable questions. Nay, I am so weak a man as to be harmed with that which others have a liberty to do. I do not yet know all the truth; I am a very ignorant Christian man. Sometimes, if I hear any rejoice in the Lord, it troubles me, because I cannot do so too. It is with me as it is with a weak man among the strong, or as with a sick man among the healthy, or as a lamp despised. "He that is ready to slip with his feet is as a lamp despised in the thought of him that is at ease;" so that I know not what to do.

GREAT. "But, brother," said Mr. Great-heart, "I have it in my work to comfort the feeble-minded and to support the weak. You must needs go along with us: we will wait for you; we will lend you our help; we will deny ourselves of some things, for your sake; we will not enter into doubtful questions before you! we will be made all things to you, rather than you shall be left behind."

Now, all this while they were at Gaius's door, and, behold, as they were thus in the heat of their discourse, Mr. Ready-to-halt came by, with his crutches in his hands; and he also was going on pilgrimage.

FEEBLE. Then said Mr. Feeble-mind to him, "How camest thou hither? I was but now complaining that I had not a suitable companion, but thou art according to my wish. Welcome, welcome, good Mr. Ready-to-halt; I hope thou and I may be some help."

READY. "I shall be glad of thy company," said the other; "and, good Mr. Feeble-mind, rather than we will part, since we are thus happily met, I will lend thee one of my crutches."

FEEBLE. "Nay," said he, "though I thank thee for thy good-will, I am not inclined to halt before I am lame. Howbeit, I think, when occasion is, it may help me against a dog."

READY. If either myself or my crutches can do thee a pleasure, we are both at thy command, good Mr. Feeble-mind.

Thus, therefore, they went on. Mr. Great-heart and Mr. Honest went before, Christiana and her children went next, and Mr. Feeble-mind came behind, and Mr. Ready-to-halt with his crutches. Then said Mr. Honest,

HON. Pray, sir, now that we are upon the road, tell us some profitable things of some that have gone on pilgrimage before us.

REVIEWS OTHER PILGRIMAGES

GREAT. With a good will. I suppose you have heard how Christian of old did meet with Apollyon in the Valley of Humiliation, and also what hard work he had to go through the Valley of the Shadow of Death. Also I think you cannot but have heard how Faithful was put to it by Madam Wanton, with Adam the first, with one Discontent, and Shame; four as deceitful villains as a man can meet with upon the road.

HON. Yes, I believe I have heard of all this; but, indeed, good Faithful was hardest put to it with Shame: he was an unwearied one.

GREAT. Ay; for, as the pilgrim well said, he of all men had the wrong name.

HON. But pray, sir, where was it that Christian and Faithful met Talkative? That same was also a notable one.

GREAT. He was a confident fool; yet many follow his ways.

HON. He had liked to have deceived Faithful.

GREAT. Ay, but Christian put him into a way quickly to find him out.

Thus they went on till they came to the place where Evangelist met with Christian and Faithful, and foretold them what should befall them at Vanity Fair. Then said their guide,

"Hereabouts did Christian and Faithful meet with Evangelist, who foretold them of their troubles which they should meet with at Vanity Fair."

HON. Say you so? I dare say it was a hard chapter, then, that he did read unto them!

GREAT. It was; but he gave them encouragement withal. But what do we talk of them? they were a couple of lion-like men: they had set their faces like flint. Do not you remember how undaunted they were when they stood before the judge?

HON. Well. Faithful bravely suffered.

GREAT. So he did, and as brave things came on't; for Hopeful and some others, as the story relates it, were converted by his death.

HON. Well, but pray go on, for you are well acquainted with things.

GREAT. Above all that Christian met with after he had passed through Vanity Fair, one By-ends was the arch one.

HON. By-ends! what was he?

GREAT. A very arch fellow—a downright deceiver; one that would be religious, which way soever the world went; but so cunning that he would be sure never to lose or suffer for it. He had his mode of religion for every fresh occasion, and his wife was as good at it as he. And he would turn and change from opinion to opinion; yea, and plead for so doing, too. But, as far as I could learn, he came to an ill end with his by-ends; nor did I ever hear that any of his children were ever of any esteem with any that truly feared God.

THEY ARRIVE AT VANITY FAIR

Now, by this time they were come within sight of the town of Vanity, where Vanity Fair is kept. So, when they saw that they were so near the town, they consulted with one another how they should pass through the town; and some said one thing, and some another. At last Mr. Great-heart said, "I have, as you may understand, often been a conductor of pilgrims through this town. Now, I am acquainted with one Mr. Mnason, a Cyprusian by nature, an old disciple, at whose house we may lodge. If you think good," said he, "we will turn in there."

MNASON ENTERTAINS PILGRIMS

"Content," said old Honest; "Content," said Christiana; "Content," said Mr. Feeble-mind; and so they said all. Now, you must think it was eventide by that they got to the outside of the town; but Mr. Great-heart knew the way to the old man's house. So thither they came, and he called at the door; and the old man within knew his tongue so soon as ever he heard it; so he opened the door, and they all came in. Then said Mnason, their host, "How far have ye come to-day?"

So they said, "From the house of Gaius, our friend."

"I promise you," said he, "you have come a good stitch: you may well be weary. Sit down." So they sat down.

GREAT. Then said their guide, "Come, what cheer, sirs? I dare say you are welcome to my friend."

MNAS. "I also," said Mr. Mnason, "do bid you welcome; and whatever you want, do but say, and we will do what we can to get it for you."

HON. Our great want a while since was a resting-place and good company, and now I hope we have both.

MNAS. For resting-place, you see what it is; but for good company, that will appear in the trial.

GREAT. "Well," said Great-heart, "will you have the pilgrims up into their lodging?"

MNAS. "I will," said Mr. Mnason. So he had them up to their

several places, and also showed them a very fair dining-room, where they might be, and sup together, until time should come to go to rest.

Now, when they were set in their places, and were a little cheery after their journey, Mr. Honest asked his landlord if there were any store of good people in the town.

MNAS. We have a few; for, indeed, they are but a few when compared with them on the other side.

HON. But how shall we do to see some of them? for the sight of good men to them that are going on pilgrimage is like the appearing of the moon and stars to them that are sailing upon the seas.

FRIENDS CALL ON THE PILGRIMS

MNAS. Then Mr. Mnason stamped with his foot, and his daughter Grace came up. So he said unto her, "Grace, go you, tell my friends, Mr. Contrite, Mr. Holy-man, Mr. Love-saint, Mr. Dare-not-lie, and Mr. Penitent, that I have a friend or two at my house who have a mind this evening to see them." So Grace went to call them, and they came; and, after salutation made, they sat down together at the table.

Then said Mr. Mnason, their landlord, "My neighbors, I have, as you see, a company of strangers come to my house: they are pilgrims; they come from afar, and are going to Mount Zion. But who," quoth he, "do you think this is?" pointing with his finger to Christiana. "It is Christiana, the wife of Christian, that famous pilgrim who, with Faithful his brother, was so shamefully handled in our town."

At that they stood amazed, saying, "We little thought to see Christiana when Grace came to call us; wherefore this is a very comfortable surprise." They then asked her of her welfare, and if these young men were her husband's sons. And when she told them they were, they said, "The King whom you love and serve, make you as your father, and bring you where he is in peace!"

HON. Then Mr. Honest (when they had all sat down) asked Mr. Contrite and the rest, in what posture their town was at present.

CONTRITE. You may be sure we are full of hurry in fair-time. 'Tis hard keeping our hearts and spirits in good order when we are in a cumbered condition. He that lives in such a place as this, and has to do with such as we have, has need of a hint to caution him to take heed, every moment of the day.

HON. But how are your neighbors for quietness?

CONTR. They are much more moderate now than formerly. You know how Christian and Faithful were used at our town; but of late, I say, they have been far more moderate. I think the blood of Faithful lieth as a load upon them till now; for since they burned him they have been ashamed to burn any more. In those days we were afraid to walk the street; but now we can show our heads. Then the name of a Christian was hated; now, specially in some parts of our town (for you know our town is large), religion is counted honorable.

Then said Mr. Contrite to them, "Pray, how fareth it with you in your pilgrimage? how stands the country towards you?"

HON. It happens to us as it happeneth to wayfaring men: sometimes our way is clean, sometimes up-hill, sometimes down-hill: we are seldom at a certainty. The wind is not always on our back, nor is every one a friend that we meet with in the way. We have met with some notable rubs already, and what are yet behind we know not; but, for the most part we find it true that has been talked of, of old, "A good man must suffer trouble."

CONTR. You talk of rubs; what rubs have you met withal?

HON. Nay, ask Mr. Great-heart, our guide; for he can give the best account of that.

GREAT. We have been beset three or four times already. First, Christiana and her children were beset by two ruffians, who, they feared, would take away their lives. We were beset by Giant Bloody-man, Giant Maul, and Giant Slaygood. Indeed, we did rather beset the last, than were beset of him. And thus it was: After we had been some time at the house of Gaius mine host, and of the whole Church, we were minded upon a time to take our weapons with us, and go and see if we could light upon any of those that were enemies to pilgrims; for we heard that there was a notable one thereabouts. Now Gaius knew his haunt better than I, because he dwelt thereabout. So we looked, and looked, till at last we saw the mouth of his cave; then we were glad and plucked up our spirits. So we approached up to his den; and, lo! when we came there, he had dragged, by mere force, into his net, this poor man, Mr. Feeble-mind, and was about to bring him to his end. But, when he saw us, supposing, as he thought, he had had another prey, he left the poor man in his house, and came out. So we fell to it full sore, and he lustily laid about him; but, in conclusion, he was brought down to the ground, and his head cut off, and set up by the wayside, for terror to such as should after practice such ungodliness. That I tell you the truth, here is the man himself to affirm it, who was as a lamb taken out of the mouth of the lion.

FEEBLE. Then said Mr. Feeble-mind, "I found this true, to my cost and comfort: to my cost, when he threatened to pick my bones every moment; and to my comfort, when I saw Mr. Great-heart and his friends with their weapons approach so near for my deliverance."

HOLY. Then said Mr. Holy-man, "There are two things that they have need to possess who go on pilgrimage—courage and an unspotted life. If they have not courage, they can never hold on their way; and if their lives be loose, they will make the very name of the pilgrim stink."

LOVE. Then said Mr. Love-saint, "I hope this caution is not needful among you. But truly there are many that go upon the road, who rather declare themselves strangers to pilgrimage than strangers and pilgrims in the earth."

DARE. Then said Mr. Dare-not-lie, "'Tis true. They have neither the pilgrim's weed nor the pilgrim's courage: they go not uprightly, but all awry with their feet; one shoe goeth inward, another outward, and their hosen out behind; there is here a rag, and there a rent, to the disparagement of their Lord."

PEN. "These things," said Mr. Penitent, "they ought to be troubled for; nor are the pilgrims like to have that grace upon them and their pilgrim's progress as they desire, until the way is cleared of such spots and blemishes."

Thus they sat talking and spending the time until supper was set upon the table, unto which they went, and refreshed their weary bodies; so they went to rest.

GRACE AND SAMUEL

Now, they stayed in this fair a great while, at the house of Mnason, who, in process of time, gave his daughter Grace unto Samuel, Christiana's son, to wife; and his daughter Martha to Joseph.

The time, as I said, that they stayed here was long; for it was not now as in former times. Wherefore the pilgrims grew acquainted with many of the good people of the town, and did them what service they could. Mercy, as she was wont, labored much for the poor; wherefore their bodies and backs blessed her, and she was there an ornament to her profession. And to say the truth for Grace, Phœbe, and Martha, they were all of a very good nature, and did much good in their places. They were also all of them very fruitful; so that Christian's name, as was said before, was like to live in the world.

While they lay here, there came a monster out of the woods, and slew many of the people of the town. It would also carry away their children, and teach them to suck its whelps. Now, no man in the town durst so much as face this monster, but all fled when they heard the noise of his coming.

The monster was like unto no one beast on the earth. Its body was like a dragon, and it had seven heads and ten horns. It made great havoc of children, and yet it was governed by a woman. This monster gave conditions to men, and such men as loved their lives more than their souls accepted of those conditions; so they came under.

Now, this Mr. Great-heart, together with those that came to visit the pilgrims at Mr. Mnason's house, entered into a covenant to go and engage this beast, if perhaps they might deliver the people of this town from the paws and mouth of this so devouring a serpent.

Then did Mr. Great-heart, Mr. Contrite, Mr. Holy-man, Mr. Dare-not-lie, and Mr. Penitent, with their weapons, go forth to meet him. Now, the monster was at first very rampant, and looked upon these enemies with great disdain; but they so belabored him, being sturdy men-at-arms, that they made him make a retreat. So they came home to Mr. Mnason's house again.

MARTHA AND JOSEPH

The monster, you must know, had his certain seasons to come out in, and to make his attempts upon the children of the people of the town. Also, these seasons did these valiant worthies watch him in, and did still continually assault him; insomuch that in process of time he became not only wounded, but lame. Also he has not made that havoc of the townsmen's children as formerly he had done; and it is verily believed by some that this beast will die of his wounds.

This, therefore, made Mr. Great-heart and his fellows of great fame in this town; so that many of the people that wanted their taste of things, yet had a reverent esteem and respect for them. Upon this account, therefore, it was that these pilgrims got not much hurt here. True, there were some of the baser sort, that could see no more than a mole, nor understand any more than a beast; these had no reverence for these men, and took no notice of their valor or adventures.

Well, the time grew on that the pilgrims must go on their way; wherefore they prepared for their journey. They sent for their friends; they talked with them; they had some time set apart, therein to commit each other to the protection of their Prince. There were again that brought them of such things as they had, that were fit for the weak and the strong, for the women and the men, and so laded them with such things as were necessary. Then they set forward on their way; and, their friends accompanying them so far as was convenient, they again committed each other to the protection of their King, and parted.

They, therefore, that were of the pilgrims' company, went on, and Mr. Great-heart went before them. Now, the women and children being weakly, they were forced to go as they could bear; by which means, Mr. Ready-to-halt and Mr. Feeble-mind had more to sympathize with their condition.

When they were gone from the townsmen, and when their friends had bid them farewell, they quickly came to the place where Faithful was put to death. There, therefore, they made a stand, and thanked Him that had enabled him to bear

his cross so well; and the rather, because they now found that
they had a benefit by such manly suffering as his was.

They went on, therefore, after this a good way farther,
talking of Christian and Faithful, and how Helpful joined
himself to Christian after that Faithful was dead.

Now they were come up with the Hill Lucre, where the
silver mine was which took Demas off from his pilgrimage,
and into which, as some think, By-ends fell and perished;
wherefore they considered that. But, when they were come
to the old monument that stood over against the Hill Lucre,
to wit, the pillar of salt, that stood also within view of Sodom
and its stinking lake, they marvelled, as did Christian before,
that men of that knowledge and ripeness of wit as they were,
should be so blind as to turn aside here.

CHAPTER 8

The Delectable Mountains and
the Shepherds

I saw now that they went on till they came at the river that was on this side of the Delectable Mountains; to the river where the fine trees grow on both sides, and whose leaves, if taken inwardly, are good against sickness; where the meadows are green all the year long, and where they might lie down safely.

By this river-side, in the meadow, there were cotes and folds for sheep, a house built for the nourishing and bringing up of those lambs, the babes of those women that go on pilgrimage. Also there was here One that was entrusted with them, who could have pity, and that could gather these lambs with His arm, and carry them in His bosom, and that could gently lead those that were with young.

Now, to the care of this Man Christiana admonished her four daughters to commit their little ones, that by these waters they might be housed, cared for, helped and nourished, and that none of them might be lacking in time to come. This Man, if any of them go astray or be lost, He will bring them again; He will also bind up that which was broken, and will strengthen them that are sick. Here they will never want food and drink and clothing; here they will be kept from thieves and robbers; for this Man will die before one of those committed to His trust shall be lost. Besides, here they shall be sure to have good nurture and training, and shall be taught to walk in right paths; and that, you know, is a favor of no small account. Also here, as you see, are delicate waters, pleasant meadows, dainty flowers, variety of trees, and such as bear wholesome fruit—fruit not like that that Matthew ate of, that fell over the wall out of Beelzebub's garden; but fruit that giveth health where there is none, and that continueth and increaseth it where it is. So they were content to commit their little ones to Him; and that which was also an encouragement to them so to do, was, for that all this was to be at the charge of the King, and so was as an hospital for young children and orphans.

DOUBTING CASTLE

Now they went on. And, when they were come to By-path Meadow, to the stile over which Christian went with his fellow Hopeful, when they were taken by Giant Despair and put into Doubting Castle, they sat down, and consulted what was best to be done; to wit, now they were so strong, and had got such a man as Mr. Great-heart for their conductor, whether they had not best make an attempt upon the giant, demolish his castle, and if there were any pilgrims in it, to set them at liberty, before they went any farther. So one said one thing, and another said the contrary. One questioned if it were lawful to go upon ground that was not the King's; another said they might providing their end was good; but Mr. Great-heart said, "Though that reason given last cannot be always true, yet I have a commandment to resist sin, to overcome evil, to fight the good fight of faith; and, I pray, with whom should I fight this good fight, if not with Giant Despair? I will therefore attempt the taking away of his life and the demolishing of Doubting Castle." Then said he,

"Who will go with me?" Then said old Honest, "I will." "And so will we, too," said Christiana's four sons, Matthew, Samuel, Joseph, and James; for they were young men and strong. So they left the women in the road, and with them Mr. Feeble-mind and Mr. Ready-to-halt, with his crutches, to be their guard until they came back; for, in that place, though Giant Despair dwelt so near, they keeping in the road, "a little child might lead them."

So Mr. Great-heart, old Honest, and the four young men went to go up to Doubting Castle, to look for Giant Despair. When they came at the castle gate, they knocked for entrance with an unusual noise. At that, the old giant comes to the gate, and Diffidence his wife follows. Then said he, "Who and what is he that is so hardy as after this manner to disturb the Giant Despair?"

Mr. Great-heart replied, "It is I, Great-heart, one of the King of the Celestial Country's conductors of pilgrims to their place; and I demand of thee that thou open thy gates for my entrance; prepare thyself also to fight, for I am come to take away thy head, and to demolish Doubting Castle."

GIANT DESPAIR IS BEHEADED

Now, Giant Despair, because he was a giant, thought no man could overcome him; and again thought he, "Since heretofore I have made a conquest of angels, shall Great-heart make me afraid?" So he harnessed himself with his armor, and went out. He had a cap of steel upon his head, a breast-plate of fire girded to him, and he came out in iron shoes, with a great club in his hand. Then these six men made up to him, and beset him behind and before; also when Diffidence, the giantess, came up to help him, old Mr. Honest cut her down at one blow. Then they fought for their lives, and Giant Despair was brought down to the ground, but was very loath to die. He struggled hard, and had, as they say, as many lives as a cat; but Great-heart was his death, for he left him not till he had severed his head from his shoulders.

Then they fell to demolishing Doubting Castle, and that, you know, might with ease be done, since Giant Despair was dead. They were seven days in destroying of that; and in it of pilgrims, they found one Mr. Despondency, almost starved to death, and one Much-afraid, his daughter: these two they saved alive. But it would have made you wonder to have seen the dead bodies that lay here and there in the castle-yard, and how full of dead men's bones the dungeon was.

When Mr. Great-heart and his companions had performed this great work they took Mr. Despondency and his daughter Much-afraid into their care; for they were honest people, though they were prisoners in Doubting Castle to that tyrant Giant Despair.

They therefore, I say, took with them the head of the giant (for his body they had buried under a heap of stones), and down to the road and to their companions they came, and showed them what they had done. Now, when Feeble-mind and Ready-to-halt saw that it was the head of Giant Despair indeed, they were very jocund and merry. Now, Christiana, if need was, could play upon the viol, and her daughter Mercy upon the lute; so, since they were so merry disposed, she played them a lesson, and Ready-to-halt would dance. So he took Despondency's daughter Much-afraid by the hand, and to dancing they went in the road. True, he could not dance without one crutch in his hand; but I promise you he footed it well; also the girl was to be commended, for she answered the music handsomely.

As for Mr. Despondency, the music was not so much to him; he was for feeding rather than dancing, for that he was almost starved. So Christiana gave him some of her bottle of spirits for present relief, and then prepared him something to eat; and in a little time the old gentleman came to himself, and began to be finely revived.

Now, I saw in my dream, when all these things were finished, Mr. Great-heart took the head of Giant Despair, and set it upon a pole by the highway-side, right over against the pillar that Christian erected for a caution to pilgrims that came after to take heed of entering into his grounds. Then he writ under it, upon a marble stone, these verses following:

> "This is the head of him whose name only
> In former times did pilgrims terrify;
> His castle's down, and Diffidence his wife
> Brave Mr. Great-heart has bereft of life.
> Despondency, his daughter Much-afraid,
> Great-heart for them also the man has played.
> Who hereof doubts, if he'll but cast his eye
> Up hither, may his scruples satisfy.
> This head also, when doubting cripples dance,
> Doth show from fears they have deliverance."

THE DELECTABLE MOUNTAINS

When these men had thus bravely showed themselves against Doubting Castle, and had slain Giant Despair, they went forward, and went on till they came to the Delectable Mountains, where Christian and Hopeful refreshed themselves with the varieties of the place. They also acquainted themselves with the shepherds there, who welcomed them, as they had done Christian before, unto the Delectable Mountains.

Now, the shepherds seeing so great a train follow Mr. Great-heart (for with him they were well acquainted), they said unto him, "Good sir, you have got a goodly company here; pray, where did you find all these?"

Then Mr. Great-heart replied:

> "First, here is Christiana and her train,
> Her sons, and her sons' wives, who, like the
>   wain,
> Keep by the pole, and do by compass steer
> From sin to grace; else they had not been
>   here.
> Next, here's old Honest come on pilgrimage,
> Ready-to-halt too, who I dare engage
> True-hearted is, and so is Feeble-mind,
> Who willing was not to be left behind.
> Despondency, good man, is coming after
> And so also is Much-afraid his daughter.
> May we have entertainment here, or must
> We farther go? Let's know whereon to
>   trust."

THE SHEPHERDS ENTERTAIN

Then said the shepherds, "This is a comfortable company. You are welcome to us, for we have care for the feeble, as well as for the strong. Our Prince has an eye to what is done, to the least of these; therefore weakness must not be a block to our entertainment." So they had them to the palace door, and then said unto them, "Come in, Mr. Feeble-mind; come in, Mr. Ready-to-halt; come in, Mr. Despondency and Mrs. Much-afraid, his daughter. These, Mr. Great-heart," said the shepherds to the guide, "we call in by name, for that they are most subject to draw back; but as for you and the rest that are strong, we leave you to your wonted liberty."

Then said Mr. Great-heart, "This day I see that grace doth shine in your faces, and that you are my Lord's shepherds indeed; for that you have not pushed these helpless ones neither with side nor shoulder, but have rather strewed their way into the palace with flowers, as you should."

So the feeble and weak went in, and Mr. Great-heart

and the rest did follow. When they were also sat down, the shepherds said to those of the weaker sort, "What is it that you would have? for," said they, "all things must be managed here for the supporting of the weak, as well as the warning of the unruly." So they made them a feast of things easy of digestion, and that were pleasant to the palate, and nourishing; the which when they had received, they went to their rest, each one separately unto his proper place.

When morning was come, because the mountains were nigh and the day clear, and because it was the custom of the shepherds to show the pilgrims before their departure some rarities; therefore, after they were ready and had refreshed themselves, the shepherds took them out into the fields, and showed them first what they had showed to Christian before.

Then they had them to some new places. The first was to Mount Marvel, where they looked, and beheld a man at a distance that tumbled the hills about with words. Then they asked the shepherds what that should mean. So they told them that that man was the son of Mr. Great-grace of whom you read in the first part of the records of the Pilgrim's Progress; and he is set down there to teach the pilgrims how to believe, or to tumble out of their ways what difficulties they should meet with, by faith. Then said Mr. Great-heart, "I know him; he is a man above many."

Then they had them to another place, called Mount Innocent; and there they saw a man clothed all in white, and two men, Prejudice and Ill-will, continually casting dirt upon them. Now, behold, the dirt, whatsoever they cast at him, would in a little time fall off again, and his garment would look as clear as if no dirt had been cast thereat. Then said the pilgrims, "What means this?"

The shepherds answered, "This man is named Godly-man, and this garment is to show the innocency of his life. Now, those that throw dirt at him are such as hate his well-doing; but, as you see, the dirt will not stick upon his clothes: so it shall be with him that liveth truly innocently in the world. Whoever they be that would make such men dirty, they labor all in vain; for God, by that a little time is spent, will cause that their innocence shall break forth as the light, and their righteousness as the noon-day."

Then they took them, and had them to Mount Charity, where they showed them a man that had a bundle of cloth lying before him, out of which he cut coats and garments for the poor that stood about him; yet his bundle or roll of cloth was never the less.

Then said they, "What should this be?"

"This is," said the shepherds, "to show you that he who has a heart to give of his labor to the poor, shall never want wherewithal. He that watereth shall be watered himself. And the cake that the widow gave to the prophet did not cause that she had ever the less in her barrel."

They had them also to a place where they saw one Fool, and one Want-wit, washing of an Ethiopian, with intention to make him white; but the more they washed him the blacker he was. Then they asked the shepherds what that should mean. So they told them, saying, "Thus shall it be with the vile person: all means used to get such an one a good name, shall, in the end tend but to make him more abominable. Thus it was with the Pharisees, and so shall it be with all pretenders to religion."

Then said Mercy, the wife of Matthew, to Christiana her mother, "Mother, I would, if it might be, see the hole in the hill, or that commonly called the By-way to Hell." So her mother brake her mind to the shepherds. Then they went to the door: it was in the side of a hill; and they opened it, and bid Mercy hearken awhile. So she hearkened, and heard one saying, "Cursed be my father for holding of my feet back from the way of peace and life." And another said, "Oh that I had been torn in pieces before I had, to save my life, lost my soul!" And another said, "If I were to live again, how would I deny myself rather than come to this place!" Then there was as if the very earth groaned and quaked under the feet of this young woman for fear; so she looked white, and came trembling away, saying, "Blessed be he and she that are delivered from this place."

THE GREAT GLASS

Now, when the shepherds had shown them all these things, then they had them back to the palace, and entertained them with what the house would afford. But Mercy longed for something that she saw there, but was ashamed to ask. Her mother-in-law then asked her what she ailed, for she looked as one not well. Then said Mercy, "There is a looking-glass hangs up in the dining-room, off of which I cannot take my mind; if, therefore, I have it not, I think I shall be unhappy." Then said her mother, "I will mention thy wants to the shepherds, and they will not deny it thee." But she said, "I am ashamed that these men should know that I longed." "Nay, my daughter," said she, "it is no shame, but a virtue, to long for such a thing as that." So Mercy said, "Then, mother, if you please, ask the shepherds if they are willing to sell it."

Now, the glass was one of a thousand. It would present a man, one way, with his own features exactly; and, turn it but another way, and it would show one the very face and likeness of the Prince of pilgrims Himself. Yea, I have talked with them that can tell, and they have said that they have seen the very crown of thorns upon His head, by looking in that glass; they have therein also seen the holes in His hands, in His feet, and in His side. Yea, such an excellency is there in this glass, that it will show Him to one where they have a mind to see Him, whether living or dead, whether in earth or in heaven, whether in a state of lowliness or in His kingliness, whether coming to suffer or coming to reign.

Christiana, therefore went to the shepherds apart—(now, the names of the shepherds were Knowledge, Experience, Watchful, and Sincere),—and said unto them, "There is one of my daughters, that I think doth long for something that she hath seen in this house, and she thinks that she shall be unhappy if she should by you be denied."

EXPERIENCE. Call her, call her; she shall assuredly have what we can help her to. So they called her, and said to her, "Mercy, what is that thing thou wouldst have?" Then she blushed, and said, "The great glass that hangs up in the dining-room." So Sincere ran and fetched it; and with a joyful consent it was given her. Then she bowed her head, and gave thanks, and said, "By this I know that I have obtained favor in your eyes."

They also gave to the other young women such things as they desired, and to their husbands great praise for that they joined with Great-heart to the slaying of Giant Despair and the destroying of Doubting Castle.

About Christiana's neck the shepherds put a necklace, and so they did about the necks of her four daughters; also they put ear-rings in their ears, and jewels on their foreheads.

THEY LEAVE THE SHEPHERDS

When they were minded to go hence, they let them go in peace, but gave not to them those certain cautions which before were given to Christian and his companion. The reason was, for that these had Great-heart to be their guide, who was one that was well acquainted with things, and so could give them their cautions more seasonably; that is, even then when the danger was nigh the approaching. What cautions Christian and his companion had received of the shepherds, they had also lost by that the time was come that they had need to put them in practice. Wherefore, here was the advantage that this company had over the other.

From hence they went on singing, and they said:

> "Behold, how fitly are the stages set,
> For their relief that pilgrims are become,
> And how they us receive without one let
> That make the other life our mark and home!
> "What novelties they have, to us they give,
> That we, though pilgrims, joyful lives may live;
> They do upon us, too, such things bestow,
> That show we pilgrims are, where'er we go."

When they were gone from the shepherds, they quickly came to the place where Christian met with one Turn-away, that dwelt in the town of Apostasy. Wherefore of him Mr. Great-heart, their guide, did now put them in mind, saying, "This is the place where Christian met with one Turn-away, who carried with him the character of his rebellion at his back. And this I have to say concerning this man: he would hearken to no counsel, but, once falling, persuasion could not stop him. When he came to the place where the Cross and the sepulchre were, he did meet with one that bid him look there; but he gnashed with his teeth, and stamped, and said he was resolved to go back to his own town. Before he came to the gate, he met with Evangelist, who offered to lay hands on him, to turn him into the way again. But this Turn-away resisted him; and having done much harm unto him, he got away over the wall, and so escaped his hand."

MEET VALIANT FOR TRUTH

Then they went on; and just at the place where Little-Faith formerly was robbed, there stood a man with his sword drawn, and his face all bloody. Then said Mr. Great-heart, "Who art thou?" The man made answer, saying, "I am one whose name is Valiant-for-truth. I am a pilgrim, and am going to the Celestial City. Now, as I was in my way, there were three men did beset me, and propounded unto me these three things: 1. Whether I would become one of them? 2. Or go back to the place from whence I came? 3. Or die upon the place? To the first I answered, I had been a true man a long season, and therefore it could not be expected that I should now cast in my lot with thieves. Then they demanded what I should say to the second. So I told them that the place from whence I came, had I not found it unsatisfactory I had not forsaken at all; but, finding it altogether unsuitable to me, and very unprofitable for me, I forsook it for this way. Then they asked me what I said to the third. And I told them my life cost more dear far than that I should lightly give it away. Besides you have nothing to do thus to put things to my choice, wherefore at your peril be it if you meddle. Then these three, to wit, Wild-head, Inconsiderate, and Pragmatic, drew their weapons upon me, and I also drew upon them. So we fell to it, one against three, for the space of above three hours. They have left upon me, as you see, some of the marks of their valor, and have also carried away with them some of mine. They are but just now gone: I suppose they might, as the saying is, hear your horse dash, and so they betook them to flight."

HOW VALIANT BORE HIMSELF

GREAT. But here was great odds, three against one.

VALIANT. 'Tis true; but little or more are nothing to him that has the truth on his side. "Though an host should encamp against me," said one, "my heart shall not fear: though war should rise against me, in this will I be confident. Besides," said he, "I have read in some records that one man has fought an army; and how many did Samson slay with the jaw-bone of an ass?"

GREAT. Then said the guide, "Why did you not cry out, that some might have come in for your succor?"

VALIANT. So I did, to my King, who, I knew, could hear me, and afford invisible help; and that was sufficient for me.

GREAT. Then said Great-heart to Mr. Valiant-for-truth, "Thou hast worthily behaved thyself. Let me see thy sword." So he showed it him. When he had taken it in his hand, and looked thereon a while, he said, "Ha! it is a right Jerusalem blade."

VALIANT. It is so. Let a man have one of these blades, with a hand to wield it and skill to use it, and he may venture upon an angel with it. He need not fear its holding, if he can but tell how to lay on. Its edges will never blunt. It will cut flesh and bones, and soul and spirit, and all.

GREAT. But you fought a great while. I wonder you were not weary.

VALIANT. I fought till my sword did cleave to my hand; and when they were joined together, as if a sword grew out of my arm, and when the blood ran through my fingers, then I fought with most courage.

GREAT. Thou hast done well; thou hast resisted unto blood, striving against sin. Thou shalt abide by us, come in and go out with us, for we are thy companions.

Then they took him, washed his wounds, and gave him of what they had, to refresh him; and so they went on together.

Now, as they went on, because Mr. Great-heart was delighted in him (for he loved one greatly that he found to be a man of his own sort), and because there were in company them that were feeble and weak, therefore he questioned with him about many things; as, first, what countryman he was.

VALIANT. I am of Dark-land; for there I was born, and there my father and mother are still.

GREAT. "Dark-land!" said the guide; "doth not that lie upon the same coast with the City of Destruction?"

VALIANT. Yes, it doth. Now, that which caused me to come on pilgrimage was this. We had one Mr. Tell-true come into our parts, and he told it about what Christian had done, that went from the City of Destruction; namely, how he had forsaken his wife and children, and had betaken himself to a pilgrim's life. It was also reported, and believed, how he had killed a serpent that did come out to resist him in his journey; and how he got through to whither he intended. It was also told what welcome he had at all his Lord's lodgings, specially when he came to the gates of the Celestial City; "For there," said the man, "he was received with sound of trumpet by a company of Shining Ones." He told also how all the bells in the City did ring for joy at his entering in, and what golden garments he was clothed with; with many other things that now I shall forbear to relate. In a word, that man so told the story of Christian and his travels, that my heart fell into a burning haste to be gone after him; nor could father or mother stay me. So I got from them, and am come thus far on my way.

GREAT. You came in at the gate, did you not?

VALIANT. Yes, yes; for the same man also told us, that all would be nothing if we did not begin to enter this way at the gate.

GREAT. "Look you," said the guide to Christiana, "the pilgrimage of your husband, with what he has gotten thereby, is spread abroad far and near."

VALIANT. Why, is this Christian's wife?

GREAT. Yes, that it is, and these also are his four sons.

VALIANT. What! and going on pilgrimage too?

GREAT. Yes, verily, they are following after.

VALIANT. It glads me at heart. Good man, how joyful will he be when he shall see them that would not go with him, yet to enter after him in at the gates into the City!

GREAT. Without doubt it will be a comfort to him; for, next to the joy of seeing himself there, it will be a joy to meet there his wife and children.

VALIANT. But, now you are upon that, pray let me hear your opinion about it. Some make a question whether we shall know one another when we are there.

VALIANT'S OBSTACLES

GREAT. Do they think they shall know themselves, then? or that they shall rejoice to see themselves in that happiness? And if they think they shall know and do this, why not know others, and rejoice in their welfare also? Again, since relations are our second self, though that state will cease there, yet why may it not be wisely concluded that we shall be more glad to see them there than to see they are wanting?

VALIANT. Well, I perceive whereabouts you are as to this. Have you any more things to ask me about my beginning to come on pilgrimage?

GREAT. Yes. Were your father and mother willing that you should become a pilgrim?

VALIANT. Oh, no; they used all means imaginable to persuade me to stay at home.

GREAT. Why, what could they say against it?

VALIANT. They said it was an idle life; and, if I myself were not inclined to sloth and laziness, I would never favor a pilgrim's condition.

GREAT. And what did they say else?

VALIANT. Why, they told me that it was a dangerous way: "Yea, the most dangerous way in the world," said they, "is that which the pilgrims go."

GREAT. Did they show you wherein this way is so dangerous?
VALIANT. Yes; and that in many particulars.
GREAT. Name some of them.

VALIANT'S DISCOURAGEMENTS

VALIANT. They told me of the Slough of Despond, where
Christian was well-nigh smothered. They told me that
there were archers standing ready in Beelzebub's castle
to shoot them who should knock at the wicket-gate for
entrance. They told me also of the wood and dark
mountains of the Hill Difficulty; of the lions; and also
of the three giants, Bloody-man, Maul, and Slay-good.
They said moreover that there was a foul fiend haunted
the Valley of Humiliation, and that Christian was by him
almost bereft of life. "Besides," said they, "you must go
over the Valley of the Shadow of Death, where the
hobgoblins are, where the light is darkness, where
the way is full of snares, pits, traps, and gins." They told
me also of Giant Despair, of Doubting Castle, and of the
ruin that the pilgrims met with there. Further, they said
I must go over the Enchanted Ground, which was
dangerous; and that, after all this, I should find a river,
over which I should find no bridge, and that that river
did lie betwixt me and the Celestial Country.
GREAT. And was this all?
VALIANT. No. They also told me that this way was full of
deceivers, and of persons that laid wait there to turn
good men out of the path.
GREAT. But how did they make that out?
VALIANT. They told me that Mr. Worldly Wiseman did there
lie in wait to deceive. They also said that there were
Formality and Hypocrisy continually on the road. They
said also that By-ends, Talkative, or Demas would go
near to gather me up; that the Flatterer would catch me

in his net; or that, with green-headed Ignorance, I would presume to go on to the gate, from whence he was sent back to the hole that was in the side of the hill, and made to go the by-way to hell.

GREAT. I promise you, this was enough to discourage you; but did they make an end here?

VALIANT. No stay. They told me also of many that had tried that way of old, and that had gone a great way therein, to see if they could find something of the glory there that so many had so much talked of from time to time; and how they came back again, and befooled themselves for setting a foot out of doors in that path, to the satisfaction of all the country. And they named several that did so, as Obstinate and Pliable, Mistrust and Timorous, Turn-away and old Atheist; with several more, who, they said, had some of them gone far to see what they could find, but not one of them found so much advantage by going as amounted to the weight of a feather.

GREAT. Said they anything more to discourage you?

VALIANT. Yes; they told me of one Mr. Fearing, who was a pilgrim, and how he found this way so solitary, that he never had a comfortable hour therein; also that Mr. Despondency had like to have been starved therein; yea, and also (which I had almost forgot) that Christian himself, about whom there had been such a noise, after all his ventures for a celestial crown, was certainly drowned in the Black River, and never went a foot farther, however it was smothered up.

GREAT. And did none of these things discourage you?

VALIANT. No; they seemed but as so many nothings to me.

GREAT. How came that about?

VALIANT. Why, I still believed what Mr. Tell-true had said; and that carried me beyond them all.

GREAT. Then this was your victory, even your faith.

VALIANT. It was so. I believed, and therefore came out, got

into the way, fought all that set themselves against me,
and, by believing, am come to this place.

> "Who would true valor see,
> Let him come hither;
> One here will constant be,Come wind, come
>   weather;
> There's no discouragement
> Shall make him once relent
> His first avowed intent
> To be a pilgrim.
> "Whoso beset him round
> With dismal stories,
> Do but themselves confound—
> His strength the more is.
> No lion can him fright;
> He'll with a giant fight,
> But he will have a right
> To be a pilgrim.
> "Hobgoblin nor foul fiend
> Can daunt his spirit;
> He knows he at the end
> Shall life inherit.
> Then, fancies fly away,
> He'll fear not what men say;
> He'll labor night and day
> To be a pilgrim."

CHAPTER 9

The Enchanted Ground

By this time they were got to the Enchanted Ground, where the air naturally tended to make one drowsy. And that place was all grown over with briers and thorns, excepting here and there, where was an enchanted arbor, upon which if a man sits, or in which if a man sleeps, it is a question, say some, whether ever he shall rise or wake again in this world. Over this forest, therefore, they went, both one and another; and Mr. Great-heart went before, for that he was the guide, and Mr. Valiant-for-truth came behind, being rear-guard, for fear lest peradventure some fiend, or dragon, or giant, or thief, should fall upon their rear, and so do mischief. They went on here, each man with his sword drawn in his hand, for they knew it was a dangerous place. Also they cheered up one another as well as they could. Feeble-mind, Mr. Great-heart commanded, should come up after him; and Mr. Despondency was under the eye of Mr. Valiant.

Now, they had not gone far, but a great mist and darkness fell upon them all, so that they could scarce, for a great while, see the one the other; wherefore they were forced, for some time, to feel for one another by words; for they walked not by sight. But any one must think that here was but sorry going for the best of them all; but how much worse for the women and children, who both of feet and heart were but tender! Yet so it was, that through the encouraging words of him that led in the front, they made a pretty good shift to wag along.

The way also was here very wearisome through dirt and slabbiness. Nor was there on all this ground so much as one inn or victualling-house, therein to refresh the feebler sort. Here, therefore, was grunting, and puffing and sighing. While one tumbleth over a brush, another sticks fast in the dirt; and the children, some of them, lost their shoes in the mire. While one cries out, "I am down!" and another, "Ho! where are you?" and a third, "The bushes have got such fast hold on me, I think I cannot get away from them."

Then they came at an arbor, warm, and promising much refreshing to the pilgrims; for it was finely wrought above head, beautified with greens, furnished with benches and settles. It also had in it a soft couch, whereon the weary might lean. This, you must think, all things considered, was tempting; for the pilgrims already began to be foiled with the badness of the way; but there was not one of them that made so much as a motion to stop there. Yea, for aught I could perceive, they continually gave so good heed to the advice of their guide, and he did so faithfully tell them of dangers, and of the nature of dangers when they were at them, that usually, when they were nearest to them, they did most pluck up their spirits, and hearten one another to deny the flesh. This arbor was called "The Slothful's Friend," on purpose to allure, if it might be, some of the pilgrims there to take up their rest when weary.

I saw then in my dream, that they went on in this their solitary ground, till they came to a place at which a man is apt to lose his way. Now, though when it was light their guide could well enough tell how to miss those ways that led wrong, yet, in the dark, he was put to a stand. But he had in his pocket a map of all ways leading to or from the Celestial City; wherefore he struck a light (for he also never goes without his tinder-box), and takes a view of his book or map, which bids him be careful in that place to turn to the right-hand way. And had he not here been careful to look in his map, they had, in all probability been smothered in the mud; for, just a little before them, and that at the end of the cleanest way too, was a pit, none knows how deep, full of nothing but mud, there made on purpose to destroy the pilgrims in.

Then thought I with myself, "Who that goeth on pilgrimage but would have one of those maps about him, that he may look, when he is at a stand, which is the way he must take?"

They went on then in this Enchanted Ground till they came to where was another arbor, and it was built by the highway-side. And in that arbor there lay two men, whose names were Heedless and Too-bold. These two went thus far on pilgrimage; but here, being wearied with their journey, they sat down to rest themselves, and so fell fast asleep. When the pilgrims saw them, they stood still, and shook their heads; for they knew that the sleepers were in a pitiful case. Then they consulted what to do,—whether to go on, and leave them in their sleep, or to step to them, and try to awake them. So they concluded to go to them and wake them; that is, if they could; but with this caution, namely, to take heed that themselves did not sit down nor embrace the offered benefit of that arbor.

So they went in and spake to the men, and called each one by his name (for the guide, it seems, did know them); but there was no voice or answer. Then the guide did shake them, and do what he could to disturb them. Then said one of them, "I will pay you when I take my money." At which the guide shook his head. "I will fight so long as I can hold my sword in my hand," said the other. At that, one of the children laughed.

THE LAND OF BEULAH

Then said Christiana, "What is the meaning of this?" The guide said, "They talk in their sleep. If you strike them, beat them, or whatever else you do to them, they will answer you after this fashion; or, as one of them said in old time, when the waves of the sea did beat upon him, and he slept as one upon the mast of a ship, 'When shall I awake? I will seek it yet again.' You know, when men talk in their sleep, they say anything, but their words are not governed either by faith or reason. There is an unsuitableness in their words now, as there was before betwixt their going on pilgrimage and sitting down there. This, then, is the mischief of it: when heedless ones go on pilgrimage, 'tis twenty to one but they are served thus. For this Enchanted Ground is one of the last refuges that the enemy to pilgrims has; wherefore, it is, as you see, placed almost at the end of the way, and so it standeth against us with the more advantage. For when, thinks the enemy, will these fools be so desirous to sit down as when they are weary? and when so like to be weary as when almost at their journey's end? Therefore it is, I say, that the Enchanted Ground is placed so near to the Land of Beulah, and so near the end of their race. Wherefore, let pilgrims look to themselves, lest it happen to them as it has done to these, that, as you see, are fallen asleep, and none can wake them."

Then the pilgrims desired, with trembling, to go forward; only they prayed their guide to strike a light, that they might go the rest of their way by the help of the light of a lantern. So he struck a light, and they went by the help of that through the rest of this way, though the darkness was very great. But the children began to be sorely weary; and they cried out to Him that loveth pilgrims to make their way more comfortable. So, by that they had gone a little farther, a wind arose that drove away the fog; so the air became more clear. Yet they were not off, by much, of the Enchanted Ground; only now they could see one another better, and the way wherein they should walk.

Now, when they were almost at the end of this ground, they perceived that a little before them was a solemn noise, as of one that was much concerned. So they went on, and looked before them; and behold, they saw, as they thought, a man upon his knees, with hands and eyes lift up, and speaking, as they thought, earnestly to One that was above. They drew nigh, but could not tell what he said; so they went softly till he had done. When he had done, he got up, and began to run towards the Celestial City.

Then Mr. Great-heart called after him, saying, "So-ho, friend! let us have your company, if you go, as I suppose you do, to the Celestial City."

So the man stopped, and they came up to him. But, as soon as Mr. Honest saw him, he said, "I know this man."

Then said Mr. Valiant-for-truth, "Prithee, who is it?"

"It is one," said he, "that comes from whereabout I dwelt. His name is Stand-fast; he is certainly a right good pilgrim."

So they came up one to another. And presently Stand-fast said to old Honest, "Ho, father Honest, are you there?"

"Ay," said he, "that I am, as sure as you are there."

HEEDLESS AND TOO-BOLD

"Right glad am I," said Mr. Stand-fast, "that I have found you on this road."

"And as glad am I," said the other, "that I espied you upon your knees."

Then Mr. Stand-fast blushed, and said, "But why? did you see me?"

"Yes, that I did," quoth the other, "and with my heart was glad at the sight."

"Why, what did you think?" said Stand-fast.

"Think!" said old Honest; "what should I think? I

thought we had an honest man upon the road, and therefore should have his company by-and-by."

"If you thought not amiss," said Stand-fast, "how happy am I! But, if I be not as I should, I alone must bear it."

"That is true," said the other; "but your fear doth further show me that things are right betwixt the Prince of pilgrims and your soul; for He saith, 'Blessed is the man that feareth always.'"

VALIANT. Well, but, brother, I pray thee, tell us what was it that was the cause of thy being upon thy knees even now: was it for that some special mercy laid upon thee, the need of prayer, or how?

STAND. Why, we are, as you see, upon the Enchanted Ground; and as I was coming along, I was musing with myself of what a dangerous road the road in this place was, and how many that had come even thus far on pilgrimage, had here been stopped and been destroyed. I thought also of the manner of the death with which this place destroyeth men. Those that die here die of no violent, painful disease: the death which such die is not grievous to them. For he that goeth away in such a sleep, begins that journey with desire and pleasure. Yea, such sink into the will of that disease.

HON. Then Mr. Honest, interrupting of him, said, "Did you see the two men asleep in the arbor?"

STAND-FAST REPULSES MADAM

STAND. Ay, ay, I saw Heedless and Too-bold there; and, for aught I know, there they will lie till they rot. But let me go on in my tale. As I was thus musing, as I said, there was one in very pleasant attire, but old, who presented herself to me, and offered me three things; to wit, her body, her purse, and her bed. Now, the truth is, I was both aweary and sleepy; I am also as poor as an owlet, and that, perhaps, the witch knew. Well, I repulsed her once or twice; but she put by my repulses, and smiled. Then I began to be angry; but she mattered that nothing at all. Then she made offers again, and said, if I would be ruled by her, she would make me great and happy. "For," said she, "I am the mistress of the world, and men are made happy by me." Then I asked her name, and she told me it was Madam Bubble. This set me farther from her; but she still followed me with enticements. Then I betook me, as you saw, to my knees; and, with hands lift up, and cries, I prayed to Him that had said He would help. So, just as you came up, the gentlewoman went her way. Then I continued to give thanks for this my great deliverance; for I verily believe she intended no good, but rather sought to make stop of me in my journey.

HON. Without doubt her designs were bad. But stay: now you talk of her, methinks I either have seen her, or have read some story of her.

STAND. Perhaps you have done both.

HON. Madam Bubble? Is she not a tall, comely dame, somewhat of a swarthy complexion?

STAND. Right, you hit it: she is just such a one.

HON. Does she not speak very smoothly, and give you a smile at the end of a sentence?

STAND. You fall right upon it again, for these are her very actions.

HON. Doth she not wear a great purse by her side, and is not her hand often in it, fingering her money, as if that was her heart's delight?

STAND. 'Tis just so. Had she stood by all this while, you could not more amply have set her forth before me, nor have better described her features.

HON. Then he that drew her picture was a good artist, and he that wrote of her said true.

MADAM BUBBLE'S INFLUENCE

GREAT. This woman is a witch, and it is by virtue of her
witchcraft that this ground is enchanted. Whoever doth
lay his head down in her lap, had as good lay it down
upon that block over which the axe doth hang; and
whoever lay their eyes upon her beauty, are accounted
the enemies of God. This is she that maintaineth in their
splendor all those that are the enemies of pilgrims. Yea,
this is she that hath bought off many a man from a
pilgrim's life. She is a great gossiper: she is always, both
she and her daughters, at one pilgrim's heels or other;
now commanding, and then preferring the excellences
of this life. She is a bold and impudent creature; she will
talk with any man. She always laugheth poor pilgrims to
scorn, but highly commends the rich. If there be one
cunning to get money in a place, she will speak well of
him from house to house. She loveth banqueting and
feasting mainly well; she is always at one full table or
another. She has given it out in some places that she is
a goddess, and therefore some do worship her. She has
her times and open places of cheating; and she will say
and avow it, that none can show a good comparable to
hers. She promiseth to dwell with children's children, if
they will but love her and make much of her. She will
cast out of her purse gold like dust, in some places and
to some persons. She loves to be sought after, spoken
well of, and to lie in the bosoms of men. She is never
weary of praising her gifts and she loves them most that
think best of her. She will promise, to some, crowns and
kingdoms, if they will but take her advice; yet many hath
she brought to the halter, and ten thousand times more
to hell.

STAND. "Oh," said Mr. Stand-fast, "what a mercy it is that I
did resist her! for whither might she have drawn me?"

GREAT. Whither! nay, none but God knows whither; but in
general, to be sure, she would have drawn thee into many
foolish and hurtful lusts, which drown men in destruction and ruin. 'Twas she that set Absalom against his
father, and Jeroboam against his master. 'Twas she that
persuaded Judas to sell his Lord, and that prevailed with
Demas to forsake the godly pilgrim's life. None can tell
of the mischief that she doth. She makes variance betwixt
rulers and subjects, betwixt parents and children, betwixt
neighbor and neighbor, betwixt a man and his wife,
betwixt a man and himself, betwixt the flesh and the
heart. Wherefore, good Master Stand-fast, be as your
name is, and when you have done all, stand.

At this course there was among the pilgrims a mixture of joy
and trembling; but at length they brake out, and sang:

"What danger is the pilgrim in!
How many are his foes!
How many ways there are to sin No living
    mortal knows.
"Some of the ditch shy are, yet can
Lie tumbling in the mire;
Some, though they shun the frying-pan,
Do leap into the fire."

CHAPTER 10

The Pilgrims at Home

After this, I beheld until they were come unto the Land of Beulah, where the sun shineth night and day. Here, because they were weary, they betook themselves awhile to rest. And because this country was common for pilgrims, and because the orchards and vineyards that were here belong to the King of the Celestial Country, therefore they were permitted to make bold with any of His things. But a little while soon refreshed them here; for the bells did so ring, and the trumpets continually sound so melodiously, that they could not sleep and yet they received as much refreshing as if they had slept their sleep never so soundly. Here also the noise of them that walked in the streets was, "More pilgrims are come to town!" And another would answer, saying, "And so many went over the water, and were let in at the golden gates, to-day!" They would cry again, "There is now a legion of Shining Ones just come to town, by which we know that there are more pilgrims upon the road; for here they come to wait for them, and comfort them after all their sorrow!" Then the pilgrims got up, and walked to and fro. But how were their ears now filled with heavenly voices, and their eyes delighted with celestial visions! In this land they heard nothing, saw nothing, felt nothing, smelt nothing, tasted nothing, that was offensive to their stomach or mind; only when they tasted of the water of the river over which they were to go, they thought that it tasted a little bitterish to the palate, but it proved sweeter when it was down.

In this place there was a record kept of the names of them that had been pilgrims of old, and a history of all the famous acts that they had done. It was here also much spoken of, how the river to some had had its flowings, and what ebbings it had had while others have gone over. It has been in a manner dry for some, while it has overflowed its banks for others.

In this place, the children of the town would go into the King's gardens, and gather nosegays for the pilgrims, and bring them to them with much affection. Here also grew camphire, with spikenard, and saffron, calamus, and cinnamon, with all the trees of frankincense, myrrh, and aloes, with all chief spices. With these the pilgrims' chambers were perfumed while they stayed here; and with these were their bodies anointed, to prepare them to go over the river, when the time appointed was come.

CHRISTIANA RECEIVES MESSAGE

Now, while they lay here, and waited for the good hour, there was a noise in the town that there was a messenger come from the Celestial City with matter of great importance to one Christiana, the wife of Christian the pilgrim. So inquiry was made for her, and the house was found out where she was. So the messenger presented her with a letter; the contents whereof were, "Hail, good woman! I bring thee tidings that the Master calleth for thee, and expecteth that thou shouldest stand in His presence, in clothes of everlasting life, within these ten days."

When he had read this letter to her, he gave her therewith a sure token that he was a true messenger, and was come

to bid her make haste to be gone. The token was an arrow, with a point sharpened with love, let easily into her heart, which by degrees wrought so effectually with her, that at the time appointed she must be gone.

When Christiana saw that her time was come, and that she was the first of this company that was to go over, she called for Mr. Great-heart, her guide, and told him how matters were. So he told her he was heartily glad of the news, and could have been glad had the post come for him. Then she bid that he should give advice how all things should be prepared for her journey. So he told her, saying, "Thus and thus it must be; and we that are left will accompany you to the river-side."

Then she called for her children, and gave them her blessing, and told them that she yet read with comfort the mark that was set in their foreheads, and was glad to see them with her there, and that they had kept their garments so white. Lastly, she gave to the poor that little she had, and commanded her sons and her daughters to be ready against the messenger should come for them.

When she had spoken these words to her guide and to her children, she called for Mr. Valiant-for-truth, and said unto him, "Sir, you have in all places shown yourself true-hearted. Be faithful unto death, and my King will give you a crown of life. I would also entreat you to have an eye to my children; and if at any time you see them faint, speak comfortably to them. For my daughters, my sons' wives, they have been faithful; and a fulfilling of the promise upon them will be their end." But she gave Mr. Stand-fast a ring.

Then she called for old Mr. Honest, and said of him, "Behold an Israelite indeed, in whom is no guile."

Then said he, "I wish you a fair day when you set out for Mount Zion, and shall be glad to see that you go over the river dry shod."

But she answered, "Come wet, come dry, I long to be

gone; for, however the weather is in my journey, I shall have time enough when I come there to sit down and rest me and dry me."

Then came in that good man, Mr. Ready-to-halt, to see her. So she said to him, "Thy travel hitherto has been with difficulty; but that will make thy rest the sweeter. But watch and be ready; for, at an hour when you think not, the messenger may come."

After him came in Mr. Despondency and his daughter Much-afraid; to whom she said, "You ought with thankfulness for ever to remember your deliverance from the hands of Giant Despair and out of Doubting Castle. The effect of that mercy is that you are brought with safety hither. Be ye watchful, and cast away fear; be sober, and hope to the end."

Then she said to Mr. Feeble-mind, "Thou wast delivered from the mouth of Giant Slay-good, that thou mightest live in the light of the living for ever, and see thy King with comfort. Only I advise thee to turn thee of thy aptness to fear and doubt of His goodness, before He sends for thee; lest thou shouldest, when He comes, be forced to stand before Him for that fault with blushing."

CHRISTIANA CROSSES THE RIVER

Now, the day drew on that Christiana must be gone. So the road was full of people to see her take her journey. But, behold, all the banks beyond the river were full of horses and chariots, which were come down from above to accompany her to the City gate. So she came forth and entered the river, with a beckon of farewell to those that followed her to the river-side. The last words that she was heard to say were, "I come, Lord, to be with Thee, and bless Thee!"

So her children and friends returned to their place, for that those that waited for Christiana had carried her out of their sight. So she went and called, and entered in at the gate

with all the tokens of joy that her husband Christian had done before her. At her departure her children wept. But Mr. Great-heart and Mr. Valiant played upon the well-tuned cymbal and harp for joy. So all departed to their respective places.

PILGRIMS RECEIVE MESSAGES

In process of time, there came a messenger to the town again, and his business was with Mr. Ready-to-halt. So he inquired him out, and said to him, "I am come to thee from Him whom thou hast loved and followed, though upon crutches; and my message is to tell thee, that He expects thee at His table, to sup with Him in His kingdom, the next day after Easter; wherefore prepare thyself for this journey." Then he also gave him a token that he was a true messenger, saying, "I have broken thy golden bowl and loosed thy silver cord."

After this Mr. Ready-to-halt called for his fellow-pilgrims, and told them, saying, "I am sent for, and God shall surely visit you also." So he desired Mr. Valiant to make his will. And because he had nothing to bequeath to them that should survive him but his crutches and his good wishes, therefore thus he said: "These crutches I bequeath to my son that shall tread in my steps, with a hundred warm wishes that he may prove better than I have done." Then he thanked Mr. Great-heart for his conduct and kindness, and so addressed himself to his journey. When he came to the brink of the river, he said, "Now I shall have no more need of these crutches, since yonder are chariots and horses for me to ride on." The last words he was heard to say were, "Welcome life!" So he went his way.

After this, Mr. Feeble-mind had tidings brought him, that the messenger sounded his horn at his chamber-door. Then he came in, and told him, saying, "I am come to tell thee that thy Master has need of thee, and that in a very little time thou must behold His face in brightness. And take this as a token of the truth of my message: 'Those that look out at the windows shall be darkened.'" Then Mr. Feeble-mind called for his friends, and told them what errand had been brought unto him, and what token he had received of the truth of the message. Then he said, "Since I have nothing to bequeath to any, to what purpose should I make a will? As for my feeble mind, that I will leave behind me, for that I shall have no need of in the place whither I go, nor is it worth bestowing upon the poorest pilgrim: wherefore, when I am gone, I desire that you, Mr. Valiant, would bury it in a dunghill." This done, and the day being come on which he was to depart, he entered the river as the rest. His last words were, "Hold out, faith and patience!" So he went over to the other side.

When days had many of them passed away, Mr. Despondency was sent for; for a messenger was come, and brought this message to him: "Trembling man, these are to summon thee to be ready with thy King by the next Lord's day, to shout for joy for thy deliverance from all thy doubtings. And," said the messenger, "that my message is true, take this for a proof." So he gave him the grasshopper to be a burden unto him.

Now, Mr. Despondency's daughter, whose name was Much-afraid, said when she heard what was done, that she would go with her father. Then Mr. Despondency said to his friends, "Myself and my daughter, you know what we have been, and how troublesomely we have behaved ourselves in every company. My will and my daughter's is, that our discouraged feelings and slavish fears be by no man received, from the day of our departure for ever; for I know that after my death they will offer themselves to others. For, to be plain with you, they are ghosts the which we entertained when we first began to be pilgrims, and could never shake them off after; and they will walk about and seek entertainment of the pilgrims; but, for our sakes, shut ye the doors upon them." When the time was come for them to depart, they went to the brink of the river. The last words of Mr. Despondency were, "Farewell, night! welcome, day!" His daughter went through the river singing, but none could understand what she said.

Then it came to pass a while after, that there was a messenger in the town that inquired for Mr. Honest. So he came to his house where he was, and delivered to his hand these lines: "Thou art commanded to be ready against this day seven-night, to present thyself before thy Lord at His Father's house. And for a token that my message is true, 'All thy daughters of music shall be brought low.'" Then Mr. Honest called for his friends, and said unto them, "I die, but shall make no will. As for my honesty, it shall go with me: let them that come after me be told this." When the day that he was to be gone was come, he prepared himself to go over the river. Now, the river at that time overflowed its banks in some places; but Mr. Honest in his lifetime had spoken to one Good-conscience to meet him there; the which also he did, and lent him his hand, and so helped him over. The last words of Mr. Honest were, "Grace reigns!" So he left the world.

THE FINAL SUMMONS

After this, it was noised abroad that Mr. Valiant-for-truth was taken with a summons by the same messenger as the other, and had this for a token that the summons was true, that his pitcher was broken at the fountain. When he understood it, he called for his friends, and told them of it. Then said he, "I am going to my Father's; and though with great difficulty I am got hither, yet now I do not repent me of all the trouble I have been at to arrive where I am. My sword I give to him that shall succeed me in my pilgrimage, and my courage and skill to him that can get it. My marks and scars I carry with me, to be a witness for me that I have fought His battles who now will be my rewarder." When the day that he must go hence was come, many accompanied him to the river-side, into which as he went he said, "Death, where is thy sting?" And, as he went down deeper, he said, "Grave, where is thy victory?" So he passed over, and all the trumpets sounded for him on the other side.

Then there came forth a summons for Mr. Stand-fast (this Mr. Stand-fast was he whom the pilgrims found upon his knees in the Enchanted Ground), for the messenger brought it him open in his hands; the contents thereof were, that he must prepare for a change of life, for his Master was not willing that he should be so far from Him any longer. At this Mr. Stand-fast was put into a muse.

"Nay," said the messenger, "you need not doubt the truth of my message, for here is a token of the truth thereof: 'Thy wheel is broken at the cistern.'"

Then he called to him Mr. Great-heart, who was their guide, and said unto him, "Sir, although it was not my hap to be much in your good company in the days of my pilgrimage, yet, since the time I knew you, you have been profitable to me. When I came from home, I left behind me a wife and five small children: let me entreat you at your return (for I know that you will go and return to your master's house, in hopes that you may yet be a conductor to more of the holy pilgrims), that you send to my family, and let them be acquainted with all that hath or shall happen unto me. Tell them moreover of my happy arrival to this place, and of the present and late blessed condition that I am in. Tell them also of Christian and Christiana his wife, and how she and her children came after her husband. Tell them also what a happy end she made, and whither she is gone. I have little or nothing to send to my family, unless it be my prayers and tears for them; of which it will suffice that you acquaint them, if peradventure they may prevail."

END OF THE PILGRIMAGE

When Mr. Stand-fast had thus set things in order, and the time being come for him to haste him away, he also went down to the river. Now, there was a great calm at that time in the river; wherefore Mr. Stand-fast, when he was about half-way in, stood a while, and talked to his companions that had waited upon him thither. And he said, "This river has been a terror to many; yea, the thoughts of it have also frighted me; but now methinks I stand easy; my foot is fixed upon that on which the feet of the priests that bare the ark of the covenant stood while Israel went over Jordan. The waters, indeed, are to the palate bitter, and to the stomach cold; yet the thought of what I am going to, and of the conduct that waits for me on the other side, doth lie as a glowing coal at my heart. I see myself now at the end of my journey; my toilsome days are ended. I am going to see that head which was crowned with thorns, and that face which was spit upon for me. I have formerly lived by hearsay and faith; but now I go where I shall live by sight, and shall be with Him in whose company I delight myself. I have loved to hear my Lord spoken of; and wherever I have seen the print of His shoe in the earth, there I have coveted to set my foot too. His name has been to me as a perfume box; yea, sweeter than all sweet smells. His voice to me has been most sweet, and His countenance I have more desired than they that have most desired the light of the sun. His Word I did use to gather for my food, and for medicine against my faintings. He has held me, and hath kept me from my sins; yea, my steps hath He strengthened in His way."

Now, while he was thus speaking, his countenance changed, his strong man bowed under him; and, after he had said, "Take me, for I come unto Thee!" he ceased to be seen of them.

But glorious it was to see how the open region was filled

with horses and chariots, with trumpeters and pipers, with singers and players on stringed instruments to welcome the pilgrims as they went up, and followed one another in at the beautiful gate of the City.

As for Christian's children, the four boys that Christiana brought with her, with their wives and children, I did not stay where I was till they were gone over. Also, since I came away, I heard one say that they were yet alive, and so would be for the help of the Church in that place where they were for a time.

Shall it be my lot to go that way again, I may give those that desire it an account of what I here am silent about: meantime I bid my reader

ADIEU.

THE LITTLE PILGRIM

The Story of a Little Girl Who Tried to Go on Pilgrimage

In a large old house, with two kind aunts,
The little Marian dwelt;
And a happy child she was, I ween,
For though at times she felt
That playmates would be better far
Than either birds or flowers,
Yet her kind old aunts, and story books,
Soothed many lonely hours.
Her favorite haunt, in the summer-time,
Was a large old apple-tree;
And oft amid the boughs she sat,
With her pet book on her knee.
The "Pilgrim's Progress" was its name,
And Marian loved it much;
It is, indeed, a glorious book,
There are not many such!
She read it in her little bed,
Beside the winter fire,
And in summer-time, in the apple-tree,
As though she would never tire.
But, unexplained, 'tis just the book
To puzzle the young brain;

And the poor child had no kind friend,
Its meaning to explain.
For though her aunts were very kind,
They were not overwise,
And only said, "Don't read so, child,
I'm sure you'll spoil your eyes."
But Marian still went reading on,
And visions strange and wild
Began to fill the little head
Of the lonely, dreaming child;
For she thought that Christian and his
        wife,
And all their children too,
Had left behind their pleasant home,
And done what she must do.
"I'll take my Bible," said the child,
"And seek the road to heaven;
I'll try to find the Wicket Gate,
And hope to be forgiven.
I wish my aunts would go with me,
But 'tis in vain to ask;
They are so deaf and rather lame,
They'd think it quite a task.
"No! I must go alone, I see,
So I'll not let them know;
Or, like poor Christian's friends, they'll say,
'My dear, you must not go.'
"But I must wait till some grand scheme
Can all their thoughts engage;
And then I'll leave my pleasant home,
And go on pilgrimage."
She had not waited long, before,
One fine autumnal day,
She saw the large old coach arrive,
To take her aunts away.

"We're going out to spend the day,"
The two old ladies said;
"We mean to visit Mrs. Blair—
Poor soul!—she's ill in bed.
"But, Marian, you must stay at home,
For the lady's ill, you see;
You can have your dinner, if you like,
In the large old apple-tree,
And play in the garden all the day,
Quite happy and content."
A few more parting words were said,
And off the ladies went.
The servants, too, were all engaged;
"The day is come at last,"
Said Marian, "but oh, I wish,
My pilgrimage was past."
She knelt beside the apple-tree,
And for God's assistance prayed;
Then, with her basket in her hand,
Forth tripped the little maid.
Behind the house where Marian dwelt,
Far off in the distance, lay
A high steep hill, which the sun at morn
Tinged with its earliest ray.
"Difficulty" was its rightful name,
The child had often thought;
Towards this hill she turned her steps,
With hopeful visions fraught.
The flowers seemed to welcome her,
'Twas a lovely autumn morn,
The little lark sang merrily,
Above the waving corn."
Ah, little lark, you sing," said she,
"On your early pilgrimage;
I, too, will sing, for pleasant thoughts

Should now my mind engage."
In clear, sweet strains she sang a hymn,
And tripped lightly on her way;
Until a pool of soft, thick mud
Across her pathway lay.
"This is the Slough of Despond," she cried,
But she bravely ventured through;
And safely reached the other side,
But she lost one little shoe.
On an old gray stone she sat her down,
To eat some fruit and bread;
Then took her little Bible out,
And a cheering psalm she read.
Then with fresh hope she journeyed on,
For many miles away;
And she reached the bottom of the hill,
Before the close of day.
She clambered up the steep ascent,
Though faint and weary, too;
But firmly did our Marian keep
Her purpose still in view.
"I'm glad, at least, the arbor's past,"
Said the little tired soul;
"I'm sure I should have sat me down
And lost my little roll!"
On the high hill-top she stands at last,
And our weary Pilgrim sees
A porter's lodge, of ample size,
Half hid by sheltering trees.
She clapped her hands with joy, and cried,
"Oh, there's the Wicket Gate,
And I must seek admittance there,
Before it is too late."
Gently she knocks—
'tis answered soon,

And at the open door
Stands a tall, stout man—
poor Marian felt
As she ne'er had felt before.
With tearful eyes, and trembling hand,
Flushed cheek, and anxious brow,
She said, "I hope you're Watchful, Sir,
I want Discretion now."
"Oh yes, I'm watchful," said the man,
"As a porter ought to be;
I s'pose you've lost your way, young Miss,
You've lost your shoe, I see.
"Missus," he cried to his wife within,
"Here's a child here, at the door,
You'll never see such a one again,
If you live to be fourscore.
She wants discretion, so she says,
Indeed I think 'tis true;
But I know some who want it more,
Who will not own they do."
"Go to the Hall," his wife replies,"
And take the child with you,
The ladies there are all so wise,
They'll soon know what to do."
The man complied, and led the child
Through many a flowery glade;
"Is that the Palace Beautiful?"
The little Pilgrim said.
"There, to the left, among the trees?
Why, Miss, 'tis mighty grand;
Call it a palace, if you please,
'Tis the finest in the land.
Now we be come to the fine old porch,
And this is the Marble Hall;
Here, little lady, you must stay,

While I the servants call."
Tired and sad he left the child,
But he quickly re-appeared,
And with him the lady of the house—
Poor Marian's heart was cheered.
"Sweet little girl," the lady said,
In accents soft and kind,"
I'm sure you sadly want some rest,
And rest you soon shall find."
To a room where three young ladies sat,
The child was quickly led;
"Piety, Prudence, and Charity,"
To herself she softly said.
"What is your name, my little dear?"
Said the eldest of the three,
Whom Marian, in her secret thought,
Had christened Piety.
"We'll send a servant to your friends,
How uneasy they must be!"
Admiringly she watched the child,
Who, indeed, was fair to see;
Around her bright and lovely face
Fell waves of auburn hair,
As modestly she told her name,
With whom she lived and where.
"How did you lose your way, my love?"
She gently raised her head;"
I do not think I've lost my way,"
The little Pilgrim said.
"This is the Palace Beautiful,
May I stay here to-night?"
They smiled and said, "We're glad our
        house
Finds favor in your sight:—
"Yes, gladly will we keep you here,

For many nights to come."
"Thank you," said Marian, "but I soon
Must seek my heavenly home.
The Valley of the Shadow of Death
Is near this house, I know"—
She stopped, for she saw, with great
    surprise,
Their tears began to flow.
She little thought the mourning dress,
Which all the ladies wore,
Was for one whom they had dearly loved,
And should see on earth no more.
Their brother had been called away,
Their brightest and their best;
No wonder, then, that Marian's words
Roused grief in every breast.
Sobs only for awhile were heard;
At length the ladies said,
"My, love, you have reminded us
Of our loved and early dead;
But this you could not know, my dear,
And it indeed is true;
We are all near to Death's dark door,
Even little girls like you."
"Yes," said the timid, trembling child,
"I know it must be so;
But, ma'am, I hope that Piety
May be with me when I go.
And will you show me your armory,
When you have time to spare?
I hope you have some small enough
For a little girl to wear."
No more she said, for Piety,
As Marian called her, cast
Her arms around the Pilgrim's neck,

The secret's out at last.
"You puzzled all," said Piety;
"But now, I see, you've read
A glorious book, which, unexplained,
Has turned your little head.
"Oh, dearly, when I was a child,
I loved that Pilgrim Tale;
But then mamma explained it well—
And if we can prevail
On your kind aunts to let you stay
Some time with us, my dear,
You shall read that book with my mamma,
And she will make it clear."
Now we'll return to Marian's home,
And see what's passing there.
The servants all had company,
And a merry group they were.
They had not missed our Pilgrim long,
For they knew she oft would play
In that old garden, with a book,
The whole of the livelong day.
"Betty," at last, said the housekeeper,
"Where can Miss Marian be?
Her dinner was in the basket packed,
But sure, she'll come in to tea!"
They sought her here, they sought her
        there,
But they could not find the child;
And her poor old aunts, when they came
        home,
With grief were almost wild.
The coachman and the footman too,
In different ways were sent;
But none thought of the narrow way
In which the Pilgrim went.

"Perhaps she followed us to town,"
Poor Aunt Rebecca said,
"I wish we had not left our home;
I fear the child is dead."
And to the town the coachman went,
For they knew not what to do;
And night drew on, when a country boy
Brought Marian's little shoe.
With the shoe in her hand, the housekeeper
Into the parlor ran,
"Oh, Mistress, here is all that's left
Of poor Miss Marian.
"It was found sticking in the mud,
Just above Harlem Chase;
I fear the poor child's perished there,
For 'tis a frightful place."
Then louder grew the ladies' grief;
But soon their hearts were cheered,
When a footman grand, with a note in his
            hand,
From the distant Hall appeared.
Aunt Ruth now read the note, and cried,
"Oh, sister, all is well!
The child is safe at Brookland Hall,
With Lady Arundel,
Who wants to keep her for a month;
Why, yes; I think she may—
Such friends as Lady Arundel
Are not met with every day.
"Our compliments, and thanks to her,
When you return, young man;
We'll call to-morrow at the Hall,
And see Miss Marian."
Then came a burst of grateful joy,

That could not be suppressed,
And, with thankful hearts and many tears,
The ladies went to rest.
We'll take a peep at our Marian now,
There in her bed lies she;
How blissful were her dreams that night,
In the arms of Piety.
Oh, that happy month at Brookland Hall,
How soon it passed away!
Cheerful and good were Marian's friends,
And who so kind as they?
And, more than all, while there she stayed
They did their best to bring
The little lamb to that blest fold
Where reigns the Shepherd King.
For many a lesson ne'er forgot,
The little Marian learned;
And a thoughtful and a happier child
She to her home returned.
Years rolled away, the scene has changed,
A wife and mother now,
Marian has found the Wicket Gate,
She and her children too.
And oh! how sweet it is to see
This little Pilgrim band,
As on towards their heavenly home,
They travel hand in hand.
When cloudy days fall to their lot,
They see a light afar,
The light that shone on Bethlehem's plain,
The Pilgrim's guiding star.
And now, dear children, whosoe'er,
Or whereso'er you be,
Who ponder o'er this strange, true tale

Of Marian's history,—
If to the Flowers of your young hearts,
Instructions dews are given,
Oh! be earnest as our Marian was,
To find the road to Heaven.

Accoucheur NOUN a male midwife or doctor ❏ *I think my sister must have had some general idea that I was a young offender whom an Accoucheur Policemen had taken up (on my birthday) and delivered over to her* (*Great Expectations* by Charles Dickens)

addled ADJ confused and unable to think properly ❏ *But she counted and counted till she got that addled* (*The Adventures of Huckleberry Finn* by Mark Twain)

admiration NOUN amazement or wonder ❏ *lifting up his hands and eyes by way of admiration* (*Gulliver's Travels* by Jonathan Swift)

afeard ADJ afeard means afraid ❏ *shake it–and don't be afeard* (*The Adventures of Huckleberry Finn* by Mark Twain)

affected VERB affected means followed ❏ *Hadst thou affected sweet divinity* (*Doctor Faustus 5.2* by Christopher Marlowe)

aground ADV when a boat runs aground, it touches the ground in a shallow part of the water and gets stuck ❏ *what kep' you?–boat get aground?* (*The Adventures of Huckleberry Finn* by Mark Twain)

ague NOUN a fever in which the patient has alternate hot and cold shivering fits ❏ *his exposure to the wet and cold had brought on fever and ague* (*Oliver Twist* by Charles Dickens)

alchemy ADJ false or worthless ❏ *all wealth alchemy* (*The Sun Rising* by John Donne)

all alike PHRASE the same all the time ❏ *Love, all alike* (*The Sun Rising* by John Donne)

alow and aloft PHRASE alow means in the lower part or bottom, and aloft means on the top, so alow and aloft means on the top and in the bottom or throughout ❏ *Someone's turned the chest out alow and aloft* (*Treasure Island* by Robert Louis Stevenson)

ambuscade NOUN ambuscade is not a proper word. Tom means an ambush, which is when a group of people attack their enemies, after hiding and waiting for them ❏ *and so we would lie in ambuscade, as he called it* (*The Adventures of Huckleberry Finn* by Mark Twain)

amiable ADJ likeable or pleasant ❏ *Such amiable qualities must speak for themselves* (*Pride and Prejudice* by Jane Austen)

amulet NOUN an amulet is a charm thought to drive away evil spirits. ❏ *uttered phrases at once occult and familiar, like the amulet worn on the heart* (*Silas Marner* by George Eliot)

amusement NOUN here amusement means a strange and disturbing puzzle ❏ *this was an amusement the other way* (*Robinson Crusoe* by Daniel Defoe)

ancient NOUN an ancient was the flag displayed on a ship to show which country it belongs to. It is also called the ensign ❏ *her ancient and pendants out* (*Robinson Crusoe* by Daniel Defoe)

antic ADJ here antic means horrible or grotesque ❏ *armed and dressed after a very antic manner* (*Gulliver's Travels* by Jonathan Swift)

antics NOUN antics is an old word meaning clowns, or people who do silly things to make other people laugh ❏ *And point like antics at his triple crown* (*Doctor Faustus 3.2* by Christopher Marlowe)

appanage NOUN an appanage is a living

allowance ❏ *As if loveliness were not the special prerogative of woman–her legitimate appanage and heritage!* (*Jane Eyre* by Charlotte Brontë)

appended VERB appended means attached or added to ❏ *and these words appended* (*Treasure Island* by Robert Louis Stevenson)

approver NOUN an approver is someone who gives evidence against someone he used to work with ❏ *Mr. Noah Claypole: receiving a free pardon from the Crown in consequence of being admitted approver against Fagin* (*Oliver Twist* by Charles Dickens)

areas NOUN the areas is the space, below street level, in front of the basement of a house ❏ *The Dodger had a vicious propensity, too, of pulling the caps from the heads of small boys and tossing them down areas* (*Oliver Twist* by Charles Dickens)

argument NOUN theme or important idea or subject which runs through a piece of writing ❏ *Thrice needful to the argument which now* (*The Prelude* by William Wordsworth)

artificially ADJ artfully or cleverly ❏ *and he with a sharp flint sharpened very artificially* (*Gulliver's Travels* by Jonathan Swift)

artist NOUN here artist means a skilled workman ❏ *This man was a most ingenious artist* (*Gulliver's Travels* by Jonathan Swift)

assizes NOUN assizes were regular court sessions which a visiting judge was in charge of ❏ *you shall hang at the next assizes* (*Treasure Island* by Robert Louis Stevenson)

attraction NOUN gravitation, or Newton's theory of gravitation ❏ *he predicted the same fate to attraction* (*Gulliver's Travels* by Jonathan Swift)

aver VERB to aver is to claim something strongly ❏ *for Jem Rodney, the mole catcher, averred that one evening as he was returning homeward* (*Silas Marner* by George Eliot)

baby NOUN here baby means doll, which is a child's toy that looks like a small person ❏ *and skilful dressing her baby* (*Gulliver's Travels* by Jonathan Swift)

bagatelle NOUN bagatelle is a game rather like billiards and pool ❏ *Breakfast had been ordered at a pleasant little tavern, a mile or so away upon the rising ground beyond the green; and there was a bagatelle board in the room, in case we should desire to unbend our minds after the solemnity.* (*Great Expectations* by Charles Dickens)

bah EXCLAM Bah is an exclamation of frustration or anger ❏ *"Bah," said Scrooge.* (*A Christmas Carol* by Charles Dickens)

bairn NOUN a northern word for child ❏ *Who has taught you those fine words, my bairn?* (*Wuthering Heights* by Emily Brontë)

bait VERB to bait means to stop on a journey to take refreshment ❏ *So, when they stopped to bait the horse, and ate and drank and enjoyed themselves, I could touch nothing that they touched, but kept my fast unbroken.* (*David Copperfield* by Charles Dickens)

balustrade NOUN a balustrade is a row of vertical columns that form railings ❏ *but I mean to say you might have got a hearse up that staircase, and taken it broadwise, with the splinter-bar towards the wall, and the door towards the balustrades: and done it easy* (*A Christmas Carol* by Charles Dickens)

bandbox NOUN a large lightweight box for carrying bonnets or hats ❏ *I am glad I bought my bonnet, if it is only for the fun of having another bandbox* (*Pride and Prejudice* by Jane Austen)

barren NOUN a barren here is a stretch or expanse of barren land ❏ *a line of upright stones, continued the* *length of the barren* (*Wuthering Heights* by Emily Brontë)

basin NOUN a basin was a cup without a handle ❑ *who is drinking his tea out of a basin* (*Wuthering Heights* by Emily Brontë)

battalia NOUN the order of battle ❑ *till I saw part of his army in battalia* (*Gulliver's Travels* by Jonathan Swift)

battery NOUN a Battery is a fort or a place where guns are positioned ❑ *You bring the lot to me, at that old Battery over yonder* (*Great Expectations* by Charles Dickens)

battledore and shuttlecock NOUN The game battledore and shuttlecock was an early version of the game now known as badminton. The aim of the early game was simply to keep the shuttlecock from hitting the ground. ❑ *Battledore and shuttlecock's a wery good game vhen you an't the shuttlecock and two lawyers the battledores, in which case it gets too excitin' to be pleasant* (*Pickwick Papers* by Charles Dickens)

beadle NOUN a beadle was a local official who had power over the poor ❑ *But these impertinences were speedily checked by the evidence of the surgeon, and the testimony of the beadle* (*Oliver Twist* by Charles Dickens)

bearings NOUN the bearings of a place are the measurements or directions that are used to find or locate it ❑ *the bearings of the island* (*Treasure Island* by Robert Louis Stevenson)

beaufet NOUN a beaufet was a sideboard ❑ *and sweet-cake from the beaufet* (*Emma* by Jane Austen)

beck NOUN a beck is a small stream ❑ *a beck which follows the bend of the glen* (*Wuthering Heights* by Emily Brontë)

bedight VERB decorated ❑ *and bedight with Christmas holly stuck into the top.* (*A Christmas Carol* by Charles Dickens)

Bedlam NOUN Bedlam was a lunatic asylum in London which had statues carved by Caius Gabriel Cibber at its entrance ❑ *Bedlam, and those carved maniacs at the gates* (*The Prelude* by William Wordsworth)

beeves NOUN oxen or castrated bulls which are animals used for pulling vehicles or carrying things ❑ *to deliver in every morning six beeves* (*Gulliver's Travels* by Jonathan Swift)

begot VERB created or caused ❑ *Begot in thee* (*On His Mistress* by John Donne)

behoof NOUN behoof means benefit ❑ *"Yes, young man," said he, releasing the handle of the article in question, retiring a step or two from my table, and speaking for the behoof of the landlord and waiter at the door* (*Great Expectations* by Charles Dickens)

berth NOUN a berth is a bed on a boat ❑ *this is the berth for me* (*Treasure Island* by Robert Louis Stevenson)

bevers NOUN a bever was a snack, or small portion of food, eaten between main meals ❑ *that buys me thirty meals a day and ten bevers* (*Doctor Faustus 2.1* by Christopher Marlowe)

bilge water NOUN the bilge is the widest part of a ship's bottom, and the bilge water is the dirty water that collects there ❑ *no gush of bilge-water had turned it to fetid puddle* (*Jane Eyre* by Charlotte Brontë)

bills NOUN bills is an old term meaning prescription. A prescription is the piece of paper on which your doctor writes an order for medicine and which you give to a chemist to get the medicine ❑ *Are not thy bills hung up as monuments* (*Doctor Faustus 1.1* by Christopher Marlowe)

black cap NOUN a judge wore a black cap when he was about to sentence a prisoner to death ❑ *The judge assumed the black cap, and the*

329

prisoner still stood with the same air and gesture. (*Oliver Twist* by Charles Dickens)

black gentleman NOUN this was another word for the devil ❑ *for she is as impatient as the black gentleman* (*Emma* by Jane Austen)

boot-jack NOUN a wooden device to help take boots off ❑ *The speaker appeared to throw a boot-jack, or some such article, at the person he addressed* (*Oliver Twist* by Charles Dickens)

booty NOUN booty means treasure or prizes ❑ *would be inclined to give up their booty in payment of the dead man's debts* (*Treasure Island* by Robert Louis Stevenson)

Bow Street runner PHRASE Bow Street runners were the first British police force, set up by the author Henry Fielding in the eighteenth century ❑ *as would have convinced a judge or a Bow Street runner* (*Treasure Island* by Robert Louis Stevenson)

brawn NOUN brawn is a dish of meat which is set in jelly ❑ *Heaped up upon the floor, to form a kind of throne, were turkeys, geese, game, poultry, brawn, great joints of meat, sucking-pigs* (*A Christmas Carol* by Charles Dickens)

bray VERB when a donkey brays, it makes a loud, harsh sound ❑ *and she doesn't bray like a jackass* (*The Adventures of Huckleberry Finn* by Mark Twain)

break VERB in order to train a horse you first have to break it ❑ *"If a high-mettled creature like this," said he, "can't be broken by fair means, she will never be good for anything"* (*Black Beauty* by Anna Sewell)

bullyragging VERB bullyragging is an old word which means bullying. To bullyrag someone is to threaten or force someone to do something they don't want to do ❑ *and a lot of loafers bullyragging him for sport* (*The Adventures of Huckleberry Finn* by Mark Twain)

but PREP except for (this) ❑ *but this, all pleasures fancies be* (*The Good-Morrow* by John Donne)

by hand PHRASE by hand was a common expression of the time meaning that baby had been fed either using a spoon or a bottle rather than by breast-feeding ❑ *My sister, Mrs. Joe Gargery, was more than twenty years older than I, and had established a great reputation with herself . . . because she had bought me up 'by hand'* (*Great Expectations* by Charles Dickens)

bye-spots NOUN bye-spots are lonely places ❑ *and bye-spots of tales rich with indigenous produce* (*The Prelude* by William Wordsworth)

calico NOUN calico is plain white fabric made from cotton ❑ *There was two old dirty calico dresses* (*The Adventures of Huckleberry Finn* by Mark Twain)

camp-fever NOUN camp-fever was another word for the disease typhus ❑ *during a severe camp-fever* (*Emma* by Jane Austen)

cant NOUN cant is insincere or empty talk ❑ *"Man," said the Ghost, "if man you be in heart, not adamant, forbear that wicked cant until you have discovered What the surplus is, and Where it is."* (*A Christmas Carol* by Charles Dickens)

canty ADJ canty means lively, full of life ❑ *My mother lived til eighty, a canty dame to the last* (*Wuthering Heights* by Emily Brontë)

canvas VERB to canvas is to discuss ❑ *We think so very differently on this point Mr Knightley, that there can be no use in canvassing it* (*Emma* by Jane Austen)

capital ADJ capital means excellent or extremely good ❑ *for it's capital, so shady, light, and big* (*Little Women* by Louisa May Alcott)

capstan NOUN a capstan is a device used on a ship to lift sails and anchors ❑ *capstans going, ships going out to sea, and unintelligible* sea creatures roaring curses over the bulwarks at respondent lightermen (*Great Expectations* by Charles Dickens)

case-bottle NOUN a square bottle designed to fit with others into a case ❑ *The spirit being set before him in a huge case-bottle, which had originally come out of some ship's locker* (*The Old Curiosity Shop* by Charles Dickens)

casement NOUN casement is a word meaning window. The teacher in Nicholas Nickleby misspells window showing what a bad teacher he is ❑ *W-i-n, win, d-e-r, der, winder, a casement.'* (*Nicholas Nickleby* by Charles Dickens)

cataleptic ADJ a cataleptic fit is one in which the victim goes into a trance-like state and remains still for a long time ❑ *It was at this point in their history that Silas's cataleptic fit occurred during the prayer-meeting* (*Silas Marner* by George Eliot)

cauldron NOUN a cauldron is a large cooking pot made of metal ❑ *stirring a large cauldron which seemed to be full of soup* (*Alice's Adventures in Wonderland* by Lewis Carroll)

cephalic ADJ cephalic means to do with the head ❑ *with ink composed of a cephalic tincture* (*Gulliver's Travels* by Jonathan Swift)

chaise and four NOUN a closed four-wheel carriage pulled by four horses ❑ *he came down on Monday in a chaise and four to see the place* (*Pride and Prejudice* by Jane Austen)

chamberlain NOUN the main servant in a household ❑ *In those times a bed was always to be got there at any hour of the night, and the chamberlain, letting me in at his ready wicket, lighted the candle next in order on his shelf* (*Great Expectations* by Charles Dickens)

characters NOUN distinguishing marks ❑ *Impressed upon all forms the characters* (*The Prelude* by William Wordsworth)

chary ADJ cautious ❑ *I should have been chary of discussing my guardian too freely even with her* (*Great Expectations* by Charles Dickens)

cherishes VERB here cherishes means cheers or brightens ❑ *some philosophic song of Truth that cherishes our daily life* (*The Prelude* by William Wordsworth)

chickens' meat PHRASE chickens' meat is an old term which means chickens' feed or food ❑ *I had shook a bag of chickens' meat out in that place* (*Robinson Crusoe* by Daniel Defoe)

chimeras NOUN a chimera is an unrealistic idea or a wish which is unlikely to be fulfilled ❑ *with many other wild impossible chimeras* (*Gulliver's Travels* by Jonathan Swift)

chines NOUN chine is a cut of meat that includes part or all of the backbone of the animal ❑ *and they found hams and chines uncut* (*Silas Marner* by George Eliot)

chits NOUN chits is a slang word which means girls ❑ *I hate affected, niminy-piminy chits!* (*Little Women* by Louisa May Alcott)

chopped VERB chopped means come suddenly or accidentally ❑ *if I had chopped upon them* (*Robinson Crusoe* by Daniel Defoe)

chute NOUN a narrow channel ❑ *One morning about day-break, I found a canoe and crossed over a chute to the main shore* (*The Adventures of Huckleberry Finn* by Mark Twain)

circumspection NOUN careful observation of events and circumstances; caution ❑ *I honour your circumspection* (*Pride and Prejudice* by Jane Austen)

clambered VERB clambered means to climb somewhere with difficulty, usually using your hands and your feet ❑ *he clambered up and down stairs* (*Treasure Island* by Robert Louis Stevenson)

clime NOUN climate ❑ *no season knows nor clime* (*The Sun Rising* by John Donne)

clinched VERB clenched ❑ *the tops whereof I could but just reach with my fist clinched* (*Gulliver's Travels* by Jonathan Swift)

close chair NOUN a close chair is a sedan chair, which is an covered chair which has room for one person. The sedan chair is carried on two poles by two men, one in front and one behind ❑ *persuaded even the Empress herself to let me hold her in her close chair* (*Gulliver's Travels* by Jonathan Swift)

clown NOUN clown here means peasant or person who lives off the land ❑ *In ancient days by emperor and clown* (*Ode on a Nightingale* by John Keats)

coalheaver NOUN a coalheaver loaded coal onto ships using a spade ❑ *Good, strong, wholesome medicine, as was given with great success to two Irish labourers and a coalheaver* (*Oliver Twist* by Charles Dickens)

coal-whippers NOUN men who worked at docks using machines to load coal onto ships ❑ *here, were colliers by the score and score, with the coal-whippers plunging off stages on deck* (*Great Expectations* by Charles Dickens)

cobweb NOUN a cobweb is the net which a spider makes for catching insects ❑ *the walls and ceilings were all hung round with cobwebs* (*Gulliver's Travels* by Jonathan Swift)

coddling VERB coddling means to treat someone too kindly or protect them too much ❑ *and I've been coddling the fellow as if I'd been his grand-mother* (*Little Women* by Louisa May Alcott)

coil NOUN coil means noise or fuss or disturbance ❑ *What a coil is there?* (*Doctor Faustus 4.7* by Christopher Marlowe)

collared VERB to collar something is a slang term which means to capture.

In this sentence, it means he stole it [the money] ❑ *he collared it* (*The Adventures of Huckleberry Finn* by Mark Twain)

colling VERB colling is an old word which means to embrace and kiss ❑ *and no clasping and colling at all* (*Tess of the D'Urbervilles* by Thomas Hardy)

colloquies NOUN colloquy is a formal conversation or dialogue ❑ *Such colloquies have occupied many a pair of pale-faced weavers* (*Silas Marner* by George Eliot)

comfit NOUN sugar-covered pieces of fruit or nut eaten as sweets ❑ *and pulled out a box of comfits* (*Alice's Adventures in Wonderland* by Lewis Carroll)

coming out VERB when a girl came out in society it meant she was of marriageable age. In order to 'come out' girls were expecting to attend balls and other parties during a season ❑ *The younger girls formed hopes of coming out a year or two sooner than they might otherwise have done* (*Pride and Prejudice* by Jane Austen)

commit VERB commit means arrest or stop ❑ *Commit the rascals* (*Doctor Faustus 4.7* by Christopher Marlowe)

commodious ADJ commodious means convenient ❑ *the most commodious and effectual ways* (*Gulliver's Travels* by Jonathan Swift)

commons NOUN commons is an old term meaning food shared with others ❑ *his pauper assistants ranged them-selves behind him; the gruel was served out; and a long grace was said over the short commons.* (*Oliver Twist* by Charles Dickens)

complacency NOUN here complacency means a desire to please others. To-day complacency means feeling pleased with oneself without good reason. ❑ *Twas thy power that raised the first complacency in me* (*The Prelude* by William Wordsworth)

complaisance NOUN complaisance was eagerness to please ❏ *we cannot wonder at his complaisance* (*Pride and Prejudice* by Jane Austen)

complaisant ADJ complaisant means polite ❏ *extremely cheerful and complaisant to their guest* (*Gulliver's Travels* by Jonathan Swift)

conning VERB conning means learning by heart ❏ *Or conning more* (*The Prelude* by William Wordsworth)

consequent NOUN consequence ❏ *as avarice is the necessary consequent of old age* (*Gulliver's Travels* by Jonathan Swift)

consorts NOUN concerts ❏ *The King, who delighted in music, had frequent consorts at Court* (*Gulliver's Travels* by Jonathan Swift)

conversible ADJ conversible meant easy to talk to, companionable ❏ *He can be a conversible companion* (*Pride and Prejudice* by Jane Austen)

copper NOUN a copper is a large pot that can be heated directly over a fire ❏ *He gazed in stupefied astonishment on the small rebel for some seconds, and then clung for support to the copper* (*Oliver Twist* by Charles Dickens)

copper-stick NOUN a copper-stick is the long piece of wood used to stir washing in the copper (or boiler) which was usually the biggest cooking pot in the house ❏ *It was Christmas Eve, and I had to stir the pudding for next day, with a copper-stick, from seven to eight by the Dutch clock* (*Great Expectations* by Charles Dickens)

counting-house NOUN a counting house is a place where accountants work ❏ *Once upon a time–of all the good days in the year, on Christmas Eve–old Scrooge sat busy in his countinghouse* (*A Christmas Carol* by Charles Dickens)

courtier NOUN a courtier is someone who attends the king or queen–a member of the court ❏ *next the ten courtiers;* (*Alice's Adventures in Wonderland* by Lewis Carroll)

covies NOUN covies were flocks of partridges ❏ *and will save all of the best covies for you* (*Pride and Prejudice* by Jane Austen)

cowed VERB cowed means frightened or intimidated ❏ *it cowed me more than the pain* (*Treasure Island* by Robert Louis Stevenson)

cozened VERB cozened means tricked or deceived ❏ *Do you remember, sir, how you cozened me* (*Doctor Faustus 4.7* by Christopher Marlowe)

cravats NOUN a cravat is a folded cloth that a man wears wrapped around his neck as a decorative item of clothing ❏ *we'd a' slept in our cravats to-night* (*The Adventures of Huckleberry Finn* by Mark Twain)

crock and dirt PHRASE crock and dirt is an old expression meaning soot and dirt ❏ *and the mare catching cold at the door, and the boy grimed with crock and dirt* (*Great Expectations* by Charles Dickens)

crockery NOUN here crockery means pottery ❏ *By one of the parrots was a cat made of crockery* (*The Adventures of Huckleberry Finn* by Mark Twain)

crooked sixpence PHRASE it was considered unlucky to have a bent sixpence ❏ *You've got the beauty, you see, and I've got the luck, so you must keep me by you for your crooked sixpence* (*Silas Marner* by George Eliot)

croquet NOUN croquet is a traditional English summer game in which players try to hit wooden balls through hoops ❏ *and once she remembered trying to box her own ears for having cheated herself in a game of croquet* (*Alice's Adventures in Wonderland* by Lewis Carroll)

cross PREP across ❏ *The two great streets, which run cross and divide it into four quarters* (*Gulliver's Travels* by Jonathan Swift)

culpable ADJ if you are culpable for something it means you are to blame ❏ *deep are the sorrows that spring from false ideas for which no man is culpable. (Silas Marner* by George Eliot)

cultured ADJ cultivated ❏ *Nor less when spring had warmed the cultured Vale (The Prelude* by William Wordsworth)

cupidity NOUN cupidity is greed ❏ *These people hated me with the hatred of cupidity and disappointment. (Great Expectations* by Charles Dickens)

curricle NOUN an open two-wheeled carriage with one seat for the driver and space for a single passenger ❏ *and they saw a lady and a gentleman in a curricle (Pride and Prejudice* by Jane Austen)

cynosure NOUN a cynosure is something that strongly attracts attention or admiration ❏ *Then I thought of Eliza and Georgiana; I beheld one the cynosure of a ballroom, the other the inmate of a convent cell (Jane Eyre* by Charlotte Brontë)

dalliance NOUN someone's dalliance with something is a brief involvement with it ❏ *nor sporting in the dalliance of love (Doctor Faustus Chorus* by Christopher Marlowe)

darkling ADV darkling is an archaic way of saying in the dark ❏ *Darkling I listen (Ode on a Nightingale* by John Keats)

delf-case NOUN a sideboard for holding dishes and crockery ❏ *at the pewter dishes and delf-case (Wuthering Heights* by Emily Brontë)

determined ■ VERB here determined means ended ❏ *and be out of vogue when that was determined (Gulliver's Travels* by Jonathan Swift) ■ VERB determined can mean to have been learned or found especially by investigation or experience ❏ *All the sensitive feelings it wounded so cruelly, all the shame and misery it kept alive within my breast, became more poignant as I*

thought of this; and I determined that the life was unendurable (David Copperfield by Charles Dickens)

Deuce NOUN a slang term for the Devil ❏ *Ah, I dare say I did. Deuce take me, he added suddenly, I know I did. I find I am not quite unscrewed yet. (Great Expectations* by Charles Dickens)

diabolical ADJ diabolical means devilish or evil ❏ *and with a thousand diabolical expressions (Treasure Island* by Robert Louis Stevenson)

direction NOUN here direction means address ❏ *Elizabeth was not surprised at it, as Jane had written the direction remarkably ill (Pride and Prejudice* by Jane Austen)

discover VERB to make known or announce ❏ *the Emperor would discover the secret while I was out of his power (Gulliver's Travels* by Jonathan Swift)

dissemble VERB hide or conceal ❏ *Dissemble nothing (On His Mistress* by John Donne)

dissolve VERB dissolve here means to release from life, to die ❏ *Fade far away, dissolve, and quite forget (Ode on a Nightingale* by John Keats)

distrain VERB to distrain is to seize the property of someone who is in debt in compensation for the money owed ❏ *for he's threatening to distrain for it (Silas Marner* by George Eliot)

Divan NOUN a Divan was originally a Turkish council of state—the name was transferred to the couches they sat on and is used to mean this in English ❏ *Mr Brass applauded this picture very much, and the bed being soft and comfortable, Mr Quilp determined to use it, both as a sleeping place by night and as a kind of Divan by day. (The Old Curiosity Shop* by Charles Dickens)

divorcement NOUN separation ❏ *By all pains which want and divorcement* *hath* (*On His Mistress* by John Donne)

dog in the manger, PHRASE this phrase describes someone who prevents you from enjoying something that they themselves have no need for ❑ *You are a dog in the manger, Cathy, and desire no one to be loved but yourself* (*Wuthering Heights* by Emily Brontë)

dolorifuge NOUN dolorifuge is a word which Thomas Hardy invented. It means pain-killer or comfort ❑ *as a species of dolorifuge* (*Tess of the D'Urbervilles* by Thomas Hardy)

dome NOUN building ❑ *that river and that mouldering dome* (*The Prelude* by William Wordsworth)

domestic PHRASE here domestic means a person's management of the house ❑ *to give some account of my domestic* (*Gulliver's Travels* by Jonathan Swift)

dunce NOUN a dunce is another word for idiot ❑ *Do you take me for a dunce? Go on!* (*Alice's Adventures in Wonderland* by Lewis Carroll)

Ecod EXCLAM a slang exclamation meaning 'oh God!' ❑ *"Ecod,"* replied Wemmick, shaking his head, "that's not my trade." (*Great Expectations* by Charles Dickens)

egg-hot NOUN an egg-hot (see also 'flip' and 'negus') was a hot drink made from beer and eggs, sweetened with nutmeg ❑ *She fainted when she saw me return, and made a little jug of egg-hot afterwards to console us while we talked it over.* (*David Copperfield* by Charles Dickens)

encores NOUN an encore is a short extra performance at the end of a longer one, which the entertainer gives because the audience has enthusiastically asked for it ❑ *we want a little something to answer encores with, anyway* (*The Adventures of Huckleberry Finn* by Mark Twain)

equipage NOUN an elegant and impressive carriage ❑ *and besides, the equipage did not answer to any of*

their neighbours (*Pride and Prejudice* by Jane Austen)

exordium NOUN an exordium is the opening part of a speech ❑ *"Now, Handel,"* as if it were the grave beginning of a portentous business exordium, he had suddenly given up that tone (*Great Expectations* by Charles Dickens)

expect VERB here expect means to wait for ❑ *to expect his farther commands* (*Gulliver's Travels* by Jonathan Swift)

familiars NOUN familiars means spirits or devils who come to someone when they are called ❑ *I'll turn all the lice about thee into familiars* (*Doctor Faustus* 1.4 by Christopher Marlowe)

fantods NOUN a fantod is a person who fidgets or can't stop moving nervously ❑ *It most give me the fantods* (*The Adventures of Huckleberry Finn* by Mark Twain)

farthing NOUN a farthing is an old unit of British currency which was worth a quarter of a penny ❑ *Not a farthing less. A great many back-payments are included in it, I assure you.* (*A Christmas Carol* by Charles Dickens)

farthingale NOUN a hoop worn under a skirt to extend it ❑ *A bell with an old voice–which I dare say in its time had often said to the house, Here is the green farthingale* (*Great Expectations* by Charles Dickens)

favours NOUN here favours is an old word which means ribbons ❑ *A group of humble mourners entered the gate: wearing white favours* (*Oliver Twist* by Charles Dickens)

feigned VERB pretend or pretending ❑ *not my feigned page* (*On His Mistress* by John Donne)

fence ■ NOUN a fence is someone who receives and sells stolen goods ❑ *What are you up to? Ill-treating the boys, you covetous, avaricious, in-sa-ti-a-ble old fence?* (*Oliver Twist* by

Charles Dickens) ■ NOUN defence or protection ❏ *but honesty hath no fence against superior cunning* (*Gulliver's Travels* by Jonathan Swift)

fess ADJ fess is an old word which means pleased or proud ❏ *You'll be fess enough, my poppet* (*Tess of the D'Urbervilles* by Thomas Hardy)

fettered ADJ fettered means bound in chains or chained ❏ *"You are fettered," said Scrooge, trembling. "Tell me why?"* (*A Christmas Carol* by Charles Dickens)

fidges VERB fidges means fidgets, which is to keep moving your hands slightly because you are nervous or excited ❏ *Look, Jim, how my fingers fidges* (*Treasure Island* by Robert Louis Stevenson)

finger-post NOUN a finger-post is a sign-post showing the direction to different places ❏ *"The gallows," continued Fagin, "the gallows, my dear, is an ugly finger-post, which points out a very short and sharp turning that has stopped many a bold fellow's career on the broad highway."* (*Oliver Twist* by Charles Dickens)

fire-irons NOUN fire-irons are tools kept by the side of the fire to either cook with or look after the fire ❏ *the fire-irons came first* (*Alice's Adventures in Wonderland* by Lewis Carroll)

fire-plug NOUN a fire-plug is another word for a fire hydrant ❏ *The pony looked with great attention into a fire-plug, which was near him, and appeared to be quite absorbed in contemplating it* (*The Old Curiosity Shop* by Charles Dickens)

flank NOUN flank is the side of an animal ❏ *And all her silken flanks with garlands dressed* (*Ode on a Grecian Urn* by John Keats)

flip NOUN a flip is a drink made from warmed ale, sugar, spice and beaten egg ❏ *The events of the day, in combination with the twins, if not with the flip, had made Mrs.*

Micawber hysterical, and she shed tears as she replied (*David Copperfield* by Charles Dickens)

flit VERB flit means to move quickly ❏ *and if he had meant to flit to Thrushcross Grange* (*Wuthering Heights* by Emily Brontë)

floorcloth NOUN a floorcloth was a hard-wearing piece of canvas used instead of carpet ❏ *This avenging phantom was ordered to be on duty at eight on Tuesday morning in the hall (it was two feet square, as charged for floorcloth)* (*Great Expectations* by Charles Dickens)

fly-driver NOUN a fly-driver is a carriage drawn by a single horse ❏ *The fly-drivers, among whom I inquired next, were equally jocose and equally disrespectful* (*David Copperfield* by Charles Dickens)

fob NOUN a small pocket in which a watch is kept ❏ *"Certain," replied the man, drawing a gold watch from his fob* (*Oliver Twist* by Charles Dickens)

folly NOUN folly means foolishness or stupidity ❏ *the folly of beginning a work* (*Robinson Crusoe* by Daniel Defoe)

fond ADJ fond means foolish ❏ *Fond worldling* (*Doctor Faustus 5.2* by Christopher Marlowe)

fondness NOUN silly or foolish affection ❏ *They have no fondness for their colts or foals* (*Gulliver's Travels* by Jonathan Swift)

for his fancy PHRASE for his fancy means for his liking or as he wanted ❏ *and as I did not obey quick enough for his fancy* (*Treasure Island* by Robert Louis Stevenson)

forlorn ADJ lost or very upset ❏ *you are from that day forlorn* (*Gulliver's Travels* by Jonathan Swift)

foster-sister NOUN a foster-sister was someone brought up by the same nurse or in the same household ❏ *I had been his foster-sister* (*Wuthering Heights* by Emily Brontë)

fox-fire NOUN fox-fire is a weak glow that is given off by decaying, rotten wood ❑ *what we must have was a lot of them rotten chunks that's called fox-fire* (*The Adventures of Huckleberry Finn* by Mark Twain)

frozen sea PHRASE the Arctic Ocean ❑ *into the frozen sea* (*Gulliver's Travels* by Jonathan Swift)

gainsay VERB to gainsay something is to say it isn't true or to deny it ❑ *"So she had," cried Scrooge. "You're right. I'll not gainsay it, Spirit. God forbid!"* (*A Christmas Carol* by Charles Dickens)

gaiters NOUN gaiters were leggings made of a cloth or piece of leather which covered the leg from the knee to the ankle ❑ *Mr Knightley was hard at work upon the lower buttons of his thick leather gaiters* (*Emma* by Jane Austen)

galluses NOUN galluses is an old spelling of gallows, and here means suspenders. Suspenders are straps worn over someone's shoulders and fastened to their trousers to prevent the trousers falling down ❑ *and home-knit galluses* (*The Adventures of Huckleberry Finn* by Mark Twain)

galoot NOUN a sailor but also a clumsy person ❑ *and maybe a galoot on it chopping* (*The Adventures of Huckleberry Finn* by Mark Twain)

gayest ADJ gayest means the most lively and bright or merry ❑ *Beth played her gayest march* (*Little Women* by Louisa May Alcott)

gem NOUN here gem means jewellery ❑ *the mountain shook off turf and flower, had only heath for raiment and crag for gem* (*Jane Eyre* by Charlotte Brontë)

giddy ADJ giddy means dizzy ❑ *and I wish you wouldn't keep appearing and vanishing so suddenly; you make one quite giddy.* (*Alice's Adventures in Wonderland* by Lewis Carroll)

gig NOUN a light two-wheeled carriage ❑ *when a gig drove up to the garden gate: out of which there jumped a fat gentleman* (*Oliver Twist* by Charles Dickens)

gladsome ADJ gladsome is an old word meaning glad or happy ❑ *Nobody ever stopped him in the street to say, with gladsome looks* (*A Christmas Carol* by Charles Dickens)

glen NOUN a glen is a small valley; the word is used commonly in Scotland ❑ *a beck which follows the bend of the glen* (*Wuthering Heights* by Emily Brontë)

gravelled VERB gravelled is an old term which means to baffle or defeat someone ❑ *Gravelled the pastors of the German Church* (*Doctor Faustus 1.1* by Christopher Marlowe)

grinder NOUN a grinder was a private tutor ❑ *but that when he had had the happiness of marrying Mrs Pocket very early in his life, he had impaired his prospects and taken up the calling of a Grinder* (*Great Expectations* by Charles Dickens)

gruel NOUN gruel is a thin, watery cornmeal or oatmeal soup ❑ *and the little saucepan of gruel (Scrooge had a cold in his head) upon the hob.* (*A Christmas Carol* by Charles Dickens)

guinea, half a NOUN a half guinea was ten shillings and sixpence ❑ *but lay out half a guinea at Ford's* (*Emma* by Jane Austen)

gull VERB gull is an old term which means to fool or deceive someone ❑ *Hush, I'll gull him supernaturally* (*Doctor Faustus 3.4* by Christopher Marlowe)

gunnel NOUN the gunnel, or gunwhale, is the upper edge of a boat's side ❑ *But he put his foot on the gunnel and rocked her* (*The Adventures of Huckleberry Finn* by Mark Twain)

gunwale NOUN the side of a ship ❑ *He dipped his hand in the water over the boat's gunwale* (*Great Expectations* by Charles Dickens)

Gytrash NOUN a Gytrash is an omen of misfortune to the superstitious, usually taking the form of a hound ❑ *I remembered certain of Bessie's tales, wherein figured a North-of-England spirit, called a 'Gytrash'* (*Jane Eyre* by Charlotte Brontë)

hackney-cabriolet NOUN a two-wheeled carriage with four seats for hire and pulled by a horse ❑ *A hackney-cabriolet was in waiting; with the same vehemence which she had exhibited in addressing Oliver, the girl pulled him in with her, and drew the curtains close.* (*Oliver Twist* by Charles Dickens)

hackney-coach NOUN a four-wheeled horse-drawn vehicle for hire ❑ *The twilight was beginning to close in, when Mr. Brownlow alighted from a hackney-coach at his own door, and knocked softly.* (*Oliver Twist* by Charles Dickens)

haggler NOUN a haggler is someone who travels from place to place selling small goods and items ❑ *when I be plain Jack Durbeyfield, the haggler* (*Tess of the D'Urbervilles* by Thomas Hardy)

halter NOUN a halter is a rope or strap used to lead an animal or to tie it up ❑ *I had of course long been used to a halter and a headstall* (*Black Beauty* by Anna Sewell)

hamlet NOUN a hamlet is a small village or a group of houses in the countryside ❑ *down from the hamlet* (*Treasure Island* by Robert Louis Stevenson)

hand-barrow NOUN a hand-barrow is a device for carrying heavy objects. It is like a wheelbarrow except that it has handles, rather than wheels, for moving the barrow ❑ *his sea chest following behind him in a hand-barrow* (*Treasure Island* by Robert Louis Stevenson)

handspike NOUN a handspike was a stick which was used as a lever ❑ *a bit of stick like a handspike* (*Treasure Island* by Robert Louis Stevenson)

haply ADV haply means by chance or perhaps ❑ *And haply the Queen-Moon is on her throne* (*Ode on a Nightingale* by John Keats)

harem NOUN the harem was the part of the house where the women lived ❑ *mostly they hang round the harem* (*The Adventures of Huckleberry Finn* by Mark Twain)

hautboys NOUN hautboys are oboes ❑ sausages and puddings resembling flutes and hautboys (*Gulliver's Travels* by Jonathan Swift)

hawker NOUN a hawker is someone who sells goods to people as he travels rather than from a fixed place like a shop ❑ *to buy some stockings from a hawker* (*Treasure Island* by Robert Louis Stevenson)

hawser NOUN a hawser is a rope used to tie up or tow a ship or boat ❑ *Again among the tiers of shipping, in and out, avoiding rusty chain-cables, frayed hempen hawsers* (*Great Expectations* by Charles Dickens)

headstall NOUN the headstall is the part of the bridle or halter that goes around a horse's head ❑ *I had of course long been used to a halter and a headstall* (*Black Beauty* by Anna Sewell)

hearken VERB hearken means to listen ❑ *though we sometimes stopped to lay hold of each other and hearken* (*Treasure Island* by Robert Louis Stevenson)

heartless ADJ here heartless means without heart or dejected ❑ *I am not heartless* (*The Prelude* by William Wordsworth)

hebdomadal ADJ hebdomadal means weekly ❑ *It was the hebdomadal treat to which we all looked forward from Sabbath to Sabbath* (*Jane Eyre* by Charlotte Brontë)

highwaymen NOUN highwaymen were people who stopped travellers and robbed them ❑ *We are highwaymen* (*The Adventures of Huckleberry Finn* by Mark Twain)

hinds NOUN hinds means farm hands, or people who work on a farm ❑ *He called his hinds about him* (*Gulliver's Travels* by Jonathan Swift)

histrionic ADJ if you refer to someone's behaviour as histrionic, you are being critical of it because it is dramatic and exaggerated ❑ *But the histrionic muse is the darling* (*The Adventures of Huckleberry Finn* by Mark Twain)

hogs NOUN hogs is another word for pigs ❑ *Tom called the hogs 'ingots'* (*The Adventures of Huckleberry Finn* by Mark Twain)

horrors NOUN the horrors are a fit, called delirium tremens, which is caused by drinking too much alcohol ❑ *I'll have the horrors* (*Treasure Island* by Robert Louis Stevenson)

huffy ADJ huffy means to be obviously annoyed or offended about something ❑ *They will feel that more than angry speeches or huffy actions* (*Little Women* by Louisa May Alcott)

hulks NOUN hulks were prison-ships ❑ *The miserable companion of thieves and ruffians, the fallen outcast of low haunts, the associate of the scourings of the jails and hulks* (*Oliver Twist* by Charles Dickens)

humbug NOUN humbug means nonsense or rubbish ❑ *"Bah," said Scrooge. "Humbug!"* (*A Christmas Carol* by Charles Dickens)

humours NOUN it was believed that there were four fluids in the body called humours which decided the temperament of a person depending on how much of each fluid was present ❑ *other peccant humours* (*Gulliver's Travels* by Jonathan Swift)

husbandry NOUN husbandry is farming animals ❑ *bad husbandry were plentifully anointing their wheels* (*Silas Marner* by George Eliot)

huswife NOUN a huswife was a small sewing kit ❑ *but I had put my huswife on it* (*Emma* by Jane Austen)

ideal ADJ ideal in this context means imaginary ❑ *I discovered the yell was not ideal* (*Wuthering Heights* by Emily Brontë)

If our two PHRASE if both our ❑ *If our two loves be one* (*The Good-Morrow* by John Donne)

ignis-fatuus NOUN ignis-fatuus is the light given out by burning marsh gases, which lead careless travellers into danger ❑ *it is madness in all women to let a secret love kindle within them, which, if unreturned and unknown, must devour the life that feeds it; and, if discovered and responded to, must lead ignis-fatuus-like, into miry wilds whence there is no extrication.* (*Jane Eyre* by Charlotte Brontë)

imaginations NOUN here imaginations means schemes or plans ❑ *soon drove out those imaginations* (*Gulliver's Travels* by Jonathan Swift)

impressible ADJ impressible means open or impressionable ❑ *for Marner had one of those impressible, self-doubting natures* (*Silas Marner* by George Eliot)

in good intelligence PHRASE friendly with each other ❑ *that these two persons were in good intelligence with each other* (*Gulliver's Travels* by Jonathan Swift)

inanity NOUN inanity is sillyness or dull stupidity ❑ *Do we not wile away moments of inanity* (*Silas Marner* by George Eliot)

incivility NOUN incivility means rudeness or impoliteness ❑ *if it's only for a piece of incivility like to-night's* (*Treasure Island* by Robert Louis Stevenson)

indigenae NOUN indigenae means natives or people from that area ❑ *an exotic that the surly indigenae will not recognise for kin* (*Wuthering Heights* by Emily Brontë)

indocible ADJ unteachable ❑ *so they were the most restive and indocible* (*Gulliver's Travels* by Jonathan Swift)

ingenuity NOUN inventiveness ❏ *entreated me to give him something as an encouragement to ingenuity* (*Gulliver's Travels* by Jonathan Swift)

ingots NOUN an ingot is a lump of a valuable metal like gold, usually shaped like a brick ❏ *Tom called the hogs 'ingots'* (*The Adventures of Huckleberry Finn* by Mark Twain)

inkstand NOUN an inkstand is a pot which was put on a desk to contain either ink or pencils and pens ❏ *throwing an inkstand at the Lizard as she spoke* (*Alice's Adventures in Wonderland* by Lewis Carroll)

inordinate ADJ without order. To-day inordinate means 'excessive'. ❏ *Though yet untutored and inordinate* (*The Prelude* by William Wordsworth)

intellectuals NOUN here intellectuals means the minds (of the workmen) ❏ *those instructions they give being too refined for the intellectuals of their workmen* (*Gulliver's Travels* by Jonathan Swift)

interview NOUN meeting ❏ *By our first strange and fatal interview* (*On His Mistress* by John Donne)

jacks NOUN jacks are rods for turning a spit over a fire ❏ *It was a small bit of pork suspended from the kettle hanger by a string passed through a large door key, in a way known to primitive housekeepers unpossessed of jacks* (*Silas Marner* by George Eliot)

jews-harp NOUN a jews-harp is a small, metal, musical instrument that is played by the mouth ❏ *A jews-harp's plenty good enough for a rat* (*The Adventures of Huckleberry Finn* by Mark Twain)

jorum NOUN a large bowl ❏ *while Miss Skiffins brewed such a jorum of tea, that the pig in the back premises became strongly excited* (*Great Expectations* by Charles Dickens)

jostled VERB jostled means bumped or pushed by someone or some people

❏ *being jostled himself into the kennel* (*Gulliver's Travels* by Jonathan Swift)

keepsake NOUN a keepsake is a gift which reminds someone of an event or of the person who gave it to them. ❏ *books and ornaments they had in their boudoirs at home: keepsakes that different relations had presented to them* (*Jane Eyre* by Charlotte Brontë)

kenned VERB kenned means knew ❏ *though little kenned the lamplighter that he had any company but Christmas!* (*A Christmas Carol* by Charles Dickens)

kennel NOUN kennel means gutter, which is the edge of a road next to the pavement, where rain water collects and flows away ❏ *being jostled himself into the kennel* (*Gulliver's Travels* by Jonathan Swift)

knock-knee ADJ knock-knee means slanted, at an angle. ❏ *LOT 1 was marked in whitewashed knock-knee letters on the brewhouse* (*Great Expectations* by Charles Dickens)

ladylike ADJ to be ladylike is to behave in a polite, dignified and graceful way ❏ *No, winking isn't ladylike* (*Little Women* by Louisa May Alcott)

lapse NOUN flow ❏ *Stealing with silent lapse to join the brook* (*The Prelude* by William Wordsworth)

larry NOUN larry is an old word which means commotion or noisy celebration ❏ *That was all a part of the larry!* (*Tess of the D'Urbervilles* by Thomas Hardy)

laths NOUN laths are strips of wood ❏ *The panels shrunk, the windows cracked; fragments of plaster fell out of the ceiling, and the naked laths were shown instead* (*A Christmas Carol* by Charles Dickens)

leer NOUN a leer is an unpleasant smile ❏ *with a kind of leer* (*Treasure Island* by Robert Louis Stevenson)

lenitives NOUN these are different kinds of drugs or medicines: lenitives and palliatives were pain relievers; aperitives were laxatives; abstersives caused vomiting; corrosives destroyed human tissue; restringents caused constipation; cephalalgics stopped headaches; icterics were used as medicine for jaundice; apophlegmatics were cough medicine, and acoustics were cures for the loss of hearing ❑ *lenitives, aperitives, abstersives, corrosives, restringents, palliatives, laxatives, cephalalgics, icterics, apophlegmatics, acoustics* (*Gulliver's Travels* by Jonathan Swift)

lest CONJ in case. If you do something lest something (usually) unpleasant happens you do it to try to prevent it happening ❑ *She went in without knocking, and hurried upstairs, in great fear lest she should meet the real Mary Ann* (*Alice's Adventures in Wonderland* by Lewis Carroll)

levee NOUN a levee is an old term for a meeting held in the morning, shortly after the person holding the meeting has got out of bed ❑ *I used to attend the King's levee once or twice a week* (*Gulliver's Travels* by Jonathan Swift)

life-preserver NOUN a club which had lead inside it to make it heavier and therefore more dangerous ❑ *and with no more suspicious articles displayed to view than two or three heavy bludgeons which stood in a corner, and a 'life-preserver' that hung over the chimney-piece.* (*Oliver Twist* by Charles Dickens)

lighterman NOUN a lighterman is another word for sailor ❑ *in and out, hammers going in ship-builders' yards, saws going at timber, clashing engines going at things unknown, pumps going in leaky ships, capstans going, ships going out to sea, and unintelligible sea creatures roaring curses over the bulwarks at respondent lightermen* (*Great Expectations* by Charles Dickens)

livery NOUN servants often wore a uniform known as a livery ❑ *suddenly a footman in livery came running out of the wood* (*Alice's Adventures in Wonderland* by Lewis Carroll)

livid ADJ livid means pale or ash coloured. Livid also means very angry ❑ *a dirty, livid white* (*Treasure Island* by Robert Louis Stevenson)

lottery-tickets NOUN a popular card game ❑ *and Mrs. Philips protested that they would have a nice comfortable noisy game of lottery tickets* (*Pride and Prejudice* by Jane Austen)

lower and upper world PHRASE the earth and the heavens are the lower and upper worlds ❑ *the changes in the lower and upper world* (*Gulliver's Travels* by Jonathan Swift)

lustres NOUN lustres are chandeliers. A chandelier is a large, decorative frame which holds light bulbs or candles and hangs from the ceiling ❑ *the lustres, lights, the carving and the guilding* (*The Prelude* by William Wordsworth)

lynched VERB killed without a criminal trial by a crowd of people ❑ *He'll never know how nigh he come to getting lynched* (*The Adventures of Huckleberry Finn* by Mark Twain)

malingering VERB if someone is malingering they are pretending to be ill to avoid working ❑ *And you stand there malingering* (*Treasure Island* by Robert Louis Stevenson)

managing PHRASE treating with consideration ❑ *to think the honour of my own kind not worth managing* (*Gulliver's Travels* by Jonathan Swift)

manhood PHRASE manhood means human nature ❑ *concerning the nature of manhood* (*Gulliver's Travels* by Jonathan Swift)

man-trap NOUN a man-trap is a set of steel jaws that snap shut when trodden on and trap a person's leg

❑ *"Don't go to him,"* I called out of the window, *"he's an assassin! A man-trap!"* (*Oliver Twist* by Charles Dickens)

maps NOUN charts of the night sky ❑ *Let maps to others, worlds on worlds have shown* (*The Good-Morrow* by John Donne)

mark VERB look at or notice ❑ *Mark but this flea, and mark in this* (*The Flea* by John Donne)

maroons NOUN A maroon is someone who has been left in a place which it is difficult for them to escape from, like a small island ❑ *if schooners, islands, and maroons* (*Treasure Island* by Robert Louis Stevenson)

mast NOUN here mast means the fruit of forest trees ❑ *a quantity of acorns, dates, chestnuts, and other mast* (*Gulliver's Travels* by Jonathan Swift)

mate VERB defeat ❑ *Where Mars did mate the warlike Carthigens* (*Doctor Faustus Chorus* by Christopher Marlowe)

mealy ADJ Mealy when used to describe a face meant palid, pale or colourless ❑ *I only know two sorts of boys. Mealy boys, and beef-faced boys* (*Oliver Twist* by Charles Dickens)

middling ADJ fairly or moderately ❑ *she worked me middling hard for about an hour* (*The Adventures of Huckleberry Finn* by Mark Twain)

mill NOUN a mill, or treadmill, was a device for hard labour or punishment in prison ❑ *Was you never on the mill?* (*Oliver Twist* by Charles Dickens)

milliner's shop NOUN a milliner's sold fabrics, clothing, lace and accessories; as time went on they specialized more and more in hats ❑ *to pay their duty to their aunt and to a milliner's shop just over the way* (*Pride and Prejudice* by Jane Austen)

minching un' munching PHRASE how people in the north of England used to describe the way people

from the south speak ❑ *Minching un' munching!* (*Wuthering Heights* by Emily Brontë)

mine NOUN gold ❑ *Whether both th'Indias of spice and mine* (*The Sun Rising* by John Donne)

mire NOUN mud ❑ *Tis my fate to be always ground into the mire under the iron heel of oppression* (*The Adventures of Huckleberry Finn* by Mark Twain)

miscellany NOUN a miscellany is a collection of many different kinds of things ❑ *under that, the miscellany began* (*Treasure Island* by Robert Louis Stevenson)

mistarshers NOUN mistarshers means moustache, which is the hair that grows on a man's upper lip ❑ *when he put his hand up to his mistarshers* (*Tess of the D'Urbervilles* by Thomas Hardy)

morrow NOUN here good-morrow means tomorrow and a new and better life ❑ *And now good-morrow to our waking souls* (*The Good-Morrow* by John Donne)

mortification NOUN mortification is an old word for gangrene which is when part of the body decays or 'dies' because of disease ❑ *Yes, it was a mortification–that was it* (*The Adventures of Huckleberry Finn* by Mark Twain)

mought PARTICIPLE mought is an old spelling of might ❑ *what you mought call me? You mought call me captain* (*Treasure Island* by Robert Louis Stevenson)

move VERB move me not means do not make me angry ❑ *Move me not, Faustus* (*Doctor Faustus 2.1* by Christopher Marlowe)

muffin-cap NOUN a muffin cap is a flat cap made from wool ❑ *the old one, remained stationary in the muffin-cap and leathers* (*Oliver Twist* by Charles Dickens)

mulatter NOUN a mulatter was another word for mulatto, which is a person with parents who are from different races ❑ *a mulatter, most as white as a white man* (*The Adventures of Huckleberry Finn* by Mark Twain)

mummery NOUN mummery is an old word that meant meaningless (or pretentious) ceremony ❑ *When they were all gone, and when Trabb and his men–but not his boy: I looked for him–had crammed their mummery into bags, and were gone too, the house felt wholesomer.* (*Great Expectations* by Charles Dickens)

nap NOUN the nap is the woolly surface on a new item of clothing. Here the surface has been worn away so it looks bare ❑ *like an old hat with the nap rubbed off* (*The Adventures of Huckleberry Finn* by Mark Twain)

natural ■ NOUN a natural is a person born with learning difficulties ❑ *though he had been left to his particular care by their deceased father, who thought him almost a natural.* (*David Copperfield* by Charles Dickens) ■ ADJ natural meant illegitimate ❑ *Harriet Smith was the natural daughter of somebody* (*Emma* by Jane Austen)

navigator NOUN a navigator was originally someone employed to dig canals. It is the origin of the word 'navvy' meaning a labourer ❑ *She ascertained from me in a few words what it was all about, comforted Dora, and gradually convinced her that I was not a labourer–from my manner of stating the case I believe Dora concluded that I was a navigator, and went balancing myself up and down a plank all day with a wheelbarrow–and so brought us together in peace.* (*David Copperfield* by Charles Dickens)

necromancy NOUN necromancy means a kind of magic where the magician speaks to spirits or ghosts to find out what will happen in the future ❑ *He surfeits upon cursed necromancy* (*Doctor Faustus chorus* by Christopher Marlowe)

negus NOUN a negus is a hot drink made from sweetened wine and water ❑ *He sat placidly perusing the newspaper, with his little head on one side, and a glass of warm sherry negus at his elbow.* (*David Copperfield* by Charles Dickens)

nice ADJ discriminating. Able to make good judgements or choices ❑ *consequently a claim to be nice* (*Emma* by Jane Austen)

nigh ADV nigh means near ❑ *He'll never know how nigh he come to getting lynched* (*The Adventures of Huckleberry Finn* by Mark Twain)

nimbleness NOUN nimbleness means being able to move very quickly or skillfully ❑ *and with incredible accuracy and nimbleness* (*Treasure Island* by Robert Louis Stevenson)

noggin NOUN a noggin is a small mug or a wooden cup ❑ *you'll bring me one noggin of rum* (*Treasure Island* by Robert Louis Stevenson)

none ADJ neither ❑ *none can die* (*The Good-Morrow* by John Donne)

notices NOUN observations ❑ *Arch are his notices* (*The Prelude* by William Wordsworth)

occiput NOUN occiput means the back of the head ❑ *saw off the occiput of each couple* (*Gulliver's Travels* by Jonathan Swift)

officiously ADJ kindly ❑ *the governess who attended Glumdalclitch very officiously lifted me up* (*Gulliver's Travels* by Jonathan Swift)

old salt PHRASE old salt is a slang term for an experienced sailor ❑ *a 'true sea-dog', and a 'real old salt'* (*Treasure Island* by Robert Louis Stevenson)

or ere PHRASE before ❑ *or ere the Hall was built* (*The Prelude* by William Wordsworth)

ostler NOUN one who looks after horses at an inn ❑ *The bill paid, and the waiter remembered, and the ostler not forgotten, and the chambermaid taken into consideration* (*Great Expectations* by Charles Dickens)

ostry NOUN an ostry is an old word for a pub or hotel ❑ *lest I send you into the ostry with a vengeance* (*Doctor Faustus 2.2* by Christopher Marlowe)

outrunning the constable PHRASE outrunning the constable meant spending more than you earn ❑ *but I shall by this means be able to check your bills and to pull you up if I find you outrunning the constable.* (*Great Expectations* by Charles Dickens)

over ADJ across ❑ *It is in length six yards, and in the thickest part at least three yards over* (*Gulliver's Travels* by Jonathan Swift)

over the broomstick PHRASE this is a phrase meaning 'getting married without a formal ceremony' ❑ *They both led tramping lives, and this woman in Gerrard-street here, had been married very young, over the broomstick (as we say), to a tramping man, and was a perfect fury in point of jealousy.* (*Great Expectations* by Charles Dickens)

own VERB own means to admit or to acknowledge ❑ *It's my old girl that advises. She has the head. But I never own to it before her. Discipline must be maintained* (*Bleak House* by Charles Dickens)

page NOUN here page means a boy employed to run errands ❑ *not my feigned page* (*On His Mistress* by John Donne)

paid pretty dear PHRASE paid pretty dear means paid a high price or suffered quite a lot ❑ *I paid pretty dear for my monthly fourpenny piece* (*Treasure Island* by Robert Louis Stevenson)

pannikins NOUN pannikins were small tin cups ❑ *of lifting light glasses and cups to his lips, as if they were clumsy pannikins* (*Great Expectations* by Charles Dickens)

pards NOUN pards are leopards ❑ *Not charioted by Bacchus and his pards* (*Ode on a Nightingale* by John Keats)

parlour boarder NOUN a pupil who lived with the family ❑ *and somebody had lately raised her from the condition of scholar to parlour boarder* (*Emma* by Jane Austen)

particular, a London PHRASE London in Victorian times and up to the 1950s was famous for having very dense fog–which was a combination of real fog and the smog of pollution from factories ❑ *This is a London particular . . . A fog, miss'* (*Bleak House* by Charles Dickens)

patten NOUN pattens were wooden soles which were fixed to shoes by straps to protect the shoes in wet weather ❑ *carrying a basket like the Great Seal of England in plaited straw, a pair of pattens, a spare shawl, and an umbrella, though it was a fine bright day* (*Great Expectations* by Charles Dickens)

paviour NOUN a paviour was a labourer who worked on the street pavement ❑ *the paviour his pickaxe* (*Oliver Twist* by Charles Dickens)

peccant ADJ peccant means unhealthy ❑ *other peccant humours* (*Gulliver's Travels* by Jonathan Swift)

penetralium NOUN penetralium is a word used to describe the inner rooms of the house ❑ *and I had no desire to aggravate his impatience previous to inspecting the penetralium* (*Wuthering Heights* by Emily Brontë)

pensive ADV pensive means deep in thought or thinking seriously about something ❑ *and she was leaning pensive on a tomb-stone on her right elbow* (*The Adventures of Huckleberry Finn* by Mark Twain)

penury NOUN penury is the state of being extremely poor ❑ *Distress, if not penury, loomed in the distance* (*Tess of the D'Urbervilles* by Thomas Hardy)

perspective NOUN telescope ❑ *a pocket perspective* (*Gulliver's Travels* by Jonathan Swift)

phaeton NOUN a phaeton was an open carriage for four people ❑ *often* *condescends to drive by my humble abode in her little phaeton and ponies* (Pride and Prejudice by Jane Austen)

phantasm NOUN a phantasm is an illusion, something that is not real. It is sometimes used to mean ghost ❏ *Experience had bred no fancies in him that could raise the phantasm of appetite* (Silas Marner by George Eliot)

physic NOUN here physic means medicine ❏ *there I studied physic two years and seven months* (Gulliver's Travels by Jonathan Swift)

pinioned VERB to pinion is to hold both arms so that a person cannot move them ❏ *But the relentless Ghost pinioned him in both his arms, and forced him to observe what happened next.* (A Christmas Carol by Charles Dickens)

piquet NOUN piquet was a popular card game in the C18th ❏ *Mr Hurst and Mr Bingley were at piquet* (Pride and Prejudice by Jane Austen)

plaister NOUN a plaister is a piece of cloth on which an apothecary (or pharmacist) would spread ointment. The cloth is then applied to wounds or bruises to treat them ❏ *Then, she gave the knife a final smart wipe on the edge of the plaister, and then sawed a very thick round off the loaf: which she finally, before separating from the loaf, hewed into two halves, of which Joe got one, and I the other.* (Great Expectations by Charles Dickens)

plantations NOUN here plantations means colonies, which are countries controlled by a more powerful country ❏ *besides our plantations in America* (Gulliver's Travels by Jonathan Swift)

plastic ADV here plastic is an old term meaning shaping or a power that was forming ❏ *A plastic power abode with me* (The Prelude by William Wordsworth)

players NOUN actors ❏ *of players which upon the world's stage be* (On His Mistress by John Donne)

plump ADV all at once, suddenly ❏ *But it took a bit of time to get it well round, the change come so uncommon plump, didn't it?* (Great Expectations by Charles Dickens)

plundered VERB to plunder is to rob or steal from ❏ *These crosses stand for the names of ships or towns that they sank or plundered* (Treasure Island by Robert Louis Stevenson)

pommel ■ VERB to pommel someone is to hit them repeatedly with your fists ❏ *hug him round the neck, pommel his back, and kick his legs in irrepressible affection!* (A Christmas Carol by Charles Dickens) ■ NOUN a pommel is the part of a saddle that rises up at the front ❏ *He had his gun across his pommel* (The Adventures of Huckleberry Finn by Mark Twain)

poor's rates NOUN poor's rates were property taxes which were used to support the poor ❏ *"Oh!" replied the undertaker; "why, you know, Mr. Bumble, I pay a good deal towards the poor's rates."* (Oliver Twist by Charles Dickens)

popular ADJ popular means ruled by the people, or Republican, rather than ruled by a monarch ❏ *With those of Greece compared and popular Rome* (The Prelude by William Wordsworth)

porringer NOUN a porringer is a small bowl ❏ *Of this festive composition each boy had one porringer, and no more* (Oliver Twist by Charles Dickens)

postboy NOUN a postboy was the driver of a horse-drawn carriage ❏ *He spoke to a postboy who was dozing under the gateway* (Oliver Twist by Charles Dickens)

post-chaise NOUN a fast carriage for two or four passengers ❏ *Looking round, he saw that it was a post-chaise, driven at great speed* (Oliver Twist by Charles Dickens)

postern NOUN a small gate usually at the back of a building ❏ *The little servant happening to be entering the* *fortress with two hot rolls, I passed through the postern and crossed the drawbridge, in her company* (*Great Expectations* by Charles Dickens)

pottle NOUN a pottle was a small basket ❑ *He had a paper-bag under each arm and a pottle of strawberries in one hand . . .* (*Great Expectations* by Charles Dickens)

pounce NOUN pounce is a fine powder used to prevent ink spreading on untreated paper ❑ *in that grim atmosphere of pounce and parchment, red-tape, wafers, ink-jars, brief and draft paper, law reports, writs, declarations, and bills of costs* (*David Copperfield* by Charles Dickens)

pox NOUN pox means sexually transmitted diseases like syphilis ❑ *how the pox in all its consequences and denominations* (*Gulliver's Travels* by Jonathan Swift)

prelibation NOUN prelibation means a foretaste of or an example of something to come ❑ *A prelibation to the mower's scythe* (*The Prelude* by William Wordsworth)

prentice NOUN an apprentice ❑ *and Joe, sitting on an old gun, had told me that when I was 'prentice to him regularly bound, we would have such Larks there!* (*Great Expectations* by Charles Dickens)

presently ADV immediately ❑ *I presently knew what they meant* (*Gulliver's Travels* by Jonathan Swift)

pumpion NOUN pumpkin ❑ *for it was almost as large as a small pumpion* (*Gulliver's Travels* by Jonathan Swift)

punctual ADJ kept in one place ❑ *was not a punctual presence, but a spirit* (*The Prelude* by William Wordsworth)

quadrille ■ NOUN a quadrille is a dance invented in France which is usually performed by four couples ❑ *However, Mr Swiveller had Miss Sophy's hand for the first quadrille (country-dances being low, were utterly proscribed)* (*The Old Curiosity Shop* by Charles Dickens) ■ NOUN quadrille was a card game for four people ❑ *to make up her pool of quadrille in the evening* (*Pride and Prejudice* by Jane Austen)

quality NOUN gentry or upper-class people ❑ *if you are with the quality* (*The Adventures of Huckleberry Finn* by Mark Twain)

quick parts PHRASE quick-witted ❑ *Mr Bennet was so odd a mixture of quick parts* (*Pride and Prejudice* by Jane Austen)

quid NOUN a quid is something chewed or kept in the mouth, like a piece of tobacco ❑ *rolling his quid* (*Treasure Island* by Robert Louis Stevenson)

quit VERB quit means to avenge or to make even ❑ *But Faustus's death shall quit my infamy* (*Doctor Faustus 4.3* by Christopher Marlowe)

rags NOUN divisions ❑ *Nor hours, days, months, which are the rags of time* (*The Sun Rising* by John Donne)

raiment NOUN raiment means clothing ❑ *the mountain shook off turf and flower, had only heath for raiment and crag for gem* (*Jane Eyre* by Charlotte Brontë)

rain cats and dogs PHRASE an expression meaning rain heavily. The origin of the expression is unclear ❑ *But it'll perhaps rain cats and dogs to-morrow* (*Silas Marner* by George Eliot)

raised Cain PHRASE raised Cain means caused a lot of trouble. Cain is a character in the Bible who killed his brother Abel ❑ *and every time he got drunk he raised Cain around town* (*The Adventures of Huckleberry Finn* by Mark Twain)

rambling ADJ rambling means confused and not very clear ❑ *my head began to be filled very early with rambling thoughts* (*Robinson Crusoe* by Daniel Defoe)

raree-show NOUN a raree-show is an old term for a peep-show or a fairground entertainment ❑ *A raree-show is here, with children gathered round* (*The Prelude* by William Wordsworth)

recusants NOUN people who resisted authority ❑ *hardy recusants* (*The Prelude* by William Wordsworth)

redounding VERB eddying. An eddy is a movement in water or air which goes round and round instead of flowing in one direction ❑ *mists and steam-like fogs redounding everywhere* (*The Prelude* by William Wordsworth)

redundant ADJ here redundant means overflowing but Wordsworth also uses it to mean excessively large or too big ❑ *A tempest, a redundant energy* (*The Prelude* by William Wordsworth)

reflex NOUN reflex is a shortened version of reflexion, which is an alternative spelling of reflection ❑ *To cut across the reflex of a star* (*The Prelude* by William Wordsworth)

Reformatory NOUN a prison for young offenders/criminals ❑ *Even when I was taken to have a new suit of clothes, the tailor had orders to make them like a kind of Reformatory, and on no account to let me have the free use of my limbs.* (*Great Expectations* by Charles Dickens)

remorse NOUN pity or compassion ❑ *by that remorse* (*On His Mistress* by John Donne)

render VERB in this context render means give. ❑ *and Sarah could render no reason that would be sanctioned by the feeling of the community.* (*Silas Marner* by George Eliot)

repeater NOUN a repeater was a watch that chimed the last hour when a button was pressed–as a result it was useful in the dark ❑ *And his watch is a gold repeater, and worth a hundred pound if it's worth a*

penny. (*Great Expectations* by Charles Dickens)

repugnance NOUN repugnance means a strong dislike of something or someone ❑ *overcoming a strong repugnance* (*Treasure Island* by Robert Louis Stevenson)

reverence NOUN reverence means bow. When you bow to someone, you briefly bend your body towards them as a formal way of showing them respect ❑ *made my reverence* (*Gulliver's Travels* by Jonathan Swift)

reverie NOUN a reverie is a day dream ❑ *I can guess the subject of your reverie* (*Pride and Prejudice* by Jane Austen)

revival NOUN a religious meeting held in public ❑ *well I'd ben a-running' a little temperance revival thar' bout a week* (*The Adventures of Huckleberry Finn* by Mark Twain)

revolt VERB revolt means turn back or stop your present course of action and go back to what you were doing before ❑ *Revolt, or I'll in piecemeal tear thy flesh* (*Doctor Faustus 5.1* by Christopher Marlowe)

rheumatics/rheumatism NOUN rheumatics [rheumatism] is an illness that makes your joints or muscles stiff and painful ❑ *a new cure for the rheumatics* (*Treasure Island* by Robert Louis Stevenson)

riddance NOUN riddance is usually used in the form good riddance which you say when you are pleased that something has gone or been left behind ❑ *I'd better go into the house, and die and be a riddance* (*David Copperfield* by Charles Dickens)

rimy ADJ rimy is an ADJECTIVE which means covered in ice or frost ❑ *It was a rimy morning, and very damp* (*Great Expectations* by Charles Dickens)

riper ADJ riper means more mature or older ❑ *At riper years to Wittenberg he went* (*Doctor Faustus chorus* by Christopher Marlowe)

rubber NOUN a set of games in whist or backgammon ❏ *her father was sure of his rubber* (*Emma* by Jane Austen)

ruffian NOUN a ruffian is a person who behaves violently ❏ *and when the ruffian had told him* (*Treasure Island* by Robert Louis Stevenson)

sadness NOUN sadness is an old term meaning seriousness ❏ *But I prithee tell me, in good sadness* (*Doctor Faustus 2.2* by Christopher Marlowe)

sailed before the mast PHRASE this phrase meant someone who did not look like a sailor ❏ *he had none of the appearance of a man that sailed before the mast* (*Treasure Island* by Robert Louis Stevenson)

scabbard NOUN a scabbard is the covering for a sword or dagger ❏ *Girded round its middle was an antique scabbard; but no sword was in it, and the ancient sheath was eaten up with rust* (*A Christmas Carol* by Charles Dickens)

schooners NOUN A schooner is a fast, medium-sized sailing ship ❏ *if schooners, islands, and maroons* (*Treasure Island* by Robert Louis Stevenson)

science NOUN learning or knowledge ❏ *Even Science, too, at hand* (*The Prelude* by William Wordsworth)

scrouge VERB to scrouge means to squeeze or to crowd ❏ *to scrouge in and get a sight* (*The Adventures of Huckleberry Finn* by Mark Twain)

scrutore NOUN a scrutore, or escritoire, was a writing table ❏ *set me gently on my feet upon the scrutore* (*Gulliver's Travels* by Jonathan Swift)

scutcheon/escutcheon NOUN an escutcheon is a shield with a coat of arms, or the symbols of a family name, engraved on it ❏ *On the scutcheon we'll have a bend* (*The Adventures of Huckleberry Finn* by Mark Twain)

sea-dog PHRASE sea-dog is a slang term for an experienced sailor or pirate

❏ *a 'true sea-dog', and a 'real old salt,'* (*Treasure Island* by Robert Louis Stevenson)

see the lions PHRASE to see the lions was to go and see the sights of London. Originally the phrase referred to the menagerie in the Tower of London and later in Regent's Park ❏ *We will go and see the lions for an hour or two–it's something to have a fresh fellow like you to show them to, Copperfield* (*David Copperfield* by Charles Dickens)

self-conceit NOUN self-conceit is an old term which means having too high an opinion of oneself, or deceiving yourself ❏ *Till swollen with cunning, of a self-conceit* (*Doctor Faustus chorus* by Christopher Marlowe)

seneschal NOUN a steward ❏ *where a grey-headed seneschal sings a funny chorus with a funnier body of vassals* (*Oliver Twist* by Charles Dickens)

sensible ADJ if you were sensible of something you were aware or conscious of something ❏ *If my children are silly I must hope to be always sensible of it* (*Pride and Prejudice* by Jane Austen)

sessions NOUN court cases were heard at specific times of the year called sessions ❏ *He lay in prison very ill, during the whole interval between his committal for trial, and the coming round of the Sessions.* (*Great Expectations* by Charles Dickens)

shabby ADJ shabby places look old and in bad condition ❏ *a little bit of a shabby village named Pikesville* (*The Adventures of Huckleberry Finn* by Mark Twain)

shay-cart NOUN a shay-cart was a small cart drawn by one horse ❏ *"I were at the Bargemen t'other night, Pip;" whenever he subsided into affection, he called me Pip, and whenever he relapsed into politeness he called me Sir; "when there come up in his* *shay-cart Pumblechook."* (*Great Expectations* by Charles Dickens)

shilling NOUN a shilling is an old unit of currency. There were twenty shillings in every British pound ❑ *"Ten shillings too much," said the gentleman in the white waistcoat.* (*Oliver Twist* by Charles Dickens)

shines NOUN tricks or games ❑ *well, it would make a cow laugh to see the shines that old idiot cut* (*The Adventures of Huckleberry Finn* by Mark Twain)

shirking VERB shirking means not doing what you are meant to be doing, or evading your duties ❑ *some of you shirking lubbers* (*Treasure Island* by Robert Louis Stevenson)

shiver my timbers PHRASE shiver my timbers is an expression which was used by sailors and pirates to express surprise ❑ *why, shiver my timbers, if I hadn't forgotten my score!* (*Treasure Island* by Robert Louis Stevenson)

shoe-roses NOUN shoe-roses were roses made from ribbons which were stuck on to shoes as decoration ❑ *the very shoe-roses for Netherfield were got by proxy* (*Pride and Prejudice* by Jane Austen)

singular ADJ singular means very great and remarkable or strange ❑ *"Singular dream," he says* (*The Adventures of Huckleberry Finn* by Mark Twain)

sire NOUN sire is an old word which means lord or master or elder ❑ *She also defied her sire* (*Little Women* by Louisa May Alcott)

sixpence NOUN a sixpence was half of a shilling ❑ *if she had only a shilling in the world, she would be very likely to give away sixpence of it* (*Emma* by Jane Austen)

slavey NOUN the word slavey was used when there was only one servant in a house or boarding-house—so she had to perform all the duties of a larger staff ❑ *Two distinct knocks, sir, will produce the slavey at any*

time (*The Old Curiosity Shop* by Charles Dickens)

slender ADJ weak ❑ *In slender accents of sweet verse* (*The Prelude* by William Wordsworth)

slop-shops NOUN slop-shops were shops where cheap ready-made clothes were sold. They mainly sold clothes to sailors ❑ *Accordingly, I took the jacket off, that I might learn to do without it; and carrying it under my arm, began a tour of inspection of the various slop-shops.* (*David Copperfield* by Charles Dickens)

sluggard NOUN a lazy person ❑ *"Stand up and repeat 'Tis the voice of the sluggard,'" said the Gryphon.* (*Alice's Adventures in Wonderland* by Lewis Carroll)

smallpox NOUN smallpox is a serious infectious disease ❑ *by telling the men we had smallpox aboard* (*The Adventures of Huckleberry Finn* by Mark Twain)

smalls NOUN smalls are short trousers ❑ *It is difficult for a large-headed, small-eyed youth, of lumbering make and heavy countenance, to look dignified under any circumstances; but it is more especially so, when superadded to these personal attractions are a red nose and yellow smalls* (*Oliver Twist* by Charles Dickens)

sneeze-box NOUN a box for snuff was called a sneeze-box because sniffing snuff makes the user sneeze ❑ *To think of Jack Dawkins — lummy Jack — the Dodger — the Artful Dodger — going abroad for a common twopenny-halfpenny sneeze-box!* (*Oliver Twist* by Charles Dickens)

snorted VERB slept ❑ *Or snorted we in the Seven Sleepers' den?* (*The Good-Morrow* by John Donne)

snuff NOUN snuff is tobacco in powder form which is taken by sniffing ❑ *as he thrust his thumb and forefinger into the proffered snuff-box of the undertaker: which was an* *ingenious little model of a patent coffin.* (*Oliver Twist* by Charles Dickens)

soliloquized VERB to soliloquize is when an actor in a play speaks to himself or herself rather than to another actor ❑ *"A new servitude! There is something in that," I soliloquized (mentally, be it understood; I did not talk aloud)* (*Jane Eyre* by Charlotte Brontë)

sough NOUN a sough is a drain or a ditch ❑ *as you may have noticed the sough that runs from the marshes* (*Wuthering Heights* by Emily Brontë)

spirits NOUN a spirit is the nonphysical part of a person which is believed to remain alive after their death ❑ *that I might raise up spirits when I please* (*Doctor Faustus* 1.5 by Christopher Marlowe)

spleen ■ NOUN here spleen means a type of sadness or depression which was thought to only affect the wealthy ❑ *yet here I could plainly discover the true seeds of spleen* (*Gulliver's Travels* by Jonathan Swift) ■ NOUN irritability and low spirits ❑ *Adieu to disappointment and spleen* (*Pride and Prejudice* by Jane Austen)

spondulicks NOUN spondulicks is a slang word which means money ❑ *not for all his spondulicks and as much more on top of it* (*The Adventures of Huckleberry Finn* by Mark Twain)

stalled of VERB to be stalled of something is to be bored with it ❑ *I'm stalled of doing naught* (*Wuthering Heights* by Emily Brontë)

stanchion NOUN a stanchion is a pole or bar that stands upright and is used as a buidling support ❑ *and slid down a stanchion* (*The Adventures of Huckleberry Finn* by Mark Twain)

stang NOUN stang is another word for pole which was an old measurement ❑ *These fields were intermingled with woods of half a stang* (*Gulliver's Travels* by Jonathan Swift)

starlings NOUN a starling is a wall built around the pillars that support a bridge to protect the pillars ❑ *There were states of the tide when, having been down the river, I could not get back through the eddy-chafed arches and starlings of old London Bridge* (*Great Expectations* by Charles Dickens)

startings NOUN twitching or night-time movements of the body ❑ *with midnight's startings* (*On His Mistress* by John Donne)

stomacher NOUN a panel at the front of a dress ❑ *but send her aunt the pattern of a stomacher* (*Emma* by Jane Austen)

stoop VERB swoop ❑ *Once a kite hovering over the garden made a swoop at me* (*Gulliver's Travels* by Jonathan Swift)

succedaneum NOUN a succedaneum is a substitute ❑ *But as a succedaneum* (*The Prelude* by William Wordsworth)

suet NOUN a hard animal fat used in cooking ❑ *and your jaws are too weak For anything tougher than suet* (*Alice's Adventures in Wonderland* by Lewis Carroll)

sultry ADJ sultry weather is hot and damp. Here sultry means unpleasant or risky ❑ *for it was getting pretty sultry for us* (*The Adventures of Huckleberry Finn* by Mark Twain)

summerset NOUN summerset is an old spelling of somersault. If someone does a somersault, they turn over completely in the air ❑ *I have seen him do the summerset* (*Gulliver's Travels* by Jonathan Swift)

supper NOUN supper was a light meal taken late in the evening. The main meal was dinner which was eaten at four or five in the afternoon ❑ *and the supper table was all set out* (*Emma* by Jane Austen)

surfeits VERB to surfeit in something is to have far too much of it, or to overindulge in it to an unhealthy degree ❑ *He surfeits upon cursed* necromancy (*Doctor Faustus chorus* by Christopher Marlowe)

surtout NOUN a surtout is a long close-fitting overcoat ❑ *He wore a long black surtout reaching nearly to his ankles* (*The Old Curiosity Shop* by Charles Dickens)

swath NOUN swath is the width of corn cut by a scythe ❑ *while thy hook Spares the next swath* (*Ode to Autumn* by John Keats)

sylvan ADJ sylvan means belonging to the woods ❑ *Sylvan historian* (*Ode on a Grecian Urn* by John Keats)

taction NOUN taction means touch. This means that the people had to be touched on the mouth or the ears to get their attention ❑ *without being roused by some external taction upon the organs of speech and hearing* (*Gulliver's Travels* by Jonathan Swift)

Tag and Rag and Bobtail PHRASE the riff-raff, or lower classes. Used in an insulting way ❑ *"No," said he; "not till it got about that there was no protection on the premises, and it come to be considered dangerous, with convicts and Tag and Rag and Bobtail going up and down."* (*Great Expectations* by Charles Dickens)

tallow NOUN tallow is hard animal fat that is used to make candles and soap ❑ *and a lot of tallow candles* (*The Adventures of Huckleberry Finn* by Mark Twain)

tan VERB to tan means to beat or whip ❑ *and if I catch you about that school I'll tan you good* (*The Adventures of Huckleberry Finn* by Mark Twain)

tanyard NOUN the tanyard is part of a tannery, which is a place where leather is made from animal skins ❑ *hid in the old tanyard* (*The Adventures of Huckleberry Finn* by Mark Twain)

tarry ADJ tarry means the colour of tar or black ❑ *his tarry pig-tail*

(*Treasure Island* by Robert Louis Stevenson)

thereof PHRASE from there ❑ *By all desires which thereof did ensue* (*On His Mistress* by John Donne)

thick with, be PHRASE if you are 'thick with someone' you are very close, sharing secrets–it is often used to describe people who are planning something secret ❑ *Hasn't he been thick with Mr Heathcliff lately?* (*Wuthering Heights* by Emily Brontë)

thimble NOUN a thimble is a small cover used to protect the finger while sewing ❑ *The paper had been sealed in several places by a thimble* (*Treasure Island* by Robert Louis Stevenson)

thirtover ADJ thirtover is an old word which means obstinate or that someone is very determined to do want they want and can not be persuaded to do something in another way ❑ *I have been living on in a thirtover, lackadaisical way* (*Tess of the D'Urbervilles* by Thomas Hardy)

timbrel NOUN timbrel is a tambourine ❑ *What pipes and timbrels?* (*Ode on a Grecian Urn* by John Keats)

tin NOUN tin is slang for money/cash ❑ *Then the plain question is, an't it a pity that this state of things should continue, and how much better would it be for the old gentleman to hand over a reasonable amount of tin, and make it all right and comfortable* (*The Old Curiosity Shop* by Charles Dickens)

tincture NOUN a tincture is a medicine made with alcohol and a small amount of a drug ❑ *with ink composed of a cephalic tincture* (*Gulliver's Travels* by Jonathan Swift)

tithe NOUN a tithe is a tax paid to the church ❑ *and held farms which, speaking from a spiritual point of view, paid highly-desirable tithes* (*Silas Marner* by George Eliot)

towardly ADJ a towardly child is

dutiful or obedient ❑ *and a towardly child* (*Gulliver's Travels* by Jonathan Swift)

toys NOUN trifles are things which are considered to have little importance, value, or significance ❑ *purchase my life from them bysome bracelets, glass rings, and other toys* (*Gulliver's Travels* by Jonathan Swift)

tract NOUN a tract is a religious pamphlet or leaflet ❑ *and Joe Harper got a hymn-book and a tract* (*The Adventures of Huckleberry Finn* by Mark Twain)

train-oil NOUN train-oil is oil from whale blubber ❑ *The train-oil and gunpowder were shoved out of sight in a minute* (*Wuthering Heights* by Emily Brontë)

tribulation NOUN tribulation means the suffering or difficulty you experience in a particular situation ❑ *Amy was learning this distinction through much tribulation* (*Little Women* by Louisa May Alcott)

trivet NOUN a trivet is a three-legged stand for resting a pot or kettle ❑ *a pocket-knife in his right; and a pewter pot on the trivet* (*Oliver Twist* by Charles Dickens)

trot line NOUN a trot line is a fishing line to which a row of smaller fishing lines are attached ❑ *when he got along I was hard at it taking up a trot line* (*The Adventures of Huckleberry Finn* by Mark Twain)

troth NOUN oath or pledge ❑ *I wonder, by my troth* (*The Good-Morrow* by John Donne)

truckle NOUN a truckle bedstead is a bed that is on wheels and can be slid under another bed to save space ❑ *It rose under my hand, and the door yielded. Looking in, I saw a lighted candle on a table, a bench, and a mattress on a truckle bedstead.* (*Great Expectations* by Charles Dickens)

trump NOUN a trump is a good, reliable person wo can be trusted ❑ *This lad Hawkins is a trump, I perceive* (*Treasure Island* by Robert Louis Stevenson)

tucker NOUN a tucker is a frilly lace collar which is worn around the neck ❑ *Whereat Scrooge's niece's sister˜the plump one with the lace tucker: not the one with the roses˜blushed.* (*A Christmas Carol* by Charles Dickens)

tureen NOUN a large bowl with a lid from which soup or vegetables are served ❑ *Waiting in a hot tureen!* (*Alice's Adventures in Wonderland* by Lewis Carroll)

turnkey NOUN a prison officer; jailer ❑ *As we came out of the prison through the lodge, I found that the great importance of my guardian was appreciated by the turnkeys, no less than by those whom they held in charge.* (*Great Expectations* by Charles Dickens)

turnpike NOUN the upkeep of many roads of the time was paid for by tolls (fees) collected at posts along the road. There was a gate to prevent people travelling further along the road until the toll had been paid. ❑ *Traddles, whom I have taken up by appointment at the turnpike, presents a dazzling combination of cream colour and light blue; and both he and Mr. Dick have a general effect about them of being all gloves.* (*David Copperfield* by Charles Dickens)

twas PHRASE it was ❑ *twas but a dream of thee* (*The Good-Morrow* by John Donne)

tyrannized VERB tyrannized means bullied or forced to do things against their will ❑ *for people would soon cease coming there to be tyrannized over and put down* (*Treasure Island* by Robert Louis Stevenson)

'un NOUN 'un is a slang term for one—usually used to refer to a person ❑ *She's been thinking the old 'un* (*David Copperfield* by Charles Dickens)

undistinguished ADJ undiscriminating or incapable of making a distinction between good and bad things ❑

their undistinguished appetite to devour everything (*Gulliver's Travels* by Jonathan Swift)

use NOUN habit ❏ *Though use make you apt to kill me* (*The Flea* by John Donne)

vacant ADJ vacant usually means empty, but here Wordsworth uses it to mean carefree ❏ *To vacant musing, unreproved neglect* (*The Prelude* by William Wordsworth)

valetudinarian NOUN one too concerned with his or her own health. ❏ *for having been a valetudinarian all his life* (*Emma* by Jane Austen)

vamp VERB vamp means to walk or tramp to somewhere ❏ *Well, vamp on to Marlott, will 'ee* (*Tess of the D'Urbervilles* by Thomas Hardy)

vapours NOUN the vapours is an old term which means unpleasant and strange thoughts, which make the person feel nervous and unhappy ❏ *and my head was full of vapours* (*Robinson Crusoe* by Daniel Defoe)

vegetables NOUN here vegetables means plants ❏ *the other vegetables are in the same proportion* (*Gulliver's Travels* by Jonathan Swift)

venturesome ADJ if you are venture-some you are willing to take risks ❏ *he must be either hopelessly stupid or a venturesome fool* (*Wuthering Heights* by Emily Brontë)

verily ADJ verily means really or truly ❏ *though I believe verily* (*Robinson Crusoe* by Daniel Defoe)

vicinage NOUN vicinage is an area or the residents of an area ❏ *and to his thought the whole vicinage was haunted by her.* (*Silas Marner* by George Eliot)

victuals NOUN victuals means food ❏ *grumble a little over the victuals* (*The Adventures of Huckleberry Finn* by Mark Twain)

vintage NOUN vintage in this context means wine ❏ *Oh, for a draught of*

vintage! (*Ode on a Nightingale* by John Keats)

virtual ADJ here virtual means powerful or strong ❏ *had virtual faith* (*The Prelude* by William Wordsworth)

vittles NOUN vittles is a slang word which means food ❏ *There never was such a woman for givin' away vittles and drink* (*Little Women* by Louisa May Alcott)

voided straight PHRASE voided straight is an old expression which means emptied immediately ❏ *see the rooms be voided straight* (*Doctor Faustus 4.1* by Christopher Marlowe)

wainscot NOUN wainscot is wood panel lining in a room so wainscoted means a room lined with wooden panels ❏ *in the dark wainscoted parlor* (*Silas Marner* by George Eliot)

walking the plank PHRASE walking the plank was a punishment in which a prisoner would be made to walk along a plank on the side of the ship and fall into the sea, where they would be abandoned ❏ *about hanging, and walking the plank* (*Treasure Island* by Robert Louis Stevenson)

want VERB want means to be lacking or short of ❏ *The next thing wanted was to get the picture framed* (*Emma* by Jane Austen)

wanting ADJ wanting means lacking or missing ❏ *wanting two fingers of the left hand* (*Treasure Island* by Robert Louis Stevenson)

wanting, I was not PHRASE I was not wanting means I did not fail ❏ *I was not wanting to lay a foundation of religious knowledge in his mind* (*Robinson Crusoe* by Daniel Defoe)

ward NOUN a ward is, usually, a child who has been put under the protection of the court or a guardian for his or her protection ❏ *I call the Wards in Jarndcye. The*

are caged up with all the others.
(Bleak House by Charles Dickens)

waylay VERB to waylay someone is to
lie in wait for them or to intercept
them ❏ *I must go up the road and
waylay him (The Adventures of
Huckleberry Finn by Mark Twain)*

weazen NOUN weazen is a slang word
for throat. It actually means shriv-
elled ❏ *You with a uncle too! Why,
I knowed you at Gargery's when you
was so small a wolf that I could
have took your weazen betwixt this
finger and thumb and chucked you
away dead (Great Expectations by
Charles Dickens)*

wery ■ ADV very ❏ *Be wery careful o'
vidders all your life (Pickwick
Papers by Charles Dickens)* ■ *See*
wibrated

wherry NOUN wherry is a small swift
rowing boat for one person ❏ *It
was flood tide when Daniel Quilp
sat himself down in the wherry to
cross to the opposite shore. (The Old
Curiosity Shop by Charles Dickens)*

whether PREP whether means which of
the two in this example ❏ *we came
in full view of a great island or conti-
nent (for we knew not whether)
(Gulliver's Travels by Jonathan Swift)*

whetstone NOUN a whetstone is a stone
used to sharpen knives and other
tools ❏ *I dropped pap's whetstone
there too (The Adventures of
Huckleberry Finn by Mark Twain)*

wibrated VERB in Dickens's use of the
English language 'w' often replaces
'v' when he is reporting speech. So
here 'wibrated' means 'vibrated'. In
Pickwick Papers a judge asks Sam
Weller (who constantly confuses the
two letters) 'Do you spell is with a
'v' or a 'w'?' to which Weller replies
'That depends upon the taste and
fancy of the speller, my Lord' ❏
*There are strings . . . in the human
heart that had better not be
wibrated' (Barnaby Rudge by
Charles Dickens)*

wicket NOUN a wicket is a little door in
a larger entrance ❏ *Having rested*

*here, for a minute or so, to collect a
good burst of sobs and an imposing
show of tears and terror, he knocked
loudly at the wicket; (Oliver Twist
by Charles Dickens)*

without CONJ without means unless ❏
*You don't know about me, without
you have read a book by the name of
The Adventures of Tom Sawyer (The
Adventures of Huckleberry Finn by
Mark Twain)*

wittles ■ NOUN vittles is a slang word
which means food ❏ *I live on
broken wittles–and I sleep on the
coals (David Copperfield by Charles
Dickens)* ■ *See* wibrated

woo VERB courts or forms a proper
relationship with ❏ *before it woo
(The Flea by John Donne)*

words, to have PHRASE if you have
words with someone you have a
disagreement or an argument ❏ *I
do not want to have words with a
young thing like you. (Black Beauty
by Anna Sewell)*

workhouse NOUN workhouses were
places where the homeless were
given food and a place to live in
return for doing very hard work ❏
*And the Union workhouses?
demanded Scrooge. Are they still in
operation? (A Christmas Carol by
Charles Dickens)*

yawl NOUN a yawl is a small boat kept
on a bigger boat for short trips.
Yawl is also the name for a small
fishing boat ❏ *She sent out her
yawl, and we went aboard (The
Adventures of Huckleberry Finn by
Mark Twain)*

yeomanry NOUN the yeomanry was a
collective term for the middle
classes involved in agriculture ❏
*The yeomanry are precisely the
order of people with whom I feel I
can have nothing to do (Emma by
Jane Austen)*

yonder ADV yonder means over there
❏ *all in the same second we seem to
hear low voices in yonder! (The
Adventures of Huckleberry Finn by
Mark Twain)*